LUNAR DESCENT

ALLEN STEELE

ACE BOOKS, NEW YORK

The author gratefully acknowledges permission to reprint the following:

Lyrics from ''Wang Dang Doodle''; words and music by Willie Dixon. Copyright © 1962 (renewed) by Hoochie Coochie Music (BMI). Administered by Bug Music Inc.

The quote by John Young from an interview published in *Footprints*, by Douglas MacKinnon and Joseph Baldanza. Copyright © 1989 by Acropolis Books, Ltd.

The quote from *The Rocket to the Moon* by Thea von Harbou (orginally published in Germany in 1928 as *Die Frau im Mond)* from a facsimile of the 1930 English-language edition. English-language edition published by World Wide Publishing Co., Inc., and the facsimile edition was published by the Gregg Press, 1977. Copyright 1930 by World Wide Publishing, Inc.

This book is an Ace original edition,
and has never been previously published.

LUNAR DESCENT

An Ace Book / published by arrangement with
the author

PRINTING HISTORY
Ace edition / October 1991

ISBN: 0-441-50485-X

Ace Books are published by The Berkley Publishing Group,
200 Madison Avenue, New York, New York 10016.
The name ''ACE'' and the ''A'' logo
are trademarks belonging to Charter Communications, Inc.

PRINTED IN THE UNITED STATES OF AMERICA

10 9 8 7 6 5 4 3 2 1

For my mother—
who let me skip school to watch the Apollo moonwalks

Acknowledgments

The author wishes to acknowledge the published research of the Space Studies Institute and the Lunar and Planetary Institute as the technological backbone of this novel, as well as the ongoing work of NASA and the National Space Society.

Among the many individuals who aided and abetted in the creation of this novel are: Michael Warshaw, Ken Moore, Bob Liddil, Michael Potter, Terry Kepner, Linda Tiernan, Larry Barnes, Paul "Tiny" Stacy, Walter Kahn, Frank and Joyce Jacobs, my sister Elizabeth Steele, cousin Alec Steele, and my ever-tolerant wife, Linda.

Special thanks to Ginjer Buchanan, Susan Allison, Deborah Beale, and Martha Millard for making it possible for me to continue writing, to Carol Lowe and Bob Eggleton for making me look good, and to Gregory Benford, Ron Miller, Sheila Williams, and Gardner Dozois for their moral support.

And, finally, my belated appreciation to a nameless civil servant at the John F. Kennedy Space Center visitors pavilion at Cape Canaveral, who patiently let me sit in the shotgun seat of an Apollo lunar rover to take notes about the vehicle and ask questions about the spacesuit-mockup he was wearing, while a tourist in a hideous Hawaiian shirt pestered me to "get outta the space car, mister, and let my kid look at it."

—Rindge, New Hampshire;
Sanibel Island, Florida
March, 1989 – June, 1990

DESCARTES STATION: GENERAL LAYOUT
Sketch courtesy of Skycorp Engineering Group
A McGuinness International Company

(1.) MAIN OPERATIONS CENTER (Subcomp A third level)
(2.) SUBCOMPLEX A (two levels)
(3.) DORM 1 (two levels)
(4.) DORM 2 (two levels)
(5.) DORM 3/VIP QUARTERS (one level; includes emergency airlock)
(6.) GREENHOUSE
(7.) EVA READY-ROOM/AIRLOCKS
(8.) SPACECRAFT MAINTENANCE (unpressurized)
(9.) TRAFFIC CONTROL CUPOLA
(10.) VEHICLE GARAGE/MAINTENANCE (unpressurized)
(11.) FACTORY DOMES (unpressurized)
(12.) MASS-DRIVER (unpressurized)
(13.) NUCLEAR POWER STATION (unpressurized)
(14.) LANDING PAD THREE
(15.) LANDING PAD TWO
(16.) LANDING PAD ONE

Not Pictured:
>   SOLAR CELL ARRAY
>   SPACECRAFT FUEL TANKS
>   MINING AREAS

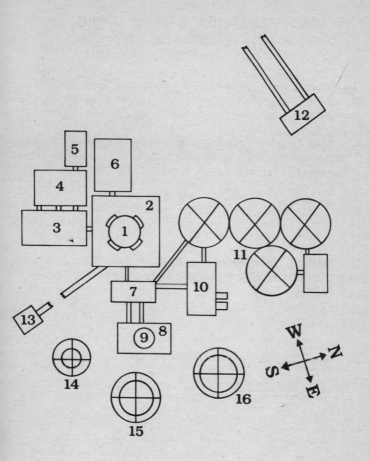

"We choose to go to the Moon . . . not because it is easy, but because it is hard."
—President John F. Kennedy

"The Descartes landing site is one of the most dazzlingly beautiful regions on the Moon. The view from Stone Mountain has got to rank as being one of the most truly beautiful views that's ever been seen by a human being. It's quite a place. I think we ought to go back as soon as we can, because's there's so little we know about it. . . ."
—Apollo 16 commander John Young

"He was alone, he, a human being from the earth, alone on the Moon, except for the company of a lunatic and a dead man."
—Thea von Harbou,
The Rocket to the Moon

PART ONE

One of These Days

Sunrise
(Montage.1)

There is a place, within sight of all the world's oceans, where the seabreeze has never flown. . . .

Descartes Traffic, this is LTV oh-five-eleven on primary approach, do you copy? Over.

High mountain ranges, colder at night than the glaciers of Antarctica, hotter at daytime than the Sahara, yet lifeless and still, never having felt the touch of snow or wind . . .

We copy, LTV oh-five-eleven, and we have you on our scope. Beacons are on and you're cleared for touchdown on Pad Two, over.

Deep canyons where water has never rushed, vast plains where neither bison nor antelope nor elephant has ever stampeded, long-dead volcanoes whose last lava flow hardened millions of years ago . . .

Shift Two, this is your final call. All work crews are to clock in by twelve-hundred hours or face late-work penalties. Shift One workers, please use Airlocks One and Two at Subcomp B for your return. Please remember to clock out before you proceed to Subcomp A.

A dead world: gray, colorless, sterile, its barren wilderness illuminated only by weak blue light cast by the half-full Earth perpetually hovering at near zenith. Yet there *is* life, there *is* motion and change. . . .

By the way, for employees on the first and second shifts, the first game between the Atlanta Braves and the St. Louis Cardinals will be shown live tonight in the rec room, beginning at nineteen-hundred hours. For the benefit of third-shift workers, the game will be simulcast on LDSM, on comlink channel four, and videotaped for your enjoyment after your shift.

In the middle of the plateau of the Descartes highlands, warm lights glow from a cluster of buried buildings and domes; more lights are in motion around it, casting strange shadows across boulders and tiny micrometeorite impact craters, as men and machines move continuously across the night-darkened, silent landscape. . . .

Sunrise coming up at twelve-oh-one hours. Repeat, we've got local sunrise in fifteen seconds, so please adjust your suit thermostats accordingly. Hope y'all enjoy the view, it's gonna be a nice one.

On a mountainside overlooking the plateau and the encampment, a lonesome, still figure stands in the darkness: a spacesuited figure, yet no light is cast from its lamps, nor does the radio cross talk reach its antenna. . . .

Descartes Traffic, this is LTV oh-five-eleven. We're on final approach at angels five, range one-five, bearing six-south by fifteen east and closing. Looks mighty nice from where we are. Time to break out the lotion and beach blankets, boys and girls. Over.

A single light in the sky, racing from east to west, is reflected in the helmet visor of the lone figure, yet it doesn't move, apparently not even noticing. . . .

Five seconds to local sunrise. Four . . . three . . . two . . . one . . .

All at once, the blinding, white-hot orb of the sun ascends above the eastern horizon, sending shadows racing away from it, and suddenly there is light on the wasteland; the gray rocks and soil are tinted with silver with just the vaguest hints of brown and orange as the sunlight moves, as a straight curtain, across the Descartes highlands, closing upon the mountain and the figure standing near its summit. . . .

Heeeey, that's gorgeous! Beautiful, just beautiful! Welcome back, Mr. Sun, we sure missed you!

The light reaches the lonely figure on the mountain, and as it does, the figure fades from sight, as if evaporating in the abrupt, harsh heat, leaving behind not so much as a single footprint to show that it had ever been there. . . .

Gonna be another beautiful day here on the Moon, ladies and gentlemen. Hope you enjoyed the show. Time to go back to work now. . . .

1. The Diversion of Spam-Can S31CO18

The next incident of piracy began early Friday morning—May 17, 2024, to be exact, just a few hours before sunrise. An appropriate time for vile acts by unspeakable men.

"Fast Eddie" Delany leaned over the railing of a catwalk high above the floor of Bay Four of Skycorp's Orbiter Processing Center and watched as the bridge crane just below his feet lowered a cargo pallet into the payload bay of the Skycorp shuttle *Jesco von Puttkamer*. He absently reached into a breast pocket of his work vest and pulled out a stick of Wrigley's spearmint as the big crane cranked and whined and beeped, the ruckus barely heard through the ear protectors clamped over his balding head. Seventy feet below, at the bottom of the vast pit formed by the tiered work platforms surrounding the shuttle, two other cargo loaders standing in the open bay of the Boeing S-202B "Humpback" reached up to grasp the leading edges of the massive pallet and gently guide it down. Fast Eddie curled the stick of chewing gum into his mouth and slid back the right sleeve of his cotton shirt to check his watch. Almost 0300. Time to get things rolling here. . . .

He looked down again to make sure the pallet was going into the stub-winged shuttle without a hitch. One of the grunts in the *Puttkamer*'s bay glanced up at him and quickly gave him the O.K. sign with a free hand. Eddie returned the gesture, then stood up from the railing and began walking down the catwalk toward the top platform of the big hangar. Up here in the rafters, he could peer above the corrugated sheet-metal walls dividing the hangar, into the bays where the other shuttles were going through the post-landing and prelaunch turnaround cycle.

In the far distance to his left the red-striped vertical stabilizer of an older ship, the Boeing S-201A *Willy Ley*, could be seen between the levels of the rear swing-away platform; the old boat had come home Saturday afternoon, and from what he had heard from the Bay Two techs during his last coffee break, its electronics were giving out almost faster than they could find and repair the faults, and whole sections of the multilayer thermal protection tiles on the lower fuselage were all but shot to shit. Somebody would have to soon make up their minds whether to keep Willy operational or decommission it for cannibalization and eventual donation of the hull to some museum. Damn shame if they took it off the flight line; the *Willy Ley* had a lot of history behind it. To his immediate right he could see the smaller, blue-and-green striped fuselage of the Orbital Services spaceplane *Deke Slayton* over in Bay Five, leased from Skycorp until Orbital Services fixed the damage suffered by its own OPC hangar, on the other side of Merritt Island, from the violent tropical storm which blew over Florida's northeast coast two weeks ago. The mini-shuttle was ready to be towed to the Vehicle Assembly Building for mating with a booster, as soon as the two almost-rival companies got the paperwork out of the way and NASA found a window in the Cape's crowded launch schedule. Fast Eddie grimaced and shook his head as he glanced away from the OS-32 shuttle. All dressed up and no place to go, aren't you, Little Deke?

But it was Bay Three, immediately to his left between the *Puttkamer* and the *Ley*, which demanded his attention. As Fast Eddie reached the stairway leading down from the work platforms to the hangar floor, he paused to rub imaginary dust from his right eye while he furtively studied the floor of Bay Three. From here he could see the blunt nose of the Boeing S-202B *Sally Ride* protruding through the forward tiers. Like the *Puttkamer*, the *Ride* was a second-and-a-half generation shuttle; raised payload bay on the top aft fuselage, no vertical stabilizer, long delta wings with tip fins, advanced avionics designed for quick turnaround at the Cape. In the trench underneath the fuselage he could see jumpsuited technicians making last-hour adjustments to the landing gear hydraulics. The doors of the humpbacked payload bay were open, and sure as hell, Eugene the Dork was waddling down the mobile ladder out of the shuttle and down to the hangar floor. Right on time.

The Dork paused on the lowermost platform to ask a question of the bay foreman—Fast Eddie could make out Lynn Stoppard's pained expression, even if Eugene missed it entirely—and to fuss over his datapad with his lightpen. Eddie took the opportunity to relish his target of opportunity. Eugene Kastner was the king nerd of Skycorp's graveyard shift at the Cape, the wanker to end all wankers. This was a guy who probably tucked his Fruit of the Loom undershirt into the waistband of his baggy shorts before he went to bed in the morning. He was an assistant scout-master for the local Boy Scout troop, took his Sunday day-off to attend the Baptist church in Titusville, voted Republican across the ballot even for municipal dogcatcher, rarely wore anything which wasn't white, gray, or brown (and secretly cheated on company dress code for management by using a clip-on tie instead of learning how to tie a decent knot), always kept a half-dozen colored pens (no two alike) in his breast pocket, and couldn't keep his weight down because his darling wife always made sure that there was a packet of Sara Lee double-fudge cookies in his dull gray lunchbox. Eugene hummed along with Muzak when he thought he was alone, stopped reading science fiction when he thought all the writers were becoming liberals, and once bared his soul to a couple of other cargo inspectors in the NASA cafeteria to tell them that, if it weren't for them, Lord knows *what* would get into the cargo canisters lifted to orbit by the shuttles during their weekly supply missions.

The last was utter hypocrisy because there were two secrets in Eugene Kastner's life, and one of them was that when he completed his meticulous inspection of the contents of the cargo bays of outbound shuttles—usually at 3 A.M., if there were no severe holdups in the launch cycle—he would retire to his office, close the door, and steal a half-hour of sleep in his desk chair. You could tell it was coming when he yawned. Fast Eddie had to smile as he watched the Dork slowly walk away from the *Sally Ride* and head for the door to Bay Four. Just before he reached the door, Eugene stopped in his tracks and yawned. He then glanced at his watch before opening the door. *Lord*, Eddie thought as he headed down the stairs, *I love a man who keeps to a tight schedule. Shows strength of character.*

But there was another, darker secret which Eugene kept: He had been bribed a long time ago to ignore certain outbound payload canisters. As unbelievable as it seemed, this prosaic Baptist Republican no-nonsense family man was on the take from someone. *The trick to finding out which Spam-can*, Fast Eddie mused as he jogged down the stairs, *is to watch the Dork carefully when he makes his inspections.*

Eddie made it to the floor just as the Dork was heading for the mobile ladder leading up into the *Puttkamer*'s payload bay. "Morning, Gene," he called out over the barrage of noise, pulling the ear protectors down around his neck. "Ready for your look-see?"

The Dork turned and cast a disdainful look at the approaching bay foreman. It was Eddie Delany's job to accompany the cargo supervisor during the inspection. Eugene knew that, but it didn't mean he had to like it, or like Eddie either for that matter. The Dork just nodded, then glanced down at his datapad. "You had trouble earlier getting the pallet into the cargo container," he said, peering over his horn-rimmed glasses at Eddie.

"Uh-huh." Eddie pointed up at the shuttle; the bridge crane had lowered the pallet the rest of the way into the payload bay and the two cargo grunts were disengaging the cables. "A couple of bolt holes were misaligned in the forward section by about a quarter of an inch either way. . . . "

"*About* a quarter of an inch?" The Dork couldn't tolerate generalizations. He preferred people to speak to him in metric terms—this was a person who, if asked on the street by a driver for directions to the nearest charge station, would tell the man how far it was in kilometers—but he had come to reluctantly accept the fact that he was working with other Americans.

"Three-point-four tenths of an inch," Eddie automatically replied. "Anyway, we got NASA to give us a waiver to drill new holes, so it isn't a problem anymore."

The Dork nodded his head, moved his lightpen across the pad and double-checked to see if a NASA waiver had indeed been issued, and nodded again. "Okay. Send me a memo on this so we can bill the supplier for the work." Then he turned and began walking up the ladder.

Eddie was about to follow him up when he heard a sharp whistle. He glanced over his shoulder and spotted Lynn Stoppard standing in the doorway to Bay Three. The other foreman quickly shook his head, then ducked back out of sight. Eddie got the message; Eugene had thoroughly inspected the payload canisters in the *Sally Ride*. If there was contraband in any of the Skycorp shuttles, it had to be in the *Puttkamer*.

The Dork was in the bucket of the cherry picker by the time Fast Eddie made it up the ladder. As Eddie watched, Eugene checked the serial number stenciled on the outside of the first of the two cargo canisters strapped to the pallet—nicknamed Spam-cans because of their general shape—against the list on his datapad, then reached down and unlocked the hatch. He pulled a tiny flashlight out of the penholder in his shirt pocket, bent over the railing and shined the beam across lashed-down plastic crates containing ball bearings, spare computer breadboards, toilet paper, glove linings, and whatnot destined for Olympus Station, the powersat construction base in geosynchronous orbit. He glanced up at Eddie, then pulled a jackknife out of his pocket, selected a box at random and sliced open the plastic sealing tape. His flashlight roved briefly over stacks of folded paper underwear. The Dork looked at his datapad again—no unauthorized jockstraps were going to make it into orbit if *he* could help it—then he clicked off the penlight and stood up. "Reseal that box and have the hatch locked down," he commanded Eddie as he moved to the second Spam-can.

Eddie watched the Dork carefully now. Ah, yes, it was happening just as it had the last time, six weeks earlier. Eugene looked at the serial number on the Spam-can, checked it against his list . . . then furtively glanced at the serial number again, slowly reading its designation as if to refresh his memory. He opened the hatch and looked inside—more crates, apparently containing more of the same stuff as in the first canister—but this time the flashlight and the knife didn't make an appearance. The Dork wasn't quite so meticulous in inspecting this particular Spam-can. Instead, he shut the hatch, and even made the uncharacteristic effort to lock down the latches himself this time.

Eugene stood up, briefly moved the lightpen across his datapad, made a grunt which was lost in the din of the hangar bay, and turned to move past Eddie. "It's okay," he said briefly—was there a vaguely guilty expression on his face?—then went tromping down the ladder again.

Eddie carefully restrained the smile he felt creeping across his face. Bingo! He looked down at the Spam-can the Dork had just "inspected," and committed its serial number to memory; S31CO18 . . . S31CO18 . . . S31CO18 . . . *That's the ticket.* Then he followed Eugene off the cherry picker.

"Make sure you get that memo to me," the Dork said to Eddie at the bottom of the ladder, tapping the edge of his datapad against Eddie's chest. Fast Eddie nodded his head, just the way the Dork himself usually nodded, and Eugene made a brief display of looking at his watch. "I'll be in my office doing some paperwork," he added. "Call me on the phone if you need me for anything." Then off he went, waddling out of the open hangar door to the prefab office complex next to the SPC, undoubtedly to consume some double-fudge cookies and to catch a few winks on company time. *Yeah*, Eddie thought as he watched the Dork walk away into the humid night. *Sure thing, Gene . . .*

Once the supervisor had disappeared, Fast Eddie walked outside and pulled a pack of cigarettes from his vest pocket. Rubbing the end of one against the bottom of the pack, he lit up, took a deep drag, and leaned back against the hangar door. Several hundred yards away, the mammoth white cube of the Vehicle Assembly Building gleamed under spotlights; a couple of miles distant from the VAB, a mobile launch platform was slowly carrying a Grumman HLV-121 Big Dummy to its launch pad in the distance. Closer by, a couple of pad rats lounged next to the big diesel tow-tractor and ground-support trucks, waiting for their cue from the Bay Four crew to haul the *Jesco von Puttkamer* over to the VAB for mating with its reusable flyback booster. By the end of next week, good old Jesse would be in orbit, making another milk run to low orbit.

Fast Eddie smoked and listened to the nightbirds in the surrounding wetlands. He loved this time of the morning, the serene cool hours before first light and the beginning of another scorching, runamok day at the Cape. *God*, he thought, *please let me stay on the graveyard shift till they retire me, because this way I don't have to deal with too many anal retentives like the Dork.*

And speaking of His Royal Dorkiness . . . Eddie checked his watch and saw that fifteen minutes had gone by since Gene had left the OPC. *He's asleep by now*, Eddie decided as he crushed his cigarette out beneath his shoe and walked back into the hangar. Even if he'd left his computer terminal on, he wouldn't notice the little bitty change about to be made to the *Puttkamer*'s cargo manifest.

His own office was a small, messy cubicle located in the rear of the hangar bay. On top of the stand-up desk was an oil-stained Digital terminal with a plastic drinking bird taped to the top of the monitor. Fast Eddie tossed aside the dogeared copy of *Penthouse* someone had left open on the keyboard and punched up the records for the *Puttkamer*. It took just a few seconds for him to locate the Humpback's cargo manifest, and there it was: cargo canister S31CO18, allegedly containing MISC. CONSMB., its destination listed as OLY. VIA OTV/PS. Beside it, in bright gold letters, was an appendix: OK/EK/5-17-24 0310.

In plain English, the line of type meant that the Spam-can contained miscellaneous consumables bound for Phoenix Station in low-orbit, where it was destined to be transferred to an orbital transfer vehicle which would carry it to Olympus Station. The gold-lettered appendix was Eugene Kastner's assurance that the Spam-can had been checked and okayed for flight. He was the only person on the graveyard shift capable of registering that appendix, since it required him to first logon a secret code number which caused the approval to be lettered in gold. Which was just fine with Fast Eddie, because everything else in the manifest could still be altered.

It took only a few deft keystrokes to change the manifest from OLY. VIA OTV/PS to DES. VIA LTV/PS and to seal the bargain with a quick stab of the ENTER key. And that was it.

Eddie cracked his knuckles and smiled with satisfaction as he studied his handiwork. Now this particular Spam-can would be taking a longer ride than anticipated by whoever had packed the thing in the first place—probably some guys on the second shift who had been paid off by the beamjacks on Olympus, just as the Dork had been bribed to overlook their little smuggling scam. The data was now in all the NASA and Skycorp databanks, and Eddie knew that Eugene wouldn't look at the manifest again; for all of his fussiness, the Dork was too busy with juggling different cargo schedules to waste time on double-checking yesterday's lists. Once he had okayed a Spam-can for flight, the case was closed.

Sure, word would soon get back to Eugene from Skycan that its illicit cargo hadn't arrived, but what was the Dork going to do about it? Calling NASA's Space Operations Enforcement Division would only serve to incriminate himself, and wouldn't the boys and girls in his Sunday-school class be shocked if Mr. Kastner got busted? Besides, once the *Puttkamer* was launched, all Fast Eddie had to do was to go back into the system and change the manifest back to the way it had been written originally, thereby confusing poor Eugene and his pals even more thoroughly. NASA and Skycorp wouldn't know the difference.

Eddie escape-keyed back to the main menu, spent fifteen minutes checking over the rest of the *Puttkamer*'s status lists, then picked up the phone and tapped the two digits that connected him with the pad rats waiting outside. "Marty?" he said into the receiver. "It's Eddie . . . yup, we're ready for rollout. Bring in the mules any time you're ready."

He hung up and walked out into the bay. Beyond the nose of the Humpback, he could hear the deep-throated growl of the tow-tractor's engines as it began backing into the door of the hangar. His team was scuttling out from underneath the fuse-lage, where they had been making last-minute checks. One man stood by each of the landing-gear wheel chocks, ready to pull them out once the tractor's yoke had been attached to the shuttle, as the rear work-platform slowly began to swing away from the back of the Humpback. The Dork was still catching zee's in his office. Fast Eddie searched in his pocket for another stick of gum and smiled again.

It was another morning in the life of a Vacuum Sucker.

The Purge
(Interview.1)

Ron Gora; former Descartes Station chief dietician:
The purge? Don't talk to me about no purge, man. I don't wanna talk about no purge. You wanna talk to me about pizza, we'll talk about pizza. We got cheese pizza, pepperoni pizza, sausage pizza, anchovy pizza, vanilla fudge pizza, any kind of pizza you want, but don't ask me about no purge 'cause I don't remember shit about . . .

What're you doing this for? A novel? Like you mean a book? Okay, okay, maybe I can remember a little bit, but only if you get my name in the book, right? That's Ron Gora, G-O-R-A, as in Ron's Genuine Italian Pizzeria. That's at 922 Pennsylvania Avenue, Washington, D.C., right down the street from the White House, and we deliver to your doorstep except on Sundays and holidays, just look it up in the phone book under *P* as in "Pizza," *R* as in "Ron's." Okay, now you can ask me about the purge. Turn that muthafuckin' thing on. . . .

See, every six months up there, like, we'd have some executive-type persons from the company come visit us. Now, most of the time we'd get plenty of warning that they were on the way, so we could get our shit together on the base for them. Y'know, clean up the dorms and the rec room, take the girlie pictures down off the walls, get rid of the still, hide the . . . well, y'know what I mean . . . and put away the cutoffs and T-shirts and pull out the regulation coveralls, take baths and maybe shave, shit like that. Make the place look good so they wouldn't get upset.

'Course, we hardly ever saw 'em once they got there. I mean, they'd get off the lander, walk through the place, take a peek in your cube, and shake your hand *(imitates a stuffy Caucasian voice)* . . . "Glad to meet you, Mr. Gora, good work you're

13

performing here, well done" . . . *(normal voice)* yeah yeah yeah, and then they'd head for the Hilton and we wouldn't see 'em again till they left. *(shrugs)* I mean, shit, they'd spend three days getting to the Moon, and once they were here they'd go hide in the Hilton—that's what we called the guest-quarters, the VIP dorm, 'cause it looked like a fucking hotel over there—for a couple of days. Yeah, okay, maybe you'd see 'em out on EVA once in a while, looking at the mine sites or the mass-driver. You knew it was them because those were the guys in the red-striped helmets who walked funny and fell down a lot and shit . . . y'know, fuck, why did they bother? They coulda stayed in goddamn Huntsville. But they were harmless, basically, so most of the time it was just a pain in the ass when they showed up.

But anyway, one day some of the guys came in on a lander. Like, just came in, boom, no warning at all. Three guys, one of 'em NASA, the other two company hotshots we never seen before. And 'cause we didn't get no warning, we didn't get a chance to clean up the place, okay? And it's right after the end of second-shift when they appear, so nobody except third-shift's working and the whole place is fucked up. I mean, they started walking through the station, and there's three-card monte going on in the rec room, some guys're getting drunk in the mess hall, and there's reefer-smoking in the greenhouse . . . maybe I shouldn't tell you about that . . . and when they get to the Hilton they find somebody screwing a girl in one of their rooms. *(laughs)* I mean, seriously, it's just the usual good-time-after-work for us, but they weren't supposed to know about any of this, right?

Right. So they hole up in the Hilton and we think the worst is over. We're thinking, y'know, they'll warn us to chill our action, dock our bonuses for the month, some shit like that, okay? But the next morning, Bo—Bo Fisk, the general manager, right?—he gets summoned over to the hotel to see 'em. They wouldn't go to MainOps, uh-uh. They carpeted him on their own turf. He's in there two, three hours, right? When he comes out he's white . . . *(snickers)* well, he was always white, but when we see him coming back through the dorm from the Hilton he's pale, okay? But he doesn't say anything. Won't tell us what's going on.

So the company guys and the NASA stiff are with us two more days, but they're crawling all over the base like cockroaches. I mean, some guy would be in the ready-room, suiting up for the next shift, and he'd look around and there's one of them watching him, writing stuff down in their little notebooks. And they spent half a day in MainOps, looking at everything in the computers. Went through my stockroom, my kitchen . . . man, pisses me off when someone I don't know goes through my kitchen . . . but nothing I could do about it, right? And all the while, they never said anything to anyone, so you didn't know if you were doing right or wrong. Not a word. Even the lander crew couldn't tell us anything, or wouldn't, at any rate. All one of 'em said to me was, "You better get your résumé in order, buddy."

Three days after they showed, there's a few of us talking it over in the rec room just before second-shift, when we knew they were by themselves in the Hilton. One guy says, "Man, it's a purge, I can feel it. We're all going to lose our jobs." Nobody really believed him, y'know. Not in the realm of possibility. But later that day, during third-shift, they take off. I mean, bang, just as sudden as they were in, they were out. The next thing we knew, they were on their way up to orbit where their AMOV's parked.

But by then, we knew what was happening, 'cause right after they launched, Bo hit the locker room, where the mailboxes were located, and stuck little envelopes in everyone's boxes. When we heard what was going on, everybody rushed in there and dug out their envelopes. If you got a white slip in your envelope, it meant your contract had been renewed, but your bonuses were suspended effective immediately. And if you got a pink slip, you didn't have to read the rest. It meant your contract was terminated and your last quarterly bonus had been annulled, and in fourteen days you were expected to climb into a zombie tank for a ride on the next LTV home. You were tuna.

Fifty-six guys got pink slips . . . half the crew, axed all at once. That included me, most of the science team, two-thirds of the miners. Even Bo himself got the bullet. Fucking goddamn moondog massacre. And Asswipe—that's ASWI, the union— wouldn't do a damn thing about it, but that was just like our worthless dickhead union for you, right? I still couldn't fucking believe it.

And that was the purge . . . huh? *(shrugs)* What do I think now? Fuck 'em with a Coke bottle, that's what I think. Hey, I can't complain in the long run, right? I still made it out of there with eleven months pay. Better than what I brought home from the Navy. I was ready to come home, man. Living on the Moon sucks, I gotta tell you. I was ready to get out of there, anyway. Three years later, and now look at me. *(laughs and slaps the counter with his fist)* I'm a successful businessman. Eleven months pay in the bank and I get to come home and start my own business, and it beats making brown rice for a buncha . . . y'know, fuck that shit. I ain't never going back to the Moon, man. Fuck that place. . . .

You like that picture? Yeah, I'm in that . . . uh-huh, that's me, the colored guy in the middle. Yeah, that's in the rec room, and that's Quack, that's Mighty Joe, that's Butch, that's . . .

Hey, look, it's been nice talking to you, but I got some customers waiting for slices here. Interview's over, okay? You wanna buy a pizza? Special for writers today, ten percent discount on pizzas with two toppings or more. I'm serious. And remember that name. That's Ron Gora, G-O-R-A, as in Ron's Genuine Italian Pizzeria. We deliver. Remember that. Ciao, dude . . .

2. Camping, Cold Beer, Ice, Good Food

Bears had raided the garbage cans again last night. Lester didn't need to find their tracks to know it had been bears. Raccoons or skunks might have tipped over the cans and strewn plastic wrappers, bottles, and paper cups all over the ground, but they couldn't have moved the broken cinder blocks he had placed on top of the lids. Only bears could do that; the long winter was finally over, and they were emerging from their dens hidden along the Presidential Range, lurching down from the mountains to the campgrounds in Crawford Notch like furry muggers looking for tourists to accost. Soon, once they had reacquired a taste for half-eaten hot dogs and unwanted Wing-Dings, they wouldn't be settling for furtive midnight forages. Lester figured that by Independence Day weekend, at least, he would be chasing one of the big bastards out of somebody's tent.

He righted the cans, then squatted down on his haunches and began to gather up the crap, dumping fistfuls of ripped, mildewed foodwrap into the cans. He was almost through with the cleanup when he heard a child giggle. Looking around, Lester saw a little boy standing next to the outhouse: about five years old, blond hair, wearing hiking shorts and a Bugs Bunny T-shirt. The index finger of his grubby right hand was exploring a nostril.

"Messy," the kid commented.

"Yep," Lester agreed. "It's a mess, all right."

The boy was with the family in Site Three, the people from New York City who had checked in two days ago. They had spent some time yesterday in the camp store, waiting out a midday rain shower; Dad had bragged that he was an investment broker from some Wall Street securities firm, trying to impress Lester with his suave urbanity, while Mom bought a load of

17

cheap Visit New Hampshire crap: coffee mugs, a bird feeder, a couple of quarts of Ye Olde Fashioned Homemade Maple Syrup, which was actually Aunt Jemima repoured into rustic-looking porcelain jugs manufactured in Taiwan. Later that afternoon, Lester had caught the kid's older brother trying to sneak out the door with a couple of candy bars stuck down the front of his jeans. Typical early-summer car campers—Lester would be seeing more by Memorial Day, next weekend—but the youngest was all right. Probably the only decent member of the family.

The boy stared at the garbage. "Didja do that?"

"Nope. The bears did. You shouldn't pick your nose."

The kid pulled his finger out of his nose, peered with scientific interest at the booger, and wiped it off on the back of his shorts. "Bears?" he asked timidly.

"That's right. Huge black bears." Lester spread his arms as far as he could reach. "Bigger than this."

The boy looked appropriately startled.

"Tell your folks to make sure they put all their trash up here and not to leave any food around your tents, or"—Lester dropped his voice menacingly—"they might come around to visit you tonight. Those bears are hungry. *Real* hungry."

The kid immediately turned and dashed into the outhouse, slamming the wooden door behind him. Lester grinned as he gathered up the rest of the trash. The boy would probably stay in the outhouse for the rest of the morning, or at least until one of his parents came searching for him.

He was replacing the cinder blocks on top of the cans when he heard car tires scrunching on the gravel in the front lot. He brushed his hands across the seat of his jeans and walked to the back door of the camp store. He paused in the storeroom to rush his hands under the sink's faucet—a vague rotten-egg odor from the water reminded him that it was time to get the well chlorinated again—then walked out into the front of the store, drying his hands on a rag.

The store was empty. Perhaps whoever had just arrived hadn't seen the self-service sign over the battery charger. Lester walked around the glass-front counter and pushed open the screen door.

A car was parked in front of the charge station: a '23 Datsun Millennium, its silver body gleaming in the morning sun, the driver's door gull-winged open. The charge cable was still on the terminal; nobody was in sight. Lester let the door slam shut behind him as he sauntered out into the gravel lot. The Millennium had Massachusetts plates; an Avis rental sticker on the rear bumper told him that it had been leased at Logan Airport. On the dashboard rested a thin, black-plastic binder; embossed on the cover was the Skycorp corporate logo.

Lester took one look at the binder and muttered, "Aw, shit."

The screen door opened, then slammed shut. Lester looked around; someone had entered the camp store behind him. As he strode back to the store, he heard the beer cooler hum a little louder as it was momentarily opened. Lester irritably pulled open the screen door and walked inside.

"That'll cost you a dollar, Arnie," he said.

Arnie Moss was leaning against the counter, tilting back the Coors he had filched from the cooler. His eyes darted toward Lester Riddell as he took a long swig; then he lowered the can and smacked his lips with exaggerated gusto. "Been on the road for four hours, Les," he drawled. "The least you can do is give me a beer."

"The least you can do is pay for it," Lester replied, standing in the doorway. "I'm on a low budget. No giveaways for anyone."

Moss belched. "Jesus. What a tightwad." He shook his head in disgust, but reached into his wallet and pulled out a dollar. He dropped it on the glass counter. "If you're that hard up, maybe I've come at the right time."

"Wait another eight years, then come ask me again."

"Maybe. Hey, join me for a cold one?" Moss cocked his head toward the cooler. "I hate drinking alone. Hell, it's your beer."

"No thanks."

Moss raised an eyebrow. "Too early?"

"No, they'd just get pissed at me at the next double-A meeting." Lester walked behind the counter and sat down on the stool next to the cash register. "And who says I'm hard up? I'd be crazy to give away beer for free."

Moss shrugged. He finished his beer with another long, open-throated swig, then set the empty can down and wandered away from the counter, looking around the store. Lester could see the place through Moss's eyes: a single long room, with dark, unpainted pine walls and a low ceiling, floor bare and dusty, narrow shelves stuffed with potato chips, canned Vienna sausage and instant coffee, batteries and paper napkins. A wire rack near the door held used paperbacks Lester had already read, marked down to half-price; an ancient TV set was on a shelf above the counter.

"Crazy isn't the word for it," Moss said, scanning the place. "Christ, what a letdown. All that training and experience, and where has it landed you? Selling toilet paper to tourists. I don't get it. . . ."

His voice trailed off as he spotted the corner of the store where an airtight wood stove had been installed. It was the most comfortable side of the store, the nook that served as Lester's parlor during the day: a frayed woolen rug, a pair of overstuffed chairs and a second-hand rocker, a wooden wire-spool that served as a table, an antique iron coal scuttle filled with magazines and more paperbacks—and the pictures on the walls.

Moss sauntered over and peered at the framed photos, then glanced at the map of the Moon tacked to the wall just above the rocker. "Now this is more like it," he said appreciatively. His gaze roamed to an old picture of Lester, taken with Beth outside the front entrance of the Johnson Space Center. "Where's Beth these days, anyway?"

"Back in Minneapolis," Lester answered stiffly.

"Uh-huh. Heard from her lately?"

"Not since she remarried. Seven years at least." Lester didn't like talking about his ex-wife. "Why are you here, Arnie?" he asked, more to change the subject than anything else.

Moss didn't reply right away. Instead, he peered closer at another picture, almost rubbing his nose against the glass: a group of spacesuited men standing on the Moon. "Yeah, I remember this one," he chuckled. "There's me and you, and Henry Wallace and . . . aw, gee, I never can remember his name. The mission specialist." He snapped his fingers a couple of times, trying to conjure the forgotten name. "You know, the ESA geologist. French guy."

"Dupree." Moss was like one of the outlaw bikers who occasionally stopped by the campground, usually on the way to the annual motorcycle races downstate in Loudon: an unwanted, bullying presence you can't get rid of but can only coldly tolerate until he decides to move on again. "Jacques Dupree."

"Yeah, that's it. Jacques Dupree." Moss pronounced the first name as *Jock*, with an irreverent hard *J*. He studied the picture. "The Descartes highlands. I was just back there recently, too."

He looked over his shoulder, as if expecting a response from Lester. Riddell wouldn't give him the satisfaction; he carefully kept his face neutral. After a moment, Moss turned his eyes back to the picture. "So, Les," he inquired, "did you get my letter?"

"Uh-huh." Lester nodded toward the woodstove. "It got kind of chilly the other night, so I used it to help fire up the stove. Thanks for the kindling."

" 'Thanks for the kindling,' " Moss repeated. He laughed and sat down in the rocker. "That's cute, Les. Mighty cute. I bet you say that to all the people who send you bills, too. Probably the reason why your credit rating is so bad."

Lester started to ask the obvious question, then stopped. Skycorp had its resources. If it wanted to get background on someone, little if anything was out of the reach of Arnie's department. Credit rating, school records, police and FBI files, marriage licenses, tax returns—the usual paper trails everyone leaves behind as their footprints through life. "Go fuck yourself," he simply replied.

Moss ignored the insult. "The salary's seventy-five thousand a year. That's not including the usual bonuses and semiannual performance risers, once monthly quotas are being met again. Half goes to you on contract-signing; the other half is payable to an escrow account at the bank of your choice. Major medical and life insurance is optional, of course, but I'm sure we can work something out. Annual contract, and that's negotiable, too. You can buy an awful lot of bug spray for seventy-five grand a year. Maybe pay off a few bills, keep the bank from foreclosure on this place. Are you *sure* you burned that letter, Les?"

Lester was sure that he wanted to lob an economy-size can of bug spray at Arnie's head. He was familiar with Moss's game: winning through intimidation, the subtle game of getting someone into a defensive position, then allowing that person to vindicate himself or herself by agreeing to whatever position Moss desired. Lester had seen Arnie use that ploy many times when they had worked together; first for NASA, later for Skycorp. It was no wonder that Moss had risen so far, so quickly, up the rungs of Skycorp's management ladder. He had become Skycorp's vice-president of lunar operations through an innate talent for being an asshole.

"If it's such a great job," he said, "why don't you take it yourself? You've got Moon experience, too. Descartes could use a nice guy like you as station general manager."

Moss snickered. "True . . . except what the station doesn't

need is a nice-guy like me. What it needs is a s.o.b. like Lester Riddell.''

Riddell shrugged. ''There's plenty of s.o.b.'s around. Ask one of them, why don't you?'' He paused. ''Besides, what's wrong with Bo Fisk? He was running things up there the last time I checked.''

The rocker creaked as Arnie leaned forward, resting his elbows on his knees and cupping his hands together. ''Well, that kind of cuts to the heart of the matter, doesn't it?'' he said slowly. ''Bo's not up there anymore because we shitcanned him. Along with half the crew, in fact.''

''*Half* the crew? That's about fifty people.''

''Fifty-six, to be exact. The biggest housecleaning since . . .'' Moss stopped himself.

''Since the company fired me,'' Lester finished.

Moss didn't say anything. Riddell *tsk*ed as he reached to the counter for a cheese snack. ''That's great, Arnie. That's fucking superb. You're offering me back my old job because the company fired someone without first considering who was going to replace him.'' He shook his head as he unpeeled the wrapper. ''Now that's what I call progressive management.''

''It was a matter of necessity.'' Arnie rocked back in his chair and rested his legs on the spool-table. ''We had to think in terms of long-range goals. It wasn't something that was pleasant. We didn't want to do it, but . . .''

''Spare me the horseshit, willya?'' Riddell angrily wadded the wrapper and chucked it into the nearest waste can. ''You probably went up there and did the job yourself. My guess is that's why you were at Descartes again recently. And now you're trying to find a way to cover yourself. 'Matter of necessity,' my ass. You fired fifty-six guys because something was broken, and you didn't think about how to fix it until after you had pink-slipped 'em. Tell me that's not the truth, Arnie.''

''That's not the truth,'' Moss said, unconvincingly.

''Yeah, and you're a liar.'' Lester pushed back his stool and restlessly paced around the counter. ''You know what got to me up there? Yeah, you've read my file. Extraterrestrial stress syndrome, or whatever the shrinks are calling it now. Two-week nights, water shortages, monotony, plus all the dope I was taking. But stress-out and substance-abuse were the symptoms, not the disease. I also didn't care for working for dickless wonders like . . .''

"Me?" Arnie completed. He shook his head. "Jeez, Les. I thought you knew me better than that."

"That right? Well, *somebody* went to the Moon to fire Bo and those guys. Tell me it wasn't you."

Arnie didn't say anything. Lester exhaled sharply. He looked down at his curled fists, discovered that he had pulped the cheese snack in his right hand without realizing it. He dropped the mess on the counter; later, he could stick it in the bird feeder by his house-trailer. Waste nothing: one of the few useful things he had learned on the Moon. "Why do you want me back up there, anyway?" he asked. "I wouldn't think Huntsville would want to send up a detox case. Aren't they afraid I'm going to start raiding the infirmary for pills again?"

Moss shook his head. "We checked you out. In fact, I stopped by the VA hospital in Manchester on the way up. No lapses, no busts, no lost weekends." A canny smile touched his lips. "And the old Les Riddell wouldn't have turned down a morning beer. One little test on my part."

"Thanks for invading my privacy. You're a real pal. You haven't answered my question, though."

Arnie Moss hesitated, then stood up and sauntered toward the door. "It's getting a little stuffy in here. Let's take a walk around your campground and clear the air a bit, shall we?"

A thunderstorm swept over the mountains late that night, one of the wild, fast-moving boomers that blitz through the White Mountains in the early summer months like an ill-tempered giant throwing a tantrum. The storm awakened Lester; for a while he lay in his narrow bed, listening to the rain as it beat fiercely on the metal roof of his trailer. When the rain quit and he could no longer see the lightning flash though the fly-specked windows of his bedroom, he tried to go back to sleep, but found that his mind wouldn't quit working. After another restless twenty minutes he gave up; he shoved back the covers, sat up in bed, and reached for the lump of clothes on the floor.

The house-trailer was parked behind the camp store. Lester had turned out the store lights when he had locked up, but as usual he had left the sign switched on: a white-and-blue Pepsi sign on a post next to the road—LESTER'S CAMPING, COLD BEER, ICE, GOOD FOOD. The sign stayed on so that stranded motorists could find their way to the pay phone next to the front door, where they could call an all-night Shell station in North Conway for help if their cars broke down.

Standing out on the center line of Route 302 in the middle of the night, Lester guessed that his sign was the only light visible for at least ten miles. The last of his campground guests had tucked themselves into their tents, and not even the long-haul truckers were on this particular highway at this time of the night. He could hear the soft gurgle of the Saco River behind him; on the other side of the highway, Mt. Bemis loomed as an indistinct hump against the dark sky. In the long, deep valley of Crawford Notch, the sole light came from a Pepsi sign, and the only thing that moved was himself.

The rain had brought out the crickets and bullfrogs; they chorused together, staccato chirps competing against sullen grumps, like nature's own jazz band working out a riff for only him to hear. Lester stuck his hands in his trouser pockets, closed his eyes, arched his back, and let his head fall back on his neck. God, the air tasted sweet: cold, like an oxygen-nitrogen mix through a hardsuit helmet, yet scented with wet pine and wildflowers. It had taken a long time for late spring to come to northern New Hampshire; the warm months didn't last long up here, and like all natives, Lester had learned to relish each moment. He took a long, grateful draw of the night air, then let it out as a steamy plume.

The wind picked up a little just then. Listening to its forceful *shush* as it moved down the long, meandering canyon, he opened his eyes to gaze upwards. The rain clouds were moving away, ghostly blue-black forms racing across the pale moonlight. The clouds parted for a moment, exposing the cool distant beauty of the first-quarter moon: a toenail in the sky, shining down across two hundred and fifty thousand miles of space.

He knew it well. Even in those few instants, he could pick up the thin wedge of the highlands west of the Sea of Tranquillity. *I'm still here*, it said to Lester. *You can't get rid of me that easily, can you? We've left some things unsaid, you and I, and I don't accept collect calls. Come back, and we'll talk to the night together. . . .*

In another moment, the clouds had moved in front of the Moon again. Yet the pay phone was still ringing; the operator was demanding more money for an unfinished call. *Sure*, Lester thought, *you can hang up and walk away, sneering as the phone company gets stiffed for a few quarters . . . but don't you wake up in the middle of the night, wondering if AT&T has purchased your soul for eighty-five cents?*

Neck sore and aching, he looked back down at the gravel parking lot and the camp store. Hey, we've got four acres of mud here at Lester's, just the place to park the car and pitch the tent. We've got ice for your cold beer, and good food if you don't mind cellophane-wrapped sandwiches which were made three weeks ago in New Jersey. There's a shelf full of worthless ceramic bullshit, a charger for your car battery, which works some of the time, and a wooden outhouse which smells as if Ethan Allen and the Green Mountain Boys were the first ones to take a dump there. And if you put all this crap together and shut your eyes, you might even begin to imagine that you're having a real wilderness experience. . . .

Unless, of course, you've really been in the wilderness. Such as having walked on the Moon. Once you've been there, the frontier never lets you go. You'll never be the same again.

We need a ramrod up there, Moss had said. *Someone with experience, because we don't have time to train a new general manager. Someone who can work with the guys who survived the purge, get 'em to toe the line and work like mules. I don't care what I said before, it's a job for a real son of a bitch, but it's gotta be one who can do it without himself getting chucked out the airlock. Not only that, but we're sending fifty-six new guys up there to replace the ones we pink-slipped. Some of 'em are fresh out of the simulators and don't know shit about what it's really like up there. You did the job before. You even did it well before you fucked up. I'm betting my own ass that you won't screw up. It's only for a year, for chrissakes. We'll even manage the campground for you while you're away and you can have it back when you return . . . we'll put it in the contract. So what do you say, Les?*

I should have told him to take a flying fuck, Lester thought. I should have kicked his conniving butt out into the highway, right in front of the next sixteen-wheeler highballing down from Maine. Jesus, I should have just said no to the bastard. . . .

He stood in the middle of his gravel lot and gazed at his store. At thirty-nine, he was no longer young, but he still had much of his youth. The years hadn't really touched him yet; there was only a little gray in his hair, and he had whittled away his beer gut when he had stopped drinking and drugging. But inside the store, he saw an old man hanging around the wood stove, sitting in a rocker beneath pictures of friends long since vanished, taken in a place a quarter of a million miles away and getting further every day. Old, gray, and bitter: hobbling out to stick a charge cable in someone else's fast car, selling Twinkies to runny-nosed kids, giving directions to Mt. Washington or the Old Man of the Mountains to another lost tourist. Dying in his trailer one day, alone and forgotten, his last chance to get back to the frontier a faded memory.

Lester stood on the highway for a long time. He finally took a deep breath of midnight mountain air, then slowly walked back to his trailer.

The business card was on top of the kitchen counter where he had dropped it, but Arnie had told him where he was staying in North Conway, so he didn't need to call Huntsville. Lester found the motel's number in the phone book; he called the front desk and asked the half-awake night clerk to connect him to Arnie Moss's room.

Moss had been dead asleep, but he had spent the evening in one of the tourist bars in town. Lester could tell by the boozy slur in Arnie's voice when he picked up the phone on the sixth ring. *'Lo?* he said.

"It's me, you disgusting drunk," Lester said. "You want me?"

Wuhh . . . Lester? Hmmm . . . for the job? Yeah, uh-huh, yeah . . .

"Okay, you got me. Be here at oh-eight hundred."

Oh-eight . . . inna morning? Tomorrow?

"No, Arnie. This morning. Today."

Hey, um, Les, can't we make it a little . . . ?

"You said you wanted an s.o.b. for a GM, didn't you?" Surprisingly, it wasn't hard for Les to keep the smile out of his voice. "See you in a few hours. Hey, and try to act sober for a change."

Then he hung up.

Profile of a Con Artist
as a Young Man   (Pressclips.1)

(Excerpt from "The Search For Willard DeWitt" by G. Luis Ortega; feature article, The Boston Globe Magazine, *September 16, 2024):*

It took a long time for the authorities to catch up to Willard DeWitt; by the time they did, he was already plotting his escape.

In that sense, he was a master criminal; he had the ability to slip in and out of his carefully selected aliases as easily as a great actor can assume different roles for the stage. Indeed, one of his high school teachers in his hometown of Albany, New York, English instructor and theater coach Paul Caswell, recalls when he took the role of Sergeant Gregovich in a school production of *Teahouse of the August Moon.* "Will was a natural for the part," Caswell says today. "Gregovich is a minor character in the play—he does little more than answer the phone and fall down drunk—but Will was able to make the role his own. In fact, he stole scenes from the leads. I would even say that he was a natural actor. He had the ability to make an audience *believe* in him." Yet the next semester, when Caswell offered to cast DeWitt as Stanley, the lead male role in *A Streetcar Named Desire*, DeWitt turned down the role flat. "He didn't say so," Caswell observes, "but I had the feeling that he thought theater was a waste of his talents."

Willard DeWitt obviously *was* already finding other uses for his talents, ones that did not limit themselves to acting. By the time he was ten years old, he had learned how to use computers; his mother, Jean DeWitt, remembers her son spending his after-school hours on his father's home computer, conversing on several different networks. It wasn't until George DeWitt, a telemarketing manager for General Electric, ran across a handful of prototype computer games in his PC's hard drive—"beta test" games as yet unreleased to the public—that his parents found out what young Willard was doing: hacking his way into the mainframes of software manufacturers and downloading their experimental programs.

Willard was given a spanking for his thievery and the software companies declined to press charges, but that didn't deter him in the long run. When he was sixteen, Pinkerton Investigations caught him writing phony checks. *Creating* phony checks, actually. The teenager would take a part-time job at a local company long enough to get one paycheck—which he would never cash—then quit. With that check as a template, he would then use his dad's desktop publishing system to produce a handful of new checks indistinguishable from the original, all drawn to phony aliases for which he had also created fake ID's. He had managed to steal about $2,000 from several Albany businesses this way before a department store chain who had employed DeWitt as a stockboy for a little less than two weeks put the Pinkerton people on to him.

Even then, DeWitt was only sentenced to two years in an Ithaca, New York rehabilitation school. It was a light sentence; he could have been tried as an adult, in which case he would have faced at least three years in prison for computer theft. "He snowed the juvenile court judge, plain and simple," says Marjorie Bennett, an Ithaca social worker who was DeWitt's guidance counselor at the school for two years following his conviction. "He was an attractive kid, and he made that judge believe that he was just a mixed-up young man instead of the cunning little hustler he really was.

"In hindsight, maybe he should have been sent up the river," she adds, "but I doubt it would have done any good. Willard was a born liar."

Bennett arranged for a standard IQ test to be administered to DeWitt, and was not entirely surprised to find that he scored 150 on the test—Willard wasn't a genius, but he had better than average intelligence. There was also his obvious charisma. Bennett says that he looked older than his age—"like a young Paul Newman"—and used his looks to good advantage. "He could charm the socks off anyone," she remembers. "All he had to do was fix those blue eyes on you and turn on the sugar machine, and you'd believe him if he told you he was the Prince of Wales."

But DeWitt wasn't about to pose as the heir to the English throne; he had a better game in mind. He earned his high-school

GED while in rehab school, convinced Bennett and New York State juvenile reform officials that he had cleaned up his act—and then, only a few weeks after he was released to his family, ran away from home. Before he went on the lam, though, DeWitt stole $25,000 from his father's savings account through computer networking: this time, the cash was transferred to a secret New York City bank account Willard had established under a bogus identity, again through the net. By the time anyone caught on, DeWitt had vanished from Albany, taking with him nothing more than a suitcase of clothes . . . and his father's Toshiba laptop computer. George and Jean DeWitt didn't see young Willard again for four years.

They might have been pleased, if only slightly, to know that their son had run away from home to go to Yale University. But it wasn't Willard DeWitt whom Yale had admitted on the false credentials and transcript DeWitt covertly sent its admissions office (obtained, again, through hackwork while he was back home in Albany): It was Willard G. Erikson. The "G" stood for "Gunnar" . . . as in Gunnar Erikson, the Norwegian billionaire entrepreneur. DeWitt passed himself off as an American nephew. Most of his father's stolen money was spent to cover the first year's tuition, paid by a check drawn on a dummy bank account in London; Willard had been busy with Dad's Toshiba.

Willard Erikson lived cheaply in a dorm for his first semester at Yale, faithfully attending classes in business administration. His high grades were apparently the one thing, perhaps the only thing, that DeWitt did not earn by hacking into a mainframe somewhere. Yale professors who remember him recall that he was alert, attentive, even creative (for instance, his advisor's file stated that Willard Erikson "will probably be as successful as his uncle"). But he also managed to seed his cover story through his classmates, so well in fact that before the end of his first semester one of Yale's leading fraternities, Alpha Beta Epsilon, actively sought him out. Willard Erikson pledged Alpha Beta; by January of his freshman year, he had moved into the frat house.

Willard Erikson was a well-liked, and trusted, member of Alpha Beta. When the fraternity's slush fund for parties inexplicably began to run low in the spring semester of '19, no one suspected it was because DeWitt was stealing them blind. He had managed to ferret out the chapter treasurer's bank passwords and transfer $7,800 to a dummy account at a different New Haven bank.

How long DeWitt might have been able to carry on this subterfuge is a matter of conjecture. He had to go on the lam again by late April, near the end of the academic year, when Yale invited Gunnar Erikson to be its commencement speaker. Not only did they make their invitation public—before Erikson's formal acceptance, the news was announced in the Yale campus paper, along with a brief mention of Willard Erikson's association with the billionaire—but the boys at the frat house began pressuring Willard to get "Uncle Gunny" over for dinner. By the time Gunnar Erikson telexed Yale to ask "Willard who?" DeWitt had fled in the middle of the night.

"We were very disappointed in Willard," recalls former Alpha Beta chapter president C. Hoyt Waxford. "Very surprised and disappointed."

But DeWitt's college career was not over. In the fall semester of 2019, Everett College—a small liberal arts school in central Massachusetts—admitted on scholarship a new sophomore, Martin Armstrong. Marty Armstrong was a student from Ohio who was known by a few to be the great-grandson of Neil Armstrong, the first man to walk on the Moon. Marty Armstrong was not only an A student, but he was also quite active in campus organizations. He wrote a column for the college paper, was active in various student groups, and in his second semester made a successful bid for election to the student senate. The following semester, Marty Armstrong, big man on campus, was elected by the senate as its new treasurer.

It was like inviting the proverbial fox into the henhouse. Over the next six months DeWitt systematically tapped the budgets of the various Everett College student groups—the college paper, the yearbook, the homecoming committee, the radio station, and so forth—a few dollars at a time, eventually stealing more than $36,000, which was hidden in four bank accounts in various parts of the state. None of his fellow students noticed the nickel-and-dime discrepancies . . . but Floyd Gerrard, the college's comptroller, did tumble to the unexplained absence of a few dollars here and there in the student-affairs budget when he was preparing the school's federal tax return. The discrepancies in the books all led back to the student senate treasurer, and Gerrard began to smell a rat.

"I remembered reading about something like this happening at a Yale fraternity," Gerrard says, "so I called [Yale's] security office and asked them to send me a picture of the kid who had posed as Gunnar Erikson's nephew." It was just a hunch on Gerrard's part, but it paid off; when the photo was faxed to him, Gerrard found himself looking at a picture of Marty Armstrong.

This time, Willard DeWitt did not escape. He was in his apartment with a couple of friends when Gerrard, Everett College president Alice Gaynor, and two members of the Massachusetts State Police arrived to arrest him on charges of embezzlement and bank fraud. "He didn't seem too surprised to see us," Gaynor recalls. "It was weird. When he opened the door and saw us standing there, his first remark was, 'I figured this would happen sooner or later.' "

DeWitt went to trial in Worcester County Superior Court in February, 2020, where he was found guilty and sentenced to four years at New Braintree Prison. Officials at the minimum-security prison report that he was a model inmate. Even when his cellmate and several others made an escape attempt while working on a road crew, DeWitt didn't run off with them, although he did nothing to deter or report their escape, either.

"He never once broke the rules," says Hal Allman, New Braintree's assistant warden. "Not so much as disobeying lights-out. So when he came up for parole in three years, he looked good in the eyes of the review board." Allman shrugs. "Maybe that's what he had planned all along."

Indeed. Willard DeWitt was paroled in November, 2023. Seeing his skill with computers, his parole officer, Carrie Smyth-Consiglio, arranged for him to get a job as a robotics programmer at a factory in Worcester. DeWitt held that job for a personal record—six weeks—before he abruptly jumped parole. Smyth-Consiglio visited his apartment in the city to find that DeWitt had completely abandoned it, leaving behind not a trace of his destination.

For six months, DeWitt completely disappeared from the radar screen. Then came the bogus-stock scandal at the Boston brokerage house of Geller Piperidge & Associates, and the criminal involvement of a junior broker named Peter Jurgenson. . . .

3. The Flight of the Imposter

The storm which had awakened Lester Riddell in his New Hampshire house-trailer careered south-southwest, out of the mountains and down the coastline into Massachusetts. By the time Lester was walking out onto the highway, the Greater Boston area was being raked by the same thunderstorm.

Two strokes of lightning split the black night sky above Boston simultaneously. One hit somewhere in Dorchester, in the no-man's-land where even the street gangs had fled from the thunderbolts and the cold, driving rain, taking shelter in the doorways of barricaded stores and housing projects; the other was its reflection, mirrored in the titanic glass wall of the Sony Tower, rising three hundred stories above the uptown streets, a black megalith that dwarfed the architectural Brahmins of yesteryear, the Hancock Building and the Pru.

The thunderclap rumbled across the rain-drenched skyline, causing the windows of Willard DeWitt's condo to shudder. It was at that moment the phone on his desk buzzed.

Standing in his darkened living room, glass of wine cradled in his hands as he watched the cold rain streak his windows, DeWitt didn't turn to his desk, didn't reach to pick up the receiver. Instead, he listened carefully. The phone buzzed again, then a third time, then a fourth . . . then abruptly stopped. DeWitt held up his left wrist and watched the luminous face of his Rolex Oyster. Exactly fifteen seconds passed, then the phone buzzed again. When it was through buzzing three more times, Willard lowered his watch and took a last sip from his wineglass.

"Damn," he said quietly.

The two unanswered phone calls had been from the computer mainframe at Geller Piperidge & Associates, the State Street stock brokerage where Peter Jurgenson was employed as a junior broker. When Willard had come aboard at Geller Piperidge ten months earlier, one of his first covert acts as Peter Jurgenson was to install his own encrypted master file in the mainframe. This file, containing his secret records, was guarded by a number of lockout and early-warning systems, one of which was programmed to call his home phone twice in quick succession if the master file was located and entered without his password. There was only one way this could occur: if a Securities and Exchange Commission bunco team were to link Geller Piperidge's mainframe to its Cray-9 icebreaker in New York. And that could only be accomplished if the SEC inspectors were at the firm's offices at this very moment, armed with a federal court order enabling them to conduct a surprise raid on the brokerage.

DeWitt put down his wineglass and strode to his cherry-oak desk. He had been anticipating this; ugly rumors had been circulating through Boston's financial community for the past few days that the feds were getting suspicious about some phony-stock transactions that had been originating from Beantown. No one knew who had been flooding the market with bogus stock, but it seemed apparent that someone, somewhere in one of Boston's many brokerages, was using his or her company's prospects lists to solicit customers under an assumed name, selling worthless securities, and hiding the proceeds in a network of dummy corporations and offshore bank accounts.

Realistically, it wasn't a matter of *who* was selling crap stock, but *which* person the SEC was after. The Boston financial community was just as crooked as Tokyo or New York or London; there were no saints on State and Tremont Streets. Heads are about to roll, went the whispers downtown. Re-evaluate your friends and cancel your lunch dates with mere acquaintances. Take a long weekend off; now is a good time to visit the Vineyard or go out to the Berkshires to reopen your summer house. Destroy any notes you would rather not have read by a federal grand jury. Get out of town. Cover your ass.

None of this greatly bothered Willard. He was an expert at covering his ass.

The drawer contained a small stack of airline tickets: all for flights originating from Logan International, all purchased two weeks in advance through the net. They were registered under a variety of aliases: Harry Papp, John Fowler, Kent Llewellyn, Mario Bodini. Every day Willard had canceled the soon-to-expire tickets and purchased new ones, charging them to any one of a revolving number of bogus Visa or MasterCard accounts. He shuffled through the tickets and picked out a Pan Am Boston-to-Orlando ticket registered under Kent Llewellyn's name, then opened his attaché case and thrust the rest of the tickets into a pocket, to be destroyed later.

The chosen ticket went into the inside pocket of the black leather jacket which he picked off the back of his desk chair, along with the packet of Amex traveler's checks he had purchased a couple of days earlier: two thousand dollars in fifties and hundreds. He pulled on the jacket, closed the desk drawer—he had already cleaned out his desk, disposing of everything that was either incriminating or which could link Peter Jurgenson to Willard DeWitt—then picked up the folded Toshiba PC and headed for the foyer closet. At the bottom of the closet was his getaway bag, perpetually packed and ready to go. He had learned to keep a suitcase packed for such emergencies from his days at Yale. Who says you don't learn anything in college?

Attaché case and Toshiba in his right hand, suitcase in his left, Willard DeWitt walked out of his condo, letting the door close and lock behind him. He barely looked back at the expensive furniture, clothes, toys and appliances he was abandoning; all that stuff belonged to Peter Jurgenson, and Jurgenson was now a ghost, an electronic specter haunting the mainframe at Geller Piperidge & Associates. Soon even that evil spirit would be exorcised. At this moment, a virus program contained in DeWitt's secret file, activated by the intrusion of the SEC inspectors, would be running through the system like a cybernetic shaman casting a cleansing spell, eradicating all mention of Peter Jurgenson and the many other aliases and dummy corporations DeWitt had utilized. The virus would even clean out the SEC's Cray-9, if it had already broken through his redundant defenses, before the virus destroyed all traces of itself. When it was done, all that would remain of Peter Jurgenson would be an empty desk at Geller Piperidge, some unpaid utility bills, and an unlisted telephone number.

Goodbye, Pete, Willard thought as he walked down the hall and took the stairs down to the front door. *It was fun while it lasted, pal. . . .*

He caught a cab on Newbury Street, just outside his building. The driver, a middle-aged Hispanic punkster wearing a studded leather vest which looked as if a cat had used it for claw-sharpening, was in the mood for conversation. He tried to initiate some small talk—"Sheeit, what do you think of this storm, man?"—but Willard answered his comments about the weather with monosyllables and grunts until the driver got the hint and left him alone to contemplate the streets through the cab's chicken-wired back windows.

The rainstorm had diminished to a thin drizzle; out on the sidewalks, people were emerging from alleys and expensive hangouts to resume their nocturnal prowling: Here, a group of college kids slumming tonight outside the safe, walled confines of the BU or Harvard or MIT campuses, loitering outside a rock club as they waited for girls, dope, or whatever other extracurricular activity might pass their way. There, two representatives of Boston's ubiquitous homeless population, squatting under the neon sign of an art gallery showing a collection of Dillon prints, hugging their damp sleeping bags to their chests and watchful for the next police cruiser. A trio of wealthy young businesswomen emerged from an Italian café, chatting gaily amongst themselves, escorted by a well-dressed gorilla from a bodyguard service. A black Cadillac nosed-dived into a rare vacant parking place, cutting off a beat-up Ford Slipstream which had been angling for the same precious spot.

The cab turned right onto Essex, then swung left through a red light onto Boylston. DeWitt pulled the Toshiba into his lap, opened the clamshell screen and switched it on. It was time for him to assume a new identity, but which one? Where to go now? Kent Llewellyn was only a getaway alias, devised solely for the purpose of making quick escapes. Beyond the plane ticket and a single credit account, there was no extensive background for this disposable persona: He was a name and some conjured numbers, that was all. Now DeWitt had to assume another verifiable, flesh-and-blood alias.

The documents crèche of the menu had a file marked AD-DRESSES. DeWitt moved the cursor to that column, tapped EN-TER, then entered the password. There were three names in the new column: Dwight LaCosta, Phillip Carson, and Jeremy Schneider.

Creating new aliases had become a necessity for DeWitt, but it was also a kind of hobby: the complete invention of new men, identities which he could slip into at a moment's notice. He had learned the knack in the rehab school in Ithaca where he had spent his wonder years, when he had participated with the other kids in fantasy role-playing games during their nightly recreation hour before lights-out. Dungeons and Dragons, James Bond, Traveler, Gurps—RP games had taught him how to concoct three-dimensional shadows of himself, complete with all the obligatory background, assets, and quirks. The lessons he had learned had been some of DeWitt's best-kept trade secrets; the well-meaning psychologists and social workers had not been able to ferret out that aspect of his profession.

DeWitt was a professional imposter; this was how he viewed his job description. As a pro, he knew the primary rules of real-life RP. A false identity must be complete—researched and documented—for it to operate faultlessly. The new persona also must be intimately assumed, much as a chameleon instinctively takes on a new color to blend into its new environment. Taking on the wrong identity, and its attendant scam, could be perilous; DeWitt had learned that lesson when he'd attempted to use the Yale scam at Everett College. What worked beautifully in one place could spell disaster in another.

The three names on his screen presented a range of possibilities. Dwight LaCosta had the background for a Connecticut real estate agent: His social and academic records were on file with the appropriate state and federal agencies, and he even had a broker's license on record with the state board in Hartford. The sixteen-year-old kid in Groton whose life had ended in 2002 when he had wrapped his ancient LeBaron around a tree would never miss his fingerprints, birth record, or Social Security number; he had been reincarnated as a young, ambitious, once-divorced realtor.

It was tempting—but, studying the file, DeWitt shook his head. He was running too hot in New England at the moment; news would be soon getting out about a fraud case at Geller Piperidge, and now was not the time to assume an identity that too closely resembled the late Mr. Jurgenson's.

Phillip Carson's persona was also unsuitable, although for entirely different reasons: Carson was still an incomplete identity. He had the makings of a publishing entrepreneur—DeWitt had tinkered with the idea of assuming Carson's role in order to buy a small newspaper somewhere out West—but his background was still too sketchy. The birth records and Social Security number were there, but the academic record and past work experience had yet to be created and inserted into the national data matrix, where would-be investors could study Carson's past accomplishments. Which was too bad; DeWitt was looking forward to an excursion into the realm of publishing. But not now, alas . . .

The cab moved up the ramp onto the Fitzgerald Expressway, hurtling through traffic toward the Callahan Tunnel entrance. The driver was taking a roundabout way to the airport, adding an unnecessary mile or two to his meter, but DeWitt barely noticed or cared. Small scams like that were hardly worth his attention; let the driver make off with a couple of bucks if it made him happy. He moved the cursor to Jeremy Schneider's name and punched up the file.

He stared at the tiny screen, scrolling down the file and scanning its contents. Now *here* was an identity which was not only complete, but which had potential for adventure in it. . . .

Jeremy Schneider. Age: 25. Birthplace: Brooklyn, New York. Occupation: communications specialist. Education: B.A. in communications, Columbia University, with a minor in space sciences. Complete birth and credit records, natch. But the most interesting part was that Schneider had recently applied to Skycorp for employment in one of its off-world operations . . . and his application had been accepted. Here was a letter from the company's personnel director, Kathleen Barry, inviting Schneider down to its Cape Canaveral office for interviews. If accepted, Schneider would be enrolled in Skycorp's six-week training program, with a possible job at Descartes Station, the lunar mining facility. The letter was only a week old; Jeremy Schneider had not yet responded.

DeWitt absently rubbed his forefinger across his chin. To be truthful, to himself—the only person, in fact, to whom Willard DeWitt had probably ever told the truth—the Jeremy Schneider persona had been created as a last-ditch getaway plan. DeWitt had no genuine interest in space; the prospect of living on the Moon was as remote and unimaginable as taking up residence on Tierra del Fuego.

However, Schneider's identity had been expressly created for a worst-case scenario: one of Willard's scams blowing apart so thoroughly that the only sure escape lay in getting off Earth entirely. It was the ultimate bailout; Jeremy Schneider existed for the sole purpose of extracting Willard DeWitt from the reach of the law. In that sense, it was a perfect trapdoor: The feds could literally search to the ends of the earth without finding him.

But it was also a dangerous passage. Escaping to space was not like heading for some remote island with a suitcase full of cash. The Moon was, after all, still a frontier—and DeWitt knew that frontiers were not always the kindest of places.

He gazed out the window as the cab soared through the sleek, echoing tube of the Callahan Tunnel. But, he had to admit to himself, his present situation was more perilous than anything he had encountered before. Ripping off gullible pensioners and overeager investors was not in the same league as stealing from the Alpha Beta Epsilon beer-kitty. He had gone after big game with the phony-stock scam, and that had meant taking greater risks. Although much of his system of dummy corporations and spectral credit-files was still intact in other parts of the financial community's computer network, the SEC might still be able to track him down if they were tenacious enough. Indeed, they might still be able to link Willard DeWitt to Peter Jurgenson.

And he still had his own face; the idea of undergoing cosmetic surgery was unnerving to him, and he viewed the prospect as a true act of desperation. Yet, on Earth, it was the face staring back at him from the cab window which might land him in prison. And the next time he went in, it wouldn't be to a minimum-security country club like New Braintree.

DeWitt pulled Kent Llewellyn's airline ticket out of his jacket pocket and stared at it. Perhaps he had subconsciously known where he was going, long before he had reached this loggerhead, when he had selected this particular ticket. Orlando was only a short drive from Cape Canaveral. By morning Kent Llewellyn would metamorphose into Jeremy Schneider, and Schneider would report to Skycorp's Florida office for an interview with the hiring office. And in six weeks . . .

The cab emerged from Callahan Tunnel and raced past the toll booths, zipping up the causeway leading to the sprawling lights of Logan Airport. The driver cocked his head toward his passenger behind the bulletproof glass. "Which airline you going to?" he asked.

"Pan Am," the man in the back seat replied. "Domestic terminal."

"Pan Am domestic," the driver repeated, swerving into the appropriate lane. His passenger had been silent the entire trip out of Boston, but there was still no reason why he couldn't get a little talk out of him now. "Where you headed?"

"The Moon," his passenger quietly responded.

"What?" The driver wasn't sure he had heard him correctly.

The man in the back seat looked away from the window. "Monterey," he said. "Little vacation."

"Oh yeah," replied the driver. "Monterey. Hear it's nice down there. Hope you enjoy your vacation."

"Thanks," said Jeremy Schneider. "I'm sure I will."

PART TWO

Return to the Moon

Getting There Is Half the Fun (Interview.2)

Ray Carroll: Skycorp LTV co-pilot, U.S.S. Michael Collins:

There's an old saying up there—you only fly to the Moon once. Now, that's technically not true, because even back in Apollo days, there were some of the old NASA flyboys—Gene Cernan, Jim Lovell, John Young—who made it to the Moon twice during the program. And since been I've assigned to the *Collins*, which has been about two years now, I've made the round trip at least once a month, which means that I've been to the Moon and back at least . . . *(shrugs)* What, at least thirty-six times now? That's not even a record. Hell, I lost count long time ago. . . .

What they really mean is that, once you're on the Moon, you're there to stay until your contract runs out and you're ready to go home. There's practical reasons for that, of course. It costs too much to get a person to the Moon to let him take a vacation back home. Last time I checked, Skycorp's overhead to send one person there is approximately two hundred fifty [dollars] per pound, which means that it costs the company about forty-five grand to send an average-size adult male to Descartes Station. That's a lot cheaper than when NASA ran the railroad, but still not cheap. The company doesn't want to spend that kind of money twice, so there's no contract-guaranteed vacations to Earth. Even the people who work in the Earth-orbital operations, like the powersat beamjacks, finally got ASWI to stipulate a one-week vacation for the guys who signed two-year contracts. But not the moondogs. On the Moon, you're there for keeps till the job is over or unless you're fired.

The second reason you don't go back is because it takes time for the body to acclimate, coming and going. The new workers tend to blunder around a lot in their first week or two at Des-

43

cartes, so they also need time to readjust to normal gravity once they return to Earth. Now, I keep up on my exercise between flights, working out on the treadmill and the rowing machine to keep my heart and muscles copacetic, because one-sixth gravity is a pernicious thing, but even then I've got my mandatory retirement coming up in three months and, hell, I'm only thirty-five and I spend most of my time in Cocoa Beach. But if you're a moondog . . . well, like I said, it can wear you out easy if you're not careful.

So that's an old saw that means something, y'know, if you're a moondog. Doesn't mean shit if you're a pilot . . . *(laughs)* But I gotta tell you, since you happened to ask, Mr. Steele . . . you don't want to fly to the Moon. Not in my ship, at least.

It takes three days to get from the Cape to Descartes Station, and for the most part, it's a pretty boring trip. I mean, I love it when I read stuff about the euphoric glory of spaceflight . . . hope you're not like one of those writers . . . because whenever I see something like that, I know it was written by someone who's never been to the Moon.

Hmm . . . *(pause)* Well, let me take that back. Launch and orbital insertion is pretty exciting, I'll admit that. I still get a kick out of riding a shuttle into space. So's looking out the window to see Earth from three hundred nautical miles. But let's be honest about it. First time up, you're liable to puke, and that's it for wonder and majesty. . . .

Star Whoops . . . that's space motion sickness, if you want to use NASA-speak . . . happens to about two thirds of the people who go up for the first time. Even some of the old hands get it. Nobody has figured out a sure-fire cure for it, though I know another pilot who drinks a pint of lemon juice and Tabasco sauce just before he goes out to the pad . . . *(chuckles)* I swear to God, I don't know how it works, but it does, for him at least. For most people, though, the first time is the roughest, because . . . *(snaps his fingers)* it happens suddenly, just like that. No incipient nausea, no cold sweats or fever. You're feeling just fine, and then you look out the window and see Africa hanging upside down, or you think *you're* upside down, and then someone floats up next to you at a ninety-degree angle, and you lose your cookies. Then you're the most godawful kind of sick you've ever been since you were a kid, and it doesn't go away for a long, long time.

The flight crew tries to do their best to make you comfortable until the rendezvous is made with Phoenix Station, and they're good old boys, but the truth is that they're secretly disgusted with you and can't wait to get your puke-face butt off their ship. Three or four hours after launch, your shuttle docks with the space station, and some nice person manages to tow you out of the shuttle and through the station to the OTV docks. It gets more embarrassing then, because you're clutching your stomach with one hand and your vomit bag with the other, and if there's anyone in the access tunnels, they're quickly backing out of your way in case you explode again. . . .

Anyway, the OTV disengages from Phoenix Station and you ride out, with several more sick people, to the LTV hangars in orbit about fifteen miles away. There's three of 'em there . . . two regular moonships, the *Collins* and the *Fred Haise*, plus the special 1st Space Infantry troop transport, the *Valley Forge*, which you can't see most of the time because they've got the hangar doors closed . . . and finally your OTV docks with one of the civilian ships. Then you get shoved through the collar into the LTV, where you're handed over to the tender mercies of the crew.

Now, I gotta be honest. If you're on the *Collins*, we're even less tolerant of you than the shuttle or space station crews, because you're baggage, and green-faced baggage at that. So you get pushed into a tiny cabin in the mid-deck, about the size of a phone booth, where you're zipped into a sleep restraint up to your armpits and handed a fresh vomit bag and threatened with bodily harm if you powerchuck on our nice clean bulkheads. A while later you feel the LTV undock from the hangar, and about an hour after that you feel the AOMV's main engine fire, and that's when you know you're on your way to the Moon.

The Star Whoops usually goes away in a day or two, as long as you don't eat anything or move your head too much. You've begun to feel better, but now you're faced with two days of excruciating boredom. Unless you've made friends with the crew . . . *(laughs)* fat chance, because we don't want to know you . . . the flight deck is off-limits, so you're confined to mid-deck, which is about the size of a small den.

Up on the flight deck, we're keeping pretty busy much of the time, and since we've got windows, we can watch Earth receding in one direction and the Moon getting closer in another. But down below . . . well, it gets pretty fucking boring for the cattle. If you've thought ahead, you tossed a nice, long paperback novel into your duffel bag before you left the Cape. If you haven't, you're shit out of luck. There's a couple of windows on the mid-deck, but they won't do you much good. The LTV is flying backwards, so you can't watch the Moon as it gets closer, and there's radar and S-band antennas sticking out from the fuselage which prevent you from getting a last good look at Earth. Cislunar space is almost dark as pitch . . . can't hardly make out any stars, despite what you've seen on the TV shows . . . so mostly all you can see beyond the glass is this great, black void. It's about as exciting as watching a dead TV screen.

So you've got two days of hanging around in the mid-deck, plenty of time to consider whether you've made a serious career mistake. You spend the time getting acquainted with your fellow passengers, reading and re-reading the moonbase orientation guide . . . which is about as exciting as reading a computer maintenance manual . . . and anticipating the next tasty meal of rehydrated beef stroganoff or reconstituted shrimp cocktail, neither of which are exactly four-star. You eventually find yourself practicing zero g somersaults, which is fun until one of us sticks his head through the forward hatch and tells you to cut it out before you break something, and after that there's really nothing left to do except to sleep. And that's how you go to the Moon . . . catching zee's.

That's why in the saying about only making the trip to the Moon once, it's considered to be a blessing. And that's another one of the reasons why, when we heard that Descartes' new GM was a NASA and Skycorp veteran who had been to the Moon twice already, we were pretty leery of him. This is his second tour of duty? He's gotta be out of his mind! Who would want to go back to *that* dump again?

4. The Promised Land

Lester awoke to the sound of an electronic cricket chirping in his ear. His eyes opened to soft, warm darkness; he pushed back the black cotton eyeshades from his face. The lights of his compartment in the *Collins'* mid-deck had been turned low; he was wrapped in a nylon sleep restraint. Lester heard the cricket chirp again, and he reached up to his ear to touch the lobe of his headset. "Riddell," he muttered.

Good morning, sir. It was the commander of the *Michael Collins*, Alli James. *We're at six minutes till AOMV separation. We thought you might want to join us up here.*

"Hmm." Lester's mouth tasted greasy, as if he had been eating bad fried chicken the night before. He ran the tip of his tongue across his front teeth, wiping away a thin, sticky sheen of grime. He could have used a toothbrush right now, but there wasn't enough time to visit the head. "Yeah. I'll be right down . . . um, up. Whatever."

Do you need help? she asked, not unkindly.

He winced. The *Collins* had been in space for two days, and during that time its crew had silently watched Descartes Station's new general manager struggle to reacclimate himself to the big and small problems of spaceflight. He had been sick as hell for the first day, and when his stomach had finally stopped flip-flopping, there had come the fight to regain his zero g reflexes. But even if he had needed help now, it would be over his dead body before he asked for it. Ready or not, he had to be the man in charge now.

"No, thanks," Lester replied. "I'll be right up." He touched the headset lobe again, signing off the intership comlink, then unzipped the bag and reached for the overhead handrail. He was fully dressed in his jumpsuit; prior experience had taught him never to get undressed for sleep, since it could hinder a person in the event of an in-flight emergency. He glanced at the luminous face of his wristwatch and saw that he had been asleep for only four and a half hours, yet he felt as if he'd caught a full eight hours of sleep. Another effect of spaceflight; in microgravity, the body requires less time to recharge. The dream of American industry realized: less rest, more work . . .

As Lester shoved aside the curtain of his compartment and floated out into the mid-deck, the recessed overhead lights brightened. Someone on the flight deck had thoughtfully decided to provide him with a semblance of morning. He passed storage bins decorated with taped-up postcards of sunny beach scenes and mountain trails, and noticed that the curtain had been pulled open in the compartment which had been occupied by the only other passenger on this trip; apparently she had also been invited to the flight deck for the landing. Across the narrow aisle, the curtain hiding the toilet was also open. He had the urge to make a visit, but he dismissed it. He could hold his bladder for another twenty or thirty minutes until they landed, and he had never enjoyed whizzing into a suction hose.

Riddell grasped the ladder with his hands and hauled himself up through the hatch onto the flight deck. The low, cramped compartment was dimly lit; most of the illumination came from tiny red and green status lights on the wraparound dashboards and from the silver-blue glow of the computer screens. The flight deck was a netherworld of thin, stark shadows; the pilot and co-pilot were two vague lumps sitting in high-backed seats in front of the angular, multipaned windows. He felt his way to an unoccupied seat behind the commander's seat on the left, lowered himself into it, and searched for the harness straps which dangled like dead tapeworms on either side.

Alli James looked around and favored him with a wide, buck-toothed grin: a homely Texarkana farm girl who had managed to get herself out of the soybean fields and onto the high frontier. "Get enough sleep?" she asked politely. Lester nodded. "Good. Three minutes to AOMV separation, better strap in tight." She turned back to her station. "How's it looking there, Ray?"

"Systems copacetic. Internal electrical is powered up, batteries on standby." The pilot's head was encased in a bulbous VR helmet; a fiber-optic cable led from the back of the helmet to the dashboard before him, and only his mouth could be seen below his opaque black visor. Inside the helmet, he was seeing the hallucinatory panorama of virtual-reality: a 3-D computer-simulated horizon, a gridwork of XYZ line coordinates, navigational beacons, guidance parameters, and artificial imagery. Like a mime artist imitating a pilot at work, Ray Carroll lifted a gloved hand, pointed his finger to an invisible console in mid-air, and made a couple of jabbing motions. Lester felt the moonship jar slightly as the RCR's on the outer hull fired to correct their trajectory.

"LTV tank pressurization complete on all four," Ray drawled. "Guidance primary is on, abort sequence is off. Status is go. Ready to decouple AOMV."

"Good deal," Alli replied. "Okay, we're on full internal. Ready to come off autopilot." As commander, Alli flew without wearing a VR helmet, to verify that Ray's electronic vision wasn't deceiving him. She reached up and snapped toggles which disengaged the autopilot, tapped a couple of digits into the flight computer, then pulled back the candy-striped safety cover from the booster-release bar above her head and watched as the digital timer on her main board counted down. "Autopilot off, manual descent system engaged. Y'all ready there?" Carroll nodded. "All right. AOMV separation minus five . . . four . . . three . . . two . . . one . . ."

Holding the yoke steady with her left hand, she yanked the release bar down with her right hand. There was a sudden jar as the pyros ignited to separate the *Collins'* lunar lander from its aerobraking orbital maneuvering vehicle, the unmanned first-stage booster which had brought them from Earth to the Moon.

James gently moved the yoke in a shallow arc; as the lander slowly turned around, the cylindrical booster floated past the windows, receding as it entered its parking orbit. Strapped to trusses behind the huge round disk of the heat shield were four squat, mylar-wrapped cargo canisters. A tug from the base would rendezvous later with the AOMV to unload the Spam-cans and bring them down to Descartes, a two-step system which saved on the LTV's reaction mass. Alli studied the AOMV for a few seconds as she fired the control jets to distance the lander from the booster. "AOMV and the Spam-cans look good," she said. "No damage."

"Distance five hundred six," Ray reported. "I read you go for LOI."

"Good 'nuff for me if it is for thee." The commander flicked back the safety cover from the engine-arm toggle and flipped it, then rested her right hand on the throttle next to her seat. "Okay, let's take her around. Primary descent engine armed and ready. Counting down for LOI burn, on my mark. Six . . . five . . . four . . . three . . . two . . . one . . . mark."

She eased the throttle forward, and there was a long, shuddering jar as the lander's main engine fired. For a couple of minutes there was the sensation of gravity. Lester felt his butt settle into the seat, and heard some unsecured object drop to the floor in the mid-deck below. Through the front windows he saw the gray, curving face of the Moon as it hove into view—upside down, about fifty miles below them and closing.

The standard flight plan for lunar descent called for the *Collins* to make a single, elliptical orbit around the Moon; since the Apollo days, this was done to effect a steady, fuel-conservative deceleration before final approach and landing. The LTV had already overshot the Descartes highlands. To the south, Lester recognized the brown-gray maria of the Sea of Clouds; to the north lay the vast plains of the Ocean of Storms, pockmarked by the crater Copernicus and, just beyond that, the shining rays of Kepler. The tiny shadow of the moonship rapidly coasted across the maria until it merged with the deeper shadows of the Cordillera mountain region when, abruptly, the ship passed the daylight terminator and they were flying over the night-shrouded lunar farside.

Riddell heard a low moan from the seat beside him. For the first time since he had entered the flight deck, he noticed the young woman strapped into the passenger seat beside him.

If Alli James was homely in a fetching sort of way, then Tina McGraw, the new Skycorp lunar worker, was just plain homely: wide face, wide body, short-cropped mouse-brown hair, and a figure which bordered on masculinity. She had said very little to Lester over the last couple of days; in fact, she had almost been rude in her stand-offish attitude. She was saying even less now. McGraw stared fixedly at a point between her knees, her jaw muscles working as she clenched her teeth. Lester smiled a little. McGraw had been battling space sickness when the two of them had transferred aboard the *Collins* from Skycorp's LEO station; it had been only yesterday that she had been able to keep anything in her stomach. Now, seeing the Moon upside down, she was fighting Star Whoops again.

"That's right," Lester said softly. "Keep your eyes on something that's not moving. I'll let you know when it's safe to look up again." McGraw nodded her head slightly, but said nothing.

The graphic readout on the dashboard computer screen between the pilots showed that the LTV was steadily rolling over on its axis; they were now traveling close to six thousand miles per hour. "Pitchover one-sixty, roll zero, yaw zero," the co-pilot murmured. "One-forty . . . one-ten . . ."

"Coming up on pericynthian," Alli murmured offhandedly. "By the way, Les, there's Hawking Station."

Lester craned his neck to peer over her shoulder. Farside was a darker-than-dark mass between them and the sun. He could see nothing . . . then, for a moment, he glimpsed the cruciform light which marked the unmanned lunar observatory. The long, dotted lines of the very-low-frequency radio telescope array spread out for fifty miles in compass-point directions from the semiautomatic observatory poised near the edge of Krasovsky Crater. "Yeah, I see it."

"Uh-huh," Alli said distantly. She was through playing tour guide; back to business. "Altitude fifty-five thousand feet."

"Roger that," Ray said. "Pitchover one hundred forward, roll minus twenty, yaw ten. Compensating for drift. Coming up on nearside terminator. Get ready for powered descent burn, on my mark." He paused. "I'm picking up LDSM's signal, too," he added with a smile. "Sounds like the Moondog McCloud show."

"Moondog McCloud?" Riddell asked.

"The jock on the lunar radio station." Alli glanced over her shoulder. "You *have* been away a while, haven't you?" She chuckled a little. "What's he playing, Ray?"

"Chuck Berry."

"Oooh! I *love* Chuck Berry. I'll put it on the cabin speakers." She touched the communications panel keypad, setting the volume low, and the opening riffs of "The Promised Land" squalled through the cabin.

"Good tunes. Okay, Ray, ready for PDI on your mark." Alli once again grasped the engine throttle. She let her left hand glide to the communications board and toggled a couple of switches without looking. "Descartes Traffic, this is Skycorp LTV oh-five-eleven, requesting clearance for primary approach, over."

"Pitch ninety-four," Ray continued. "Ninety-three, ninety-two, ninety-one . . . mark." Alli moved the yoke forward again, the main engine fired again, braking their approach for landing. They could see only stars through the window; the lander was flying backwards now, its forward hull facing away from the lunar surface.

Sunlight abruptly broke through the windows, casting long, quick-moving shadows across the cabin before the photosensitive filters kicked in and reduced the glare. Riddell checked the screen again; the simulations confirmed that the ship had passed over the terminator. They should be somewhere over the highlands region separating Smyth's Sea and the Sea of Fertility by now, just south of the equator. He glanced at McGraw, who was cautiously beginning to raise her head. "Not yet, Tina," he said quickly.

McGraw caught a glimpse of what was going on, then hastily ducked her head again. "Oh boy," she murmured. "Tell me when we're off the roller coaster."

If either the pilot or co-pilot was aware that one of their passengers was on the verge of spacesickness just behind them, they were too busy to say anything about it now. "Good PDI burn," Ray said, still staring ahead at a place only he could see. "Altitude fifty thousand feet, range one thousand eighty miles and closing."

"Roger that," Alli said. She was listening to the tinny voices in her headset. "We copy, Descartes Traffic, thank you. *Collins* is go for primary approach, over." She glanced at the computer screen. "Want to take us in, Ray?"

"My pleasure." Ray raised his hands in front of him, touching invisible buttons in midair. Minute shudders ran across the hull as the moonship slowly moved into a vertical position, its RCR's firing to correct its course. Through the windows, the lunar horizon again moved into view. Below them stretched the dark-gray expanse of the Sea of Fertility. "Altitude forty thousand feet, range eight hundred ten miles and closing."

"Can I look up now?" Tina asked.

"It depends," Lester said nonchalantly. "On the plus side, we're flying rightside-up." McGraw raised her head, saw a normal looking horizon through the windows, and sighed gratefully. "On the other hand," Lester added, "you'll be interested to know that a blind man is flying the ship."

"Hey!" Ray said, affecting a helpless voice as his hands groped in the air. "Where's the dog-gone controls?"

Alli looked over her shoulder at McGraw. "Don't worry," she said. "It makes him feel useful. We've only crashed once doing this." McGraw stared at the back of Ray's helmet, glanced at the stark moonscape rushing past them, then wordlessly fixed her eyes on the floor again.

"We're now on final approach," Ray said. "Altitude thirty-two thousand two hundred feet, range three hundred fifty miles and closing."

"Your manual control is good," Alli replied. "Descartes Traffic, this is LTV oh-five-eleven on final approach, requesting landing instructions, do you copy? Over." She listened for a few moments. "We copy, Descartes. Touchdown approved for Pad One. We're on the beam and copacetic for landing. Over."

"Affirmative on that," Ray responded. "Altitude twenty thousand five hundred feet, range two hundred miles, and we've got visual acquisition."

The edge of Mare Nectaris was marked by the giant impact crater Theophilus and the long, snakelike crevasse of the Cyrillus Rill. The terrain was becoming rock-strewn and cratered once more, gradually rising to the highlands plateau. Far off on the curve of the horizon, they saw the red beacon lights and the tiny, white-on-gray sprawl of the lunar station. Ray's left hand clutched the throttle and slowly inched it forward, further braking the *Collins'* descent, as his right hand gripped the yoke.

"Altitude twelve thousand feet, range one hundred miles," he said as he carefully guided the moonship down. "Radar on and locked into the landing grid."

"We copy, Descartes Traffic, thank you," Alli said to the voice in her ear. "Traffic has us in their pattern and reports we're looking fine." She reached up and simultaneously clipped down a row of four toggles. They felt a slight tremor run through the moonship; she watched her status screen, then double-checked it against the lights above the toggles, which turned green. "Landing gear deployed and in position."

"Altitude one thousand five hundred feet, range twelve miles and closing," Ray said.

Lester could see the station better now: low, square and rectangular mooncrete buildings clustered together under bulldozed soil, interconnected by subterranean tunnels and above-ground crosswalks. The high MainOps tower and the aluminum-gray domes of the factory complex, gleaming in the midday sunlight, were almost all that could be seen of the base above the radiation-shielding regolith-pack. In mid-distance from the short horizon, he could make out tiny dozers and regolith combines slowly roaming the strip-mined plains to the north and northwest. Furthermost away, beyond the heavily tracked and trailed land, the long rails of the mass-driver stretched westward across twenty miles of high lunar plateau, crossing under the shadow of Stone Mountain.

Gazing down at the complex, he could only admire the work that had gone into the expansion of the base. A lot of moondogs had busted their asses getting the new base built. In 2016, when he had last been here, Descartes Station had been little more than a double row of prefab modules, nine in all. The mass-driver had yet to be built; a couple of tall refinery stacks and three dozers and a few rovers were all that had been available for the mining operations. Skycorp and NASA had persuaded the public into thinking Descartes was a mining town back then, even though the place was less developed than a mid-twentieth-century Antarctic base.

Lester shook his head in admiration; he had seen the pictures and layouts of the new base, but it had taken until this moment for him to believe it. They had done a lot with the place in the last eight years. Now Descartes Station was, in all truth, a company town.

The song on the radio ended, replaced by a guttural, fast-talking voice: One could imagine a Southern yahoo behind the microphone, babbling away as he fondled a pint of Wild Turkey between his legs, deliriously imagining himself to be the reincarnation of Wolfman Jack as his voice howled Top-40 shuck and jive across the pitted wastes. *Ow! Yeah! Baby baby baby! The father of rock 'n' roller, Mister Chuck Berry, courtesy of El-Dee-Ess-Em, home of the moonrocks . . . !*

"You've got to be kidding me," Lester muttered.

Now the moonship was directly above Descartes Station; the pilots were working together in concert, calling out angles of descent, nursing the engine thrust, letting the *Collins* gradually descend to the landing pad below. They felt the gentle tug of lunar gravity as the lander slowly descended on its engine-thrust.

Moondog McCloud's voice dropped to a conspiratorial growl.

That one was going out by request from some of the boys, to the—a solemn, reverential tone of voice now—*honored and most worthy passenger of the LTV arriving at Pad One even as I speak. . . .*

"I think they know you're coming," Alli murmured, grinning as she watched her dashboard. "Two-fifty and down, push it a little left by ten, down two bills . . .' "

"I'm flattered," Lester said, grinning from ear to ear. He was indeed; maybe this wasn't going to be so tough after . . .

The DJ's voice again rose to a hysterical scream. *Yowsuh, our new GM! The boss! The chief! The Ayatollah of the Moonah! The big BM the GM! Let's have a big LDSM welcome for Mister Lester Riddell!*

Then—at the moment the landing gear touched down on the scarred mooncrete landing pad, bringing a proud and embarrassed Lester Riddell back to the Moon—there came over the radio the sound of a loud, wet, and enthusiastically rude Bronx cheer. . . .

Alli James reached over to the com panel and snapped off the cabin feed. "Now wasn't that interesting?" she said drily.

Tina McGraw, finally raising her eyes from the floor, glanced at Riddell. So did the pilot and co-pilot, looking over the back of their seats at him. There was a long, frozen moment of silence in the moonship's flight deck.

"That wasn't very funny," McGraw said.

Lester just stared ahead at the windows.

Alli broke the pall by unclipping her checklist from beneath the dashboard. "Engine arm off. Controls auto. Gear sensors nominal change, gyro stable." She paused to flip toggles, then added with terse formality, "Welcome back, Mr. Riddell."

Lester's eyes came back into focus as he turned away from the window. There was no way he was going to take this kind of abuse. *Your first command decision, pal . . .*

"Patch me into MainOps," he said. Alli nodded and tapped a key on the communication panel; Lester touched the lobe of his headset. "Descartes Control, this is Lester Riddell, the new general manager. I want a meeting of all station personnel in the mess deck at thirteen hundred sharp. That's *everyone*, no excuses accepted. Call in all shifts. Absentees will be docked for one day's pay."

He switched off before he could get a reply; he didn't care to hear it. He released the headset and watched Ray and Alli go through the post-touchdown checklist. *I'll show you who's the Ayatollah of the Moonah*, he thought. *I'll show you who's in charge of the promised land.*

Yes, But Does She Know Anything About Igneous Formations? (Pressclips.2)

(Excerpt from "Susan Peterson—The Playboy *Interview";* Playboy, *March, 2022:*

The question that millions of men around the world have about you is . . .

I've heard it already. Why have I quit modeling to go to the Moon? *(sighs)* I thought I answered that a long time ago.

One more time, please . . .

If it'll help cut down on all those fan letters asking me to pose in a teeny-weeny little thong again, sure. *(laughs)* For starters, the Moon in general, and lunar geology in particular, was my first interest in life, not being a super-model. When I was a little girl I decided that, one way or another, I was going there. But I grew up in the poor-black area of Kansas City, and my folks didn't have enough money to send me through college . . . Dad was a city sanitation worker, which is not a high-paying profession. This meant that even after I managed to earn a high-school scholarship to go to college at Washington University in St. Louis, I didn't have any money to keep myself in school. My grant paid for the tuition and that was it. I still had to eat, and once I moved out of the dorm, pay rent for an apartment.

So you decided to go into modeling.

Well, I didn't really decide for myself. I mean, I never considered myself to be any sort of raving beauty. I was never a cheerleader or a prom queen in high school. But one of my roommates encouraged me to apply for work at a local modeling agency where she was part-timing herself. I was reluctant about the whole thing, but when she pointed out that they would be essentially paying me good money just to stand in front of a camera *(shrugs)* . . . well, it was either that or wait tables, so I went to the agency and, much to my surprise, they hired me.

And it sort of went from there. I worked in St. Louis for about a year, posing for local department stores ads, before I was discovered by a talent scout for the Ford Agency in New York.

You make it sound as if it was accidental.

It *was* accidental! Honestly, I never once considered myself to be a professional model, not even after I went to work for the Ford Agency. To me, it was moonlighting to earn money to get myself through school. It was just a job that paid better than most others. When you consider that lunar geology is Ph.D-track academic work—because you really can't find meaningful employment in this particular field without having earned a doctorate—I needed to keep employed almost constantly, especially after the scholarship ran out before I even received my B.S. And if that meant posing in fishnet bikinis for ten thousand dollars an hour, well . . .

Grin and bare it?

Why not? It paid my way all through postgraduate school.

So you didn't consider it glamorous work?

Are you kidding? Look . . . in the middle of a major research project or the writing of my thesis, I would have to drop everything and catch a plane to, say, Hawaii for a *Sports Illustrated* photo shoot. This is in January, so the Pacific Ocean at Maui is frigid at that time of year—it only looks warm in the photos—but they've got me peeled down to the buff, wearing this little spandex thing which leaves me next to stark naked, standing up to my waist in forty-six-degree surf. You ever wonder how swimsuit models make their nipples stick out? It's because they're so goddamn cold, that's why!

You're talking about when you were on the cover of the '18 Sports Illustrated *swimsuit issue. . . .*

Yeah, right. That sexy smile was because my teeth were chattering. Modeling is a twelve-hour-day job . . . and don't believe for a second it's not a job, because for each picture that actually gets printed, there's a few hundred exposures that end up on the darkroom floor. Half of them are in contortionist positions that only double-jointed persons should try, and the other half are in poses which would have made Masters and Johnson blush. By the end of the day, you're sore all over . . . and the next morning, you start it all over again. No, it's not glamorous. It's bloody hard work.

You once complained, in an interview published in Ms., *that modeling was demeaning side-work for a scientist.*

Yes, it is. I still stand by that statement. Look, I didn't ask to be African-Asian, beautiful, and stacked. Nature gave me this body, and I was able to utilize those looks as a way out of a bad financial predicament. In that sense, working as a Ford model was a blessing from heaven. But I didn't like what I was doing because of the major drawback.

Which was?

The eternal stereotype of beautiful women is that if they're good-looking, they must be stupid, too. *(winces)* Maybe it's because most guys are nervous about great-looking women who have brains. I mean, it was difficult as hell to have any meaningful relationship with men outside my lab at Washington U., because even though I could have had any man I wanted, most of them thought I had to be some bimbo . . . and that's just not my style, because I'm not going to play down my intelligence just for some guy's attention. So I'd go out on a date with somebody . . . I was getting fixed up with blind dates for a while . . . he'd ask me what I did besides modeling, and I'd start talking about how I was currently studying the volcanic origin of basalts from lunar maria, and these shutters would click down over their eyes. "Oh, God, she's smarter than I am . . . I can't handle this." End of relationship. Call me a cab. *(laughs)* And you can't go out on dates with your colleagues because you have to work with them in the lab. Job-fostered romances are nothing but poison. So, yeah, it was hard to be a researcher and a model at the same time. Practically impossible, in the long run, because your colleagues resent you for being famous, and your public doesn't want you to be intelligent.

Is this the answer to the question of why you quit modeling?

Took me a while to formulate the answer, didn't it? *(laughs)* Yeah, it is, but only a little bit. As it turned out, my contract with the Ford Agency happened to come up for renewal at the same time that I was finishing up my doctoral work at the university. The Lunar and Planetary Institute in Houston wanted me aboard as an associate, and Skycorp was offering me a contract to do basic research at Descartes Station, so . . . *(shrugs)* There wasn't really much of a choice, as I saw it.

Was the salary that they offered you comparable to your modeling fee?

Oh, nowhere even close! But it wasn't a question of salary. As I said before, lunar geology had been my calling in life. Why should I give up a chance to live and work on the Moon . . . my lifetime dream . . . just for a few more years of having the bottom of a swimsuit run up my ass? Besides, by that time I was twenty-nine years old. In the high-profile modeling world, that meant I was almost over the hill. I don't think there really was that much of a choice.

You were engaged for a short time to tennis champion Bill Cooper. That broke off as soon as you announced your intention to quit modeling. Did he want you to continue being a model?

I . . . (sighs) Hey, that's a personal matter between Billy and me. I don't want to comment on it here.

It's been said that he wanted you to stay in modeling, and that he broke it off when you opted for a full-time career as a research scientist.

No comment. It's nobody's business but our own. The breakup was peaceful, that's all anyone needs to know. Next question.

A lot of people believe that you were crazy for opting out of modeling when you were at the top of your profession.

My profession is science. Modeling was how I paid the bills. I was more than happy to get out of it when I could.

Your nickname in the modeling field was "Butch" . . .

Still is. That's what everyone calls me. Butch Peterson.

How did you get the name?

Because I was hard to work with. Maybe it's my mean streak. Maybe they meant "bitch" and somebody just misspelled it. Who cares? I like the name. Describes my character accurately. I'm a tough cookie.

Tough enough for the Moon?

Well, Skycorp's sending me up there in about five weeks, on a joint-operating agreement with the Lunar and Planetary Institute, just as soon as I complete my training at the Cape. Three years with the Descartes Station science team. We'll get to find out, won't we? (laughs) Hey, and if it doesn't pan out, I can always pose for a centerfold in *Playboy*, right?

5. The Usual Gang of Idiots

"You know, of course, that he's going to want to change everything," said Mighty Joe Young.

He was watching from the traffic control cupola on top of the LTV maintenance center. Out on Pad One, under the glare of the ring of landing beacons, ground vehicles moved in on the *Michael Collins* as hardsuited pad rats dragged fuel lines and power cables across the reinforced mooncrete apron toward the LTV. Mighty Joe dispassionately watched the scene through the triple-thick windows. "This guy's going to be nothing but trouble," he added sourly.

Casey Engel, the pad operations manager, didn't look up from his console. "Give him a chance, willya?" he answered softly as he watched a bank of TV and computer monitors. "He's company, but I heard he's been here before. He might be a blessing in disguise, for all we know."

"I doubt it." Mighty Joe shook his shaggy head. Joe Young resembled the cinematic ape after whom he was nicknamed: six-foot-six, 275 pounds of hard muscle covered by hairy, sunburned skin, heavily bearded and long-haired except for the beginnings of a bald spot on the crown of his head, which he kept covered with a baseball cap from a Florida alligator farm called Gatorama ("the only place in the world with more lizards than Skycorp," he was fond of telling people). Most of the time Mighty Joe was grinning, as if all the universe were a great cosmic gag and he was the only one who knew the punch line. Now he was glowering through the windows at the moonship.

"Bullshit," he groused. "Fucking company's up to something. First we get a work slowdown, then we get fifty new guys sent here in the last few weeks, and now *this* guy shows up." He thrust a hairy finger at the spacecraft. "I'm telling you, pal

61

of mine, there's a shitstorm coming. I can smell it and I can feel it.''

"Umm.'' Casey was barely paying attention to the tug pilot. Cupping his right hand over his ear, he listened to the voices in his headset. "Yeah, we verify that, Ray,'' he said. "Engines are safed and we've got you on external power. You're go to pop the hatch any time you're ready.'' He glanced over his shoulder at Mighty Joe. "Sorry, Joe. You were saying . . . ?''

"Nyahh . . . forget it.'' Mighty Joe looked away from the *Collins* toward the other side of the landing field, where his own ship was poised on Pad Two. A couple of other pad rats were working on the tug, their arms thrust deep within service hatches leading into the guts of the big, ugly spacecraft, prepping the ship for its next flight in a few hours. He smiled as he gazed upon the tug, once known as the *Harrison Schmitt* until he had rechristened it. Slightly smaller then the LTV on Pad One, but with larger DPS engines and trusslike strongbacks running along its lower fuselage, it resembled an albino toad which had just crawled out of a sandbox. Gray lunar dust was caked on its sides; its wide flight-deck windows and mid-deck airlock hatch gawked at him like an amphibian face. There were too many moonships named after old, dead astronauts already, and the tug was the only thing on the Moon bigger and uglier than himself. Its registered name had been insolently crossed out with two red swaths of paint, and its unofficial name had been crudely painted below: *Beautiful Dreamer*. No one got the inside joke behind the new name, which suited Mighty Joe Young just fine. Let the uncultured peasants lose sleep over it.

"Listen, the *Dreamer*'s still having trouble with Main Bus A,'' he said as he watched the pad rats crawling around the tug. "Probably a short in one of the conduits or something, maybe down in the mid-deck I think. The last flight up we had to keep switching over to the backup cells. I put in my report. Has anyone gotten around to fixing it yet?''

Casey sighed. "I dunno . . .''

Mighty Joe stared at the back of Engel's head. "You *don't know*? Hell, Casey, I gotta fly that thing with a faulty electrical system! *Why* don't you know?''

Casey nodded toward the tug. "See that kid on the left? That's one of the new guys Skycorp sent us this month. I brought it to his attention and he told me he'd look at it once he read the section in the service manuals.''

"Once he read the . . . ? Jesus and Mary, what was the kid doing before they sent him up here, flying model rockets in his backyard?"

The pad supervisor looked at him irritably. "Now that you mention it, he's got an NAR patch on his vest." Casey tapped a finger against the National Association of Rocketry patch on the right sleeve of his jacket. "Just like this one."

Mighty Joe grimaced. "Okay, okay, I'm sorry. Just get him to fix my damn ship, all right? That busline bothers me, and I gotta fly with it." He paused, again watching the activity on the field. "Just tell me one thing. Is the *Dreamer* going to launch on time?"

Casey waited until he had monitored the securance of the fuel line against the side of the *Collins*. A moondog climbed a ladder on a landing gear strut to manually push its collar into position and lock it firmly into place; when he was done, he turned and gave Casey a thumbs-up from across the pad. The controller nodded, double-checked his computer screen to make sure the seal was airtight, then touched a couple of buttons on his board to start the pump cycle. "You're go for launch," he replied without looking at Young, "but your window doesn't begin till fifteen-hundred. It's been moved back."

Mighty Joe took a deep breath and carefully counted to ten before he replied. He had a bad temper; everyone told him so, and he was trying to overcome a tendency to jump all over people. "May I ask," he queried as politely as he could, "whatever the hell for?"

Casey didn't say anything. He studiously watched the post-touchdown procedure until Joe laid a huge hand on his shoulder and squeezed just a little bit. Casey winced and testily shook off Mighty Joe's paw. "Lay off, willya? It's not my call. The new GM radioed MainOps just after they landed. He wants a general staff meeting in Mess at thirteen-hundred. We're all supposed to be there in one hour. No exceptions. So that means you don't launch till fifteen-hundred."

"What the *fuck*?"

"Hell, I don't know!" Casey snapped. "I'm just telling you what I heard. Anyone who doesn't show gets their pay docked for the day." He glanced over his shoulder at Young. "The best I can do is fifteen-hundred if I'm going to get you guys up without a scrub. I ran the flight-plan through the computer. You'll still make the pickup with the *Collins* AOMV, no problem."

"No problem." Joe let out his breath, then balled his right fist in his left hand and cracked his knuckles. "No problem," he repeated. "Okay."

He nodded his head lazily and turned to saunter toward the open hatch of the pressurized passageway leading back to the main building. He waited until he heard Casey's relieved sigh; then he turned back. "But remember," he added. "I want a clean launch at fifteen-hundred. Got it? No holds, no scrubs. And I want that main busline fixed. Everything copacetic, right?"

"Uh-huh. Yeah. Right. You got it, Joe."

"Delightful. I'm ever so fucking glad to hear it." Mighty Joe bent low and turned his wide shoulders to squeeze through the hatch into the tunnel. Great, he thought. Nothing to do but sit around and beat off until launch-time.

If he had ever doubted it before, he didn't doubt it now. The new GM was going to be nothing but trouble.

There was a portrait of Alfred E. Neuman, cut from the cover of an issue of *Mad*, taped to the door of the Lunar Resources lab. Below it was a handprinted sign: "The Usual Gang of Idiots," with the names of the Descartes Station's science staff listed underneath. Once there had been five names on the roster, but now there were only two: Susan Peterson, Ph.D., and Lewis Walker, M.D. The three other names had been crossed off the list.

The string of brown prayer beads made a soft, rhythmic snapping noise, like tiny castanets, as they moved through Monk Walker's fingers: *click . . . click . . . click . . . click . . . click . . .* Butch Peterson usually found it a soothing background sound, like the random music of wind chimes tinkling in a summer breeze. It was the sound of Monk's mind at work. Now the prayer beads sounded disturbed, restless. Butch stared for a few more moments at the raw data from the most recent local geological survey before she finally gave up. She swiveled her chair away from her desk terminal and stared at Monk Walker.

The chief physician was sitting on a stool next to the window, gazing out at the lunar plain. Windows in Subcomp A were rare; much of the base lay underground and most of the above-ground structures were buried by regolith, so space for windows had to be scalloped out from beneath the soil. They were lucky to have this one window in the science lab, and luckier still to have such a good view. The gentle slopes of Stone Mountain rose on the southeastern horizon, with the crescent Earth hanging overhead, but she sensed that he wasn't really looking at the scenery. She looked at the small string of beads in his right hand and noted that they were moving outwards from his palm. In the Buddhist tradition it meant that the object of Monk's meditation was external, outside of himself.

Butch had learned not to interrupt Walker's meditations; if he wanted to speak, he would interrupt himself. No one else on the Moon received this kind of courtesy from Butch Peterson. Indeed, she itched to make some sort of smartass remark—*Playing with yourself again?* or *Try chewing your nails, it's quieter*—but she deferentially kept her silence.

Monk's gaze presently moved from the window to her, and the clicking of the beads paused as he raised a questioning eyebrow. "Yes?" he asked.

She smiled and shrugged slightly. "Penny for your thoughts?"

"I'm driving you crazy again? Sorry." He considered her remark. "They're probably not worth even a penny."

"Naah. Your penny-ante thoughts are worth a nickel to anyone else's." Butch moved the mouse across the pad so that the cursor touched the SAVE function; then she tapped the button to close the file. Might as well, she thought. Can't get a damn thing done today, anyway. "How about some tea?"

She stood up from her chair and arched her back as she asked the question, wrapping her arms behind her and letting her head tip back, feeling her breasts stretch against her washed-out Royals sweatshirt. A standard modeling pose, remembered from the old days, but it felt good. A sexy stretch; the grand old dames at the Ford Agency would have been proud. If she had done this outside the privacy of the lab, at least seventy-five guys in Descartes—not counting the small handful of gays—would have been driven apeshit.

But not Monk. The only deliberately celibate man on the Moon was sitting right here in her lab. Butch spied on Lew Walker out of the corner of her eye; his expression was totally neutral. Butch Peterson could have jumped up on her workbench and started a striptease, and Monk would have warned her that she might fall off and bruise herself . . . or dismissively turned to look out the window and started playing with his beads again. Her stretch didn't do a thing for him. He nodded his close-cropped head. "Tea sounds good."

She let out her breath and dropped her arms. "Thanks, Lew," she murmured gratefully.

He blinked. "What for?"

"Never mind." Butch walked over to the plastic flask mounted above an electric burner. Their combined daily drinking-water ration was collected in the flask; she picked it up and examined the scale. "Only about a liter left. Want it now or later?"

Monk thought about it. "Now. Just make it a small cup. Use this morning's tea bag, please. No sense in letting it go to waste."

"One secondhand cup of tea coming up." She dropped two moist, leftover tea bags in their respective drinking mugs—his had the seal of the University of Massachusetts stamped on the enamel, hers bore the *Cosmopolitan* logo—and switched on the burner. As the precious water began to boil, Butch turned and leaned against the bench, folding her arms across her chest. "It's about the new general manager, isn't it?"

The beads clicked between his fingers. "Sort of, but not quite . . ." He shook his head. *Click.* "I can't put my finger on it, but I don't have a good feeling about this meeting." *Click-click.* "I don't know any more than you do about Riddell, but Skycorp couldn't have picked a worse time to install a new GM. There's a lot of ill feeling toward the company right now."

Butch pulled her long hair back behind her neck and reached for a hairband on her desk. "If you're expecting me to sympathize with Huntsville, you haven't been paying much attention lately to current events. I've been swamped since the purge, and I don't believe a word Arnie Moss or Ken Crespin says about a new science team."

"Why don't you?"

"C'mon. The writing's on the wall. Basic science is the bottom priority now. The only reason they kept me around is because the legal department couldn't find a way to wriggle out of the joint-operating agreement with LPI."

Walker slowly nodded. "Uh-huh . . . and that's what's scaring me. Have you checked the newsfeeds lately?"

She shook her head, and he continued. "I looked at the *Wall Street Journal* on-line edition yesterday. . . . "

"You reading the *Wall Street Journal*?"

He shrugged. "If you want to keep up on the news, you have to read everything. Even if it doesn't have a crossword puzzle." He smiled briefly. "Anyway, there was a small item yesterday about some sort of agreement being hammered out between Sky-corp and Uchu-Hiko. Nobody seems to know what's going on. Or if they do, they're not talking about it.''

Peterson shrugged. "The Korean project? That's old news.''

Click. "No, it can't be just the Korea powersat.'' *Click.* "It's something else again.''

Peterson frowned as she tied back her hair. It could be an expanded powersat construction program . . . but if it was, Sky-corp had picked a strange bedfellow to negotiate an agreement with: The Japanese space company Uchu-Hiko was its closest competitor. Despite its current financial troubles, Skycorp had managed to successfully complete the West European solar power satellite system with its own resources. The capital infrastructure for building the new SPS for the United Republic of Korea was already in place, so the company didn't need to invite aboard its top rival in the space industry for any future projects, even though Uchu-Hiko had been making noises about expanding its base from launch services and zero g manufacturing to high-space construction. Then again, Korea had become Japan's closest trade partner in the last few years. . . .

Butch gave up. She had never been able to comprehend the intricate business dealings of the space industry. "You might have a point,'' she conceded. "What is it, then?''

The beads stopped clicking. Monk waved his hand briskly. "Don't worry about *what* it is. That's really not the point. It's the *how* that bothers me. . . . ''

She shook her head. "I don't follow you.''

"Whatever Skycorp has in mind, it's no small project. And if that's the case, Descartes isn't ready to handle it.''

"Uh-huh. Okay . . .''

"Right. Look at the situation here. We've had firings, a bonus freeze, a work slowdown, and an embargo on nonessential goods. That's all in the last few months. Half of the work force—the ones who survived the purge—is demoralized. They've even stopped thinking of themselves as employees. In their minds, they're wage-slaves being yanked around by the company . . .''

"I second that emotion,'' she interjected.

". . . and the other half doesn't know which end is up,'' Monk continued. "Huntsville obviously rushed the new guys through training. Some of these kids must have thought they were taking jobs in the Virgin Islands, they're so unprepared. I've been seeing guys in the infirmary who were suffering from dehydration because no one told them how to handle water-rationing, or nearly breaking their legs because they don't know how to walk in one-sixth gee.''

He stopped and sighed. ''Remember the kid I treated two days ago, the one who blacked out during EVA?'' Butch nodded. ''Turned out he didn't know how to interpret the mix indicator in his suit. He thought that his oxygen intake remained constant, no matter how much work he was doing outside, so he overcompensated the nitrogen intake. He was singing 'Happy Trails' when they caught up with him. Any longer and he might have tried to take off his helmet. Nobody told him how to watch his levels.''

Butch gazed out the window at the pockmarked plains as Walker went on. ''And now there's some new deal being hatched. We're going to hear about it in a few minutes, I'm sure. Whatever it is, these kids aren't ready to handle it.''

''They're not kids,'' she murmured, turning to look at him.

Monk smiled at her. ''C'mon, Sue. Some of those guys had your *Sports Illo* cover stapled to their bedroom walls when they were trying to figure out who to take to the senior prom. We're not talking about people with acquired wisdom and maturity.''

''And you?'' she teased.

''I told you already. I was . . .''

''Right. Running an antique movie projector in Tibet for the Dalai Lama. He loved Marx Brothers movies. You told me.'' Peterson went back to looking out the window. Beyond the domes of the factory subcomplex and the regolith strip mines, she could see the rails of the mass-driver leading westward out into the lunar desert. When she had first arrived here a little more than a year ago, the mass-driver had been operating almost twenty-four hours per Earth day, the spherical cargo cans hurtling down through the electromagnetized track until they reached escape velocity at the ramp at the end of the line. That level of activity hadn't been seen in the last two months; the mass-driver was only working part time now.

''Ready or not, they're going to get it,'' she said, more to her own reflection in the window than to Walker. ''If only we knew what kind of guy the company's sent us . . .''

''Hmm?'' *Click-click.* A pensive pause. ''Perhaps we could find out,'' Monk said slowly. ''Maybe we could ask for a private meeting.''

Butch looked sharply at him. ''Today?''

"Why not? You're senior scientist, I'm the chief physician. He should get to know us, right?" Monk hopped off the stool and walked past her toward the workbench. "We could try to catch him right before he goes to the mess hall," he said as he picked up the flask and poured hot water into his tea mug. "Strictly low-profile, of course. A little get-together in his office, perhaps."

"Roll out the welcome wagon?" She held out her mug. "Here."

"It's the only welcome wagon he's going to get." He poured water into her mug. "Someone should talk to him about our problems here. I'm not going to count on the Huntsville boys giving him all the messy details."

Butch sipped her tea and nodded. The general manager's office was directly across the corridor from the lab; that was probably his next stop after he desuited in the ready-room. "Sure, why not? Maybe we can ask some straight questions then."

"Maybe. Just don't count on straight answers." Monk tucked his beads into a vest pocket and headed for the door. "Let's try it anyway. C'mon. Let's park ourselves over there."

Peterson blinked. "Your keycard's set for the GM office door? You never told me."

"Sure. I'm the doctor, remember? Bo Fisk coded me on the card." The former holy man shrugged as he opened the door. "This qualifies as a medical emergency. I'm trying to prevent Lester Riddell from cutting his throat at the staff meeting."

Willard DeWitt's sleep-niche in Dorm 1-A was the same size as every other individual's in Descartes: six feet across by eight feet deep by nine feet high. With the bunk folded up against the aluminum wall, there was just enough room for him to sit at his fold-down desk or to open his wall-locker; he couldn't do both at the same time. He had been in jail cells which were larger . . . and, indeed, the dorms resembled prison cell blocks: cold, efficient, sterile, meant for sleeping and privacy and little else.

It scarcely mattered to him, though. His niche had one saving grace: a private communications/computer terminal built into the wall above the desk. It had a phone for making long-distance calls to Earth—although comsat-time was rationed, just like everything else, and enormously expensive—and he had discovered that the terminal had a serial port into which he could jack his Toshiba laptop, the only personal item he had brought with him to the Moon. The computer was meant for mundane tasks like checking the base's bulletin board and keeping a personal diary, yet he had already found a way, by interfacing his Toshiba through the serial port, to crack into the base mainframe. Through this back door, he could annex the base's central tele-communications system. A couple of minor systems tests had convinced him that he was capable of uploading and download-ing data with any networked computer on Earth; diverting the phone bill somewhere else was simple enough after that.

Sitting now at his desk, gazing silently at the blank surface of his clamshell screen as he absently rubbed his recently bearded chin, Willard had to grin. No one here knew better, but putting him in a room alone with a modemed computer was like leaving a little kid alone with a box of Hershey bars.

Beyond the claustrophic walls of his niche, he could hear the ruckus of the all-male dorm swirling around him. Men talked, laughed, argued, shouted down the narrow aisles to each other. Niche doors opened and slammed shut, the sounds reverberating through the cramped block. At the end of his aisle, there was the hollow sucking sound of a commode being flushed in the head; from the ceiling-mounted speaker above his head, the sexy beauty of an old Koko Taylor number rumbled in from the blues portion of Moondog McCloud's daily radio show. All the shifts were coming in for the general staff meeting in the mess hall. Descartes Station was jumping at noon, and so was his imagi-nation.

The blank screen stared back at him like a painter's canvas awaiting the first, crucial brush stroke. He was a quarter of a million miles from home, far out of the reach of the SEC and the FBI and the IRS and everyone else. No one knew anything about Jeremy Schneider, the new third-shift communications of-ficer. His cover was foolproof, at least so far. True, if the ham-mer came down again, he had nowhere to run or hide, but that was only a minor consideration, really. After two weeks of being here, he was beginning to itch again for another profitable scam. But what to do with so much potential at his fingertips?

The fact is, Will—he reluctantly admitted to himself—you're addicted to this sort of thing. You've got money squirreled away in several discreet bank accounts back on Earth, probably as much as Jeremy Schneider may earn in the next year in this hellhole. Yet the acquisition of wealth has never been the point, has it? You *like* your complex game of cops-and-computer-robbers, don't you? Hell, you *love* it!

And that's what it all comes down to, isn't it? Sure, you could lie low in this place for the next twelve months: doing Jeremy Schneider's boring job, playing poker for tobacco chews with the boys, watching dumb TV shows in the rec room, griping about the terrible food, going out for an occasional stroll on the surface, waiting for the heat to die down back home. But you'll probably go crazy that way, won't you? Because, in your own way, you're an artist, and artists go nuts when they can't practice their art. Face it, pal, you need to . . .

The Koko Taylor number ended and Moondog McCloud growled through the ceiling speaker. *Oh, lordy lordy yeah, Missus Koko Taylor, rounding off the Blues Hour here at LDSM, the voice of Descartes Station. Now listen here, boys and girls, don't forget the general staff meeting at thirteen-hundred hours in the mess hall. You know where that is, now, don't you? If you've forgotten, better ask your buddy, 'cuz the new GM tells us he ain't gonna accept no excuses for bein' tardy or absentee, if y'know what I mean. . . .*

A deep-throated chuckle. *But if you're one of our occasional listeners out there who just so happens to pick up our signal quite accidentally . . . that's right, Olympus Station, we're talking about you . . . don't worry. None of you freeloaders are required to attend.* Another chuckle. *Just think about it, folks! We're going out at the speed of light throughout the universe! This radio show will someday, somehow, be heard across the galaxy! I'm FAMOUS! I'm BAD! And I'm not even in the Arbitron books! I'm . . .*

The voice suddenly dropped to a disappointed mutter. . . . *Moondog McCloud, here at the last radio station in the solar system. Drop a note in the box in the rec room if you have any requests, okay? Until I get a real job, here's the Rolling Stones with the theme song of our little mandatory meeting today, by request from Slow Mo and the Bulldozer Patrol. . . .*

Another oldie banged over the speaker. As Mick Jagger began singing "Under My Thumb," the windows of Willard DeWitt's mind drifted open as if caught by a criminal breeze. His head lolled back on his neck, sagging against the stiff back of his chair, as something Moondog McCloud had just said echoed through his brain: the whisper of an idea, concealed in the off-hand remark of the only disk jockey in outer space.

For the next eight minutes, the mind of Willard DeWitt played
and pummeled and tinkered with the rough machinery of a perfect scam. He sat absolutely still, his body so inert that if he'd
relaxed any further he would have started drooling, entranced
with the vision of a perfect scam: *if I can . . . if he will . . . if
we can do this . . . and then this . . .*

The door to his next-door neighbor's locker abruptly slammed
shut. Willard's head rocked forward. He automatically shifted in
his seat, cleared his throat, stretched his arms to smooth out the
sleeves of his sweatshirt. The stream of consciousness had ebbed
to a trickle, but still he heard the water of an idea falling over
rocks, gliding downstream.

Finally he switched off his computer, pushed back the chair
and stood up. He gazed down at his desk, and as Mick sang
about a cheating heart coming back to him, a smile slowly spread
across Willard's face.

He had his next scam.

Good Luck, McDuck
(Video.1)

From "Welcome to Descartes Station," a Skycorp training film. Copyright © 2023 by Hi-Quality Film Productions Inc., Flint, Michigan:

(MUSIC UP. Skycorp logo appears, then FADE TO the Narrator; behind him is a large model of the Moon.)

Narrator (on screen): "Hi! I'm Jeff Larson. You probably remember me from when I played Ralph Sweeney, the happy-go-lucky lunar miner in the TV series *Moonbase Blues*. But what you're about to see isn't science fiction, and we're not about to visit a Hollywood sound-stage. I'm pleased to welcome you to Descartes Station. . . . "

(POV the summit of Stone Mountain; camera PANS LEFT across the terrain until it STOPS at Descartes Station. An INSET appears in the RIGHT BOTTOM CORNER of the screen, revealing a map of the Moon: Landmarks are HIGHLIGHTED on the map as they are mentioned. The inset disappears, then the camera slowly PULLS IN on the base.)

Narrator (V.O.): "This is Descartes Station . . . your home away from home for the duration of your employment with Skycorp. Although two other outposts exist on the Moon . . . Skycorp's man-tended Permaice Extraction Facility near Byrd Crater at the lunar North Pole, and the automated Stephen Hawking Lunar Observatory at Krasovsky Crater on the lunar farside . . . Descartes Station in the largest permanently manned station. So let's take a good look at the place, shall we . . . ?"

(Stock footage of: NASA moonships landing in the Descartes highlands, the first prefab "modular" habitat, Skycorp construction crews building the new structures, etc.)

Narrator: "The first lunar base in the Descartes highlands was established in December, 2005, as a temporary NASA base camp. After Skycorp was formed in 2010, the corporation purchased the facility from the United States Government, and beginning in 2011, additional prefab modules were added to the base, now called Descartes Station. The base continued to expand until 2020, when it was decided that modular construction no longer suited the permanent colony's growing needs. The new base uses 'mooncrete' slabs as the primary building material, with Mylar liners added to the interior walls to ensure atmospheric integrity. In addition, all structures except the control towers, the nearby SP-100 nuclear reactors, and the factory domes are covered with lunar soil, or regolith, for additional protection against radiation. The third-generation facilities at Descartes Station were erected between 2021 and early 2023. As a result, your moonbase is a brand-new, state-of-the-art habitat. . . . ''

(A schematic diagram of the moonbase's layout gradually FADES IN over the stock footage. As the narrator speaks, the described areas are highlighted in bright red.)

Narrator: "As you can see from this diagram, Descartes Station is actually comprised of several interdependent subcomplexes, which are connected by access tunnels. Oh, and by the way, all the subcomplexes are designed to automatically seal off from one another in the highly unlikely event of a loss-of-pressure emergency. Just thought you'd like to know. . . .''

(MONTAGE of still shots from Subcomplex A interior: Main-Ops, mess hall, rec room, atrium, etc.)

Narrator: "In the center is Subcomp A. It has three levels. On top is the tower for Main Operations, the command center sometimes known as MainOps. Below it, on the first level, are various crew facilities . . . the mess hall, medical clinic, men's and women's locker rooms, the rec room, and various small offices and science labs. The second level, which is underground, is comprised mainly of the life-support center . . . including the water reclamation, waste-recycling center, and water and oxygen storage tanks . . . as well as storage rooms, the lower level of the medical clinic, and the emergency shelter for solar storms. All three levels are reached through a central stairwell, which also serves as a botanical atrium. Looks like a nice place to visit during your off-hours, doesn't it . . . ?''

(Camera DOLLIES through an open hatch and moves down an access tunnel into one of the dorms. As the camera moves

past rows of sleeping niches, the schematic diagram reappears in an INSET in the UPPER LEFT CORNER.)

Narrator: "This tunnel takes us into your living quarters—Subcomp D, also known as the Dorms. As you can see, this subcomplex is comprised of three separate buildings. Dorm One, on both A and B levels, serves as the bunkhouse for men, with a total of eighty niches. Dorm Two-A, the top level, is the living quarters for women, with twenty niches. Dorm Two-B, the lower level, has mixed-gender living quarters for base administrators. Each level has its own lavatories, which the residents of each level share in common. Dorm Three is reserved as a temporary residence for visitors to the station, and is not usually occupied. Total available occupancy at Descartes is for one hundred and twenty-eight persons, although the population rarely reaches that number. All niches are single-person. . . . "

(The diagram fills the screen; then an INSET appears in the RIGHT TOP CORNER, which EXPANDS to show footage of the interior of the Greenhouse. CLOSE-UP of a tomato vine. CUT TO the diagram again, and ZOOM IN on the factory subcomplex. CUT TO still-camera MONTAGE of the subcomplex interior: factory domes, electrostatic scrubbers, access tunnels, control cupolas, etc.

Narrator: "Adjacent to the Dorms in Subcomp D is the Greenhouse, an inflated structure buried beneath the regolith, where various crops are hydroponically cultivated for crew consumption . . . mmm-mmm, don't those tomatoes look swell! To the right of MainOps is the place where many of you will be earning your paychecks . . . Subcomp C, the lunar factories. Entrance to the factories from the surface is made through electrostatic scrubbers, which remove dirt from your hardsuits, or through pressurized access tunnels from MainOps and Subcomp B, which we'll describe momentarily. After lunar ore is separated at the receiving station, it is sent either to the ilmenite factory, where lunar oxygen and hydrogen are extracted, or to the raw materials factories, where silicon, aluminum, and rare elements are extracted in turn. The raw materials are in turn made into final products . . . such as milled aluminum rolls, photovoltaic solar cells, and breathable oxygen . . . and shipped by tractor to the mass-driver station for launch into space. You will receive more detailed instruction on each of these facilities later in your four-week training period. . . . "

(INSET appears in LEFT BOTTOM CORNER, expanding to

show the schematic diagram again. Camera ZOOMS in on Subcomp B. FADES to footage of the EVA ready-room, airlocks, and scrubbers, interior of spacecraft maintenance hangar and vehicle garage, an LTV landing on a pad, etc.)

Narrator: "Finally, we come to Subcomp B—the EVA operations center. From the tunnel to MainOps, you first enter the EVA ready-room, where you suit-up, get checked out by suit inspectors, clock out on the job, and exit the base through one of four airlocks. When you come back in, of course, you'll enter through electrostatic scrubbers, just as with the factory subcomplex. You'll be seeing a lot of this place, for sure! Two additional airlocks lead down to the spacecraft maintenance hangar and to the unpressurized garage for ground vehicles. Two landing pads are used by incoming and outgoing orbital spacecraft, such as the lunar transfer vehicle which will bring you to the Moon, and the third pad is used by long-range lunar transports, or LRLT's. A pressurized tunnel from the ready-room leads to the pad operations cupola . . ."

(CUT TO the Narrator in the same setting as seen in the beginning of the film.)

Narrator: "Wow! Sure looks like a great place to live and work, doesn't it? Well, I'm certain that you have a lot of questions now for your Skycorp training instructor, so I won't keep you waiting. Look for me on your next training film. I'll be seeing you then. In the meantime, as Sweeney would say . . . 'Good luck, McDuck!' "

(Narrator winks and smiles. FADE TO Skycorp logo, then FADE OUT.)

6. First Impressions

Moondust, caught in an electromagnetic dust devil of positive and negative polarities, swirled around Lester and Tina McGraw as they stood in the airlock scrubber. Since they hadn't been out on the surface for more than a few minutes after disembarking from the *Collins*, there was little of the fine gray dirt for the scrubber to pick off their suits and suck down the tubes below the gridded deck. Gradually the little tornado subsided as Lester watched the status panel above the exit hatch of the cylindrical compartment. When the scrubber was done, the orange light went out and the pressurization cycle started; a few minutes later, the amber light switched to green and the exit hatch automatically popped open.

"Okay, we're here," Lester said to McGraw. She said nothing; small talk was obviously not something in which she indulged. *Fair enough*, Riddell thought as he pushed open the hatch and stepped out of the airlock, hauling his duffel bag over his left shoulder and carrying his airtight aluminum briefcase in his right hand. *But you're going to make yourself awful lonesome up here unless you learn to start speaking to people.*

The ready-room was a long compartment with low ceiling crossed with airducts and conduits, its walls lined with airlocks through which moondogs were entering in a steady trickle. As soon as he came out of the airlock, a suit tech—a skinny kid with acne scars, wearing a Seattle Mariners sweatshirt—came up to guide him to the nearest de-suit rack; he was there more to hold him to the floor, by firmly pressing down on his shoulders, than to lead him. The kid babbled as he turned Riddell around to back him into the rack: "Glad to meet you, sir, my name's Bill, welcome back to Descartes Station, if there's anything I can do, just let me know and . . ."

"Bill, stop brown-nosing and get back to work." The suit tech at the rack was a muscular woman with crew-cut red hair; in spite of the ready-room's chill, she wore only a tanktop above her loose khaki trousers. She took the aluminum attaché case and duffel bag from Lester's hands and carelessly dumped them on the floor, then buckled Lester's arm and legs into the rack. Bill scuttled away to help McGraw. "Okay, take a deep breath and hold it," she ordered Lester, then reached to the suit's chest unit and switched off the air and coolant circulation. She took her time; Lester nearly turned blue before she unlocked his neck collar and pulled off his helmet.

"Feel better?" she asked perfunctorily as she placed the helmet on the rack's overhead shelf. Lester took a deep breath, then let it out as a steamy froth. The air had the faint burnt-gunpowder odor of lunar dust; apparently the scrubbers couldn't keep all the dirt from getting inside the base. The smell was exactly as he remembered it. With the helmet off, he could see better, too. The walls of the ready-room were streaked with grime. It had been a long time since this place had last been cleaned.

The suit tech didn't wait for an answer; presumably, if a moondog didn't keel over and pass out on the floor, it meant he was feeling just great. "Good," she said as she rolled a step-ladder behind the rack and unlatched the suit's rear hatch. "Okay, okay, wiggle your ass back and duck your head forward. . . ." He did so, and suddenly felt her strong hands grab his hips and pull back. "Good, good. Now pull up your right leg first, pull it straight out of there and put it behind you on the ladder . . . yeah, okay, now the left. . . ."

It took about fifteen minutes for Lester to get out of the hard-suit; he was long out of practice with the de-suit procedure, and his assistant was helpful but impatient with his slow progress. When he was out of the suit, standing in the cold room in his thin, watertube-lined nylon undergarment and feeling like a turtle who had just been robbed of his shell, the woman pulled a pair of twenty-pound ankle weights off the rack and briskly handed them to him. "Put these on," she told him, "toss your pissoir in the bin over there next to the time clock. You know how to clock out, don't you?"

"Yes. I do." Lester juggled the ankle-bracelets in his hands. "What's your name?"

"Smith," she said. "Lana Smith. Just call me Smitty." The last was added without a trace of warmth or Irish humor.

"Right." Lester paused. "Do you know who I am, Smitty?"

Smitty rested her hands on her hips. "Yeah, you're the new GM. And this is the ready-room."

"That's right. . . ."

She nodded, her face completely blank. "Uh-huh, that's right. What'd you expect, the Marine Corps marching band? Look, I gotta job to do here and there's two dozen guys waiting in line behind you. You've taken up too much of my time already, so why don't you try to hustle . . . sir."

Lester said nothing. He kneeled and clipped on the ankle-bracelets, which would keep him from bouncing off the floor with each step in one-sixth gee. When he stood up again, another tech was wheeling his suit away to the row of carapaces lined up against a wall, and Smitty was already backing another moondog into a de-suit rack.

He picked up his attaché case and duffel bag and walked across the chill mooncrete floor, passing Tina McGraw as she wormed the rest of the way out of her own hardsuit. He set down his luggage again, unsnapped the unisex urine-collection cup from his groin, and tossed the pissoir into a hamper next to the time clock. His keycard was in a pocket on his right wrist; he pulled it out, passed it in front of the lens of the clock until he heard it beep, then walked toward the open hatch to the narrow tube-shaped passageway to Subcomp A.

Nobody had been waiting to greet him; the two men walking down the passage in front of him and the guy following behind seemed to be keeping their distance. *Uh-huh*, Lester thought as he strode into Descartes Station. *It figures. Now let's see what the locker room is like. . . .*

The men's locker room was located on the second level of Subcomp A, and could have been transplanted in its entirety from a YMCA in any large city in America, down to the aroma of sweaty socks which permeated the large room.

Rock music from the overhead speakers was all but drowned out by the clamor of moondogs talking and aluminum locker doors being opened and banged shut. CRT's suspended from the low ceiling displayed duty rosters and general announcements; posters of guitar-brandishing rock stars and nude movie starlets were taped to the Mylar-padded walls. The door to the adjacent infirmary was open; inside, a couple of guys were being treated for suit-chafes and minor sprains and bruises. In the shower room at the end of the central aisle, several men were taking lukewarm sponge-baths, rinsing off with quick spurts of cold water from the showerheads. Taped to the door of the women's locker room was a poster of Moon Maid, from the Dick Tracy comic strip; the door cracked open a few inches and a woman with a towel wrapped around her chest peeked through to beg for an extra bar of soap. Whistles and hoots rang through the room; red-faced but grinning good-naturedly, the woman retreated and the door slammed shut.

The camaraderie stopped when Lester reached a short row of lockers, one of which bore the nameplate GENERAL MANAGER. As he entered the area, barely anyone noticed, but when he slipped his keycard into the door's slot and tapped his ID number into the keypad, moondogs on either side of him suddenly vanished from sight. He shoved his duffel bag into the locker, changed out of his longjohns, and pulled on the light-blue Skycorp jumpsuit he found inside; someone had at least taken the trouble to put a fresh jumpsuit of his size in the locker. He was uncomfortably aware of men furtively walking past, pausing and casting a quick look in his direction, then hurrying on. No one stopped to introduce themselves; there was no overt hostility, but no welcome either.

As he pulled out a pair of high-top sneakers and shut the locker, he noticed something on the outside of the door which he hadn't seen before: a strip of white plastic tape under the "General Manager" plate, with the name B. FISK printed on it. Scrawled in ballpoint pen below the name: "Gone but not forgotten."

Lester started to reach up to peel off the tape, then thought better of it, and let his hand drop. He could always get rid of the former GM's name, but doing it now might send the wrong message.

He sat down on the bench and began to lace up his shoes. As he fitted the laces through the eyes of the hightops, he overheard two men talking on the other side of the row of lockers:

"Goddamn frigging company. I wonder what this shit's about now. . . ."

"Yeah. Fuckin' A. . . . "

"I swear, if they're announcing another slowdown or a bonus squeeze . . ."

"Fuckin' A, yeah. . . ."

"I'm gonna quit. I mean it. Call in the Section Four-D clause on the contract and catch the next LTV outta here, man. . . . "

"Right! Fuckin' A!"

"Yeah. Right after I collect my six-month bonus . . ."

Another voice entered the conversation as a low, unintelligible murmur. "Where?" the second voice asked. "Over there? Shit!" And suddenly the gripe session came to an end.

Lester stood up, brushed off the seat of his pants, picked up the attaché case, and headed out of the locker room. He followed the corridor through an open hatch and past the infirmary into the office section, located halfway between the mess hall and the rec room. Once again, he noticed the walls: the handprints, the long-since expired tax notices still taped to the walls, the graffiti—"Skycorp Sux"; "Eat my piss-cup"; "Larry + Amad are queers & so are u"; "Vacuum Suckers! Now and Forever!"; "Blow me!" and so forth. There was litter on the floor, some within reach of recycling chutes. At the intersection of two corridors, near the spiral staircase leading into the atrium and down to the underground level of the subcomplex, he observed that the lighting seemed a little darker; stopping and gazing up, he saw that one of the recessed light fixtures was inoperative, bashed in as if someone had recently punched his or her fist through the panel.

As with everything he had seen since he had arrived, Lester silently took note of the damage, adding it to a general pattern of neglect and abuse. Descartes Station hadn't looked this bad even when it was being run by junkies. The base resembled a housing project in an urban combat zone. And the company had sent him here to be the new janitor. . . .

His office was located at the end of the corridor. Lester paused a moment before the door, which was slightly ajar, then pushed it open, and found a lovely young woman sitting behind his desk with her feet propped up on its plastic top.

"Hi," she said, smiling serenely at him, then self-consciously swinging her feet down. "I'm Butch . . . um, Dr. Susan Peterson, senior research scientist. I'm . . ."

"Right." Lester walked into the office—*his* office, he reminded himself—allowing the door to stand open behind him. "How did you get in here?" he asked evenly.

"Hmm? Oh. Monk Walker . . . that's Dr. Walker, our chief physician . . . has a keycard coded to your lock."

"Where's Dr. Walker now?" The office was small; he was able to walk to the front of his desk in a couple of strides. He deposited the attaché case flat on the desktop and placed both hands on it. "That's my chair you're sitting in, by the way."

Peterson raised an eyebrow, but she stood up. "Sorry," she said, taking a step around his desk, "but it's the only chair in here, and we were waiting for you to show up, so . . ."

"What makes you think you can come in my office any time you want?" Lester tapped his finger on the desktop. "What makes you think you can put your feet up on my desk?"

Butch Peterson's gaze simmered. "Listen, let's take this one question at a time. . . ."

"No, Dr. Peterson," Lester said, "you listen. One, I don't like arriving at my office to find some stranger has broken in. Two, I don't appreciate finding the same stranger sitting in *my* chair, behind *my* desk, as if they own the place. And three, I don't like somebody telling *me* to listen. Now are we straight on all that . . . ?"

Someone behind him cleared his throat. "If you're going to chew out anyone, Mr. Riddell, please let it be me. I'm the one who opened the door and let Butch in."

Lester turned to find a small man with a close-shaven head and a benign smile standing just outside the door. "You're Dr. Walker?" he asked.

The man nodded briefly. "Yes, I am . . . but really, we don't go by formal titles here. I'm Monk and she's Butch." He hesitated, then added, "If you wish, we can call you Mr. Riddell, but we'd prefer to call you Lester. If that's okay with you, of course. May I come in?"

Lester shrugged and sighed in exasperation. "You've already unlocked my door and let yourself in. Why not?" He sat down on the edge of his desk and waved his hand to his computer terminal. "Want me to open up my files for you, too? Or do you already know my password?"

Monk Walker smiled and shook his head as he stepped into the room. "I think we're getting off to a bad start here," he said gently. "Let's try this again. I apologize for letting Butch in here. It was entirely my idea. I was here myself for a while, but I was summoned to the infirmary to deal with a few minor injuries. Butch said she'd wait here for you. I thought that would be all right, since it was our intention to welcome you to the base, but . . ."

He held up his hands. "I can see that was a rash decision. We intruded on your privacy. Again, my most sincere apologies. It won't happen again."

Lester studied the mild little man. He was smooth, well-spoken, and disarming, characteristics, sometimes, of a person who cannot be trusted. Lester had encountered his share of bullshit artists, including some who could charm your wallet right out of your back pocket, but in this case, he could detect nothing but sincerity.

He glanced over his shoulder at Butch Peterson. Her dark, narrow eyes—as a guess, he pegged her heritage as part African-American, part Filipino or Malaysian—still smoldered like blue-hot flames from a camp stove. Yet as she caught his gaze she slowly nodded her head, silently adding her own reticent apology. An attractive woman; he now regretted having snarled at her by way of introduction.

He let out his breath. True, this first encounter was off to a rocky start—but these were the only friendly faces he had met since his arrival at Descartes, and his first impressions of the base had been less than kind. "Apologies accepted," he said. "And I'm sorry for jumping on you both. It's been a hell of a day."

Although his chair was now vacant, Lester didn't sit down right away. Instead, his eyes traveled around the tiny office; little more than a closet, really, but more room than in his first "office" at Descartes Station, a tiny screened-off part of the old command module. There were a few pictures on the wall, mostly leftovers from Bo Fisk's tenure, but a couple that dated back to eight years ago: a low-orbit photo of the original base—the huddled row of tunnel-connected modules he remembered all too well—and the photostat of an old *New York Times* newspaper clipping, dry-mounted on a piece of fiberboard, yellow and stained with age. Lester stepped closer, a grin involuntarily spreading across his face as he recognized an old memento.

"Aw, I remember this," he murmured. "I'd forgotten it was up here."

"Oh?" Monk rested his back against the door and crossed his arms. "I've seen it many times, but Bo never said anything about it. I thought it was here just because of the headline."

The story in the clipping was dated November 16, 1989; it was headlined "Moondog Returns From the Hippie Years." In the photo below was an old man with a flowing white beard, rapping a drumstick against a kettledrum that was almost as big as he was. His closed eyes and solemn face, the black cap and flowing brown robes, gave him the appearance of a medieval mage. The photo was captioned "Moondog at a rehearsal in Brooklyn."

Still smiling, Lester tapped a finger against the clipping. "When we started the base, when the first crew was here, somebody started referring to us as 'moondogs'. . . . I don't know who it was, but it wasn't me. Anyway, it was a good name and it stuck, but although it seemed to ring a bell with everyone, nobody could figure out what it meant."

"You mean you didn't invent it yourselves?" asked Butch. "I always thought the term originated here."

"No, it didn't originate here," Lester replied. "Someone picked it up from someplace, but we couldn't put our finger on where the word came from." He flashed upon the often-drunken bull sessions in the old wardroom, when the subject of What's a moondog? had arisen time and again during bored conversation, and chuckled. Those were the good times.

"The best we could figure was that it was an archaic term," he continued. "Something from the sixteenth century, maybe."

"The clipping . . ." Monk prompted.

"Well, one of the crew that was here then decided to research the matter," Lester continued. "Our resident computer jockey used a few hours of Earth-link time to query the Library of Congress and other databases. It took a while, but eventually he tracked down this old news story." He gazed fondly upon the old man in the picture. "Turned out there was a blind, eccentric musician in the last century nicknamed Moondog. He was a street person in New York. Liked to walk the streets of Manhattan wearing a Viking helmet, but was known locally as an amazing—if weird—symphonic composer. Sort of a Big Apple legend. Even made a few recordings and once conducted the Brooklyn Philharmonic. We had a tape of his music here for a while. . . . Have they ever played it on your new radio station here?"

"Moondog McCloud play anything but rock or blues?" Butch snorted. "Are you kidding? This is the guy who once played old Frank Zappa tapes for ten hours straight, nonstop. . . ."

"And the guys here loved it," Monk finished.

"Yeah, I know what you mean. Too bad that the tape was lost. Anyway, that's the closest we came to figuring out the origin of the word 'moondog.' We got that guy to generate a photostat of the *Times* story he found that told about Moondog and we . . .''

Lester's voice trailed off as he recalled the hacker who had made the discovery. Sam Sloane. He had unearthed the original Moondog not long before he was lost while exploring the Descartes region on his own. Sam used to go out on solo excursions to get away from stoned-out wrecks like Lester himself—and he'd suffered a long, lonely death because not one of two dozen moondogs at the old Descartes Station happened to notice that he was long overdue from his EVA. Lester was as much to blame for Sam's death as anyone else, if not more so. He had been the boss back then; it had happened on his watch. If he hadn't been so fucked up . . .

"Was it Sloane?" Monk asked. "Sam Sloane?"

"Huh?" Lester was startled from his train of thought. "How did you know that?"

Walker shrugged. "Lucky guess. But we . . ." He coughed; he seemed reluctant to go further. "Well, we know about Sam Sloane. Kind of a folk legend, you might . . ."

"C'mon, Lew, don't be such a schmuck. You can't believe that, can you?" Peterson crossed her arms and sat down on the edge of the desk. "Some of the guys claim they've seen a ghost while on EVA," she continued impatiently, looking at Riddell now. A cynical grin curled her lips. "A mysterious figure in an old-style suit, wandering the edges of the base at night . . ." She raised her hands and fluttered them around her face. "*Woooo-weeee-wooooooo . . .*"

"Well, I believe it," Monk said.

"Well, I think it's a bunch of shit," Butch shot back. She looked at Lester. "What do you think?"

A ghost on the Moon, he thought. *Right. Sam's ghost . . .*

A faint chill ran down from the base of his neck. He didn't like thinking about it, and there were far more important matters facing him right now. He glanced at his watch. "Look, we've got the meeting coming up in a few minutes," he said quickly, "and I've got to get ready." Abruptly, he sat down and opened his briefcase. Looking up again, he found Butch and Monk still watching him. "Is there anything else?"

The two scientists glanced at each other. "No, I don't think so," Peterson replied. "We thought we might have a few more minutes, maybe get to know each other before . . ."

"Sorry, no." Lester shook his head. "It's nice of you guys to stop by and introduce yourselves, but . . ." He sighed and spread his hands. "Seriously, I've got to get ready for the staff meeting. I wasn't even planning to hold it until the minute we landed. So, y'know . . . I need to get prepared."

Butch blinked, but said nothing. "All right," Monk said, edging out into the corridor. "We'll have plenty of time later to become acquainted."

"Yeah. Okay. Right." Lester looked first at Monk, then at Butch, then back at Monk again. "See you at the meeting. Right?"

"Right," Butch said tersely. She turned and marched past Monk out of the office. Monk let her pass, then cast a faint smile upon Lester before he carefully closed the door. The door swung shut behind them, but not before Lester heard Butch whisper: "He's doomed. . . ."

He leaned back in his desk chair and let out his breath. Just a couple of minutes until the meeting . . . barely enough time to prepare himself for the inevitable confrontation.

Doomed? he thought. Christ, lady, by the time I get through with these guys, they're going to be organizing a lynching party. He let his eyes drift to the narrow window and gazed out over the bleak yet startling landscape.

"Doomed," he repeated aloud.

Okay, maybe so. Just all I ask, dear God, is please don't let anyone get killed again like Sam did. Not while I'm here.

7. Attitude Correction

This is, Lester thought as he surveyed the crowd in the mess hall, *going to be harder than I expected.*

The mess hall was a long narrow room, its Mylar-padded walls painted a utilitarian shade of gray, with hard, sheet-metal tables and benches arranged in straight lines down the cement floor. It was tonelessly lighted by fluorescent fixtures that dangled from the mooncrete ceiling between the omnipresent pipes, conduits, and airducts. A couple of recessed windows looked out onto the drab moonscape; travel posters taped to the walls— San Francisco's Telegraph Hill, Yellowstone National Park and the Great Smoky Mountains, Chicago's Lake Shore Drive, an anonymous beach scene somewhere in Hawaii—fought a lame battle to lend color to the room.

Even more colorless were the faces that turned toward Lester the moment he walked in. Conversation diminished to mutters and grumbles as he strode to the front of the room; not a respectful silence, but rather an obligatory absence of noise. Lester was reminded of a friend's account of having attended a bullfight in some South American nation when the country's unloved dictator showed up for the games; no one cheered for the old murderer, but no one dared make catcalls either. The arena had simply fallen silent until *el presidente* had been seated in his box, then the aficionados resumed their roaring.

The moondogs seated at the tables—most of them male—were a lean and sullen bunch, with hard faces reminiscent of old-time West Virginia coal miners and oil-rig operators from the Alaskan North Slope. The jumpsuits of those wearing Skycorp blues had been altered, with sleeves cut off at the armpits and various patches sewn on the front pockets. Most of the crowd was dressed in football jerseys and perspiration-stained sweatshirts, frayed jeans and hightop sneakers, baseball caps and bandannas. On most of the tables were empty vegetable and coffee cans, into which, every now and then, someone spit a rancid stream of tobacco juice. Cigarettes were banned on the Moon—smoke tended to gunk up the filters of the air circulation system—but there was enough contraband Red Man and Bull Durham stockpiled in their lockers to last a generation. Brown stains on the floor showed that some of the tobacco-chewers didn't bother to aim for the cans.

The moondogs sat at the tables and leaned against the walls, watching him watching them, waiting for their new boss to make the first move. Their stoical faces expressed their silent thoughts: *What a pain in the ass . . . Who does this guy think he is? . . . Okay, let's get this over with. . . .* Near the door, Butch Peterson and Monk Walker silently waited for him to start. He caught a quick wink from Walker, but that was the only reassurance he had. Yes indeed, this was going to be a tough audience, and there was nothing to do but brazen it out.

Lester cleared his throat tentatively. "Umm . . . good afternoon," he began. "I'm Lester Riddell and . . . uh, I'm the new general manager."

"So what?" someone in the back of the room muttered.

Lester ignored it. "I'm . . . ah, glad to be here. . . . "

"Big fucking deal." Scattered laughter.

"And I'm looking forward to working with you over the next year. . . . "

"Yo' momma's looking forward to working with you. . . . "

The laughter grew louder now; the faces before him went from noncommittal apathy to mean-spirited enjoyment in watching the new GM squirm. Lester fought to contain his temper; he paused and took a deep breath before going on. "And I hope we can . . ."

"Say *what*?"

"He said his momma's coming up here to run the place."

"Sheeit, I believe it. . . . "

"Maybe she can get our bonuses back. . . . "

"And maybe she can go down on us, too. . . . "

Okay, Lester thought, that's *it*.

He snatched the spittoon off the table in front of him and swung his arm back. "And I hope we'll learn to *respect* each other!" he yelled, and pitched the can out in the direction of the last voice.

Men ducked and howled obscenities as the can hurtled over their heads, spraying brown slime across their shoulders and backs. It hit the San Francisco travel poster with a loud CLANG! and splattered mucus across the poster and the table beneath it as it ricocheted across the room. Moondogs jumped to their feet, staring at the wall, then at Lester, then back at the wall again. Suddenly, the mess hall was deathly quiet.

At the targeted table, a huge black man slowly stood up and started moving toward Lester. Head shaven, with a trim mustache framing his scowling mouth, he was not much smaller than a shopping mall; his clenched fists looked as hard as bricks, "Muthafucker, I'm gonna . . ."

"You're going to *what*?" Lester shouted back. He didn't wait for the giant to get to the front of the room; instead, he quickly strode down the aisle between the tables. Men and women quickly got out of his way as he advanced on the moondog. Lester met him before he left his table.

"Tell me about it," Lester demanded. "*What* are you going to do?"

The giant glared down at Lester, and Lester stared straight back at him. Blood pounded in Lester's ears like kettledrums; he barely noticed the expectant silence in the mess hall. If he swings, Lester thought distantly, he'll plaster me like a tomato across the floor. . . .

"Do you know my mother?" Lester snapped. "Huh? Have you ever *met* my mother?"

The big man said nothing, just kept staring at Lester. "You can say what you want about me," Lester continued, lowering his voice to a tone of restrained menace, "but unless you want your ass kicked, you leave my mom out of this."

A young black man sitting at a nearby table politely cleared his throat. "Excuse me," he said, smiling as he peered at Lester over the top of his rimless glasses, "but do I understand you correctly in that you're saying you're going to kick Tycho's ass?"

Lester didn't move his eyes from Tycho's face. "That's right," he said evenly. "If Tycho makes any more remarks about my mother, I'm going to kick his ass."

"That may be difficult," the young man replied, smiling a little, "but that's beside the point. You're saying that, even if he happens to inquire about your mater's *health*, you're going to attempt to kick his ass?"

"My mother's been dead for ten years," Lester said, still not looking away from Tycho. "And, yeah, I'm going to kick his ass. And it won't be an attempt, either."

The kid crossed his arms. "Still," he pontificated, "I'm not sure how you can be . . ."

"Shaddup, cool." Tycho looked away from Lester to cast his chill gaze on the young man, who immediately shut up. The big moondog looked back at Lester. "Too bad about your mother, man," he rumbled. He paused, then quietly added, "I'm real sorry about that."

Then, without another word, he turned around and went back to his chair. Lester silently let out his breath. *Thank you, Jesus, for not letting me die. . . .*

He turned and looked across the mess hall. *"Now!"* he shouted. "If I've finally gotten your attention, maybe you can start this meeting!"

Lester began to walk slowly back down the aisle. "Let's get a couple of things straight," he continued, allowing his gaze to sweep across the faces. "I'm the new GM, and I've had as much shit as I'm going to take from you people. If you don't like me, then keep in mind that I don't like you very much either. In fact, there's nothing in my contract which says that I have to treat you as anything but a bunch of low-life grunts for hire. The difference between me and you is, I've got the power to fire you if I feel like it, and there's not *one fucking thing* you can do about it."

"Fuck you," someone in the back of the room murmured.

"No, you're the one who's fucked," Lester retorted, not bothering to look round. "Your ASWI local contract gives me the right to terminate your employment whenever and for whatever reason I please, so don't even think about getting the union to bail you out. In fact, the union doesn't give a wet shit about you guys. You're an embarrassment. They let Skycorp screw you in the contract talks last year because ASWI wanted to get concessions for the Olympus Station beamjacks instead, and you were an expendable giveaway. And as for Skycorp, the reason why the company sent me up here was for me to be a hardass. They spent righteous bucks to send every one of you up here to do a job and for me to make sure you do it, and now they want their money's worth. I'm only too happy to oblige."

He reached the front of the room again and turned around to look them over. "Make no mistake about it, pilgrims. I'm not your buddy, I'm not your pal, and I'm not going to let things slide the way Bo Fisk did. And you've gotten me pissed off already. From the moment I landed here, I've gotten nothing but attitude from you guys. I've had a chance to look around this place, and it's a goddamn sewer. Now, I'm going to clean this place up and get it working right again, and I'll be only too happy to purge the whole work force if I don't get some cooperation from you people. Have we got this straight?''

No one said a thing. Lester leaned against a table and crossed his arms. ''You people have been hired to do a tough, lousy job,'' he went on in a calmer tone of voice. ''Things were getting sloppy here. You got away with it for a while, but Skycorp found out how much this base was fucking off, so they cleaned house. If you were here then, you're still here only because you weren't screwing around on company time—and that's twenty-four hours a day the way I see it, because they pay you and me too well for us to be fooling around. Understand?''

A few coughs, some hushed murmurs, but no reply. The crowd watched him ''If you were jerking around and just weren't caught,'' Lester went on, ''don't count on getting away with it with me. And if I hear any more shit like I got on the radio coming in, you're outta here.'' He snapped his fingers for effect. ''Fired, and I don't give a rat's ass what it does for your sick grandmother or the kids you're putting through school. Do I *still* have your undivided attention?''

A few heads were nodding. Mostly, the response was as if a harmless puppy had suddenly turned dingo: stunned disbelief. ''If you're new here,'' Lester went on, ''that's no excuse, either. Skycorp couldn't find anyone decent to work in this godforsaken hole, so they hired you instead.''

''What about you?'' someone loudly asked.

''I'm here because they couldn't get anyone else dumb enough to take this job,'' Lester answered honestly.

For the first time since he walked into the room, people laughed without malice. *Good*, he thought. *I'm beginning to get somewhere.* . . .

''Okay, you've got the ground rules. Now here's the lowdown.'' Lester propped a foot up on the table and wrapped his hands around his knee. ''As of first-shift tomorrow, we're coming out of work-slowdown. Everyone on all three shifts is back on the job.''

A moment of silence . . . then cheers rang through the room as the moondogs whistled and stamped their feet. ''Hot fucking damn!'' a man at one of the front tables yelled. ''We're gonna get paid again!''

Lester nodded and waved his hand. ''Yeah, yeah, I know you've been spinning your wheels, and not everyone's been getting full-time pay. That changes at oh-eight-hundred local tomorrow. But before you start counting your money, you better know that there's another side to this. . . . ''

The room lapsed into silence again. ''We're going to continue making aluminum and photovoltaics for the powersats, because Skycorp's going ahead with the Korean project,'' Lester continued. ''Same product as always. But what has changed is . . . there's going to be more of it.''

He took a deep breath. ''Tomorrow morning, there's going to be a press conference in Huntsville, where a major announcement will be made. I'm authorized to spill the beans to you guys early. Skycorp is going to tell the press that it's made an agreement with Uchu-Hiko, and that they will be cooperating on a separate SPS project.''

Lester looked around the room, and saw that he had everyone's complete attention. He indulged in a pause before letting the other shoe drop. ''They're going to start building a powersat for Japan.''

''Say *what*?'' somebody asked.

''You heard me the first time,'' Lester said. ''Uchu-Hiko wants a powersat for Japan and Skycorp's going to make it for them. But this time they're going to do it just a little differently. Since the Korean project is already go, the company is going to build the Japanese SPS concurrent with the Korean SPS.'' He held up two fingers. ''So that's two powersats that are going to be made by the boys at Skycan at the same time. And I don't have to tell you where all the raw materials are coming from, either.''

Now there were murmurs and low whistles from the crew. ''How come Uchu-Hiko came to us?'' someone in the crowd asked. ''I mean, why don't they just do it themselves?''

''Because we've already got the resources in place,'' Lester replied. ''They have a space station, but it isn't big enough to house a construction crew. And we've got the experience from building three of these suckers so far. Once the first phase of the Korean project is finished, Olympus Station is going to start work on Phase One of the Japanese powersat. Since they'll both have the same equatorial orbit, they can be built side by side.

But even before then, we're expected to have stockpiled everything they'll need to start the first phase. Aluminum roll for the skeleton, oxygen for the beamjacks, glass, photovoltaics. The works. Everything they need to hit the ground running. So, for us, the first phase of the Japanese SPS starts tomorrow, at least a year before the actual construction begins. That means we're expected to be producing and stockpiling materials for Japan's SPS in addition to the stuff for the Korean powersat.''

The silence was an abyss into which he could have fallen. Men and women were glancing skeptically at each other. ''What's this about stockpiling?'' Tycho suddenly asked. ''You mean we're going to be making the stuff, then just letting it sit there?''

Lester nodded. ''Uh-huh. It's not going off the mass-driver until the first phase begins up there.'' He shrugged. ''Call it twelve months at least, though I've been told it might be as close as six, because Skycorp's going to be hauling ass with the Korean powersat.''

''Okay.'' Tycho stretched back in his chair. ''That's fine with me, just as long as we get our bonus pay back. Know what I mean?''

Lester's mouth tightened. Now for the hard part . . . ''The bonuses and performance risers will be—'' He stopped himself. ''They *may* be reinstated. No promises.''

Tycho's mouth dropped open as anger surged through the mess hall. ''What do you . . . ?''

''Listen to me,'' Lester said. ''The union's backing the company up on this. No bonuses unless we earn the money. We're going to have to work for it.''

As he expected, the noise level rose still higher. Lester quickly held up his hands. ''Just *listen* to me!'' he yelled. ''Skycorp has zero confidence in this base right now. In fact, they're about an inch away from selling the base to Uchu-Hiko. . . . ''

''*What?*'' at least half the people in the room shouted in unison.

Tycho was out of his chair again. ''You gotta be shittin' us—!''

''Just shut up and listen!'' Lester yelled. When the room finally quieted down one more time, Riddell went on. ''The Japanese may be a co-partner in this deal, but the word from the inside track is that they're still unhappy with the deal they made with Skycorp. They want Descartes Station, and if the boys in

Huntsville start to think we're not worth the grief, they'd be just as happy to sell this whole place to Uchu-Hiko. I'm sure you know what that means.''

"No," another moondog said. "I don't know what that means. So our paycheck comes from Tokyo instead of Alabama. Big fucking deal.''

"No." Lester shook his head. "It means you get a pink slip and two weeks severance pay and a ride home. I'm telling you, Uchu-Hiko won't play with a losing hand. They'll buy the capital assets from Olympus and get rid of us. Then they'll bring in their own team to get the job done. It must be a tempting option for Huntsville, or Arnie Moss—''

"Oh, fuck, *that* bastard . . . ?''

"—wouldn't have told me about it," Lester finished. "The Japanese space workers still aren't unionized. They'd probably work for less." He shoved his hands into his jumpsuit pockets and shrugged. "Hell, I dunno. Maybe they won't even bother with space workers. Maybe they'll just go teleoperation instead and replace us with a bunch of robots. It'll be slower and less efficient to do it that way, sure, but perhaps they'll figure it beats the hassle of supporting a human work force.''

"I don't fucking believe it," someone grumbled.

"You better come to believe it," Lester replied, nodding his head. "The bottom line, folks, is that we're going to have to work like dogs if we're going to regain the bonuses you guys had before the purge, or even to keep our jobs in the first place. Now, there's a bright side to this. . . . ''

"Oh, *please* . . .'' someone else said. "I can't take too much more of this healthy optimism.''

Lester ignored the jab. "We're on a probation period for the next six weeks. Our fiscal first-year production quota is going to be one hundred fifteen thousand tons of finished material. If we can ship twelve thousand tons of material within that six-week probation period—that's twelve thousand tons shot down the mass-driver by August twelfth—we'll be awarded bonuses commensurate with those six weeks *plus* full pay and bonuses for the period during the work slowdown, just as if we had been receiving monthly bonuses all along. A new performance riser also kicks in, with a five percent increase in net pay if we meet the annual quota.''

A few appreciative murmurs and whistles. "Not bad," Smitty said. "But what if we don't meet the quota?''

"We start asking Seki, here, for Japanese lessons," another moondog finished.

A middle-aged Japanese-American man sitting next to him grinned. "I don't think it'll do you any good," he said.

"What about supplies?" asked a young woman wearing a black beret. "We sent the company a personal-items list about three months ago, and they said everything on it was suspended from export. What's going on?"

Others murmured support. Another tough question. "They're still suspended," Lester said. The murmurs turned into outraged shouts. "Nothing nonessential gets shipped up unless it's life-critical," Lester finished, ignoring the protests. "Mail gets delivered, but no 'care' packages. So if you were expecting home-baked cookies or comic books, forget it."

"What the hell are they trying to prove?" a big hairy guy in the back of the room demanded. "I mean, what the fuck?"

"Yeah!" someone else shouted. "You tell 'em, Mighty Joe!"

"It's because they're trying to put pressure on you guys, that's why," Lester shot back. "Huntsville figures you've been taking it easy for too long, so they want to make life as uncomfortable for you as they can."

Before the voices could rise again, he held up his hand. "Hey, hey, I didn't make the rules. I don't like it either, but that's the way it is. Write a letter to the board of directors if you want, but don't take it out on me. It's like the bonus situation. If we get through the probation period and meet the six-week quota, the nonessentials get shipped up here again."

More pissing and moaning, but at least no one was calling him names again. Lester paused and cleared his throat. "Umm . . . and if you haven't guessed already, this is a dry town again. The rules prohibiting liquor and recreational drugs are back in force. No booze or dope under any circumstances. Possession is grounds for termination of your contract."

That was one regulation Lester was fully in favor of, but there was no sense in letting the crew know that. The atmosphere in the mess hall was becoming nastier every second. "Who's gonna stop us?" someone in the back of the room yelled.

That's a good question, Lester thought. It occurred to him that Descartes was still without a new security chief. The last one had been nailed in the purge; he had been caught looking the other way when the drinking and doping had been going on.

Skycorp had yet to tell Lester if a replacement was on the way up. *If the company thinks I'm going to double as the security chief*, Riddell thought, *they're dead wrong. I can't run this place and be the resident arm-breaker, too.*

He ducked the last question. It was time to wrap this up before the scene got any uglier. "That's it," he said, getting up from the table. "You'll be seeing me around. New maintenance and clean-up schedules will be posted tomorrow on the computer, so check your niche terminals. That's part of your job, too, and your pay will be docked if you don't report for cleanup detail. If you have any questions, my office is right down the hall, across from the labs. Second shift goes back to finish their regular clock, and third shift reports on schedule."

Hardly anyone was paying attention. The moondogs were getting up from their benches, talking among themselves as they either headed for the door or wandered to the coffee pots for a refill. Lester suddenly felt exhausted. It had been a grueling day so far. All he wanted to do was find his office and lock himself inside for a few hours. A quick nap, maybe . . .

"Excuse me," a familiar voice behind him said. "Mr. Riddell?"

Lester looked around; it was Tina McGraw. Besides himself, she was the only person he had yet seen who was wearing an unaltered Skycorp jumpsuit. "Hi, Tina," he said wearily. "What can I do for you? And call me Lester, okay?"

Her thin lips pursed disapprovingly, as if she disdained using an informal tone of address. "I need to speak to you, please," she said softly. "In private."

He sighed and rubbed his eyes. "Sure, sure, but can it wait? I need to take a break. This meeting . . ."

"I understand." She shook her head. "But no, it can't wait. It's very important that we speak at once."

Before Lester could respond, McGraw dipped her right hand into the pocket of her jumpsuit and pulled out a small leather folder. Stepping a little closer, she hid the case in her palm and flipped it open to quickly show him what was inside.

The folder contained the silver oval badge of a field officer from NASA's Space Operations Enforcement Division. She held it open just long enough for Lester to see the badge, then snapped it shut and tucked it back in her pocket.

"As I said, we need to speak immediately," the new Chief of Security whispered, in a tone which implied that it was no longer a request. "Will you accompany me to MainOps, please?"

The Vacuum Suckers
(Interview.3)

Anne Noonan; former Skycorp lunar-tug payload specialist:

What were we doing, hijacking Spam-cans? *(pause)* Good question, and since I no longer work for Skycorp I don't think I'll get in any trouble for answering it, but let me tell you about the Vacuum Suckers first, okay? Maybe that'll help explain things.

The Vacuum Suckers are the Hells Angels of space. . . . Maybe that makes you nervous, but that's about the best way to describe them, because they sure ain't the Kiwanis Club. The way I've heard the story, the club got started on Olympus Station about five or six years ago by some beamjacks working on the second SPS project. There was a blowout caused by a collision with some space junk, and two of the bunkhouse modules were holed. One blew out all at once and the other developed a slow leak, and there were three beamjacks trapped in the module which was losing its atmosphere. There was no seal-kit in their module, they didn't have any hardsuits or rescue balls, and the hatch to the pressurized module on the other side of them was jammed. They were capable of opening the hatch to the adjacent bunkhouse, but that was the one which had completely lost pressure. The module on the far side of that bunkhouse was pressurized.

Anyway, it's the kind of situation which calls for desperate thinking, and that's exactly what these guys did. They deliberately blew the hatch on their own module, got themselves shot through the unpressurized module, and managed to open the hatch to the opposite module and get in before their lungs ruptured. They were exposed to hard vacuum for almost a full minute, which in theory is the absolute maximum for human tolerance. Somebody told me that Arthur C. Clarke once wrote a sci-fi story based on nearly the same premise, but that was even before the first satellite was put in orbit. Nobody had ever tried it in real life.

At any rate, they pulled it off and survived to tell about it. It took a lot of guts, and it got into the record books and so forth, and pretty soon people started calling these guys "the vacuum suckers." So that's how the club got started. *(shrugs)* You can take it with a grain of salt, but that's the story I've heard.

Anyway, it's sort of a fraternal club for pro spacers. Membership is strictly invitational. By tradition, you have to have two other working spacemen nominate you for membership, and it's only open to people who are actively employed in a hands-on capacity in space or in ground-support, so that's why you don't see any administration types wearing Suckers colors. And you have to have exhibited . . . well, "grace under pressure" is probably the right phrase, although Mighty Joe used to call it "having more balls than brains." Not everyone who works up there gets invited into the Suckers, but once you're in, you're a member for life. . . .

(Nods and jabs a finger) And the Vacuum Suckers are the closest-knit group up there, pal. I don't care what anyone says about 'em. Out there, there's no one I'd rather have working with me. That's the gospel truth. A Sucker will risk his or her own ass to keep you alive, and that's more than can be said for anything ASWI will do for you in a pinch. Especially the union . . . they're worthless as far as I'm concerned. You can quote me on that. The Suckers don't have union dues, they don't give you a card or send you a newsletter, but at least you can count on them, which is more than I can say for Asswipe.

Hmm? How did I get in? Naw, it wasn't for doing anything spectacularly brave, except maybe for flying with Mighty Joe. Or maybe just for being on the crew of a lunar tug, which is a hell of a hard assignment in the first place, even when your pilot isn't certifiable. *(shrugs)* I handled cargo for five flights of the *Beautiful Dreamer* without bitching about Joe's driving, and that was enough to earn the respect of him and Rusty Wright, the co-pilot. They were both in the Suckers, so they nominated me for membership. *(grins)* I have to admit, I was touched when I was told I was in. Gender notwithstanding, it meant I was one of the boys.

Like I said, it's not an official club by any means. No written charter or secret handshake or similar bullshit. There's just that embroidered patch that goes on the back of your jumpsuit or vest. That, and the respect of your fellow spacers. You're a pro among pros when you're in the Suckers. Skycorp and the other companies kind of wish we'd go away, and ASWI has never been crazy about us, either, though there was never anything they could legally do to break up the club or prevent Suckers from being hired or rehired.

(Grins) Not that they don't try. We've sort of got a rep for breaking rules. Like, there was a time when the guys at the Mars base wanted some real turkey for Christmas dinner, and they . . .

Hmm? Oh, sorry. Didn't mean to get carried away like that. I mean, you put a tape recorder in front of me and it's just talk talk talk, y'know, right? . . . Okay, it happened like this. . . .

Skycorp cut nonessential supplies to Descartes Station following the purge. You know about that, right? Huntsville said it was to preserve payload mass for shipment of volatiles, but nobody was buying that shit. The company was just going it as a punitive sort of thing, to get back at the moondogs for messing around while Fisk was in charge, and there wasn't a thing our good-for-nothing union could do about it since there was this little clause in the contract which gave Skycorp the right to make cutbacks in nonessential supplies. Shows how much our union reps screwed us over when they were negotiating our contract, doesn't it?

Anyway, this meant that we weren't being sent anything except the bare necessities—food, medical supplies, some parts replacements which we couldn't salvage from Honest Yuri's, that sort of thing. I mean, it wasn't as if they were trying to starve their employees on the Moon *(laughs)*. . . . Okay, so they were, or at least it felt that way since the cutback mostly affected recreational materials. No new books or magazines or comics were getting to us, f'rinstance. CD's of current movies were no longer coming our way. Harry Drinkwater, the DJ at the radio station . . . that's Moondog McCloud's real name . . . wasn't getting new music for his show. Since they had taken to reinforcing the regulations against liquor, our usual contacts at the Cape couldn't slip a few bottles into the Spam-cans scheduled for the outbound LTV's. Skycorp inspectors were now opening them up just prior to launch.

And sometimes the stuff which got designated as "nonessential" was just plain stupid. Some jerk in Huntsville apparently decided that it wasn't important to send new brassieres to the female moondogs . . . y'know, as if the ones we had were made of some indestructible fabric . . . so bras got put on the list. Maybe that sounds trivial to you, but ask any woman you know how she feels about never getting new lingerie. I got by for several months wearing one of three bras every day, and I'm here to tell you that the goddamn things start to rot after a while.

Then we got word through the grapevine that the beamjacks on Skycan were still getting "nonessential" supplies, and that made us curious. Skycan had more goof-offs in its crew than we ever had. So what were they doing, getting comics and movies and junk? So we got a couple of Suckers who worked at the Cape to do some snooping around, and it turned out that some guys on Skycan who *weren't* Suckers had managed to bribe an inspector at Skycorp's SPC to overlook certain Spam-cans which were scheduled to be shipped by OTV to Olympus.

Now that really got us riled. I mean, if there's anyone who should be pulling off a scam like that, it should be Vacuum Suckers, not some low-life short-timers on Skycan. *(laughs)* I mean, Jesus, the nerve of some people!

Anyway, as it turned out, at the end of one work shift there were a few of us sitting around a table in the rec room, griping about what we had just learned. Somebody says . . . and I'm not saying who it was . . . he says, "Gee, if there was only some way of getting *their* Spam-cans off their OTV's and loaded onto *our* LTV's."

Well . . . *(chuckles)* that's when Mighty Joe got up from the table and said that he had a phone call to make. And, to make a long story short, that's how we got into the piracy business.

Does that answer your question?

8. Pirates

"Descartes Traffic, this is flight Delta Tango One-Two-One, standing by for launch."

We copy, Delta Tango One-Two-One. Stand by for initiation of final countdown sequence, over.

Strapped into the pilot's seat of the tug's flight deck, Mighty Joe watched through the narrow canopy windows as the hard-suited ground-crew dragged the fuel lines away from the landing pad toward the nearby LO2/LH2 tanks. One of them turned and gave him a quick thumbs-up; Joe returned the gesture, then looked at his co-pilot. Russ Wright was moving down the pre-launch checklist, switching on the auto-abort sequencer and checking the pressurization of the fuel tanks. Without looking up, Rusty also gave him a thumbs-up: The tug was ready for flight.

"Jesus, what takes them so long?" Joe muttered impatiently. He gazed through the canopy again, this time to peer at the turretlike MainOps tower on top of Subcomp A. Always another frigging hold-up. He blew out his cheeks in disgust, then clicked on the radio again. "Descartes Traffic, this is the *Beautiful Dreamer*, on standby for launch," he repeated. "C'mon, guys, we've got a schedule to meet here. What are you waiting for?"

The voice that came back over the comlink was the same, unchanged monotone. *Delta Tango One-Two-One, please remain on standby, over. Launch authorization is not, repeat, is not given. Over.*

Joe glared at the MainOps tower. "Blow it out your—"

"Oh hell, Joe, cut it out." Wright stretched forward against his harness to hastily squelch Mighty Joe's radio, cutting the pilot off in mid-curse. The pilot glared at him. "Just cool off, willya?" Rusty added, tipping back his Giants baseball cap as

he settled into his seat. "I could use another few minutes anyway. I'm having trouble getting electrical out of backup mode."

"What's the problem?" Mighty Joe leaned forward and
checked the main console between their seats. The status light
on the electrical system showed that internal power was still
coming from the backup system instead of the main batteries.
Joe snapped the toggle switch back and forth a few times.
"Aw, it's the goddamn Main Bus A again," he muttered.
"Looky . . . cut off Main A for a second, switch over to Main
B, cut in the backups, then switch back to Main A. That should
jimmy the thing."

Rusty shrugged, but followed Joe's suggestion. The status light
instantly switched on to main batteries. "Nice trick," Rusty
said. "I thought you told them to get Main A fixed."

"I did." Mighty Joe slouched back in his seat, absently pulling the bill of his Gatorama cap over his eyes. "They got some
reject from the Young Astronauts maintenancing this thing now
who doesn't know how to read the service manuals." He laced
his fingers together, cracked his knuckles, and sighed. "I swear
to God, this whole fucking operation's gone into the toilet since
they canned Fisk. Can't get off the fucking ground without a
fucking act of Congress. . . . "

"Gee, Joe, you've got such a way with words." Anne Noonan, watching from the passenger seat behind them, tightened
her harness. "You know, they say guys who use the word 'fuck'
all the time are supposed to have male potency problems."

Rusty looked over his shoulder at the cargo specialist; Joe just
stared straight ahead at the lighted dashboard. "Keep it up,
sweetheart," he growled, "and you're getting out to push." He
shook his head in disgust. "Come to think of it, it might help."

"You know, you're always a grouch when you're in a hurry,"
Wright observed. He double-checked the CRT screen in front of
him, then touched his own headset. "Descartes Traffic, this is
Delta Tango One-Two-One. We've got Go status for launch. I
repeat, that's green for Go. On standby and requesting permission for launch, over."

There was a long pause, then the voice of the MainOps
TRAFCO came over their headphones. *Roger that, Delta Tango
One-Two-One. You have permission to launch. Countdown ini-
tiates at sixty seconds, on my mark. Three . . . two . . . one
. . . . mark. T minus sixty seconds and counting. Over.*

"Now that's more like it." Mighty Joe glanced at his co-pilot. "How did you do that?"

Rusty smiled. "You just have to learn to ask politely, that's all."

"Fat chance," Noonan said under her breath.

"I heard that, crew slut," Joe growled.

"Pay attention to the controls, monkey dick," she replied easily. She absently brushed back her short black hair and sighed. "I swear, one of these days I'm going to find a real pilot to fly with."

Mighty Joe ignored the final remark from his cargo specialist. He switched on his radio again. "*Thank* you, Descartes Traffic," he said with exaggerated politeness. "Delta Tango One-Two-One on final countdown." His voice dropped to a whisper as he added, "And it's about time, you lazy assholes."

He rested his right hand on the attitude control stick and ran his eyes across the array of status lights and computer screens to make sure all systems were copacetic for launch. Rusty reached to the manual abort switch and flipped back its red-striped cover, getting it ready in case of a launch emergency and the remote possibility that the onboard computer's auto-abort sequence might jam. Unlike the LTV flight crews, no one aboard the *Beautiful Dreamer* wore VR helmets during launch or landing, even though Mighty Joe or Rusty could easily patch into the tug's virtual-reality computer subsystem. VR was kid stuff, too much like playing a computer game; any pimplehead back home could buy a game disk that would do the same thing. A real pilot relied on his knowledge, his eyes, his hands, and his gut instincts. Maybe it was the old-fashioned way, but that's what flying was all about. You can't be a true Vacuum Sucker by dicking around with candy-ass cybershit.

Four . . . three . . . two . . . one . . .

"Ignition and liftoff," Mighty Joe said, and shoved forward the thrust bar. The tug's four Rockwell main engines ignited soundlessly, white-hot jets of flame pressing against the scorched mooncrete pad, and the squat spacecraft rose quickly into the black sky.

Inside the flight deck, there was barely a sensation of movement. In the near-vacuum of the Moon, the tug soared upwards with the smooth, effortless ease of an ascending elevator, rocking only slightly in its ascent. The *Dreamer* punched through the thin, localized haze of dust held above the ground by the

Moon's negligible atmosphere, thrown up by the base's mining operations. Another fraction of an inch of dust was added to the tug's outer hull; even out here, industrial activity was polluting the natural environment.

Mighty Joe held the attitude controller steady, guiding the *Dreamer* upwards as he stared at the three-dimensional flight path painted for him on the navigational computer's CRT screen. Ten miles, fifteen, twenty, twenty-five miles . . . he glanced out his window for a glimpse of Descartes Station dwindling below him, a cluster of regolith-covered molehills surrounded by dingy gray lunar highlands. Rusty Wright's voice was a reassuring drone, telling him that fuel pressurization and electrical systems were nominal, beginning the 30-second countdown to main-engine cutoff. Mighty Joe nodded, smiling in spite of himself. This was the rush for which he positively lived: taking a hunk of graphite-polymer, steel, and aluminum, and riding the big ugly fuck into space. And they say you can't have fun on the Moon anymore. . . .

Exactly half a minute later, Joe reached out and pulled down the engine-control bar. The dull, subaudible vibration of the engines slowly grumbled down to a stop. Rusty checked the computer screen and the gyroscope. "Okay," he reported. "MECO complete. Ascent continuing, bearing X-ray forty-four, Yankee minus two-zero, Zulu nine-niner-six. Coming up the pike for orbital insertion and everything's just A-OK."

We copy, Delta Tango One-Two-One, Descartes Traffic responded. *Your launch looked good. Sorry for the delay, gentlemen. We had a software glitch that needed correction down here. Over.*

Mighty Joe snorted and cupped his mike with his left hand. "Somebody had to visit the john," he said to his crew. He uncovered the mike again. "Roger that, Descartes Traffic, we fully understand your problem. *Beautiful Dreamer* on course for orbit and rendezvous with AOMV *Collins,* over."

We copy, Beautiful Dreamer. Thank you for your indulgence. Hearing that, Joe laughed out loud. There was a short pause before the TRAFCO's voice resumed, sounding slightly miffed. *Confirm that AOMV Collins is in standard orbit Lima November one-zero-zero-nine. Repeat, that's Lima November one-oh-zero-niner. Should be coming up over the horizon now. Over.*

Wright carefully typed the orbital parameters into the navaids computer's keypad. Mighty Joe checked the readout, making certain the coordinates were correctly entered, then snapped the autopilot's toggles. "We copy, Descartes Traffic," he replied. "*Dreamer* on course for Lima November one-zero-zero-niner. Thank you very much and we'll be signing off for now, if you don't mind. Catch you on the flip side. Delta Tango One-Two-One over and out."

He switched off the radio. Fortunately, NASA regulations permitted him to cease radio communications with the base when he felt like it, so he could eliminate the distraction of endless chatter with TRAFCO. "And good riddance to all that happy shit," he muttered. "Okay, let's see about bringing home the goodies."

Mighty Joe reprogrammed the flight computer to give him a three-dimensional layout of all orbital objects above the lunar nearside. The AOMV stage of the *Michael Collins* was clearly visible near the left edge of the screen, designated by its blue alphanumeric code-letters, but he wasn't concerned with its immediate whereabouts. Instead, he typed in a set of commands which logoned the navaids course-calculation subsystem. "Now, where is this sucker going to take us?" Joe asked no one in particular.

"Hmm?" Rusty glanced up from his situation. "Why worry about it?"

"Just a little change of plan here . . ." Mighty Joe's voice trailed off as he studied the screen. Feeling Rusty's and Anne's eyes on his back, he looked up at them. "I want us to get that Spam-can we're looking for in the cargo bay and checked out before we land again."

"Hey!" Noonan yelled. "What do you mean 'us'? You mean I gotta put that thing in the mid-deck?"

"Yeah, and bring it back out again." Before the cargo spec could protest, Joe raised his hand. "Just wait a second and listen. We got that new GM down there, and you heard his speech about him wanting to make everything at the base a straight act. Now, what do you imagine will happen if we open that can while he's standing around?"

Noonan's mouth closed. She slowly exhaled and grumpily lay back in her seat. "Okay, all right, so you've got a point." She shook her head and gazed up through the docking window. "Bet you're doing this just for that monkey-dick crack."

"Naw, hold it a minute, Annie," Rusty said. "He's got a good idea, but we've got to get the timing perfect." He leaned over the console, stroking the tip of his blond mustache as he peered at the swift-moving track of the *Collins'* estimated trajectory. "Let's just look at this thing and figure out how to make the offload without someone getting suspicious."

A constant signal transmitted by radio beacon by the moonship's AOMV stage was received by Descartes Station's space traffic control computers and automatically relayed back to the tug through the ground-based telemetry link. It took a lot of the guesswork out of orbital rendezvous, since the base and tug computers could handshake and agree where a particular object lay in a standard orbit—in this case, a slightly elliptical orbit a little more than fifty miles above the lunar surface. In the subroutine Mighty Joe had plugged in, the computers could also estimate with a low degree of error the trajectory the AOMV would take for each minute of its orbit above the Moon.

"Look at this," Rusty said. The blue-tinted object twice circled the lunar polar projection, crossing the dark-shaded eastern terminator, moving on a dotted hemispherical trajectory, moving again into the western terminator, and finally crossing the eastern terminator again. The co-pilot, who had been studying the swift-changing set of numbers at the bottom of the screen, jabbed his finger at the display the third time the AOMV crossed the eastern terminator. "That's it," he said softly, and tapped the keyboard's HOLD button with his finger. "Check out the numbers, Joe."

Mighty Joe studied the coordinates. "Yeah, yeah . . ." He nodded. "I think that's the ticket, all right. Beauty. Three orbits in two and a quarter hours should give us enough time to get it in the cargo bay and unloaded. We can offload right here at the east terminator if we cut it right." He pointed at the blue light's estimated XYZ axial coordinates shortly after it crossed the eastern terminator. "Think we can hack it?"

"No sweat." Rusty had already begun to enter the parameters for rendezvous and linkup with the *Collins* into the navaids computer. "Might be close, though," he added as he bent over the keypad, fixated on the readout. "Seriously. It's shaving the fuel supply a bit close, and we'll have to work fast to get the stuff unloaded in the cargo bay without them catching on. . . . Three orbits, that's okay, but if we have to go into four there might be a few questions and . . . lemme see, if we've got the return crew coming up at oh-nine-hundred tomorrow and . . ."

He mumbled to himself for a few moments. Joe and Annie

stared silently at him until Rusty suddenly twitched and looked up at them again. "Yeah, sure," he murmured. "We can pull it off. Sorry. Just thinking out loud. Don't worry about it."

"No problems, Russ?" Annie asked quietly. "Just like the last two times? You're sure?"

The co-pilot blinked and nodded, then returned his attention to the keyboard. They had gotten used to Rusty's becoming obsessed with the more abstract aspects of orbital mechanics. Mighty Joe looked over his shoulder at Anne Noonan. "We better hope they have some marijuana stashed in that thing," he said solemnly. "Flying with this guy straight is beginning to get on my nerves."

"Hey, at least I can count on his calculations." Annie was already unbuckling her seat harness. "If we had to rely on you, we'd be on our way to Mars right now."

She gently pushed herself out of her seat, did a midair somersault with her knees bent in, then guided herself with outstretched hands toward the mid-deck hatch. On the back of her utility vest, a skull wearing a space helmet sneered at the pilots. The lower rim of the Vacuum Suckers patch was embroidered with the words: AD ASTRA PER BULLSHITUM. "I'm going down to get in the iron lady," Noonan said. "Let me know the second we're hard-docked and I'm outta here."

"Okey-doke," Mighty Joe replied. He was admiring the view of her rear end. So round, so smooth, so positively aerodynamic . . . "Hey, are you sure you're eating right?" he asked lasciviously, stretching a hand out toward her buns. "Seems like you're gaining a little weight right around . . ."

"Back off, bub!" Noonan kicked backwards with her left leg, almost landing the sole of her foot square in Joe's face. He dodged and yanked his hand back as she twisted the latch and opened the hatch.

"Adolescent sexist . . ." she muttered as she vanished into the mid-deck cargo hold.

Mighty Joe chuckled as he turned back around to his console; Rusty looked up at him and shook his head. "One day, you're going to push it just a little too far with her," he said quietly. "And man, I wanna be around to watch when it happens."

"Don't hold your breath." Mighty Joe reached up and toggled the switches that opened the jaws of the *Dreamer*'s forward docking adapter, readying it for linkup with the *Collins*. He chuckled again, watching through the windows as the flanges of the docking collar slowly spread open. Beyond the prow of the ship, he could already see the elongated spot of light which was the AOMV, slowly coasting above the limb of the Moon. And now for the second nifty part of this job . . .

"Episode Five!" he exclaimed. "Space Pirates! When we last saw Flash, he and Dale were about to bang the daylights out of each other, when Ming's cutthroat pirate fleet suddenly . . ."

"Yeah." Rusty reached up to swing the periscope down from the ceiling bulkhead. "Shiver me timbers and all that stuff."

When Les Riddell came up the central stairwell into MainOps, he was astonished by the size of the new command center. Eight years ago when he had been in charge of Descartes, the command center had been a narrow module little larger than the interior of a mobile home; five people couldn't fit in there together without constant jostling and elbow-rubbing. He had always remembered the old command center as a claustrophobic, vaguely depressing place: cramped, littered with food wrappers and dogeared logbooks, fitted with partly disassembled instruments which looked as if Skycorp had bought them secondhand at a going-out-of-business sale held by the Chinese space program.

The new MainOps, by comparison, appeared as if it feasibly could be converted into an additional rec room. The large, circular compartment had a twelve-foot ceiling, carpeted floors, upholstered swivel chairs in front of the work stations, even a raised dais in the room's center for the general manager's station. Four recessed, wall-sized windows, made of photosensitive lunar glass and spaced equidistant from each other around the room, looked out over the base and the highlands. The indirect lighting was subdued without provoking eyestrain; the consoles were sleek aluminum desks, with push-button covers that slid over the keypads when they were not in use. Someone had even taken the trouble to hang small pots of ivy and fern on the walls that were not occupied by computer screens and TV monitors.

In all, MainOps had the efficiency of a supertanker's bridge combined with the ambience of a den. Lester stopped in the doorway to admire the room. Skycorp's engineers had obviously learned some lessons over the past few years about designing a user-friendly work environment, even if the rest of the base was coldly utilitarian. It figured that Skycorp would make things as comfortable as possible for the command staff, while failing to

take into consideration the living areas and work places occupied
by the rest of the personnel.

Behind him, at the top of the spiral staircase, Tina McGraw
coughed and gently prodded his back, shaking Lester from his
reverie. The new security chief was impatient to get down to
business. Riddell took a couple of steps farther into the command center, and McGraw immediately pushed through the open
hatch past him, stalking into the circular aisle which led behind
the duty stations.

"I want a Mercator projection of near-lunar orbit on the main
screen," she said briskly to no one in particular. "Three-
dimensional projection, including the positions of the *Schmitt*
and the *Collins'* AOMV and their trajectories. Now."

The eight shift officers in the command center looked over
their shoulders; first at McGraw, then at Riddell. The expressions on their faces registered the same unspoken thought: *Who
the hell is this woman, and aren't you the guy who's supposed
to be giving orders around here?* Lester walked in front of Mc-
Graw, gently yet firmly pushing her out of his way.

"This is Tina McGraw," he explained. "She's with the NASA
enforcement division . . . our new security chief." He paused,
then added, "Skip the Mercator projection and give us a Lam-
bert sphere only, please. But put the tug and the AOMV on the
chart, too." He glanced at McGraw and pointedly added,
"Please."

The young Japanese-American man at the Traffic Control
station tapped instructions into his keyboard as Lester walked
up the three steps to the dais. McGraw followed him onto the
platform. As he settled into the command chair—*his* chair—
and touched the studs that recessed the panels into their slots,
he caught a fleeting glimpse of McGraw's irritated face. *Tough
shit, lady*, he thought. *I'm the head honcho around here, not
you. . . .*

Lester logged himself in, adding McGraw's name to the computer record almost as an afterthought, listing her as "Security
Chief." He then put on a headset, fitting the right earpiece
against his ear and draping the rest of the unit loosely around
his neck. A spherical projection of the Moon and its near-space
environment had already appeared, both on a wall-screen above
the TRAFCO station and on a smaller screen on his console. A
blue and a red point of light moved in circular orbits around the

Moon, tracing broken lines as they moved toward an intercept point near the eastern terminator.

"Focus on the tug, please," Lester asked. At first, nothing happened. The traffic control officer gazed straight ahead at his console, his headset clamped firmly to his ears. Lester opened his mouth to repeat the request more loudly, then stopped and examined his headset. It was one of the newer bone-conduction units which had replaced the old acoustical headsets. Damn, Lester thought. Have they changed *everything* in this place?

He repositioned his own headset so that the bone-phone rested firmly against his jaw and repeated the order. This time the TRAFCO heard him; his fingers danced on his keypad and a window opened on the screen for a zoom-in shot of the *Beautiful Dreamer*. The red spot, designated by alphanumeric code, appeared in the close-up frame, rapidly closing in on the blue spot of the *Collins'* first-stage booster. As the two spacecraft crossed the eastern terminator at the D'Alembert Mountain range, the dotted lines subtly changed, depicting their computer-estimated trajectories. Lester had to remind himself that he'd left the AOMV behind only a few hours earlier. Given the events that had taken place since, it seemed as if it had been much longer. Hell, it had been a long day. . . .

He examined the screen for a moment, then swiveled around in his chair to face McGraw. "Okay," he said, "there's the tug we just launched and there's the *Collins*. Looks like a routine cargo-recovery mission to me. You were saying something about piracy?"

Tina McGraw's narrow eyes bored into the projection on the wall-screen. "Why can't you get more than an estimation of their trajectories over the farside?" she asked. "And why did you ignore my request for a Mercator projection?"

"We don't have radar installations on the other side of the terminator capable of reporting a cohesive picture," Lester replied casually. He settled back in his chair and knitted his fingers together; he had to admit he was beginning to enjoy vexing the security officer. "That's because navigational radar dishes over there would interfere with the VLF radiotelescope at Hawking Station. They've got very sensitive instruments working full time at Krasovsky Crater, and any radar we'd put on farside would foul their reception."

McGraw frowned. "I see," she said, in a tone which suggested that she really didn't understand.

"You can't get a Mercator projection without those navigational radar dishes," Lester continued, "because you need far-side radar to give you an accurate fix on something's trajectory in order to establish its flightpath. All we can do is display its position over the nearside and give a best-guess computer estimate of where it is when it crosses the terminator to the farside. It's a necessary compromise."

McGraw appeared less than satisfied with Riddell's explanation. Yet she said nothing and stolidly watched the screen. Lester watched as her narrow eyes squinted to slits, her mouth pursed in a pugnacious scowl. There was much about McGraw which reminded Lester of pushy small-town cops he had met in the past, the type who couldn't get enough of throwing their weight around. "It'll do," she said simply. "We'll just watch and see. Give me . . ."

She glanced at Riddell and deferentially rephrased her request. "Can you *please* ask your TELMU to see if he can locate an orbital object with a radio beacon transmitting at 103.5 kilohertz? If he finds it . . ."

She stopped; an enigmatic Cheshire-cat smile grew on her face. "*When* he finds it," she corrected herself, "ask him to match that object with the appropriate image on the screen."

What in the bloody hell was going on here? Yet instead of asking, Riddell turned around in his chair until he found the young, blond-haired man sitting at the TELMU station. He started to call to him, then paused. If he wanted to establish himself as being the head man, it would help if he started calling his people by their given names. Simply yelling "Hey, you!" wasn't a good way to gain anyone's confidence. Funny how those things were coming back to him. *Maybe I did want this job back after all*, he mused as he tapped into the logbook again.

He found the name of the telemetry officer now on watch: *Schneider, Jeremy.* "Schneider," he said, and the TELMU's head cocked slightly as he heard the general manager's voice in his headset. "See if you can locate an orbital object which is transmitting at 103.5 kilohertz. When you get it, pass it over to TRAFCO . . . ah, Shimoda . . . for him to plot on the screen. Got it?"

"Yes, sir." Schneider bent over his console, but his fingers hesitated for a few moments before they went to work. Lester noticed the meticulous way in which Schneider entered the instructions; he obviously was still learning the commands. *Must be another new guy*, Lester thought distractedly.

"There," McGraw said suddenly. "You see?"

Riddell glanced back at the screen. Something odd had happened. A second window had opened on the screen; the numbers showed that the frequency-search had discovered just such an object. The *Collins'* AOMV was now depicted in a lapsed-time sequence just before it had crossed the eastern terminator. As Shimoda eliminated the unnecessary second window—now the blue blip of light had a second alphanumeric code scrolled beneath it as it circled the farside of the Moon—Lester glanced again at McGraw and noticed that she had a distinctly smug look on her face.

McGraw looked down at him. "That's a transmitter which was covertly placed in a Spam-can before it was loaded on the *Sally Ride*, Mr. Riddell," she explained, reading the expression on his face. Lester couldn't help but notice that she had reverted to formality in addressing him. "It was supposed to be on a Spam-can manifested for an OTV to Olympus Station. I wonder how it ended up on the *Collins* instead?"

Lester stared back at her, then looked back at the screen. He had been on the *Ride*, too, when he had taken it up to Phoenix Station. McGraw had already been at Phoenix when he had arrived, come to think of it. Too many things were getting weird too fast. "How did . . . Why was a transmitter put aboard the . . . ?"

"I'll explain the details later," McGraw said impatiently. She leaned over the back of a vacant chair and watched the big screen intently. "The important fact right now is that the Spam-can has a homing transmitter aboard which allows us to track it."

Lester rubbed his chin between his thumb and forefinger as he watched the tracks of the two spacecraft intercept over the lunar farside. He was getting sick and tired of McGraw's attitude. She had hidden her identity from him for the three days that they were aboard the *Collins*, then presented herself as the new security chief as if she were the head of a Central American secret police force, following which she attempted to run his command center as if he were a puppet leader. Now she was operating on a hidden agenda which suggested that Skycorp and NASA had plotted something in advance, a weird sting operation in which he was expected to obediently play a passive role.

Something strange was happening here, and he didn't like what he had seen of it so far.

"Okay, McGraw," he said softly, "what's going on?"

McGraw's catty smile broadened a little. "Just wait and see," she replied. "Somebody's in for a big surprise."

Classified Information (Interview.4)

Angelo deCastro: assistant director, Corporate Security Division, Skycorp (Huntsville headquarters):

(NOTE: This interview was conducted in the presence of NASA Space Operations Enforcement Division public affairs officer Leslie Hieronymous, who interjected at points on behalf of the space agency.)

deCastro: We knew . . . um, that some sort of smuggling activity was taking place at our Cape Canaveral operation. *(spreads his hands)* Really, Mr. Steele, the company has always had a problem with contraband making its way into space, such as the time in '17 when something like four hundred cases of beer managed to get smuggled up to Olympus Station in an OTV, so it's never been anything new to us. We've always tried to keep it under control, but it's difficult to keep an eye on every single payload canister which gets shipped up there. In this particular case, though, we were able to nip it in the bud mainly because we received information from a reliable source at the Cape that . . . um, certain restricted items were being put into the cans when they were being loaded in the shuttles at the company's Shuttle Processing Center . . . Pardon me?

Hieronymous: I'm sorry, that information is classified.

deCastro: Ah . . . Yes, right. I can't confirm or deny if there was an informer involved. All I can tell you is that we received word that the items were being put aboard so-called Spam-cans which were scheduled for launch in company-owned shuttles, and that one of the company's supervisors had been bribed by the same persons to overlook those payload canisters when it came time for him to inspect the shuttle's cargo bay. This supervisor, along with the other . . . ah, parties involved, were eventually dismissed from our employment and turned over to

115

NASA's Space Operations Enforcement Division for arrest and subsequent prosecution under federal law. On that particular point, I'm . . . um, not at liberty to discuss the matter in further detail.

Hieronymous: The case against the alleged suspects is still in litigation.

deCastro: Right. Anyway, once this was discovered, the Corporate Security Division worked with NASA to find out the final destination of the contraband items, and that's when we made a second interesting . . . um, discovery. Apparently the restricted items were originally intended to be sent to Olympus Station. That is, that was the original . . . ah, intent of the parties involved, and that this had been going along for quite some time. But in their last two attempts to illicitly ferry the contraband to Olympus, the designated Spam-cans had not made their way to the space station, although they had been launched from Cape Canaveral. Instead they went *(waves his hand)* somewhere else entirely.

This led us to believe that, in some way, we were dealing with two—not one, but *two*—entirely independent smuggling operations, with the second one parasitically feeding off the labors of the first group. *(smiles)* That was when it became quite interesting . . . um, from a law enforcement standpoint. We had no direct clues to tell us where the hijacked Spam-cans had been sent, because whoever from the second group had arranged the diversion at the SPC had been able to doctor the cargo manifests so that the canisters appeared to have been shipped to Olympus, although the persons in the first group told us, once we interrogated them, that those two Spam-cans never got to Olympus at all. Understand? I mean, are you following me so far?

That led us to several alternative scenarios. *(holds up his forefinger)* One, the contraband cargo was being sent back to Earth, by nearly the same means, for resale. We ruled that out almost immediately, since most of the contraband . . . booze, for instance . . . had little or no resale value back on Earth. Didn't make sense. *(holds up a second finger)* Two, the contraband was making its way to our installation at Arsia Station on Mars, or *(holds up a third finger)* three, it was going to Descartes Station on the Moon. Given the closer . . . um, proximity of the Moon base as opposed to the Mars base, we decided to focus our attention on Descartes Station.

This presented us with a difficult situation, given the fact that

Descartes Station had recently been through a shakeout of its
personnel and that we had a new General Manager coming
aboard at the base at the same time that we were pursuing our
investigation. Fortunately, NASA was also placing a field officer
up there at the same time to act as the base's new security chief
. . . um, that's right, Ms. McGraw . . . and she was willing to
act as the point man in our investigation. . . .

Hieronymous: Point woman . . .

deCastro: Excuse me, point woman . . . um, in our investigation. So when she was transferred to her new assignment, she
went in a covert low-profile role, appearing to be just another
new lunar worker on her way to the Moon, in hopes of gathering
additional information. But, mainly, she was to observe the covert sting operation we had put in place. In this operation, which
we code-named Operation Blue Moon, we placed . . .

Hieronymous: Sorry, sir, this operation is still classified information.

deCastro: Um . . . right. It's still classified information.

Hieronymous: Sorry.

deCastro: Sorry. Well, um . . . *(coughs)* do you have any
more questions?

9. Booby Trap

Damn, it's dark out here, Annie said. *Gimme some more light, Joe, willya?*

Mighty Joe reached to his left and flipped a switch which turned on another bank of the exterior hull searchlights. Through the canopy windows he could see the stark white glare reflecting off the gold Mylar foil wrapped around the AOMV's hull. Two spots of light shined on the opaque cockpit of Noonan's work capsule, hovering alongside the *Collins*. "See better now?" he asked politely.

Fine, thanks, Noonan replied over the comlink. He couldn't see her through the windows of the tiny, bottle-shaped RWS, but he could watch the long, triple-jointed arms of its remote manipulators imitating her hand movements. She had already transferred most of the Spam-cans to the tug; they were lashed to the strongbacks on the *Dreamer*'s lower fuselage, giving the tug the vague appearance of a worker bee carrying pollen sacs to the hive. The empty cargo cradles yawned open behind the *Collins'* aerobrake heat shield. Once the AOMV was reunited with its lander, the moonship would be heading back to Earth orbit; although it would never land on the planet itself, it would make an aerobraking maneuver in the upper atmosphere before rendezvousing with its LEO hangar near Phoenix Station.

Annie had unlocked the final Spam-can—the one in particular which had been diverted from delivery to Olympus Station—and had the massive canister gripped by the arms' pincers. *Okay, we got it*, Noonan said. *Ready to bring it aboard?*

"Affirmatory on that." Joe double-checked the status lights for the cargo bay, making sure that the hatch was still open, and then glanced at the event timer. Rusty silently pointed at the CRT screen between them, where a three-dimensional image of

118

their position over the lunar farside was displayed. They were completing their third orbit now; things were getting a little tight. "We need to hurry it up, sweetheart," he added. "Big Russ here tells me we're T-minus-eleven to coming over the terminator again, and I'd rather not . . ."

Okay, okay, I heard you already. The RCRs on the sides of her work capsule flared briefly, pinpricks of matchlight against the dark bulk of the Moon in the background, and the little one-person vehicle glided sideways toward the stern of the tug, shoving the Spam-can along in front of it. *Tell me again at T-minus-five if we're still cutting it close, but otherwise shut up and lemme work.*

Joe watched as the work capsule moved closer to the open cargo hatch. A floodlight beam briefly caught the words "Wonder Woman" painted in a bright red slash on the fuselage, just below a hand-painted picture of the comic-book superheroine. He waited a moment, then said, "Annie . . ."

What, damn it?

"You're still a bitch," he finished sweetly.

He heard her sigh over the comlink . . . but she didn't say anything. Mighty Joe grinned. Noonan caught a lot of flak from him, most of it of the sexist variety, but he had to admit to himself that she was one hell of moondog. If there was a bitch out there next to the *Dreamer*, it was the little work capsule, not the woman who piloted it. It took a special touch to fly the damn things; the reaction control jets were notorious for being overly sensitive, and even with the aid of a virtual-reality control system, operating the remote manipulators was a lot like trying to juggle balls while wearing plaster casts on both arms.

After the *Dreamer*'s last payload specialist had completed his contract, and before Annie had come aboard, Mighty Joe and Rusty had flown pickup missions for six weeks without a cargo rat. They had done the grunt work themselves in that period, and by the time Noonan had arrived for duty, the two men were on the verge of having fistfights over whose turn it was to fly the capsule. Noonan had just climbed in, shut the hatch, flown out, and got her first non-simulated Spam-cans transferred and latched down without any sweat. . . . Then she had climbed out and told them that they were both clumsy jerks and to bathe before the next time they climbed in *her* RWS, if she even let them. "It stinks like a jockstrap in there," she had said.

"It's a woman's job," he murmured aloud.

"Say what?" Rusty asked, looking up from his navigation console. He was working out the flight plan for the *Dreamer*'s return to Descartes.

"Never mind. Just thinking aloud . . ."

But I appreciate it, Annie said. She sounded sincere. *Thanks, Joe.*

"Don't let it go to your head, toots," he growled back. He watched as Noonan slowly maneuvered the canister toward the starboard cargo hatch; it was a tight fit, and she had to move gradually to keep the blunt forward end from bashing into the tug's fuselage or the hatch doors.

"Five minutes," Rusty said.

Mighty Joe glanced up again. In the far distance, beyond the edge of the RWS, the farside terminator hove into view as a white-silver crescent, the ragged western edge of Hirayama Crater outlined by the half-light cast by the rising Earth. Once over the Hirayama, he knew from experience, they would again be within range of Descartes' traffic radar; MainOps would be expecting them to make the braking thrust for return and touchdown. If they had to delay, any excuses given for making another orbit might arouse suspicions, and that was the last thing Mighty Joe wanted from the new GM.

"Annie, I don't mean to be an asshole," he urged softly, "but can you hurry up? It's getting a bit tight, if you know what I mean."

Why, what's your rush? she replied breezily. She had the Spam-can almost one third of the way inside. *Five minutes, four minutes, what's the . . . ?*

"Move it, Noonan!" Rusty snapped.

All right, all right! she yelled back. *Take it easy, I'm coming.* There was a pause, then: *Hang on to something, this could be rough.*

"Annie, what . . . ?" Rusty began.

The elbows of the capsule's manipulators folded against the canister's back end. Joe suddenly realized what Noonan was about to do and managed to grab his armrests just before the RCR jets on the back of the capsule flashed again and the manipulators shot out in the opposite direction. The Spam-can was brutally shoved the rest of the way into the cargo deck; Noonan was obviously counting on the cargo deck's capture-and-support cradle to keep the massive object from breaking something inside. Lights flashed on the dashboard and an annunciator rang as the tug's RCR's fired once, automatically compensating for the shift of inertial mass. Joe's hands darted for the alarm override.

"Goddammit, Annie!" he shouted. "Watch the—!"

Keep your shorts on, Joe. It's okay. The work capsule was slowly backing away from the hatch, its manipulators disengaged and floating free. *There, see? Nice and neat. The cradle caught it and everything. Now close the hatch and prep the RWS sleeve. I'm coming in.* She paused. *That fast enough for you guys?*

Pilot and co-pilot exchanged a glance; Rusty let out his breath and Joe shut his eyes and let God know he was grateful for not allowing some reckless wench to wreck his ship. "Uh, yeah, that's an affirmative," Rusty said. "Superlative. Now c'mon in and let's get ready for touchdown."

"Three and a half minutes till we're over the terminator," Mighty Joe rumbled. "Good deal." He closed the cargo deck hatch and started the repressurization cycle, then unbuckled his seat harness and carefully pushed himself out of his chair. He felt the back of his shirt unstick from the upholstery as he moved. Damn, had he been sweating that much? "I'm going below to help Noonan out of the capsule," he said shortly, hoping Rusty didn't notice.

"Uh-huh. Sure. You want to check out the goodies." Rusty shook his head as he programmed the autopilot for the return leg of the trip. "Just make sure that if there's a bag of pot in that thing, it has my name written on it."

"You'll have to arm wrestle me for it, bub." Legs dangling upwards, Mighty Joe grabbed the recessed floor rungs and pulled himself toward the mid-deck hatch. "I'll let you start taking us down. I'm gonna go see what the lady's done brought home."

The pirated Spam-can took up most of the space in the mid-deck cargo hold; it hung within the nylon net of the cradle like a huge moth strangled in a spider's web. As Mighty Joe came down the ladder, he glanced once at the open service panel leading to the conduits for the main electrical busbars. When Main Bus A had started acting twitchy, Rusty had taken the precaution of unscrewing this particular service panel and leaving it off, exposing a candy-striped U-bar within the recess. If an emergency arose which could not be controlled from the flight deck, someone could get down here and cut off Main A by throwing the manual circuit breaker. Next to the open panel was a strip of white masking tape, scrawled with the words DON'T TOUCH THIS!!

Just looking at it made Joe irritated. *Somebody's got to get in here and fix this frigging thing.* He shook his head and pushed off the ladder, gliding across the compartment toward the captured Spam-can. Before Mighty Joe opened it, though, he went to help Noonan out of the RWS where it had docked inside its sleevelike berth. Like the hardsuits the moondogs wore, the RWS was zero-prebreath; Annie didn't have to spend hours in decompression, waiting for differing atmospheric pressures to adjust to each other. By the time Joe reached the berth, Noonan had opened the topside hatch and was pulling herself out, looking like someone emerging from an old-fashioned iron lung.

"Well, *you* certainly were a pain in the ass today," she complained, giving him a dirty look. She removed her bulky VR helmet, shook out her hair, and tossed the helmet back into the capsule's tiny cockpit before kicking the topside hatch shut. "I was half inclined to accidentally let that thing slip out of my hands."

"Sorry," Joe said. "Maybe I got a little carried away there."

"Yeah, maybe you did." Annie pulled her communications headset out of her vest pocket and pulled it over her head, then shoved Mighty Joe aside as she pulled herself along the overhead handrail to the Spam-can. "Well, it's aboard at any rate, so let's pop the hatch and see what Santa brought us good little boys and girls."

Joe cocked an eyebrow. "It's the first week of July, sweetheart."

"Haven't you ever heard of Christmas in July? Car dealers get a lot of mileage out of it. Now hurry up and open the damn thing."

"Now you're talking sense." Mighty Joe pushed himself over the top of the Spam-can and located the recessed valve that unsealed the O-rings which kept the canister sealed and airtight. He twisted it counterclockwise; there was a slight hiss of escaping air, and the long, refrigerator-door-size hatch popped open slightly. One by one, Joe flipped open the three latches, then grabbed the main rung and pulled it up. "Let's see what . . ."

"Hush!" Annie snapped. "You hear something?"

"Naw, I don't . . ."

Before he could react, Annie brutally shoved him away from

the hatch. As Mighty Joe reflexively grabbed for a ceiling rung, he started to yell at Noonan. And then he heard, from within the open hatch, a tinny electronic *tickatickatickatickaticka*. . . .

"*Duck!*" she screamed and threw herself backwards.

Mighty Joe barely had time to double up, when there was a sharp, loud *bang!* and something within the Spam-can exploded.

Pieces of ceramic shrapnel and bright blue ink exploded from within the canister. The dye sheeted across Joe's shoulders and forearms and the front of Annie's suit, plastering half of the cargo bay with sticky blue goop, as fragments of the bomb ricocheted off the interior of the cargo bay. Something behind them made a loud *snap!* and . . .

"GAAAH!" Mighty Joe howled as his shoulders caught the worst of the dye-bomb's discharge. "Fuck!" he screamed. "What the holy fuck was that?"

All at once, alarms started going off in the mid-deck, a harsh, white-noise blare mixed with a high, whining *beep-beep-beep-beep*. Recovering herself, Noonan absently wiped blue dye from her chin and stared into the open Spam-can. She looked up at Joe and started to laugh—the tug pilot looked as if he had walked under a housepainter's ladder just in time to have a bucket of blue paint spill over his head—then caught herself. The air was suddenly tinged with an acrid, ozone-laced odor . . . and, over that, a faint smell like burning tires. . . .

She looked at the open service panel at the same time as Mighty Joe, to see blue-green smoke billowing from the lacerated electrical conduits. Unable to control herself, she screamed as Joe launched himself at the fire-extinguisher station.

What the hell's going on down there? Rusty's voice shouted in their headsets. *Is everyone . . . ?*

"Fire in the hull!" Joe yelled. "Fire in mid-deck! Shut 'er down! Shut 'er down!" He ripped the fire extinguisher from its plastic tie-downs, twisted around in midair, and jammed the nozzle toward the fuming service hatch.

Main A and B down! Rusty shouted. *Repeat, Main A and B are . . .*

"I know, I know!" Mighty Joe squeezed the extinguisher's valve within his fist. The nozzle *squonked* and a white blast of carbon dioxide knocked him backwards, his ass slamming into the Spam-can as he struggled to direct the frigid jet against the electrical fire. Crystalline snowflakes spit from the sides of the panel and drifted in the air; the alarm continued to howl as

Noonan pushed herself forward, making a grab for the fire extinguisher to steady it in Joe's hands.

I heard an explosion! Rusty shouted. *Is everyone okay down there?*

"I got it, leggo!" Joe yelled in Annie's face. He pushed himself forward again, directing the nozzle toward the fire. It was almost smothered, but he wasn't about to take any chances. "Get topside now!" he shouted at Annie.

Suddenly the mid-deck lights went out; an instant later the rose-red emergency lights kicked in on their batteries. *Main A and B off-line,* Rusty said. His voice was almost ironic in its calm. *We're on backup. What's . . .*

"Okay, okay!" Joe shouted back. "Goddammit, Noonan, get up the ladder and lemmee handle this!" He held the nozzle on the frost-blanketed service panel as Noonan scrambled for the ladder. When the fire extinguisher's blast petered out and the pressure-gauge hit the red zone, he tossed it aside, reached into the bin and yanked down the icy circuit-breaker bar, just in case the automatic circuit beakers Rusty had flipped in the flight deck hadn't done the job. He then kicked off the deck and swam for the ladder.

Before he went up, though, he stopped and reached up to the ceiling for the cradle's unlocking lever. One hard yank and the ceiling hooks that held the nylon net unlocked; the Spam-can hung free, still loosely wrapped in the webbing. A necessary precaution, if he was going to do what he already suspected would have to be done.

It took only a sharp heave on the rungs to propel himself up into the flight deck. He almost collided with Annie as he shot through the hatch; she yelled an obscenity which Joe ignored as he pushed her aside and clumsily dove headfirst for his seat. "Get that hatch fastened down!" he shouted back at Annie.

"Calm down," Rusty murmured. He was bent over the main console, his eyes twitching back and forth over the myriad readouts and dials. The flight deck was dimly lit by the red emergency lights and the blue glow of the dashboard screens, but as Joe buckled into his seat, the compartment was suddenly awash in the bright white glow of sunlight. Glancing up, he saw the Sun rising over the limb of the Moon; they were over the western terminator now. "What's going on down there?" Rusty demanded.

"Dye-bomb in the Spam-can," Annie said. Her voice was

hoarse from shouting. She had shut the mid-deck hatch and dogged it, and was now hauling herself back into her seat. "Banks use 'em to mark cash heisted by bank robbers. . . . "

"Yeah, except this sumbitch shrapneled and nailed the main busbars. Lucky shot . . . or whatever you wanna call it." Joe reached up to pull down the bill of his Gatorama cap, only to find it missing entirely. It must have been knocked off down there. Fire in the mid-deck, dye-bomb in the Spam-can, his ship on auxiliaries, and now, on top of that, he had to lose his lucky cap. Somebody was going to pay for this shit.

"Never mind that now," he said. "What's our current status, Rusty?"

"Backup electrical is copacetic, fuel pressure is nominal," Wright replied, "but I don't know how much longer we can hold it, hoss. We're a hurtin' puppy."

"I hear you. Mid-deck temperature?"

"Up a bit. Two hundred degrees above nominal. Could be external, though. Fuselage heating." Rusty glanced at Joe; their eyes met and both men silently shook their heads. The tug's sensors would have compensated for the move into daylight again. Joe might have only extinguished part of the electrical fire; even as they spoke, more of the busbars could still be burning, deep within the pressurized part of the mid-deck. If that hypothetical spark were to reach the fuel tanks . . .

"Want to go for an abort?" Rusty asked. He reached out and flipped back the safety cover from the MAN. ABORT switch.

"Uh-uh," Joe snapped. "Belay that shit. I say we go for a blowout on the mid-deck."

"Blowout?" Noonan shouted. "Are you out of your—?"

"Shut up, Annie!" Mighty Joe didn't even glance in her direction. He locked eyes with his co-pilot. "Abort or blowout. That's the choice."

The abort procedure meant that the lower hull of the *Dreamer* would be jettisoned from the tug, and the upper stage's emergency DPS, located beneath the main crew compartment, would be fired for a crash-landing. There were two big problems with that idea. First, the emergency descent system had only enough fuel for a low-altitude abort; it was designed primarily for take-off emergencies below twenty-five nautical miles, and the *Dreamer* was almost fifty miles above the Moon's surface. A crash-landing, therefore, might not be survivable; the fuel supply would be exhausted long before they made it to the ground.

Second, they were still no closer to Descartes Station than the eastern edge of Smyth's Sea, thousands of miles away from the base. Ditching there, assuming they could survive the landing, would put them out in seldom-explored boonies—not a good place for a rescue mission.

On the other hand, deliberately blowing out the pressurized mid-deck meant that the fire would be extinguished once and for all. That was for damn sure; hard vacuum is the ultimate fire-stopper. It was also a dangerous maneuver, known to astronauts as a feasible, not-in-the-book option which could be successfully accomplished, as it had been on a few legendary occasions—*if* the craft's fuselage survived the trauma. There had also been a couple of instances in which an emergency blowout had resulted in the rupture of the crew compartment, and the guys who had been through that hadn't lived to tell anyone about the experience. Also, the reaction from the sudden blast could put the craft into a hell of a delta-V, potentially putting them in something akin to a uncontrollable spinout by an aircraft on Earth. Again, lunar pizza. But there wasn't enough time for any of the *Dreamer*'s crew to get into their hardsuits, and they were flat-broke when it came to other choices.

Rusty knew the risks of both procedures. He nodded once, then flipped the safety cover back over the ABORT switch.

"Okay, then," Joe rasped. "We're going for a blowout." He reached up and snapped back the four toggles which would arm the emergency pyros on the mid-deck cargo hatch. An alarm began to howl, unnecessarily warning them that the mid-deck was still pressurized.

He looked back over his shoulder at Noonan. Annie was pale-faced, but strapped in tight; she grimaced and gave him the thumbs-up. "Get us out of this alive," she whispered, "and I swear you'll get the sex of your life out of me. . . . "

No time even for a comeback; right now, he could have cared less if Noonan had promised him an orgy with her sister, her mom, and all her cousins. He turned back to his console and laid his finger on the FIRE toggle. "All right, gang," Joe said, "here goes. Three . . . two . . ."

He didn't bother to reach the bottom of the countdown before he snapped back the toggle. From below the flight deck there was a hard, loud BANG!! and the *Beautiful Dreamer* suddenly rocked sideways as if an angry god had drop-kicked them over the gates of Hell. Through the windows he saw the curved, pitted horizon veer sharply to the right, and as he grabbed the attitude controller and fought the son of a bitch, he heard Rusty shouting . . .

"Mayday! Mayday! Descartes, this is Delta Tango One-Two-One, going down! Mayday—!"

Jesus Christ, Mighty Joe silently prayed as his craft hurtled toward the Moon, *get me outta this one.* . . .

10. Heroes Are Hard To Find

The *Harrison Schmitt*—or the *Beautiful Dreamer*, Lester reminded himself, if one cared to acknowledge its rechristening—had come down in a boulder field about three hundred yards east of Descartes Station, not far from the landing pads. It had not been a smooth landing, although the crew had managed to walk away from the tug; the starboard landing gear had settled on a trunk-sized rock, causing its main strut to buckle. *Beautiful Dreamer* was therefore in a lopsided position, listing sharply to the right. One look at the tug and Les knew that the spacecraft would have to be cut apart, its upper and lower stages dismantled by mobile cranes and hauled back in sections to the base, before anyone could even begin to make the tug flightworthy again.

Terrific, he thought. First day on the job, and somebody totals a spacecraft. I can't wait to report to Huntsville about this one. *Sure, Les, no problem. Big Mac has an assembly line in St. Louis already geared up to build you another tug. Just as soon as the insurance companies cough up the $600 million it takes to make the things, and NASA's Commercial Spaceflight Review Board gets through reaming us. No sweat . . .* Arnie was going to have a duck when he heard about this.

Some of the rescue team was siphoning the remains of the tug's fuel into a tank on the back of a rover. From what he could make out from their cross talk on the comlink, there was not much LOX left in the tanks; the tug had landed with little less than a minute's worth of fuel to keep it in powered flight. Other moondogs were wrenching down the Spam-cans and loading them onto another couple of rovers. Lester carefully shuffled around to the tug's starboard side—he didn't trust himself yet to try hop-skipping, at least not until his lunar reflexes returned—and gazed up at the mid-deck cargo hatch above him. One of the two hatch doors had been all but completely sheared away by the explosive decompression the pilot had deliberately caused. It hung from its bottom hinge like a barn door that had been torn down by a stampeding bull. Inside the hold, he could see the moving lights of the rescue team's helmet lamps as they prowled the grounded spacecraft.

Riddell glanced at the trio of rovers parked around the base of the *Dreamer*. Off in the distance, he could see a fourth rover trundling toward Descartes Station, taking the tug's crew back to the base. They had been laconic when they had emerged from the tug and climbed down the ladder, unwilling to answer questions with anything more than noncommittal monosyllables. Les shook his head inside his helmet. They'll talk eventually, he thought. But not before I murder the sumbitch pilot for bringing his ship back in such sorry-ass condition.

But he still had to give credit to the sumbitch for having the foresight not to attempt a landing on one of the landing pads. Given the condition of his craft, he could have lost control and crashed into the base itself, possibly killing dozens of people. Better to ditch in a boulder field than to take that sort of chance. Smooth flying, indeed. Lester had to admire the guy—what's-his-name, Young—for keeping his act together in this sort of emergency.

If, indeed, there *had* been an emergency . . .

Mr. Riddell, you should come up here to see this. The voice in his headphones belonged to Tina McGraw. The security chief had come out to the crash site with the rescue team. She was inside the *Dreamer* with a couple of moondogs, at her insistence. *I want to show you something.*

I'm sure you do, Lester answered silently. "Okay, I'm on my way," he said aloud, heading for the ladder which had been unfolded from the fuselage.

He climbed up to the open flight deck airlock hatch, feeling the familiar chafing of the hardsuit's rotary joints against his skin. Inside the tug, he found the mid-deck ladder and climbed down into the cargo hold. Portable lamps had been hung from handholds along the ceiling and bulkheads, casting a shadowy glare over the compartment. The torn nylon remnants of the payload cradle hung from the ceiling like Spanish moss on the trees in the Georgia bayou; the cradle itself had been ripped away by the sudden decompression of the cargo deck.

Lester stopped to look at an open service panel; blackened

power cables showed where the electrical fire had erupted, apparently from an uncontained short circuit. A rescue worker with a 35mm camera was kneeling in front of the panel, taking pictures of the ruined busbars. When he stood up, Lester noticed how tall the moondog was; he glanced at the ID tag clipped to the front of his suit's overgarment. The badge read "Samuels, A.T.," but when the moondog turned around, Lester recognized Tycho's face through the unpolarized faceplate of his helmet.

"Umm . . . How's it going there, Tycho?" Lester asked, feeling a little uncomfortable. It was only a couple of hours earlier that he and the huge moondog had nearly come to blows in the mess hall.

Tycho gazed impassively back at him. *Not bad,* he rumbled into Lester's headset. *How's it going yourself?*

Lester shrugged, although the gesture was meaningless inside the hardsuit's carapace. "I'd rather be somewhere else, to tell the truth," he answered. "Hey, if any of those pictures turn out right, let me know. We'll make 'em into postcards or something."

Tycho smiled a little. *Yeah, proper,* he said and turned back to his work. Score another small victory, Lester thought. Maybe I'll get somewhere with these guys yet. . . .

Mr. Riddell . . .

"Yeah, hold on. I'm coming." The general manager turned toward another hardsuited figure in the cargo deck. "Tina, I thought I told you to call me Lester. I don't know how they do things at the Cape, but up here everyone works on first name basis."

We'll discuss protocol later, if you don't mind. McGraw was standing next to the shredded remains of the cradle. *Notice that the cradle's missing.*

Lester sighed. "Gee, Tina, the cradle's missing. If you hadn't pointed that out to me, I might have never noticed."

Her helmet turned toward him; he could see her thin-lipped face through the faceplate. *Look at the way the nylon's been stretched near the ceiling hooks,* she said. *Something was in the cradle when it was jettisoned.*

"Uh-huh. Like your hijacked Spam-can. Sure, Tina . . ."

She scowled at him. *I see that you're still unconvinced,* she said tightly. *Then tell me why the pilot opted for a dangerous maneuver like a sudden decompression. I don't see why he didn't use his fire extinguisher instead.*

Lester looked around at the empty fire-extinguisher bracket. "Looks to me like he did," Lester said. "It probably went out the hatch along with everything that was in here.

McGraw looked unconvinced, but before she could repond Lester went on. "Do you know anything about electrical fires? Let me tell you, they're a bitch to contain, especially when you've got one in a pressurized cabin. They spread fast, and if you don't knock 'em out in a hurry they can get worse. This one"—he pointed toward the service panel Tycho was photographing— "was not far from the inboard reserve tank. If it had hit the tank, this tug wouldn't be here now and we'd be combing through the wreckage somewhere out in the boonies, trying to find what was left of the crew."

She pointed at the empty bracket. *Then why didn't the fire extinguisher work?*

"Oh, it probably did work. But if I had been the pilot, I would have wanted to make sure, too, and nothing puts out an onboard fire like blowing the hatch. Sure, it's not prescribed in the manual, but any pilot working for Skycorp will tell you about blowing the hatch. Oldest trick in the book . . . or not in the book, rather."

Lester shrugged again, surprised at himself for defending the pilot's actions when he himself was ready to kick the guy's butt. Maybe it was a reaction to McGraw's warm and ingratiating personality. "It's dangerous as hell," he added, "but at least you can be certain you've knocked out your fire."

Then the stretched nylon . . .

"How the hell should I know?" he said. "Sudden decompression does weird things. Guys the size of Tycho over there have been sucked clean out through holes no larger than their heads. When Young blew the hatch, it must have been like a hurricane in here."

He batted at the dangling fabric with the back of his hand. "You said that Skycorp put a dye-cartridge in their Spam-can, rigged to explode when the thing was opened. Okay, where's the dye?"

Because they faked an emergency! McGraw snapped back at him. The frustration was plain to see on her face. *They managed to make it look as if an electrical fire had occurred, then jettisoned the canister! The blowout sucked the dye out of the compartment! Okay? I just told you how they did it! And then there's the radio beacon we monitored at MainOps. We picked up a signal. You're the GM! Now what are you going to do about it?*

Looking at McGraw's face, Lester saw again what kind of law officer he was dealing with: the overeager cop, the fanatic type usually found in small towns, hanging out in patrol cars late at night near the only stoplight in the village, waiting for someone to fail to use their left turn-signal even if it's three o'clock in the morning and there's not another car in sight. Lester had met the type before; New Hampshire was teeming with them. McGraw was hungry for a bust.

"So what about the beacon?" he replied with what he knew was maddening calmness. "You used 103.5 kilohertz. That's not an uncommon frequency. It could have been cross-feed from just about anything this tug normally uses in its telemetry with TRAFCO. Hell, it could have even been a stray signal from one of our own satellites, or even from an Earth comsat."

Get off it, Riddell, she shot back. *You know what's going on here.*

"No," he replied evenly, "I don't. Want to tell me about it? I mean, you've been so open about everything else so far, so why stop now?"

McGraw stepped closer, as if by reducing the distance between them she could make her voice more clearly heard over the comlink. *I'm going to swat these guys,* she hissed. *Are you going to help me, or are you going to get in the way?*

Holy shit, Tycho muttered, *it's Quick-Draw McGraw.*

Lester suddenly remembered that they were on a common channel; all the moondogs in close range had been able to eavesdrop on their exchange. Scattered chuckles, only barely subdued, came over the comlink. Everyone recognized the reference to the old Hanna-Barbera talking-horse sheriff whose visage—as Lester's childhood memory suddenly reminded him—bore a vague yet uncanny, ludicrous resemblance to the face of his new security chief. *Tycho,* he said to himself, *you've got a rare sense of humor.*

The comment hit home with McGraw; the scowl on her face deepened and she looked ready to throw a punch at Abraham T. Samuels. Lester was barely able to restrain his own instinctive smirk. Better defuse this quick; he pointed to his helmet and held up three fingers, signaling McGraw to switch to another comlink channel for privacy. She complied; when she had switched to Channel Three and there was silence in his helmet again, Lester went on.

"Look, Tina, you better face facts," he said. "You've got nothing on these guys, even if they did pull a number here. This stuff about ripped nylon webbing and an intercepted radio signal doesn't make a foundation for a solid case. Nothing you can take to the bank, at least."

She hesitated, apparently mulling it over. *And what about you?* she asked at last. *What do you think?*

"Me?" Lester paused to assess his own situation. It was not a good one: between a rock and hard place. On one hand, he could take a hard line and side with McGraw; like it or not, even circumstantial evidence could be made to stick if Skycorp and NASA wanted culprits. As GM, he could make the facts stick if he wanted them to stick. But somehow that gnawed at his guts. *Eight years ago,* he considered, *you might have tried to pull the same heist yourself . . . but this time, it's your call.*

"Maybe they did, maybe they didn't," he replied. He slowly let out his breath. "Look, Tina, I don't know if I even give a damn. There's a lot worse things I have to worry about right now. . . ."

NASA wants to know who's behind the hijackings, McGraw demanded. *Circumstantial or not, we've got the evidence to put a stop to this. We can . . .*

"What?" he asked. "Try to nail some guys for petty horse-shit like diverting Spam-cans? I mean it, there's more important matters for us to deal with right now. Neither of us are doing any good for ourselves or for the job we're supposed to be doing if you pursue this any further."

She didn't say anything, but she looked away at the empty fire-extinguisher rack, apparently chewing over his words. "Look," he continued, "I've got to run this base and I'm going to need your help if I'm going to handle these guys. We're not going to win any respect if we both spend our first day here playing tough cops on the block. Like it or not, we've got to win their respect first. We have to get them to . . ."

Okay, okay, McGraw said impatiently. She shut her eyes and shook her head. *What do you suggest? Let it go?*

"Yeah," Lester said. "Let it go. Drop the whole matter. We could do worse. I don't know who's been stealing Skycorp's Spam-cans, but if it was these guys, you can't prove it."

He paused. "And I don't like the way NASA and Skycorp

tried to nail whoever's been doing it. Slipping an explosive de-
vice, even if it's just a dye-bomb, into a Spam-can is the most
lunatic notion I've ever heard of. Somebody down there wasn't
thinking straight.''

It was intended to go off when it was opened on the ground,
she countered. *We assumed that the can would be brought into
the base for . . .*

"Sure," Lester said. "Great idea, but nobody knew that for
certain. Sounds like someone made one assumption too many.
For all we know, that might have been what started the fire in
the first place . . . and, yeah, I think they did have a real fire in
here. In any case, I'd like to find the joker who came up with
this silly-ass idea and punch his clock.''

Then . . .

"We're going to drop it," he said flatly. "*Finis.* Case closed.
I don't want to hear about it anymore.'' Without waiting for a
response, Lester turned and started to climb back up the ladder.
Then another thought, overlooked until now, occurred to him;
he stopped and stepped off the ladder.

"One more thing," he added, addressing McGraw. "I'm the
GM around here, not you. I need your help, but I'm not going
to put up with any more of your secret-police bullshit, and I
don't have to, either. If you don't believe me, re-read the operations manual and your contract. My authority supersedes yours
. . . and I can even fire you if I feel like it. Now, have we got
that straight?''

Tina's eyes narrowed and her mouth pursed into a straight
line. For a moment she said nothing . . . then she nodded, so
stiffly that her spine might have been replaced with an oak board.
Yes, Mr. Riddell, I understand you, she replied tersely.

"Good. And I told you to call me Lester." He paused. "One
more thing. The next time I see you on-duty, you better be
wearing a uniform. I want everyone to know who you are and
what you do here. No more Gestapo stuff out of you. You're
going to play a straight game with my people from here on out.
Got that?''

Her mouth twitched, but she nodded again. Without another
word, Lester turned back toward the ladder. As he grabbed the
rungs, he noticed Tycho motioning to him. He remembered that
he was still on restricted frequency and switched over again to
the common band. "Yeah, Tycho?" he asked.

How much longer you want us to keep up with this? the moondog asked. He held up his camera. *I mean, I got a whole disk of film here. Is that enough for you and . . . uh, Quick-Draw?*

Through the corner of his helmet, the GM saw McGraw quickly turn away. She must have switched over in time to catch Tycho's remark. Lester knew that in a place like this nicknames once conferred tended to stick, and Tycho had just pegged her with a great one. Good, he decided. Maybe getting an embarrassing moniker might help to keep her in line.

"That's okay," he replied, trying to keep a straight face. "Just relieve the team and call in the cranes to get this tub broken down. For the time being, I'm putting you in charge of the salvage operation. Okay?"

Tycho grinned back at him. *You got it, man,* he said. He moved away from the service panel; as he did, Riddell noticed something in the spot where he'd been standing.

Lester peered closer. In the oval of light cast by his helmet lamp, he saw an irregular streak of bright blue dye, like a blotch of Day-Glo paint that had dribbled off the edge of a Ciccotelli canvas. But it was a safe bet that the great abstract artist had never been near this spacecraft.

He glanced in McGraw's direction, but the security chief hadn't noticed his interest. Tycho, though, was watching him. After a moment, the moondog stepped over and stood on top of the spot again. The general manager looked up at him; Tycho's face was absolutely impassive. Lester hesitated, then began to climb up the ladder.

It had taken a lot of smooth-talking and bartering of favors—including three hours of Moon-to-Earth phone-time to two guys and a week's worth of mess-hall desserts to another—before Mighty Joe had finally managed to get thirty minutes of hot-water ration allocated to him from several moondogs, enough for the pilot to take a long shower. It was no mean feat; the once-a-week hot showers were a valuable commodity to the crew, who normally had to make do with cold-water sponge baths. But it was worth every fruit salad and bowl of Jell-O he sacrificed if it helped to keep him out of shit creek.

But even after fifteen minutes of scrubbing under scalding water, the bright blue splotches left from the dye-bomb had yet to completely disappear except from his beard. Though he had scoured his face, forearms, and hands to the bone, each time he looked in the hand mirror propped up under the showerhead, he could still see faint traces of blue on his skin, like birthmarks.

He cussed and reached for the soap again. Damn, what did they put in that stuff, anyway? A little old-fashioned turpentine might have done the trick, but there was none to be found on the base. It didn't help his sour mood to know that Annie Noonan was probably doing the same thing over in the women's locker room next door. Their opaque helmets and quick exit from the *Dreamer* had kept the new GM from spotting the marks . . . but he couldn't get out of here until that stuff was gone for good. He quickly soaped his arms and face again, and was idly entertaining the horny notion of seeing if Annie needed help with *her* scrubbing—shouldn't be a total loss, after all, and it wouldn't be the first time a guy had invaded the ladies' showers—when he heard a voice behind him.

" 'Out, damned spot . . .' "

"Huh?" Mighty Joe glanced over his shoulder. The new general manager was standing at the entrance to the shower room, leaning against the tiled wall.

Oh, fucking *shit*—! Joe quickly turned his back to Riddell, ducking his head beneath the hot rush of water. "Uh . . . Hi, Mr. Riddell. What's that you said?"

"Hm?" he replied. "Oh, that. Just a line from Shakespeare. *Macbeth*, if I remember correctly." There was a pause, and then Mighty Joe could hear the whisper of cloth moving across skin. "Hey, that shower looks good. Mind if I join you?"

Joe's mouth dropped open. Hell, yeah, he minded! But before he could think of an excuse—if a decent excuse even existed for refusing to let the station general manager into the shower— Riddell had dropped his clothes on the bench next to the showers and had sauntered into the long stall.

"Nothing like a shower to finish the day, right?" Lester went to the showerhead next to Mighty Joe, shoved his keycard into the slot, and pushed the buttons on the waterproof pad to give him five minutes of cold water. He pulled the sponge and soap out of the bin beneath the showerhead. "Ahhh . . ." he said as the frigid water hit his face and shoulders. "That's the way I like a shower. Nice and icy, right?"

"I guess. If you say so." Carefully keeping his back turned to Riddell, Joe peeked over his shoulder at the new boss. The GM's eyes were closed as he ducked his head under the water. *Maybe I can ease out of here without him noticing. . . .*

"So where did you dump the Spam-can?" Riddell asked as casually as if he had asked about Mighty Joe's home town. "It must have been as soon as you crossed the terminator again." He pulled his head out from under the cascade. "You were running out of time, so my guess is that you blew the cargo bay hatch as soon as you crossed the D'Alembert Mountains. Or maybe you made it as far as Lenz Crater."

"I don't know what you're talking about," Joe said. Suddenly the hot water seemed to have turned as cold as a tray of ice cubes.

"Sure you do." Riddell shrugged nonchalantly. He could have been talking about a baseball game from last week. He started to soap his chest and armpits. "Well, it doesn't matter where it went down. We can always find the wreckage."

"It's Greek to me, Mr. Riddell."

"Naah, don't bullshit me. 'Course you do. And call me Lester." He cast a knowing grin at Mighty Joe. "Must have been a helluva kick when you blew the hatch, though. My bet is that you got lucky with the electrical fire. See, I know about the dye-bomb in that thing. Somehow it caused the main buses to short out and it gave you a good excuse for blowing out the hatch and ditching the tug the way you did. By the way, thanks for missing the base and landing out there. That was good flying, pal. I mean it. My compliments."

Mighty Joe felt his face getting hot. "Sure thing, Lester," he muttered. *Screw the shower. Let's get out of here.* " 'Scuse me . . ."

He reached out to turn off the water—and Riddell's hand shot out to grab his wrist. Before Mighty Joe could resist, Riddell had turned it over, exposing his blue-dyed forearm. He then looked up into Mighty Joe's face and studied it closely. "Wooeee!" he exclaimed. "That dye-bomb did a hell of a job. If you work a little harder, you might be able to get the rest off before Quick-Draw McGraw finds you."

Mighty Joe felt awe seeping through into his anger. This guy wasn't hustling him; from hard facts or guesswork, he *knew* what had happened aboard the *Dreamer*. In any case, there was no point in dicking around now. Riddell had him cold. "Who the fuck is Quick-Draw McGraw?" he asked sullenly, jerking his arm out of Lester's grasp.

"That's our new security chief," Riddell replied. "NASA enforcement division. She came in on the *Collins*, same as I did.

Take my word for it, she's a real pain in the ass. She'd just love to start her new job by busting you and your crew.''

"Uh-huh. I see." The shower timer *pinged* and the water stopped running, but Joe barely paid attention, ignoring his towel and the cool breeze from the air vent on his wet skin. "So why aren't you helping her?''

Riddell frowned. He rocked his head back and forth on his neck as he quickly moved the soap and sponge around his chest and armpits. "You got this thing started before I even signed onto this job, so I consider this is as one more burden I inherited from Bo Fisk, regardless of whether he condoned it or not. And maybe I can even see the reason why you did it, if it's for the reasons I suspect.'' He paused to step under the water again. "What have you been getting out of those cans, anyway?''

Mighty Joe couldn't help smiling. "Some stuff. Not a whole bunch.'' He hesitated before deciding to offer the supreme sacrifice. "Got a fifth of Jack Daniel's in my locker if you want it,'' he added quietly. "It's all yours.''

"I don't want to hear about it,'' Riddell snapped. For a few moments he rinsed the soap from his body. Mighty Joe wondered how he could take the cold water without complaining. Most new guys raised hell the first time they took an ice-cold shower in here. Then again, he reminded himself, Riddell isn't entirely new to the Moon, is he? He probably remembers when moondogs got to take cold-water sponge baths only once a week.

"Here's the bottom line,'' Lester went on. "It stops here, right now. I won't let anything I know slip to Quick-Draw if I can be sure that's the last Spam-can that gets diverted. I don't know all the details, I don't know who else was involved, and I honestly don't care. But I do know enough to get you and the others canned. Maybe sent home with federal marshals waiting for you when your shuttle lands at the Cape. Am I making myself clear so far?''

"Real clear,'' Mighty Joe mumbled.

"Good. So you can bet your furry ass I'm going to be watching it.'' Riddell *whoofed* as the chill water hit his chest. "Damn, that's cold . . . and before you ask why I'm doing this, it's only because we're short-handed and I need anyone I can get to keep this place running. Even a fuck-up like you.''

"Yeah,'' Joe growled. "Thanks a heap.''

Lester darted a look at him the moment his own timer pinged. He pulled the keycard out, then reached over, and slipped it into

Mighty Joe's shower. "Here, have ten more minutes on me," he said as he reentered the hot water program. "Might as well make sure McGraw doesn't spot any ink when she sees you next time."

Steaming water gushed out of the shower again. Amazed, Mighty Joe stared at Lester as the new GM walked, dripping wet and hugging his shoulders, out of the shower stall. "Mind if I borrow your towel?" he asked. Joe nodded his head. "Thanks. See you around, flyboy."

He then walked out into the deserted locker room, picking up his clothes as he headed for his own locker in the back of the room. Joe sagged face-first against the wall and slowly let out his breath. Christ almighty, that had been a close one!

He was still leaning against the wall when he heard the door to the women's locker room open. He didn't pay much attention, though, until he heard the sound of bare feet smacking onto the tiled floor behind him. He started to turn around when a pair of unmistakably feminine hands were laid on the back of his shoulders.

"Hey, big guy," Annie Noonan said quietly. "Care to scrub a lady's back for her?"

Joe looked around just in time to see the bath towel she had wrapped around her body drop to the wet floor. "Uhh . . . yeah, I might be able to," he murmured, letting his eyes travel down the length of her nude body. God, she looked better in the raw than he had ever fantasized.

She had managed to get the dye off herself, but he barely noticed. "I was just thinking about you," he said, unable to take his eyes away from her body. "This is kind of a new attitude, isn't it?"

Noonan smiled as she draped her arms around his neck and pulled herself under the hot water. "Kinda," she said, grinning up at him. "I still think you're adolescent and sexist, but I made you a promise, didn't I?"

She curled her fingers through the hair on the back of his head as her face went serious. "We could have been killed up there, you know," she murmured, her mouth growing into a pout. "It was that bad, wasn't it?"

"Yeah," he admitted as he let his hands circle her slender waist. Her small, elegant breasts pressed against his chest as he drew her to him. "It was a close one all right. I'm sorry about that, kiddo. Didn't mean to scare you like . . ."

"Aw, shaddup, you big galoot," Annie whispered as her lips found his. Her kiss was long and exquisitely passionate. "Just think of it as sort of a hero's reward," she added when she broke the kiss. "You know what they say about heroes, don't you?"

"Uh-uh." He moved his hands down to her ass, grabbed hold of her buttocks and picked her up. Her long legs straddled his hips, allowing him to hold her above the floor as she guided him toward the warmest place of all. "No, I don't know. What about 'em?"

"Heroes are hard to find," she said in his ear.

PART THREE

After Midnight

Postmarked the Moon
(Montage.2)

Dear Becky:

Glad to hear that the paycheck got there in time to cover the electric bill. Don't let it slide so long next time, O.K? Did they cut off the juice, or did you manage to work something out first?

Anyway, the good news is that we've just about met the six-week production quota I told you about, so that means the next check should be a little larger, since we're getting our bonuses. At least that's what the new general manager told us last month. We still haven't heard for sure, though, if Skycorp will still keep their end of the deal—no, I still don't trust them—so don't go on any shopping sprees till I tell you. . . .

It's morning at midnight: 0800 GMT on Tuesday, July 13, 2024, at Descartes Station. The first shift of the day is about to begin, in the middle of the two-week lunar night.

The first bars of the national anthem, recorded on an aging cassette which has been wrung through the heads too many times already, rasps through the ceiling speakers in the dorms, a tired *dah-duh-duh-duh-duuuh* and *dum-de-dum-dum-dum-duuuh*, which stirs Lester Riddell from his sleep. He lies in his bunk for a long time—legs curled up against his chest, hands clutching the baggy pillow against his neck, feeling the coarse warmth of the brown wool-polyester blanket wrapped around his stiff body, his bare feet sticking out from under the sheet, cold and numbed. As his eyes focus at random on the luminescent, ever-changing readout of the niche's computer terminal—rows of cryptic symbols, graphs, and code numbers flashing on and off, apparently telling him that everything is static, unchanging, A-OK on the base—the tape goes *dee-dee-dah-dee-dah-SQUONNNK!* and there's a half-instant of high-pitched feedback until Moondog

143

McCloud's smoky voice mutters, *Naaawright, that's enough of that stuff, let's try a little music instead.* . . .

Oh, please . . . Lester scrunches his eyes tightly shut, dreading whatever is to come from McCloud's eclectic tastes this morning. God help them, he might have decided to subject everyone to an old Residents or Plasmatics cut—last Thursday morning it was Sid Vicious' version of "My Way"—but instead the mellow tremor of Miles Davis' trumpet cuts through the fog. Lester takes a deep breath, slowly lets it out, and watches as the ceiling lights gradually sharpen in intensity like a false dawn. He hears around him from other cubicles the sullen squeak of bedsprings releasing their weight, the hollow thump of feet landing on floorboards. Time to get going. He rolls over and places his feet on the cold floor. . . .

. . . Did I tell you that we've got a former fashion model working here? No kidding! The girl who was on the Sports Illustrated *cover you had taped over your desk at UMC, the one in the purple bikini under the waterfall—"Maui Zowie." Yeah, that Susan Peterson!!! I'm not lying: she's a scientist up here! Didn't you read that interview with her in* Playboy? *I don't know how old she is now, but I swear she's got a great ass! Hey, and don't believe me if you don't want to, but I think she likes me. Watch it, pal. You'll get hair in your palms if you start thinking like that, nyuk nyuk nyuk.* . . .

Butch Peterson snaps her ankle-weights into place, then stands up from the bunk and steps up to the chinning bar mounted just above the door of her niche. Wearing only the panties and tank-top she slept in, she reaches up, grabs the bar, and begins to do twenty quick ones, her morning regimen. One . . . two . . . three . . . four . . .

Perspiration soon beads her forehead and chest, running in rivulets down the front and back of her top. Eight . . . nine . . . ten . . . eleven . . . Her mind is already at work, going over the results of the polar geological survey she has just completed. She's going to have to talk to Les about letting her go up to Byrd Crater for an inspection of the permaice extraction facility. It's not a prospect that particularly excites her, except maybe for the fact that it gives her an excuse to get away from the base for a day or two.

Fourteen . . . fifteen . . . sixteen . . . She grits her teeth with the exertion. Face it, kiddo, you're going stir-crazy here. Even if it's just going up to the north pole again, it might be worth the trip just to give yourself a change of scenery. Eighteen, nineteen . . .

. . . Skycorp must have been desperate to send up the replacement workers we've received last month. Specially trained personnel? Who do they think they're kidding? These are guys out of die-tool factories, pool halls and chop-shops; I can't imagine how they were recruited for a job like this. Every shift there is a mishap of one sort or another, whether it be loss-of-oxygen accidents, sprained ankles and wrists, machinery broken because of lack of proper instruction—it's really pathetic, like a bad TV sitcom sometimes. I know we needed the money to send the kids to college, but I'm sincerely beginning to wonder if this was a serious mistake.

Don't worry—I'm looking out for myself. That's my Number One priority. I refuse to let myself be harmed because some tobacco-chewing yahoo from East Podunk was screwing around on the clock. Just keep the money in the bank where it belongs, darling, and don't quit your job at the shoe store. The kids are old enough to take care of themselves while you're at work. I'll be home in only five months, and we'll put this ordeal behind us.

I really miss you, too, Doug. . . .

In the infirmary, Monk Walker is already laying out bandages, antiseptic, sutures, and low-level painkillers in preparation for the long day ahead. Through the door leading to the locker room, he can hear moondogs from the third shift returning from work—lockers opening, men talking and cussing. He hums along in time with the Miles Davis cut on the radio, thankful for a little bit of good music before the daily barrage of rock and roll begins.

The prayer beads around his left wrist click softly as he begins to change the sheets on the cot, and he briefly remembers the silence of the Tibetan Himalayas in the morning: the way the low morning clouds curled around the columns of the great monastery at Lhasa, the melodic sound of drums and chimes being beaten by the Gyuto monks—all very long ago and far away. He thinks of the smiling face of his teacher and former patient, the Dalai Lama, the mornings they spent together, sipping tea and discussing the ways of the world, and finds himself longing for those simpler times . . . and reaches for the dosimeter logbook, in which he keeps a written record of each moondog's radiation exposure.

Keep your mind on the present, he reminds himself. This isn't Lhasa. . . .

. . . I swear to God, Chuckie, this job is beginning to suck something big-time. Remember how you told me this would be easy, workin on the moon? "Anythings got to be better than stayin on the assembly line?" (you sez that—I remember!) Ha-ha-ha and fuck you too, and I mean it. If its so fuckin easy, why ain't you up here, you low piece of shit? (Just kiddin—honest!) Anyway, we're workin a hundred times harder now that this new GM is here, and even tho the sun went down last week (the nights are two weeks long here, remember?) we're still pullin three eight-hour shifts a day, and I'm workin like a cocksucker now, but you think fuckin Skycorp is goin to give us back our bonus pay? Not a fuckin chance!

Dont try sendin me any more doobies in the mail again, cuz fuckin NASA and the company clamped down on all the illicit contraband thats been sent up here. And stay away from my sister, you asshole, cuz if I find out you've been banging her while I'm up here, I rip your head off and shit down your neck. . . .

Mighty Joe gently unlocks Annie Noonan's arms from around his neck and pushes her aside in the narrow bunk. The sleeping woman whispers something unintelligible as she rolls over, pulling the covers around her nude body. Joe looks down at her and fondly pats her rump, then stands up and stretches his back. *Good God,* he thinks as he hears it crack, *many more nights like this and the woman's going to throw my spine out of place.*

He grins saucily. *And you're not going to hear me complaining, either. Sure is weird, having a steady girlfriend again.* He knuckles sleep out of his eyes. So long as she doesn't get serious on him or anything, he doesn't mind.

"Aw, well," he says softly. "Time for that glorious first piss of the day." Scratching his ass, he reaches for the door and pulls it open—just in time to catch one of the other women who share the females-only dorm on her way back from the head. She shrieks at the sight of his naked body and dashes down the corridor as Mighty Joe slams the door shut.

Christ! He had forgotten he had been sleeping in Annie's niche again. . . .

. . . You know how much Dad meant to me. I loved him as much as you or anyone else in the family, and if I could have been there for the funeral, you know I would have made it. That's the truth. But Skycorp's contract prohibits me from coming back for any other reason than serious injury, mental unfitness, or being fired or laid off. Dad knew that when I signed on, and he told me to go ahead, even though he knew he didn't have that long to live. I'm sorry, sis. That's the way it is. I've said kaddish for him. Please lay flowers on his grave for me until I get back. . . .

Willard DeWitt, sitting behind his desk in his niche, shuffles through a stack of printout next to his Toshiba laptop, scanning information he has already collected and collated over the past couple of weeks. He absently curls his lower lip between his thumb and index fingers. Ah, yes. Most interesting indeed.

DeWitt has been up all night, working through the graveyard shift on his secret plans; he's ready to turn in and catch a few hours of sleep before reporting in at MainOps for duty on the second shift. But his mind continues to work, spinning along the endless permutations of his scheme. He'll stay awake for a little while longer. He turns back to his keyboard and scrolls to the end of the file to enter some new data. At the top of the screen is printed the filename for his latest entrepreneurial endeavor: MOONTUNES. . . .

. . . And to really put the cherry on the sundae, there's a new security chief up here. Her name is McGraw—nicknamed Quick-Draw, get it?—and she seems to regard herself as The Law up here, meaning that she's a pain in the ass. We weren't even sure whether she was a man or a woman when she first showed up . . . there's something weirdly androgynous about the way she walks, talks, etc., like a bull dyke who was once a national champion on the mud-wrestling circuit.

The funniest part is her uniform: a dark-blue NASA Space Enforcement Division outfit with a straight black clip-on tie (a tie! Can you believe it?) with every zipper and snap spit-polished and perfectly in place, badge pinned just above the left breast pocket (though she really doesn't have any breasts to speak of), ankle-weights at precise height on her boots, cap set on her head with the bill exactly straight ahead, never tipped back or pulled forward. And her belt! She's always got a riot-stick, Taser, Mace and tear-gas dispensers, first-aid kit, two (count 'em, two) sets of handcuffs, beltphone, flashlight, utility knife, emergency oxygen mask, dosimeter, lock-remover, universal keycard, and God knows what else stashed in the pouches (we're betting a suicide pill, in case we get invaded by aliens). She clanks when she walks down the corridor—like Clint Eastwood, Batman, and your cousin Darienne all rolled into one. Weirder than shit, man.

But McGraw's all right in some ways. One of the gays—yeah, we got a few up here, but they're all right—told me that she caught him and his friend going at it in the storeroom. He was giving head to his boyfriend when she walked in, and all she did was give 'em a lecture about safe sex and hand Mike a condom (from the pouch on her belt, of course). "I'm glad she didn't make a scene about it," he told me, "but do you know how nasty those things taste?"

Tycho Samuels, encased in his hardsuit, stands in the Number Two airlock and waits patiently until the cell decompresses. The status-light over the hatch switches from amber to green; after a quick glance at the digital pressure gauge to make certain that the airlock is in hard vacuum, he grasps the lockbar between his gauntleted fists, yanks it down, and shoves the hatch open.

Beyond the hatch, caught in the shadowless glare of the scaffold-mounted floodlights, is the Moon. Within the privacy of his helmet, Tycho's face breaks into a seldom-seen smile. This is the part of the job he loves the most: stepping *out there* for the first time each day. The strange, pitted landscape below his feet, Earth hovering high above his head . . .

This is what he came here to find. Its harsh beauty is indescribable; he has tried to put it in words, in his letters to his father back in Nashville, but writing is a skill he has never mastered. But it's a world away from the Jefferson Street projects where he was born and raised; even if he goes back there, he intuitively knows that he will never be the same again.

Tycho steps out onto the Moon, heading for the rover which will take him out to his job at the mass-driver plant . . . then, impulsively, he bends his knees, swings back his arms, and leaps into the starlighted sky, just the way he used to jump-shoot on the basketball court in his old neighborhood. Straining against his bulky suit, he stretches out a hand and, for just a brief second, touches the blue-green face of the Earth.

Yeah! Dunk-shot! Tycho scores another two points! And the crowd goes wild. . . .

. . . You should see what Earth looks like from up here. You wouldn't believe it. I'll send pictures.

Love, as always . . .

11. Wang Dang Doodle

First-shift began much like any other: in the EVA ready-room, the last few moondogs squirmed and grunted into their sour-smelling hardsuits, waited for the suit techs to check them over, slam shut their back hatches, and wave them along into the line in front of the airlocks. Outside the base, they climbed onto the beds of rovers—shoving against each other for room, swearing at the long-suffering driver, guts roiling from yet another taste-less powdered-eggs-reconstituted-hashbrowns-and-freeze-dried-sausage breakfast hastily shoveled down in the mess deck. Finally the rovers started up and began crawling out to the rego-lith fields a quarter of a mile away.

The habitat slowly receded in the distance; narrow slits of light from the windows cast long shadows from the nearby fuel tanks and the antenna grove. Floodlights on the landing pads reflected dully off the hulls of spacecraft being worked on by the pad rats. The rovers paused next to the long aluminum rails of the mass-driver, stretching toward the western horizon, to let off a few workers; out behind the rim of Spook Crater to the south, they could see the faint glow of the searchlights on the twin SP-100 nuclear reactors at the bottom of the crater. It was nothing they hadn't seen before; they bumped along in the back of the rover, gripping the bed rail for support, and mentally counted the days until they could get the hell off the Moon.

Over their suit radios, if they switched to Channel Four and pinned the cross-talk switch on Channel Two so that they could still hear one another, LDSM played the blues. Willie Dixon's ferocious growl came through their headsets:

"Tell Automatic Slim,
To tell Razor totin' Jim,

To tell Butcher knife totin' Annie,
To tell Fast-talkin' Fannie. . . . "

Out in the regolith fields, the lights of vehicles slowly roamed across a terrain that vaguely resembled furrowed New England pasture land covered by the first heavy snow of winter. Rovers shuttled men back and forth, bulldozers shoved rocks and boulders aside, immense caterpillar-treaded combines scooped up the tough regolith and deposited the powdery fines into the bins of tractors—to be taken back to the Dirt Factory at the base for processing for oxygen, aluminum, and silicon—leaving behind straight low hedgerows of coarser till-soil.

"That we're gonna pitch a ball,
Down to the union hall,
We're gonna rump and trump till midnight,
And fuss and fight till daylight,
We're gonna pitcha wang-dang-doodle all night long,
All night long . . . "

Beneath the untwinkling starlight, hidden from the Sun, men and machines labored against the ancient topsoil deposited by millennia of meteorite impact and tectonic movement, gradually stretching the expanse of worked-over ground further north, strip-mining the rich highlands foot by foot. Dust thrown up by the mining operations lingered above the ground; it gave the fields a perpetual gauzelike haze which coated their white suits with a gray film, making it necessary for everyone to stop now and then to rub the tips of their gloves across their faceplates to clear their vision.

"Tonight we need no rest,
We're gonna really throw a mess,
We're gonna break out all the windows,
And kick down all the doors,
We're gonna pitcha wang-dang-doodle all night long,
All night long . . .
All night long . . . "

"Christ, I love this job." Mighty Joe tamped the last knotty bud of his private stash of California sinsemilla into the battered mini-waterpipe he had carried with him since his Navy days and fumbled in a hipside cargo pocket for a lighter. "Y'know that, Seki? I fuckin' love this job."

"Yeah, uh-huh. I love this job too." Seki Koyama reached up to the little Sony radio suspended by its strap over his driver's seat and turned down the volume a tad. Through the narrow windows of the combine's pressurized compartment, he could see a 'dozer struggling to move a boulder out of his way. He downshifted to first gear and touched the lobe of his headset. "C'mon, Jenny, get that thing outta there already," he muttered. A pause, then he added, "Any time and any place, but move the rock first, okay?"

"Don't worry about it." Mighty Joe held the pipe steady against the sudden forward lurch of the massive vehicle. A tiny speck of marijuana was knocked loose from the pipe's lip and slowly fell toward the floor between his knees; he reached down and caught it before it landed. "No, I mean it. I love having to sneak out in a suit just to smoke a little weed. I love having Quick-Draw kick down my niche door to look for drugs when I'm trying to sleep . . . and I'm telling you, I really enjoy the presence of your company."

"Just light the thing, willya? Damn, what takes her so long?" Koyama shifted to neutral, almost causing Joe's helmet to topple from its perch on the sill above the dashboard. "Might as well," he said, shoving the helmet back in place before it fell. "Gives us a little time to enjoy the last of your stash." The Japanese-American combine operator inched back his bucket seat a little and loosened the harness. "That *is* the last of it, right?"

"Sad to say, it most certainly is. Treasure it." Mighty Joe nicked on the butane lighter, held it over the pipe's bowl and gently baked the nub as he sucked on the stem. He took a big hit of the acrid smoke—the pot was more than three months old, hardly fresh at all—and held it in his lungs as he capped the bowl with his thumb and passed it to Seki. He half-closed his eyes and waited till his chest felt like it was ready to explode, then slowly exhaled, letting out a pale stream of smoke, which swirled around the tiny cabin and was promptly sucked through the vent above their heads.

Pretty soon we're going to be scraping the residue from this thing's air-filter and trying to smoke that, Joe thought. *Goddamn Skycorp. Goddamn NASA.* It had been six weeks since he had crashed the *Dreamer*. Although he and his crew still had their jobs, it had definitely been the end of the party for their smuggling operation. Even if he wanted to attempt getting more dope up here, he couldn't pull it off. Their Cape Canaveral connection had fallen to the feds, and even though Fast Eddie had managed to get away from the NASA investigators, he was unwilling to risk his neck again for a good long time, if ever. The Skycorp inspectors had discovered the pot crop being cultivated in the greenhouse during the purge, and Quick-Draw had been making regular searches of the hydroponics tanks to make certain the new farmers hadn't gotten any frisky ideas. Unless someone else had their own stash hidden somewhere, this was the last marijuana to be found on the Moon.

"Oh, yeah!" Seki exclaimed. The Willie Dixon tune had made a clean segue into the bump-and-grind of the Doors' "Roadhouse Blues" and Seki reached to turn up the volume. "My theme song," he said, exhaling through his nose and passing the pipe back to Mighty Joe. " 'Keep your eyes on the road and your hands upon the *wheee-ahl,'* wah-*wahh*!" he sang off-key, slapping his bare hands on the thighs of his suit.

"Like the Doors, huh?" Mighty Joe said as he took a last hit and clamped his thumb and forefinger over the bowl and stem to extinguish the pipe. Seki only needed a hit to get him high, and Joe's pot was precious enough to have him stretch the load. "McCloud's got something about the oldies. Sometimes I wish he would play some more new stuff."

"Fuck all the new stuff. I'm telling you, rock died in '11 when the Beat Snails broke up. But Jim Morrison . . . man, that's my favorite person in history." Seki rocked his head back and forth with his eyes closed as his palms kept time with the music. "Y'know, they said that he didn't really die back then? Did you ever hear that story?"

"Yeah, I heard that." Joe found the film capsule where he had tucked it in the crotch of his suit and began to tap the dregs of the pipe into it. "Naw, he didn't die," he went on. "At least not when everyone said he did. He ran a seafood joint down in Florida till he died. . . ."

He stopped to search his memory. "Three or four years ago, I think. Yeah. Just before I signed on with Skycorp."

"Aw, come off it. . . ."

Mighty Joe shook his head. "No, I'm not kidding. Jim Morrison was this crazy old dink who ran a beachside seafood shack on Captiva Island, where I used to live. A hangout for the locals, right? He had this recipe for Cajun-style steamed shrimp that would make your eyes water. . . .''

Koyama laughed. ''Can't be the same Jim Morrison. . . .''

''Sure was. Sometimes on Saturday nights he'd get plowed and bring out this beat-up old Les Paul guitar he kept in the storeroom, sit down at one of the picnic tables outside and start banging out Doors numbers for us. 'L.A. Woman,' 'People Are Strange,' 'Horse Latitudes,' '20th Century Fox' . . . maybe you'd think he was putting you on at first, but when you heard that voice you *knew* it was him.''

''You're a liar.''

''Seriously. Then he would tell us again how he had faked the whole death scene in Paris 'cause he was sick of doing concerts and the press and shit. All that Lizard King crap, the cops always on him 'cause he had flashed his dick once during a show . . . he'd had enough, that's all.'' Joe unsnapped a pocket on his suit and thrust the pipe and his minuscule stash back into it. ''We kept trying to talk him into jamming with one of the local bands, just so's we'd get to hear 'The End' done properly, but he wouldn't have none of it. Nice old fart, even if he did steal my girlfriend.''

Seki cracked up. ''Ah, *c'mon!* He would have been in his nineties.''

''Shit, that didn't stop him. I'm telling you, Old Jim was the sex dynamo of the Gulf Coast. He was bedding ladies young enough to be his granddaughter and they'd always come back the next day saying that he was the greatest lay of their lives. My girlfriend told me he'd . . .''

''Shh!'' Seki suddenly signaled Joe to quiet down as he cupped his right hand over his headset. He listened for a second, then solemnly looked askance at Mighty Joe. ''Umm, roger, we copy that, MainOps, he's right here with me . . . brought out some coffee just a few minutes ago.''

Another pause. ''Okay, I'll put him on right now.'' He nodded his head toward Mighty Joe. ''Lester wants to talk to you on Three.''

''Goddammit,'' Joe muttered irritably. ''Why did you tell him I was here?'' But he pulled his headset up from around his neck and carefully laid the bone-phone against his jaw. ''MainOps, this is Young.''

Joe, this is Lester, he heard the general manager say. *What are you doing out there in the fields?*

"I brought some coffee out to Seki, that's all." Mighty Joe grinned at Seki. "Just making a little wake-up call, sir. Gets kinda lonely for him out here."

Seki had to cover his mouth with his hand to keep from guffawing over the comlink. *You're supposed to be helping the pad crew with the repair of your tug,* Lester said sternly. *If Seki needs a coffee break, he can wait until his shift is over. Your place is back here at the base.*

Joe rolled his eyes but refrained from making any smart-aleck remarks. Lester was sounding pissed-off this morning. "Ah, yeah, we copy that, Lester. I'm coming right over to Subcomp Bravo this minute."

Negatory on that, Joe. That's why I was looking for you in the first place. I've got a little LRLT flying job for you. I want you in MainOps in fifteen minutes . . . and no more coffee breaks on the way, you got that? The combines aren't a doughnut shop for you. Over.

Mighty Joe clenched his left fist and yanked it up and down over his lap; Seki smirked and nodded his agreement. "Roger that, MainOps," Joe replied. "Over and out." He tapped the headset lobe with his finger and added, "You jerkmeat corporate tool."

"He sounded a little pissed." Koyama reached behind him and popped the airlock hatch as Joe shrugged out of his shoulder harness and reached under the seat for his suit gloves. "Flying job? I thought he had you grounded till the *Dreamer* was fixed."

"Guess that's come to an end," Joe said sullenly as he thrust his left hand into a gauntlet and locked down the wrist joint, but he was secretly pleased. He had gone to half-pay during the *Beautiful Dreamer*'s downtime, but what he had really missed was flying. Rusty and Anne had been taking the other tug, the *Edgar Mitchell*, up to low-orbit for the weekly rendezvous-and-supply junket while he had been stuck in the dirt, which was six weeks too long for his regular aviation fix. Any chance to get off the ground again, even if it was only for an LRLT bus-hop, was fine by him.

"I don't get it, though," he thought aloud as he fitted on his right glove. "We don't have another LTV rendezvous for at least four days, and that's nothing Wright and Noonan can't take care of themselves. A crop-duster flight is something he can get anyone else to handle. What's he want me for?"

"Guess you'll be finding out soon enough." Seki picked up

Mighty Joe's helmet and waited for the pilot to finish the pre-EVA checkout of his suit. "Hey, what's with you and Noonan, anyway? I heard you guys were some kind of hot number lately."

"For me to know and you to mind your own friggin' business about." Joe took the helmet from Seki, held his breath and ducked his head into it, then clamped down the collar-ring. Once the suit was repressurized, he let out his breath and switched on the comlink. "Okay, lemme out of here. I gotta go see what the man wants."

"You're ten minutes late, Joe," Lester said from the command station as the pilot tromped up the stairs into MainOps.

"Fire me, then. I don't give a shit." Joe sauntered down the curving aisle past the work stations, idly glancing through the windows at the distant mass-driver. On a wall-screen was a close-up of the mass-driver station: a cargo canister—shaped like a giant soccer ball with an engine at one end, lying on a launch sled—came off the loading line and began to accelerate down the long, floodlighted track. As it diminished to a tiny spot, it reached the ramp at the end of the track and shot off the launch sled. Mighty Joe looked through the windows again, just in time to see the distant canister bulleting into the black sky, its RCR's already firing to maneuver it along its cislunar glide path to Olympus Station. On the screen, another canister was coming on the rail.

"Joe . . ." Lester repeated.

"Awright," he said, turning away from the window. "I'm coming. Take it easy." Riddell was seated behind the center console on the raised dais; somewhat to Joe's surprise, Butch Peterson sat in the chair next to him, with her long legs crossed and a datapad in her lap, wire-rimmed reading glasses perched on the edge of her elegant nose. Lord, he thought absently, I've always had a thing for women who wear glasses . . . and if Annie could read minds, she'd castrate me for what's in my head right now.

Riddell stared at him over the edge of his console and seemed ready to say something, but instead motioned for Joe to come up the steps. "What's your schedule for Thursday?" he asked.

"Schedule?" Young walked up the steps, leaned against a bulkhead and shoved his hands into his trouser pockets. "Lessee. I've got an urgent meeting with my broker, then there's a producer from Paramount who wants to film my life story. And after that, there's going to be an orgy in the Hilton . . . y'all are invited, of course. Think you can be there, Butch?''

Peterson didn't even look up at him. She pushed back her glasses and glanced at Riddell. ''Did we have to ask this guy?'' she said with quiet disgust.

The GM shook his head. ''Emerson is down with the flu, Quack is on permanent rescue standby, Wright is assigned to the *Mitchell* for an LTV rendezvous, and everyone else is tied up. He's the only LRLT-rated pilot available on short notice.''

Mighty Joe's attention was caught by a geologic survey map of the north polar region which was displayed on two of the GM's screens. Noting the interest in the pilot's eyes, Riddell explained, ''Dr. Peterson has been reviewing the latest findings from our Byrd Crater facility. Butch, if you want to . . . ?''

''Not particularly,'' Peterson said. She sighed and reluctantly turned around in her chair. ''To make it simple, I've been analyzing the recent core samples and satellite pictures from the permaice facility at the north pole. There's substantially less ice showing up in the samples than in previous batches, which gives us some reason to be concerned. Understand?''

''Uh-huh,'' Joe murmured. He did indeed understand, despite Peterson's condescending attitude. Ancient deposits of permaice lay below the topsoil of the lunar north pole, scattered there by a comet which had struck the Moon millions of years earlier; since sunlight never reached much of this permanently shadowed region, a significant quantity of this ice had never melted. Its existence had been confirmed by a Space Studies Institute lunar probe in the 1990's and had been one of the major discoveries that helped push the industrial development of the Moon. It was a natural resource, not just for water, but also for hydrogen: one of the most crucial volatiles used on the Moon, and also one of the most expensive bulk-item imports from Earth.

But the full extent of the lunar permaice had never been fully understood; if this natural well was drying up, nothing would replace it besides praying for another comet to strike the Moon, which was pretty unlikely within the next few thousand years.

''I can guess the rest,'' Joe said. ''You want me to fly Butch up there for a checkup, maybe to make sure the robots aren't drilling in the wrong place or something.''

''Yes and no,'' Lester said. ''I'm going with you, too. I skipped the last chance to go up to Byrd, when Emerson made a pickup a couple of weeks ago. In fact, I haven't been up there since I got here.''

"Right . . .''

"Good.'' The GM turned back to his console. "I want you to get a crop-duster ready for flight by Thursday at oh-eight-hundred. Water tanks and all. Should be just a one-day trip. Any problem with that?''

"Just a little one,'' Mighty Joe said. "We might not have a flightworthy crop-duster.''

Riddell said nothing, but only waited for him to elaborate. Joe rested his butt against the edge of the desk. "To get the *Dreamer* off the ground again, we've had to cannibalize parts from the LRLT's.'' Riddell started to say something, but Joe held up his hand. "Wait a minute before you start yelling at me again. It's not as bad as it sounds. For the most part they're interchangeable parts, modular stuff we can take off one boat and put on the other within a few hours. No big deal. We do it all the time. But in this case, if you want to have a tug *and* a LRLT on the flight line by Thursday, we're going to have to get a little creative, since we'll be missing a backup fuel pump for the crop-duster.''

Lester blinked. "I don't get it,'' he said. "If you're missing a backup fuel pump for the LRLT, why didn't you request one from Skycorp?''

Joe grimaced. "We did . . . seven weeks ago, even before the *Dreamer* crashed. But because it was a standby unit then, our pals in Huntsville put it on the soon-come list.'' Before Lester could ask, Joe added, "That's as in, 'Yeah, it'll soon come.' Like, don't hold your breath.''

Lester closed his eyes and shook his head slowly. "Okay, I get it. So what do you mean by getting a little creative?''

Before the pilot could answer, the phone on Riddell's desk buzzed. Lester held up a finger, signaling Mighty Joe to wait, as he picked up the receiver. "Riddell,'' he said. "Yeah, uh-huh . . . damn . . . okay, Tina, I'll be right down. Don't do anything till I get there unless you have to. . . . ''

He put down the phone and stood up. "Gotta go some-where,'' he said as he quickly moved past them both and hopped down the steps from the dais. "Butch will brief you on the rest. Just get that crop-duster flight-ready by Thursday, okay?'' In a few quick steps he strode down the aisle and disappeared through the stairwell hatch, ignoring the duty personnel's questioning looks at his abrupt departure.

Peterson watched him go, then looked around at Mighty Joe. Joe just shrugged. "Hell if I know," he murmured. "None of my business anyway."

The geologist sighed. "That's the whole problem with this place," she said. "Everyone's only looking after their own business." She looked down at her datapad; then, as a thought seemed to cross her mind, she looked sharply up at Joe again. "That remark you made about finding a creative solution to the fuel pump problem . . . you're not talking about getting one from Honest Yuri, are you?"

Mighty Joe only smiled and looked away, pretending to be gazing out a window. "Oh *God!*" she yelped. "Don't tell me you're going to get one from Honest Yuri!"

"Okay," he said agreeably, patting her knee and turning to walk down the steps from the platform. "I won't tell you I'm getting one from Honest Yuri."

He looked over his shoulder in time to see Butch drawing back her arm to heave her datapad at him. "Now now *now*," he scolded, wagging his finger at her. "You heard what he said. Get a crop-duster flight-ready by Thursday. And it's your trip, after all."

Peterson brought her arm down, dropped the pad on the desk, and sagged in her chair. "No," she whimpered helplessly, covering her face with her hands. "Not spare parts from Honest Yuri . . ."

12. A Little Gratuitous Violence

The rec room was located on Level One of Subcomp A, downstairs from MainOps and at the opposite side of the building from the mess hall. It wasn't a very large room—only about half the size of the men's locker room—nor was it very comfortable. The floor was uncarpeted, the walls were decorated with framed antique *Weekly World News* tabloids (WW2 BOMBER FOUND ON MOON—*Now scientists know how it got there!* and HUMAN SKELETON FOUND ON MOON—*'Absolutely mind-boggling,' say shocked scientists* and MOON LANDING WAS A HOAX!—*NASA made $30 billion movie to fool the world*) and it was furnished mainly with wire-mesh chairs and tables which had been converted from discarded fiberoptic cable spools. The inevitable food-can spittoons for the tobacco-chewers were scattered across the tables, surrounded by greasy brown spots where moondogs had misjudged their aim. The single, slitlike window looked out upon the dusty, micrometeorite-pitted domes of the Dirt Factory.

The rec room had all the ambience and charm of a bus station lavatory, but it was the closest thing the Descartes crew had to a social area. A soda machine dispensed cans of Pepsi and Nehi and tasteless nonalcoholic near-beer; there was a holographic games table, a small shelf of broken-spine paperbacks and ragged magazines with cover dates from last year, an exercise machine in the corner, and a wall-screen TV.

The TV was hooked up to a high-gain antenna on the roof which received signals from the lunar comsats, which in turn intercepted TV signals from a variety of Earth-orbiting satellites in the geosynchronous Clarke Belt. This arrangement had its benefits and drawbacks. On the plus side, it meant that Descartes Station could pick up virtually any commercial TV network on

Earth that used communications satellites. But as the Moon gradually orbited the Earth, the signal from one comsat was lost and was replaced by another. Sometimes it happened quickly, in mid-program; a crowd of moondogs could be watching a Bruins hockey game when, all at once, it was replaced by a turgid British costume-drama or a dumb Israeli cop-show like *Yitshak & Menachim.* This meant, overall, that the available viewing time for turgid or dumb TV fare from the good ol' U.S.A. was limited to a few weeks a month, and was jealously fought over by moondogs who were off-shift.

Every now and then, it led to serious disagreements.

As he strode down the corridor to the rec room, Riddell heard the argument even before he caught sight of Quick-Draw McGraw. The security chief was standing outside the open door; she held her Taser ready in her right hand, and she looked up as the general manager approached. From within the room Lester could hear voices shouting:

"Listen, asshole, you want music, you listen to the fucking radio—!"

"Fuck you, buddy! We were here first, so get the fuck outta—"

"Fuck *you* too! We're here to watch this every fucking . . . hey hey hey, put down that—!"

There was a loud *spang!* as a spit-can was hurled across the room. "Don't mess with me, you spic muthafucker, or I'll—!"

"Who're you calling a spic?" *Crash!* "Huh? You ___ ___'ling me a spic?"

"Yeah, I'm calling you a spic!"

"You watch your mouth, man, or I'll tear off your dick! Now you get the fuck outta here before I—!"

Lester didn't have to ask what was going on. He stopped next to Quick-Draw, careful to put his back to the corridor wall to keep out of the line of fire. "What shows are they trying to watch?" he asked quietly.

Quick-Draw contemplated Lester's question. "I don't see how that matters," she murmured, not looking away from the door. "If they go on like this, they'll . . ."

"Just tell me what they're fighting over," he demanded. He glanced at the Taser in her hand and shook his head. "I want to see if we can arbitrate this thing before you go in shooting."

Quick-Draw let out her breath. "Ummm . . . Jesus and his

friends want to watch *Ouch, That Hurts!* And I think Bee-Pee and his buddies want to see *The Drunk Brothers Rock 'n' Roll Keg Party.*'' She shook her head before he could ask the obvious next question. ''And don't ask me who got there first. I arrived only after they started throwing chairs at each other.''

Lester sighed. No point in trying to settle the dispute on the grounds of artistic merit; both shows appealed to the lowest common denominator of human intelligence. *Ouch, That Hurts!* was allegedly a sitcom, but if there was any situation in the show or any comedy, it escaped Lester's detection. Essentially it involved a roomful of loud, stupid people screaming at each other and beating one another over the heads with frying pans, fire extinguishers, ashtrays, toaster ovens, or whatever else the show's writer had dreamed up for the current episode. It made old Three Stooges flicks look like high Shakespearean drama. *The Drunk Brothers Rock 'n' Roll Keg Party* was a variety show; its hosts were two alcoholic motorheads who sat around in a beer-splattered studio introducing one insipid rock video after another, guzzling quarts of warm beer and cheap fortified wine between videos, and conducting slurred interviews with musical acts like 101 Virgins or Wazted Minds. The most intriguing part of the program was seeing which of the Drunk Brothers would barf first, Guido or Ramrod.

In any case, neither show had sufficient socially redeeming qualities to make Lester feel comfortable about settling the dispute on the basis of aesthetics: both shows were fit only for morons. Another spitton ricocheted off the wall near the door; Quick-Draw ducked as brown saliva sprayed past the doorway.

''Why don't I just zap them all and get it over with?'' she hissed.

Lester was tempted—but he reminded himself that he was still trying to get the respect of the crew. Quick-Draw's Taser would settle the argument quickly, but he didn't want these guys to wake up with horrendous headaches, claiming that the new GM had used storm-trooper tactics on them. Getting tough in a situation like this was a no-win solution; like it or not, it called for diplomacy.

He shook his head. ''Uh-uh,'' he muttered. ''Just cover me . . . and use that thing only if you think I'm about to get clobbered in there.''

McGraw looked apprehensive, but she nodded her head; she

knew who was in charge here. "Your funeral," she whispered, and added, "Good luck."

That took him by surprise. It was the closest she had come to making a gesture of good will toward him. He was about to say something, but noticed that she was watching the room again, the Taser held upward between her hands, ready for fire. Wondering if she was right, Lester took a deep breath and walked into the rec room.

The place had been thoroughly trashed, as if a pack of speed-crazed baboons had been set loose. Tables were overturned, chairs had been thrown around, spittoons seeped their vile contents on the mooncrete floor. The combatants faced off from opposite sides of the big-screen TV (on which Guido was slumped into a chair guzzling a bottle of Irish Wild Rose, mumbling "Stay tuned for more rock 'n' roll!" as his wild-eyed brother pawed at the plastic dress of some hysterically giggling bleached-blond ingenue). On one side were Jesus Cinque and his friends; the thin, pock-faced Latino held a chair in his hands as if preparing to hurl it at the opposite group, led by a Mississippi cracker named B.P. Carruthurs, known as Bee-Pee for short. The shouting died down as the general manager sauntered into the gap between the two groups.

"Hey! Lester!" Jesus said innocently. He self-consciously lowered the chair a little, as if to say *Me? Throw this chair? Aw, c'mon—!* "Listen, Les, this son of a bitch tried to . . ."

"Shaddup," Riddell said calmly.

"Mister Riddell, sir," Bee-Pee drawled, "the real cause of this is because Jesus over here . . ."

"I said *shaddup*," Lester snapped. Not a word from either side. Okay, you've got their attention. Now you've got to do something with it. . . .

He paused to take a breath. "Gentlemen . . . and I use the term reluctantly . . . in the short time I've been here, I've seen a lot of stupid shit from you people, but this really takes the prize. If I had any sense, I would just as soon have Officer McGraw lock the door and let you kill each other." He shrugged and rested his hands on the back of the only remaining upright chair in the room. "But since we're desperate and we need you guys to do your job, I can't really do that."

There were a few chuckles from both sides of the room—except for Jesus and Bee-Pee, both of whom had murder in their eyes. "So why don't you decide who gets to watch the show?" Jesus rumbled. "I mean, I can live with that, right?"

Riddell glanced at Bee-Pee. Carruthers was still glaring at Jesus, but he shook his head with the committed expression of someone who still wanted to watch his cultural icons, Guido and Ramrod. Lester pretended to think it over, then shook his head.

"No . . . no, I'm afraid that won't work," he mused, rubbing his chin between his fingers. "It's a no-win situation for me, because if I choose one way or another, somebody goes away a sore loser and I get the blame." He sighed and shook his head. "There's only one way to handle this. . . ."

Riddell suddenly grabbed the chair he had been leaning on and swung it up over his head. Everyone immediately backed away, certain that he was about to hurl it at them, but instead Lester turned toward the TV itself. "If you don't make up your minds in one minute," he said, "I'm going to throw it right through the screen."

Everyone stared at him in utter disbelief. "Hey, man, you wouldn't dare . . ." Jesus began.

"I wouldn't?" Still holding the chair above his head, Lester twitched his arms a little, as if practicing for his throw. "I don't watch TV, so I don't care one way or another if the thing's wrecked. Sixty seconds . . . fifty-nine . . . fifty-eight . . ."

Bee-Pee grinned. "Yeah, but if you try that, what's to stop us from taking you down first?"

Good point. Lester hadn't thought of that. Yet before he could muster a reply, he heard Quick-Draw stride across the room to stand behind him. She didn't say anything, but when he glanced over his shoulder he saw her holding her Taser in firing position, swiveling her hips to point the weapon first one way, then another.

"Need I say more?" he murmured. "Fifty . . . forty-nine . . . forty-eight . . . forty-seven . . ."

"You're crazy as shit," someone behind Jesus murmured.

"Yeah, I'm crazy," Riddell said. "You guys are driving me out of my fucking mind. Don't you think this is a good way of getting back? Thirty . . . twenty-nine . . . twenty-eight . . ."

Everyone shouted at once. "Hey!" Jesus protested. "You jumped the count!"

"My arms are getting tired," Lester said. "So what? They're my rules, anyway. Twenty-six . . . twenty-five . . . Better make up your minds, boys, I got work to do . . . twenty-four . . . twenty-three . . .''

Now both sides were staring anxiously at each other. Lester could easily imagine what was going through everyone's minds: *He won't do it, he won't do it, he won't do it . . . but what if he does? I don't want to back down, but if we don't and if they don't, oh Christ the TV gets smashed and then what happens? . . . how do you explain this to everyone else, like the guys on third-shift when they get back from work? . . . maybe we should back down . . . but wait, they're beginning to sweat, maybe they'll say something first. . . .*

"Twenty," Lester counted. "Nineteen . . . eighteen . . . Gee, my arms are sure getting tired. Maybe I ought to just chuck this thing and get it over with. . . . ''

"No!" everyone screamed at once.

On the screen, some heavy-metal band was leaping around on a blue-lighted, fogged stage, cavorting around nude teenage girls bound with leather straps, lip-synching imbecilic lyrics having something to do with Satan screwing all the dogs in the pound and, oh baby, don'cha wanna be my bitch. Lester was tempted to pitch the chair through the screen right there. The music industry had been pandering this sort of adolescent crap for a couple of generations now.

"Fifteen . . . fourteen . . . thirteen . . .'' Lester yelled above the noise. "Think about it, guys. The company won't send us another set if I kill this one. No more sitcoms, no more mini-series, no more cop shows or doctor shows or lawyer shows. You'll miss the World Series. You'll never find out who killed what's-her-name. Ten . . . nine . . . eight . . .''

You won't throw it, he thought to himself. The TV's worth its weight in water. Yet, at the same time, he knew he *had* to throw the chair. He couldn't wimp out, not now. If he did, no one here would ever take him seriously again.

"Six!" he shouted.

"You won't do it!" Jesus yelled. His hands were bunched into fists; he took a step forward, and stopped dead as Quick-Draw's Taser swung around in his direction. "You're not going to throw it, man!"

"Yes I will!" Lester shouted back. "I'm not waiting! Five . . . four . . .''

"Ouch, That Hurts!" Bee-Pee howled.

"Turn off *The Drunk Brothers*!" Jesus shouted simultaneously.

"I can't hear you!" Lester yelled. "I'm going to throw it. Three . . . two . . ." He swung the chair back, getting ready to chuck it straight across the room. In his mind's eye, he could already see the chair hitting the screen, punching through Ramrod's smirking face, shredding the image . . . "I swear to God, I'm going to throw it—!"

"*Ouch, That Hurts!*" everyone screamed at once, a single voice of pure fear and desperation.

Lester stopped. The chair was still raised high above his head. Time seemed to have stopped dead. He looked one way, then another. Every eye in the room was fixed on him.

Then, very slowly, he lowered the chair to the floor and let go of it, then walked to the TV set and apathetically stabbed the channel selector with his finger. The scene instantly switched to a roomful of actors pummeling each other with rubber chickens to the beat of canned laughter. Funny as someone snoring during a eulogy.

Riddell didn't look at anyone as he turned and walked away from the TV. "You guys are pathetic," he mumbled as he strode past Quick-Draw and headed for the open door. "Ready to kill each other for a damn TV show."

He got to the door, then turned around and looked back at the silent crowd. "The next time I hear about this happening," he added, "there won't be a countdown."

The men in the rec room stared back at him. "Hey, Lester . . ." Jesus called out.

Lester stopped and looked around. "Were you really going to throw that chair?" Bee-Pee asked.

Riddell didn't say anything. Instead, he turned again and walked out of the room. It was time for him to make an important phone call.

He was halfway down the corridor, almost to the sanctuary of his office, when he heard something he couldn't believe. Actually, it was something he didn't hear. There was a sudden absence of noise: The TV had been switched off; there was dead silence from the rec room.

Lester turned around to see Quick-Draw standing in the corridor not far behind him. She smiled and nodded her head toward him.

He thought for a moment about going back to say something

to her. The impulse passed, though, and instead he continued walking to his office.

Honest, Les . . . I don't know what to say. Arnie Moss, seated at his office desk, shrugged with irritating nonchalance. *I mean, you know I would say yes if I could, but you know I don't have that kind of clout around here.*

Lester faced his fingers together on his desktop as he stared back at the phone screen. "Oh, of course not." he said bitterly. "You're only the vice-president in charge of lunar operations. No authority whatsoever." He tapped a finger on a thick binder stuffed with computer printout. "Have you even looked at my weekly production reports? Or did you toss them out while you were emptying the trash cans and vacuuming the floors?"

There was a two-second delay before Riddell's words reached Huntsville from the Moon. When they did, Moss's face changed visibly. He glared at Lester. *No reason to get nasty about this,* he replied evenly, obviously forcing himself to maintain a bland manner. *I've seen all your reports. Your people have done very well. You yourself should be proud of the job you've done. Those reports represent a lot of hard work.*

"Damn straight it's been hard work," Lester retorted. He picked up the binder and shook it in front of the phone lens so that it filled Moss's screen. "Lunar oxygen, aluminum rolls, solar cells . . . we've met the six-week production quota in all areas. These guys have been busting their humps for the last month and a half because of the carrot-and-stick treatment you've given 'em." He dropped the binder back on the desk. "Okay, today's the deadline. We've done our part. Now how about keeping your end of the deal?"

Moss was looking distinctly uncomfortable; his next pause went longer than the usual two-second delay. This wasn't a situation out of which he could easily bluff his way. *Like I said, Les . . . if this was something I could rubber-stamp myself, I'd do it in a second. Your people would have their bonuses with my blessings.*

"Bonuses *and* reinstatement of production risers *and* shipment of nonessentials," Lester pointedly reminded him. "You've got a lot of promises to keep, sport. They're not going to be very happy if you dump 'em like this."

Moss's eyebrows rose. His mouth turned into a lopsided grin. *Hey, it ain't just me. You're the one who took it to them. I'm a quarter of million miles away . . . nobody's going to throw a plate of food at me during dinner in the mess hall tonight.*

Riddell sucked in his breath. "They won't do that. They know who makes the decisions around here. Besides, you're not dealing with children up here." No point in telling him that he had just broken up a fight over who got to watch something on TV. Lester shook his head and held out his hands. "C'mon, Arnie, level with me for once. Who do I have to talk to in order to get a straight answer about this? Ken? Rock? It's a simple goddamn decision, for chrissakes."

Again, a longer-than-necessary pause. *It's Crespin and Chapman and all the rest of the board. They've got to review your production figures, and you know what that takes. Meetings, memos, departmental reports, more meetings . . . you know this is a bureaucracy. Takes time to get anything done. You're acting like my kid when it's allowance day and he wants his five dollars.*

"What do you make your boy do?" Lester shot back. "File a one-hundred-page report on how many fetal pigs he's dissected in biology class?"

Moss grinned. *No. He's just got to show me his report card.* The grin faded. *There's also the matter of the tug your pilot crashed, and the missing Spam-cans. They're not satisfied with the final report you made. Look . . . I know and they know the Vacuum Suckers were behind that whole thing, but they were counting on you to prove it. You gave us this song-and-dance about a faulty electrical system and pilot error and stray telemetry signals, and maybe it was enough to get NASA off everyone's backs, but the guys upstairs are still pissed off about the whole thing.*

"So they're pissed off. Who cares? That was six weeks ago. The piracy stopped, didn't it? And besides, it doesn't have a thing to with the six-week production quota and the bonus situation. I've just about . . ."

Again, Lester stopped and took a deep breath. He wasn't getting anywhere by getting tough with Moss; he should have realized that his old buddy didn't intimidate easily. Time to try a little old-fashioned groveling. "C'mon, Arnie," he begged. "Tell me something I can take back to these guys. You're right . . . it's allowance day, and the kids want their bucks. Maybe you aren't able to give me a straight answer right now, but at least tell me *when* you can give me something concrete. Next week? Two weeks? Monday? What?"

Moss sighed and looked away from the camera, apparently lost in thought. Finally he looked back at the screen. *I'll give you a call soon, Les*, he said slowly. Despite the inexactitude of his answer, for the first time during their conversation Lester sensed that Arnie was being candid with him. *There's a lot of complicated shit going down here right now and . . . well, I don't know if I'm at liberty to discuss the details with you.*

Lester frowned; a shiver ran down his back. "Details? Arnie, are you talking about Uchu-Hiko?" He waited; no reply. "Hey, is this something with the Japanese? What the hell is going on down there?"

Moss avoided looking at the screen. *Uh-uh. Nothing like that. Hey, I gotta go. I'll get back to you soon as I know something definite, okay?* He leaned slightly forward in his seat, reaching for the base of his phone.

"Arnie?" Lester said. "Hey, Moss! Don't hang up! What are you trying to . . ." Then his phone screen went blank, replaced by lines of luminescent type which told him how long the call had taken, the amount of money it had cost, and how much time he had left on his telephone budget. Seventeen minutes on an AT&T comsat, he thought, and not a damn thing resolved.

Lester settled back in his chair, propped one foot up on the edge of his desk, and let his head fall back. Nothing resolved, but something learned nonetheless. Some bad kind of weirdness was coming down the road . . . but he was damned if he knew exactly what it was.

The Mouth of the South
(Pressclips.3)

Excerpted from "Hellraiser—Harry Drinkwater, The Last Angry DJ In America" by J.R. Presley; Rolling Stone, *November 7, 2023:*

The radio disc jockey who later became known to fans and enemies alike as the "Mouth of the South" first came to public attention in 2002, when he was a second-year law student at Vanderbilt University in Nashville, Tennessee.

By his own account, Harry Drinkwater led an unremarkable, even typical, college career: attending classes during the day, studying in his dorm room or in the library at night until about ten o'clock, after which he sometimes wandered down to Elliston Place to indulge in his favorite hobby, watching new session-musician bands try their licks at the legendary Nashville rock venue, the Exit/In. Drinkwater's ambition was to be a public defender in his hometown of Charlotte, North Carolina; that was his goal until the day he happened upon a student demonstration on the Vandy campus.

"There were about twenty students in front of the president's office," Drinkwater recalls. "This was right after the Duck River nuke outside Manchester had its near-meltdown, and these guys were protesting Vandy's investment in Southern Nuclear Utilities, the plant's owner. They were actually being pretty peaceful about it—carrying placards, chanting slogans, that sort of thing—but there were about a hundred or so frat boys standing around them. Throwing beer cans at 'em, yelling obscenities, making rude gestures at the girls. I was just standing there—watching, not participating either way—when all of a sudden the frat animals charged the demonstrators and began to beat the holy crap out of them. And because I just happened to be there, a couple of them decided to jump me, too."

Drinkwater laughs. "So there I am, with one of these nean-derthals having me in a full nelson and the other tenderizing my stomach with his fists, and I look up to see [former Vanderbilt University President] Gilbert Gallagher standing in his office window, watching the whole thing and laughing his ass off. And right then I kind of decided it was time for a career change."

The next day, Drinkwater went to Vandy's student-operated campus radio station, WRVU-FM, and applied for an unpaid position as an announcer. As luck would have it, the station's general manager at the time was Kate Humphrey, who would later become the program director of WJBR-FM in Boston (and one of Drinkwater's many bosses in his career).

"Harry made no attempt to hide what he wanted to do on the air," Humphrey says. "He wanted a soapbox for his views. But he knew his music, and I was angry about the breakup of the demonstration myself, so once we got him his license and he had been trained, we put him right on the air. The only ground rules I gave him were to say nothing which would break FCC rules or cause the university to shut us down."

As he would many more time in the future, Drinkwater ig-nored those ground rules. At almost every stop-set, Harry Drinkwater railed against Gallagher, the university's board of directors, its regents and trustees, the frat system to which a majority of the underclassmen belonged, and anyone else whose stance rankled him. More than once, Vandy's administration at-tempted to shut down WRVU, only to be stopped either by fac-ulty members or liberal trustees who—despite the fact that they themselves were often categorically attacked by Drinkwater—believed in the student DJ's right to express his opinions.

Although Drinkwater was once attacked in WRVU's studio by a gang of irate fraternity members, he also became a celebrity, both on and off campus. His play-list was his own selection; his choice of music included an eclectic mix of the best oldies as well as the prime cuts of cutting-edge new groups. In compari-son to the bland, homogenized play-lists of Nashville's com-mercial rock stations, Drinkwater's alternative-AOR show was a welcome change. At the height of his career at WRVU, Drink-water was easily one of the most popular radio announcers in Music City—no small feat for a college jock in a major radio market.

Nonetheless, it was a short career, lasting less than ten months. The FCC suspended the station's license (after Drinkwater called Gallagher "a Nazi motherfucker" on the air) and the former law student was expelled, for bad grades as well as bad attitude. But by then an article on Drinkwater had already appeared in *CMJ*, attracting the attention of Jules Fontana, the general manager of WXKQ-FM in Atlanta.

"We were at the dead rock-bottom of the Arbitron and Birch books," Fontana recalls. "We had just lost our morning-drive person, and the owner was threatening to fire everyone and switch our format to country. I sorta knew it was a risk to hire Drinkwater, but I figured, 'Hey, what have I got to lose?' "

Within two months of his expulsion from Vanderbilt, Harry Drinkwater became the new morning announcer at WXKQ. At six A.M. on December 1, 2003, Atlanta was rudely shaken out of bed by the Red Hot Chili Peppers' "Nobody Weird Like Me," followed by a tirade against Santa Claus as being a wholly-owned subsidiary of Coca-Cola. And this was only the beginning.

"God, did I have fun in Atlanta!" Drinkwater cackles. "They're still talking about me there. . . . " Considering some of his exploits, that's not an idle boast. In his role as an activist-DJ, Drinkwater's favorite gag was to call various Atlanta public officials—the mayor, the chairman of the city council, the chief of police, the superintendent of public works, and so on—at their homes at the earliest possible hour and ask them blunt on-air questions about their jobs. He took a remote-broadcast team to the executive offices of the McGuinness Corporation (the Atlanta-based owner of his old foe, Southern Nuclear Utilities) and camped out in the reception area of CEO Michael Edgerton's office for twelve hours, giving half-hour updates to his audience about the upcoming unscheduled interview, until McGuinness' security staff finally lost patience and threw them out of the building.

He delivered coffee and doughnuts to skyscraper construction crews and did a remote broadcast from the Atlanta sewer system. His guest-shows were also memorable: He asked the sexagenarian former film star Warren Beatty if he was "getting any good ass lately" ("Sure, with your sister" was Beatty's playful response), discussed comic books with Nobel laureate Harlan Ellison, told Ku Klux Klan leader Newt Cahill to "go suck on an exhaust pipe," and allegedly had sex with Gina LaMotta in the record library during a *long* station break.

During his nine-year tenure, WXKQ steadily rose in ratings

and on-the-street listenership. By 2007, it had become the top station in Atlanta, and Harry Drinkwater had become a household name in the Deep South. Yet Drinkwater had simultaneously become a curse to the station's management and ownership. "There's an unwritten code in radio," Jules Fontana explains, "and that is, 'Never piss off your advertisers.' Harry knew that code, and he did his best to break it every chance he got."

Drinkwater didn't spare any company, local or national, that bought air-time on WXKQ. Car dealerships, fast-food chains, soft-drink makers (including the Atlanta-based Coca-Cola), the manufacturers of jeans and pimple cream and condoms, and the U.S. Army—all caught Drinkwater's ire for real or imagined offenses. Until, one day, the ad agencies which represented all these clients collectively went to WXKQ's management and issued a simple ultimatum: "He goes, or we go." Guess who went?

"Well, I was fed up with Atlanta anyway," Drinkwater says unconvincingly.

He was quickly snapped up by WJBR in Boston, hired by his old college friend, Kate Humphrey, over the misgivings of the station's owners. Since WJBR's evening format did not allow for on-air interviews, Humphrey thought it was safe to put Drinkwater in the afternoon-drive slot. "I told Harry that anything he said was okay, as long as it didn't concern our advertisers," she says. "He kept his promise . . . but I forgot to mention sports."

Within a few weeks of coming on board with WJBR, Harry Drinkwater was regularly attacking a hallowed Boston institution, the Red Sox baseball team, which was currently experiencing one of its worst all-time losing streaks. It's okay for a native Bostonian to dump on the Red Sox, but not for a newly arrived Southerner. After three bomb-threats and the torching of Humphrey's car, Harry Drinkwater was out on the street again.

Harry returned below the Mason-Dixon line, and over the next decade gradually began to work his way through the ranks of FM-rock radio stations. On the strength of his résumé, he was hired by WBNT in Louisville, WCCS in Macon, WDPW in Charlotte, WEUP in Memphis, WNEP in Jackson, WOQQ and WRLT in Bowling Green, and WSST in Shelbyville. In recent years, he has taken on a number of pseudonyms—Marvin Gardens in Memphis, Ben Dover in Jackson, I.P. Freely in Bowling Green. At all these stations, his style has remained consistent. And he has been fired from them all, always for opening his mouth. His average tenure has been twelve months, although in Charlotte he lasted three weeks, and in Memphis he lasted one day (he made fun of the local Elvis Presley tourist industry).

At each station, he played music which fit the appropriate formats, kept the FCC-required logbooks in perfect order, showed up on time for his air-shifts and never missed station meetings, never brought booze or drugs into the studio or invited groupies into the station. He has rarely even been known to argue directly with management or other staff members ("I just quietly disagree," he says with a chuckle). Almost everyone who was interviewed for the article has described Harry Drinkwater, in terms of his off-the-air behavior, as "polite" or "friendly" or "gentlemanly."

"But I read the papers," Harry admits, "and I keep my ear to the ground. I know what people in the community are saying at the lunch counters and the mass-transit stations. They want a voice. They *need* a voice, and not one that's going to be silenced just because the owner of the local Pizza Trough gets pissed off. As a lawyer, I would have been mediocre . . ."

He pauses and waves his hand around the air-studio of WBTV-FM, a small-market radio station in Cedar Key, Florida, where he is the current overnight jock (as Sugar Ray Monsoon). "But as a DJ," he continues, "I can reach the ears of many more people than I could make speeches to in some dead courtroom. I can keep up the good fight. Sure, it always cost me, but I can change some minds. . . ."

The Homeboys CD which was been playing in the CD rack begins to fade. Harry Drinkwater quickly excuses himself, swivels back to the console, clears his throat, and switches on his mike. The management at his current post has already become weary of his monologues about the hardships of the local shrimp-fishing industry; they may have him canned by the time this article sees print.

Where will Harry Drinkwater go next? He's beginning to use up all his medium-market stations in the South; he's *persona non grata* throughout major-league Dixie radio. Yet it's difficult to ignore a copy of the current issue of the *R&R* which lies open on the counter next to a stack of CD's. It's turned to the classifieds page in the back; a display ad, with a photo of the Moon, has been circled with red ink from Harry's logbook pen. . . .

13. Radio Free Luna

Long before Harry Drinkwater said No—absolutely, positively, without exception *no*—Willard DeWitt knew that he was looking upon the face of a soulmate: a person who had hardwired reality *his* way.

While DeWitt—that is, Jeremy Schneider, hopeful media broker and entrepreneur—recited his spiel about establishing Moondog McCloud as the host of a new syndicated alternative-AOR radio program called MoonTunes, he watched Drinkwater carefully. Moondog McCloud's hands prowled restlessly across the mixing board, potting up one CD deck to segue in a new Flaming Carrots number while potting down "Lost in the Supermarket" by the Clash, shoving a PSA tape (Gina LaMotta on safe-sex habits) into the cart machine, then abruptly changing his mind and hastily replacing it with another PSA (Albert Crenshaw on watching your cholesterol); now nervously adjusting the big Electrovoice mike dangling in front of his face, then hunting through the box of CDs at his feet, apparently searching for something to match the Flaming Carrots, even though there was a stack of unused albums by everyone from the Who to the Yummy Nummins to Dagwood Bumstead right next to his elbow. All the while saying *no . . . no . . . no . . .* as if it were a mantra.

Even as DeWitt talked, keeping on with the now-useless prattle about estimated audience penetration and possible Arbitron ratings escalation, he let his own eyes roam around the studio. LDSM had been established in a vacant office in Subcomp A, almost directly adjacent to the mess hall. The smallest available office, it was in fact little larger than a walk-in closest. The narrow room barely had enough space to contain a tiny wraparound console, a shelf of CD's and tapes, a single chair, the transmitter rack behind the console, and the ceaselessly buzzing Associated Press line-printer. Scrolled paper was heaped on the floor around and behind the chair, with pertinent scraps of news piled high on the desktop in front of the six-channel soundboard, burying the FCC-required logbooks. The mooncrete walls were lined with sheets of pitted foam-rubber which DeWitt recognized as having come from the insides of cargo canisters: crude but effective acoustic baffles. On top of the foam were stapled promotional posters of a dozen throwaway one-album rock bands—Area 18, Veronica and the Bar Sluts, Cleveland, Wha???, Bathtub Slime, the Dinks—some of whom were never played on the station.

Drinkwater was heavyset, with the build of a welterweight boxer past his prime. He had a mop of curly black hair and a greasy beard just beginning to turn gray at the jawline, framing the expressive mouth of a professional talker. His eyes, though, were what captured DeWitt's attention the moment he walked into the studio. Drinkwater had the hooded eyes of a perpetually angry young man who was not going quietly into middle age. He was, Dewitt decided, a person much like himself. A rebel. Yet while DeWitt was exercising his own anger at the system by covertly robbing it blind, Harry Drinkwater was tilting at windmills. Maybe he had destroyed a few windmills in his time, too . . . but there were a lot of windmills, and some of them had awfully big vanes.

"Be quiet a minute," Drinkwater said. "I've gotta make an ID." He switched on the mike, suddenly silencing the thud-and-blunder of the Flaming Carrots on the monitor speakers, and waited a few moments until the song began to fade out. "Yesirree bob!" he abruptly chortled as he potted up the mike. "The Flaming Carrots here on LDSM, the moon rock sound of the high frontier! We got some moldy goldy oldies by the Talking Heads and R.E.M. comin' up in just a few seconds, right after this important, I mean *urgent*, public service announcement!"

He stabbed the PLAY button on the cart machine, potted down the mike and switched it off, then turned down the volume on the PSA tape. "Christ almighty," he grumbled as he shrugged off the headphones, "even if they won't send me any new CD's, you'd think the damn company would at least ship up some new PSA's. Getting sick of hearing this cholesterol shit over and over." He waited a half-minute until the PSA had stopped, then cleanly segued in R.E.M.'s "Stand."

As McCloud turned to grab a Talking Heads CD out of the stack on his desk, he added, "That's some interesting idea you have about syndicating my show, Jeremy, but I'm afraid I'm not real keen on being a big-time jock. I'm just some guy who likes doing this on a small-scale level, if you know what I mean."

"Uh-huh," DeWitt replied. He had already gotten the message. Yet, instinctively, he knew that it wasn't for the reasons that Harry Drinkwater had cited. Not that DeWitt had ever seriously intended to market Moondog McCloud as a syndicated radio announcer; Drinkwater's cooperation had only been necessary to add credibility to the scam he had been perpetrating.

The idea was complex, but it had begun with a fairly simple observation. The paychecks issued every two weeks to Descartes Station personnel were direct-deposited into banks of their choice on Earth. But Skycorp also had a group-investment program in place; its employees were offered the opportunity to have money taken from their checks, before they were deposited, and put into stock investments handled by Skycorp's primary broker, the multinational New York firm of Empire Securities.

At least half of Descartes Station's moondogs took advantage of the deal, in hopes of increasing their income by playing the stock market. Yet, DeWitt had noted, none of them paid the slightest bit of attention to *exactly* what their money was doing in the market. Empire Securities was investing their cash in everything from maglev-train projects in Germany to housing projects in Chicago to a chain of pool halls in London, buying and selling like maniacs on half-a-dozen exchanges worldwide. This was the way the stock market usually worked; no surprise there.

DeWitt had studied the last six-month prospectus from Empire and had noticed these things; he had also noticed that the moondogs rarely glanced at their stock reports. More than half of the time, the prospectus each one received by fax went straight into the recycling bins. The rest of the time, they glanced at the reports in the rec room or in the mess hall, grunted without understanding the material, and tossed them into an unread pile of other reports in their niches. They didn't care where the money was invested, as long as the balance sheets showed a positive result, even if it was measured only by pennies.

All great scams begin with a simple notion. Willard's began with a deceptively easy question: *How can I get them to invest their money in something which belongs to me?* Which led to the next question: *What do I have which they will want to buy?* Just by listening to the radio, he found the answer.

First, he would get McCloud hooked on the idea of becoming a syndicated DJ, establishing him as the on-air talent for Radio Free Luna, billed as the "world's first rock show from outer space." Then DeWitt would establish Radio Free Luna as the first product of MoonTunes Ltd., a private commercial radio syndicate. On the surface, MoonTunes would be offering Radio Free Luna to radio stations back on Earth. This was calculated to stir up some excitement among the moondogs at the base, once the news was deliberately leaked. One of their own was about to make the big time. Hometown boy makes good and all that stuff.

Once the excitement had built to a fever pitch, Jeremy Schneider would make his surprise announcement: Stock in Moon-Tunes Ltd. would be offered to prospective investors among the crew. In fact, they could purchase shares from a small yet established New York brokerage called Gamble, Hutton & Schwartzchilde, which was handling transactions for MoonTunes. And as it happened, Gamble, Hutton & Schwartzchilde was an associate brokerage of Empire Securities. Therefore, all the moondogs had to do was instruct Empire to invest part of their investment capital with Gamble, Hutton & Schwartzchilde; this was as simple as touching a couple of keys on the terminals in their niches when the biweekly pay notices were faxed by the company.

All it took was a certain amount of hubris and sweet-talking by Jeremy Schneider. He had little doubt that he could convince people that MoonTunes was a viable investment. Moondog McCloud was beloved by the station's crew; if they were sure that their own DJ would be a big hit with the folks back home, the Descartes Station investors were certain not only to get their money back, but also to turn a considerable profit on the deal. And since they needed only to invest a fraction of their hard-earned money from each pay period—DeWitt had learned how deceptively small "five percent" could sound—no one would feel that their stake in this venture put them at great risk.

Except that Gamble, Hutton & Schwartzchilde existed only as an account number within the vast memory of Empire Securities' computers. It had taken DeWitt a considerable amount of hacking, using his Toshiba laptop computer to establish a secret back door into Empire's computers through the comsat system.

Yet once he had managed to do so, it had been relatively simple to ferret out the information he desired. Gamble, Hutton & Schwartzchilde had been a minor company specializing in penny stock until it had gone bankrupt six weeks ago. The company had been dissolved and its meager capital assessts sold to another brokerage. Yet, through the negligence of some overworked systems keypuncher, its name and account number had not been eradicated from the memory of Empire's computer mainframe. In name only, therefore, it still existed.

DeWitt secretly purchased the defunct company for exactly one dollar, then created an entirely fictitious board of directors and listed the revived firm as a company dealing in "space and media futures." He had then patiently waited to see what might happen, but nobody at Empire Securities appeared to notice: Gamble, Hutton & Schwartzchilde continued to exist as a tiny, unnoticed cog in a vast machine stretching from New York to London to Tokyo to Rio to Johannesburg.

The alleged president and CEO of Gamble, Hutton & Schwartzchilde, Elliot Entwhistle, was one of DeWitt's phony identities, created long ago as a standby entity. Entwhistle was supposedly a wealthy investment banker in Houston, complete with an account in a large Texas bank. A secret, well-guarded subroutine in the Empire Securities computer was programmed so that the money received from investments in Gamble, Hutton & Schwartzchilde would automatically be transferred via computer network to the Houston bank, into Entwhistle's account.

The New York computers did not know that Gamble, Hutton & Schwartzchilde and Elliot Entwhistle existed only as ghosts; they would obediently follow instructions planted in advance by DeWitt. The legitimate flesh-and-blood bankers who rubber-stamped the transactions would never notice the primary transaction; Empire Securities bought and sold, on a daily basis, stock in excess of several billion dollars on behalf of their clients. A couple of hundred thousand bucks diverted, over a year's time to a small brokerage handled by their own holding company, would be ignored, lost in the fathomless paperwork and number-crunching. And the investment-minded moondogs at Descartes Station would receive a regular series of faxed letters from radio stations on Earth, all of whom wanted to syndicate Radio Free Luna—all completely fictional, of course, but necessary to maintain the verisimilitude of the bogus company.

The moondogs would also receive authentic-looking stock

certificates from Gamble, Hutton & Schwartzchilde; these would be ground out by a desktop-publishing program that DeWitt had managed to steal from a California software firm which specialized in such things. Only a skilled security hacker hired by Empire Securties could ever crack the elaborate system DeWitt had established, and DeWitt had taken pains to eliminate any loose ends that might draw the attention of Empire's counter-hackers.

The whole thing would look, sound, and feel like a completely légitimate stock transaction . . . but all the money invested in MoonTunes through Gamble, Hutton & Schwartzchilde would be electronically transmitted to the Texas bank account of Elliot Entwhistle. In the meantime, the puppet strings would be manipulated from DeWitt's comsat-linked laptop computer on the Moon, protected by layer upon layer of cutouts. If all worked well, this scheme would take almost exactly twelve months to complete. Then, after those twelve months, Jeremy Schneider's contract with Skycorp would expire. He would not renew his contract, but instead would ship back to Earth . . . and disappear from existence almost as soon as he touched ground on the shuttle landing strip at Cape Canaveral.

Within two days, the reclusive Elliot Entwhistle would resurface in Houston, where he would liquidate his bank account, taking the money away in cash and vanishing once again. Within at least an hour of that, a secret pass-phrase would be activated along the computer network, activating a well-buried cybernetic worm which would obliterate all traces of MoonTunes Ltd., Gamble, Hutton & Schwartzchilde, and Elliot Entwhistle . . . leaving behind several dozen bewildered moondogs with stock certificates worth exactly zip, and not one clue as to where their money went. Except maybe some confused recollections about a dependable, honest-looking young entrepreneur named Jeremy Schneider who had convinced them to purchase stock in MoonTunes Ltd. Except that Jeremy Schneider, too, had ceased to exist.

It was a lovely scam. It had taken weeks of unflagging effort to put all the pieces in place, hacking out the programs which would establish the dummy companies and identities, using the covert comsat link from his niche to crack the necessary bank accounts and corporate files. It was a masterpiece of criminal art; from the Moon, the beginnings of an invisible, untraceable financial network had been established on Earth.

• • •

Except that the first piece of the mosaic adamantly refused to fall into place: the cooperation of Harry Drinkwater.

Without Moondog McCloud's involvement from the very beginning, there could be no MoonTunes Ltd., no Radio Free Luna, no enticement for the wage-slaves of Descartes Station to kiss away part of their investment cash to Gamble, Hutton & Schwartzchilde. Yet, much to his own surprise, DeWitt found that he could hardly care less if his scam was now dead as the proverbial doornail. For the moment, at least, he was fascinated by Harry Drinkwater.

"I would have thought the fame might interest you," DeWitt prodded. "The chance to go gain some notoriety, perhaps . . ."

There was a fleeting expression of distaste on Drinkwater's face. The DJ glanced askance at DeWitt as he slipped another CD into the vacant player and cued up the next song. "Fame sucks," he murmured, concentrating again on his show. "Take my word for it. I've tried it before."

"Then, the money you could make . . ."

"I make enough." Drinkwater reset the levels on the mixing board and picked up the program log and a pen. "If you want to make serious money, you don't go into this business," he continued as he started updating the log. "Go jump into bed with the Japs if you want to make money up here. They want to own this place. Why don't you throw in with them? Don't try some crazy-ass notion about starting up some radio network on the Moon. That's got to be the dumbest thing I've ever . . ."

Abruptly, the pen paused on the checklist. Drinkwater looked up from the logbook and fixed his eyes on his visitor. DeWitt started feeling vaguely uncomfortable; he suddenly realized that Drinkwater, for the first time since he had walked into the studio and started making his pitch, had been sizing him up, too.

"Dumbest thing I've ever heard," Drinkwater repeated softly. "And you don't look like a dummy. Not by a long shot." His eyes traveled back to the logbook, but his attention never left DeWitt. "What's your game, Schneider?"

DeWitt swallowed a hard stone in his throat. "I don't know what you mean."

Harry Drinkwater shook his head. "Sure, you know what I mean," he said easily, still looking at the logbook. "I don't know what it is, but it ain't radio. Maybe I'm getting a little slow, and maybe I didn't catch on when you first walked in here, but I still know a con man when I see him."

He smiled a little. "I've seen plenty," he continued, "and you fit the profile. The fast talk, the smooth pitch, the get-rich-quick scheme leading into the I've-got-everything-figured-out routine." Drinkwater chuckled and shook his head again. "Yeah, boy. You must have been hot shit in Great Falls or wherever you hail from, but I didn't fall off the potato wagon yesterday." His smile grew broader. "I've interviewed con artists like you before. They get easy to spot after a while. And, pal, you don't even rate."

DeWitt felt his hands begin to tremble. He nervously tucked them in his trouser pockets. "I don't . . ."

"Hush." Drinkwater's voice was the easy whisper of a viper. He signed his name at the bottom of the page and tossed the logbook aside. "I don't want to hear it," he went on, now looking straight up at DeWitt, transfixing him with angry black eyes. "You've got some kinda scam going. I don't know what it is and I don't really care, except that I don't want you coming my way with it again. Just let me give you a word of warning. . . ."

He rested his elbows on the console, laced his hands together, and pointed both index fingers straight at DeWitt. "If you do anything . . . if you even *try* anything . . . that's going to hurt or rip off the guys working here, I'm going to cut off your balls and shove 'em down your fucking throat. You got me straight on that, Jeremy Schneider?"

DeWitt fought the impulse to run straight out of the studio. In his career, he had been threatened in a hundred overt and subtle ways, but never before had he met someone who, without a doubt, meant every word of what he'd said. This was not the rhetorical teeth-gnashing of a college frat boy or a yuppie or even a cell block thug trying to cadge a cigarette. This was a threat from someone who meant serious business, and it felt like ice water had just been pumped into his guts with an enema bag.

He nodded stiffly, and Drinkwater responded with a slight nod of his own. "There's good people working here," the DJ continued. "They don't deserve whatever you've cooked up for them. Do they?"

Good Lord, was this guy telepathic or what? DeWitt quickly shook his head. Drinkwater relaxed a little. He sat back in his chair, folding his hands in his lap, still staring straight at DeWitt. "Okay," he said. "Now get out of here, con man. I've got work to do."

If Drinkwater had slapped him—if he had taken a CD and

frisbeed it across the studio at him, if he had ripped off his
testicles and pushed them bleeding down his throat—DeWitt
could not have been hurt more than by those few dismissive
words. He had met someone very much like himself, a person
with whom he felt an untouchable, yet distinct bond—and had
been written off as a cheap swindler. Harry Drinkwater had re-
jected him as beneath contempt.

Drinkwater reached forward to the soundboard to segue the
next song. The conversation was concluded. DeWitt eagerly
turned around and started to open the door. He couldn't wait to
get out of there. But as he opened the door, he heard Drinkwater
say, "Just one more thing . . ."

DeWitt stopped and looked around. "Is it about money?"
Drinkwater asked. "Is that all it's about? Tell me the truth."

DeWitt took a deep breath. There was no sense in lying to
those eyes. "No. It's not," he admitted.

The black, unwavering gaze lingered on his face. "It's the
hunt, isn't it? The game. That's what you're all about. Isn't it?"

DeWitt nodded his head very slowly. "I sort of thought so,"
Drinkwater said. "What's your name?" DeWitt started to reply,
but the jock cut him off. "No, don't tell me it's Jeremy Schneider," he said. "You don't look like a Jeremy Schneider to me,
and con artists don't use their real names. Tell me your real
name. The one your momma gave you."

DeWitt hesitated. This was the hardest question anyone
had ever put to him. How could he trust this guy? How could
he . . . ?

"Willard," he blurted. "Willard DeWitt."

"Very good." Drinkwater nodded approvingly. "Don't worry.
You're safe as long as you play straight with me. You're not with
the feds, are you, Willard DeWitt? You're not working with the
company?"

DeWitt quickly shook his head. "Are you any good at what
you do?" Drinkwater asked.

"I'm not the best . . ." DeWitt admitted, then stopped. "But
I'm working on it."

Another long pause; Drinkwater's eyes never left his face.
Then, unexpectedly, a wide grin spread across Moondog Mc-
Cloud's bearded face. "C'mon back in and shut the door, Willard," he said. "I think I got an idea. You'll love it. You may
even make some money with it, too."

DeWitt stared back at him. Drinkwater smiled and nodded his

head; it was an invitation to dance with the devil. The con man turned to shut the studio door, and as he did, he heard the DJ's chair scoot back on its casters along the floor. He quickly turned around, half-expecting an attack, only to find Drinkwater standing up behind the console. He held out his hand for him to shake.

"Sit down," he said. "We've got some things to talk about."

○
○
○
○
○
○
○
○

The Art of the Moon
(Pressclips.4)

Excerpt from "A Canvas as Large as the Universe—The New Space Art" by Lowell Weishaupt: Atlantic Monthly; July, 2028:

Historians and aficionados of space art generally agree that the first true work in the genre was produced by the twentieth century pulp artist Frank R. Paul; it was a painting of Jupiter, which appeared on the cover of the March, 1930 issue of *Astounding Stories*. In the decades that followed, many other artists would follow in Paul's footsteps: Lucien Rudaux, Chesley Bonestell, Ludek Pesek, Ron Miller, Pat Rawlings, David Hardy, Adolf Schaller, Andrei Sokolov, and David Egge are among the names most frequently cited as seminal artists in the field. The roster includes painters as renowned as Bob McCall, whose work ranged from vast murals on the walls of the National Air and Space Museum to postage stamps issued by the U.S. Postal Service, and as obscure as Morris Scott Dollens, whose best work is nonetheless prized by collectors.

Yet it was a long time, even after the beginning of the Space Age, before artists ventured into space itself. Although two early astronauts, Alan Bean of the U.S. and Alexei Leonov of the U.S.S.R., became astronomical painters in their own right, their best work did not begin until their flying careers had long since ended, when both men were working from fading memories of their experiences. NASA made an admirable effort to promote realistic and abstract space art with the short-lived NASA Fine Arts Program—with some noteworthy results such "Blockhouse 34" by James Wyeth and "Power to Go" by Paul Calle—but these paintings were rarely seen outside of limited runs at municipal galleries and small-press portfolios; some of the best works were on permanent display only in the sterile corridors of the NASA headquarters building in Washington D.C., seen only by government bureaucrats on their way to lunch.

For the most part, though, astronomical art largely remained in the realm of science fiction magazine covers, industrial promotional work, and movie backdrops. Some of Bonestell's best astronomical paintings, for example, can only now be seen in videotapes of 1950's SF movies such as *War of the Worlds*, *Destination Moon*, and *The Conquest of Space*. With the arguable exceptions of Bean and Leonov—who did all their work on the ground—it took many years for true space art to emerge.

Despite the prognostications of futurists and science fiction writers, it was not until 2023 that the first impressionistic art was actually produced in space. Although many astronauts carried sketchbooks into orbit, beginning with the first wave of shuttle flights by NASA in the 1980's, it was some time before a dedicated, trained artist actually journeyed into the cosmos, to create his work on-site in real-time. Yet it eventually occurred, and although the Mars paintings of Milos Capor are considered to be the touchstone of the field today, most contemporary observers agree that the first off-Earth space art was done by a lunar hermit best known by his signature—"Yuri."

Yuri was Gregor Gagarin, a Russian immigrant from Soviet Georgia to the United States, who made the dubious claim (thus far unproven) to being a descendant of Major Yuri Gagarin, the first man in space. Gagarin lived up to his supposed-ancestor's name by becoming an industrial space pilot. After working for Skycorp as a so-called beamjack in 2017 and 2018, Gagarin left the company and, along with several other former employees of Skycorp, Glavkosmos, and Arianespace, started the private space-salvage company Cheap Thrills, Inc. in 2019. At the age of twenty-nine, when he was the co-pilot of the company's "flagship," the orbital tug appropriately christened *Cheap Thrills*, he began to produce his first serious art.

Gagarin had taken art as an elective while an engineering student at Stanford University. According to popular legend, he started drawing sketches aboard the *Cheap Thrills* during the long hours in Earth orbit while the tug was making mid-course corrections to home in on a piece of debris or a defunct satellite which the company had been hired to salvage. Others claim that his first sculptures were produced in a bunkhouse module on Olympus Station, where he stayed between salvage missions; these are reported to be abstract miniatures, as befitting the close confines of his quarters. At any rate, very few of these sculptures and sketches remain in existence, and those which do are now in the hands of private collectors who rarely, if ever, exhibit them to the public.

In 2021, the National Transportation Safety Board of the FAA revoked Cheap Thrills, Inc.'s license when the company was found guilty of hijacking defunct U.S. government communications satellites and reselling them to private firms. Gagarin was not among those indicted in the conspiracy, but his first tenure in space ended with the bankruptcy of the company. After spending fourteen months on the ground, Gagarin managed gather the capital to reacquire the title to the *Cheap Thrills* and convert it into a small lunar tug, through the addition of landing gear and an uprated propulsion system. Orbital salvage was still a desirable enterprise in deep space, especially so on the Moon; industrial activities had put thousands of tons of garbage into lunar orbit, where it posed a hazard to navigation.

According to several sources inside Skycorp, Gagarin made the giant space company an offer it could scarcely refuse. In return for salvaging discarded OTVs, broken satellites, and similar space refuse, and repairing the junk for reuse by Skycorp's lunar mining facility at Descartes Station, all Skycorp had to do was furnish Gagarin with an independent habitat near Descartes Station, which could serve both as a junkyard and as a studio. Except for negotiable costs of life-support, materials, insurance and taxes, no other payment was necessary. Simply put, Skycorp would act as a patron of the arts in return for Gagarin's services as a salvager. Skycorp considered it to be a highly profitable arrangement; it was then considering several other bids by start-up companies eager to take the place of Cheap Thrills Inc., but each was tendering contracts of up to five billion dollars. Gregor Gagarin's arrangement, by contrast, was a bargain.

Thus, in late 2022, Gagarin took the *Cheap Thrills*—now whimsically rechristened the *Vincent's Ear*—and migrated to a small base camp in the Descartes highlands of the Moon, about fifteen miles northeast of Descartes Station. He received his supplies on a regular basis from the base; in return, the base received refurbished equipment collected from his salvage missions. Otherwise, Gagarin kept out of contact, rarely if ever to be seen at the base itself. For most of four years, Gregor Gagarin—now known by the inhabitants of the base only as ''Honest Yuri''—isolated himself on the Moon, producing the first true collection of painted and sculptural art to be made off the planet Earth.

He was also considered by his closest neighbors, the moon-dogs of Descartes Station, to be completely insane. . . .

14. The Night Gallery

As the lunar truck rounded the side of the last hillock, the beams of its headlights fell across the nine-foot-tall figure of a man standing alone on the plain. His outstretched right arm hovered menacingly above the tread-worn road in a gesture which unmistakably signified *Go back.*

Seeing it, Anne Noonan jerked in her seat. *"Gaaagh!"* she yelped, the Thermos mug of coffee in her hand dancing out of her grasp. The coffee spilled in her lap—she was still wearing her hardsuit, fortunately, or she might have been scalded—and the cup landed at her feet, unnoticed, as she stared through the canopy at the giant that seemed to have materialized in front of the vehicle.

Mighty Joe was laughing in the driver's seat next to her. He stopped the truck and looked over at her. "Kinda takes you by surprise, doesn't it?"

Noonan reflexively put her hands over her chest and sucked in a deep breath, trying to steady her thudding heart. "What the hell is that thing?" she demanded. Then she glared angrily at Joe. "You knew it was there? Why didn't you *warn* me? Look what I did!"

"Hey, you spilled your coffee, not me." Joe stopped laughing, but he was unable to hide his grin. He searched under the seat for a rag and handed it to her. "If I had told you, it would have taken all the fun out of it." He dodged as she swatted at him with the rag. "C'mon, Annie, don't take it so seriously. Didn't you ever go into the funhouse when you were a kid?"

"Yeah," she murmured irritably, mopping up the coffee on her suit. "I ran screaming out of there when Dracula jumped out of the ceiling and never went to a carnival again. I've got a low threshold for being scared."

She looked out through the canopy windows again, examining the statue more carefully. The figure was made of discarded scraps of aluminum and steel and graphite-plastic polymer; the limbs were landing struts, the torso reconfigured parts of spacecraft fuselage, the head a battered half of an oxygen tank, all crisscrossed with pieces of rebars and wrapped with wiring. It was hauntingly beautiful . . . but nonetheless unsettling, even on second glance. "That's one of Yuri's works?" she asked. "He's got some kinda sick sense of humor."

"Don't feel alone," Joe confessed. "I just about dropped a load in my shorts the first time I saw that thing." He grabbed the gearshift and put the truck into drive again. "And if you think that's weird, wait'll you see what's up ahead."

The truck slowly trundled forward again on its huge wire-mesh wheels, towing behind it the tandem-trailer for the auxiliary fuel pump Mighty Joe intended to collect from Honest Yuri's junkyard. They were in the heavily cratered region northwest of Descartes Station, on the other side of Stone Mountain: wilderness area on the edge of the Descartes plateau, where hardly anyone ever ventured. Yet there were signs of habitation here. As they passed the statue, they could now see in the distance the glimmering lights of a couple of old-fashioned habitat modules. Between them and the base camp, vague forms were scattered like humps along the roadway, the distant lights reflecting dully off their surfaces.

As Noonan peered into the darkness, trying to make them out in the deep lunar night, Joe touched the node of his headset mike. "Hey, Yuri," he said. "It's Joe. I've got a visitor, like I told you. We've just passed the Sentry. ETA in five minutes. Okay?"

Noonan touched her own headset, expecting to hear a reply, yet heard only the patter of static. She was about to say something, but Mighty Joe reached out to the dashboard to click off the radio. "He knows we're here," he said softly. "Now let's see if he wants to—"

All at once, on either side of the roadway, lights suddenly flashed on; navigational beacons from old spacecraft, red and blue and white and gold, buried in the regolith and concealed behind rocks, forming a runway a half-mile long straight to the distant habitat. "I guess he does," Joe finished.

Annie glanced sharply at her boyfriend. "What does he want to do?"

Mighty Joe reached up and switched off the cab's interior lights, then the front headlights. Now the only light came from the varicolored beacons before them and the weak purple glow of the dashboard panels, which illuminated the mysterious smile on his face. Despite a continual blast of hot air from the floor vents, the pressurized cab seemed colder now. "Show off the Night Gallery," he replied in a hushed voice. "Enjoy. This is all for you."

She was about to make a nervous reply, but the words caught in her throat as she looked to her right. Bathed in the bright red glare of a beacon, a gargoyle crouched by the side of the road. Catlike legs of aluminum seemed to ripple with restrained fury, claws of junked RWS manipulators dug into the dry gray soil, dagger-toothed jaws of welded titanium snarled agape, round eyes of glass seethed murderously at her. A cyborg monster from her worst nightmares, dead metal yet uncannily alive . . . she was not comfortable again until it was past them.

Annie looked away, only to find another life-size statue on her left. In a dim gold sheen of light, a human-shaped robot—sticklike arms and legs with landing gear pods for its feet and manipulator claws for its hands, a narrow, boxy torso and skeletal hips, a sleek metallic skull with cantilevered jaws and multifaceted eyes thrown back on a high neck made of a single steel bar—was impaled on a crucifix made of a narrow mooncrete slab. Jesus Christ as a robot as a mortal in pain; the crystal eyes, reflecting the gold light, searched the star-filled sky in eternal suffering: *Father, why hast thou forsaken me?* It had been many years since Noonan had set foot in a church; seeing this, lines from ancient hymns echoed in her mind, and she suddenly remembered the horror she'd felt as a child when a rather sadistic Sunday School teacher told her the grisly details of the Crucifixion. Like the biblical event which inspired it, the sculpture was both beautiful and gut-wrenching.

"What the hell is—" She stopped herself, consciously amending her words. "What is this, Joe?"

Mighty Joe said nothing. The truck rolled past the Christ-robot. On the right, out of the corner of her eye, Annie could see a blue glow illuminating another sculpture. She didn't want to look at it . . . nonetheless, her eyes were drawn to the next work. . . .

"He makes these out of old spacecraft," Joe said. Annie almost jumped again at the unexpected sound of his voice, but he didn't seem to notice. "Much of the stuff that he salvages from space he refurbishes and sells back to the company. Even the *Dreamer*'s got some used parts from Honest Yuri's junkyard. The rest he brings out here, welds together into what you're looking at. . . ."

Two humanoid figures—lacking exact detail and androgynously shaped, yet undoubtedly a man and a woman—were copulating on the side of the road. Both were standing; she held on to his hips as her thighs thrust against his pelvis, he was balanced in the opposite direction, legs spread wide apart. His hands clasped the small of her back as she arched her spine backwards, her mouth perpetually agape in the first instant of an orgasm forever suspended in time and space. It resembled, in a strangely familiar way, the time she and Joe had first made love in the shower room. Annie blushed and giggled despite herself . . . .

"Like that, huh?" Joe said drily. "He paints, too, but that stuff gets sent back to Earth for exhibition. He's got a reputation for his astronomical art. But this . . . well, this is his private work. Only a few photos have been sent to Earth, and not many people from the base come out here. Yuri tends to be too weird for most folks. Maybe that's the way it should be. You shouldn't see what goes on in an artist's head. Sometimes it's a little scary. . . ."

Now, on the left: A small platoon of robotic soldiers, all sharp angles of metal and glass like a three-dimensional Picasso painting, stood at attention by the side of the road as if in perpetual review for a spectral general. At first each burnished soldier seemed exactly alike, but as the truck moved closer, Noonan could see subtle differences in each androidal form: a slouch here, a stray piece of wiring there, a misshapen head which seemed to be discreetly checking the polish on its boots. Ten-*hut!*

Annie watched the soldiers pass by them. In the red glow of the beacons, for the first time, she could perceive the vague forms of other, half-visible sculptures set back from the roadway. There were more statues lurking out there in this airless, lightless gallery of the night; other erotic dreams, other forgotten nightmares, other monsters and martyrs and phantom armies. She had the urge to make Mighty Joe stop the truck, to allow her to put on her helmet and gloves, to make him depressurize the cab and guide her through this strange landscape. At the same time, she was frightened of what else she might find out there. Things which no person—no *sane* person, at least—should ever see.

Joe seemed to be reading her mind. "Have you ever checked the map of this area?" She shook her head. "The old Apollo 16 landing site is right over there," he continued. "Yuri took me out to see it once."

"Did he . . . uh, use some of that stuff to . . . ?"

"For the sculptures? No, he's got the place perfectly preserved." He chuckled. "It's incredible. The old LEM descent stage, all the experiment packages, even the rover . . . right where they were left behind. There's not even a footprint around it which wasn't made by John Young or Charlie Duke. He went back and raked over the ones which other folks have made since then. Not even Tranquillity Base is so well-kept." He smiled again. "That's why he chose this particular place. Says there's a lot of great power in these hills."

They were almost at the habitat now. She could make out the tilted rows of the solar collectors and a communications dish within a tangled lot strewn with rubbish and junk: half-disassembled OTV's, stripped-down satellites, the huge cylindrical form of what looked like an old third-stage rocket booster. Beyond the habitat she could make out the hulking mass of Honest Yuri's spacecraft, squatting on its tripod landing gear. Near the edge of the junkyard was a final sculpture: a single anthropomorphic form, a hunchback with his right arm raised straight forward to the road. His right hand was curled into a gnarled, wiry fist, except for the upraised middle finger. Sort of a no-welcome mat, she guessed. Or a gesture of defiance. "Why are you telling me this?" she asked.

Mighty Joe stopped talking. He looked at her appraisingly before he grabbed the gearshift and pulled it back to neutral. "I dunno," he said. "Maybe I'm just trying to prepare you for meeting Yuri."

He switched on the interior lights again, then unbuckled his harness and reached behind his seat for the shelf where his helmet and gloves rested. Noonan hesitated, then unbuckled herself and reached for her own gear. "Do you take all your girlfriends out here?" she asked.

Joe favored her with a gentle smile. "Got no other girlfriends, babe." Then his smile faded. "Yuri and I . . . well, we understand each other and we get along, but I'm not ready to call us friends. Just keep your mouth shut and follow my lead, okay?"

Noonan raised an eyebrow. "Mad genius type, huh?"

"Yeah." Joe pulled on his gloves. "He's a genius. And he might be mad."

Mighty Joe was surprised: Yuri had cleaned up the place since the last time he had been here. On his previous visit, two months ago, the floors had been littered with discarded sketchbook pages and blotched with oil paint; the counters and chairs had been buried beneath paper plates, logbooks, and welding torches, and the head had smelled as if one of Yuri's gargoyles had crawled in there to die. Just before they opened the airlock, Joe had warned Annie not to say anything about Honest Yuri's sloppy housekeeping ("Breathe through your mouth if you think it'll help"). Once inside, however, he found the two habitat modules as shipshape as one could reasonably expect of a hermit artist's domicile. Cluttered, yes—for all of Yuri's skill with scrap-metal sculpture, it had apparently never occurred to him to build a couple of extra shelves—but at least it no longer looked like the Studio That Time Forgot. Yuri must have gone on a cleaning jag recently.

Yuri himself was nowhere in sight. Holding their helmets and gloves in their hands but still wearing their hardsuits, Joe and Annie stood in the narrow entryway just beyond the airlock and looked around. "Maybe he's out making another sculpture," Noonan whispered. She studied a poster-print of Monet's "Poplars (Autumn)," which was magnetically tacked above the kitchen counter and nodded appreciatively. "At least he's got good taste."

"Yeah, well, wait'll you see his collection of *Penthouse* centerfolds," Joe murmured. "He's got to be here, because he turned on the gallery lights." He raised his voice and yelled, "Hey, Yuri!"

In reply, a voice barked from the lateral hatch leading to the adjacent module: "Here!" A pause, then: "In the studio! Leave your stuff at the door!"

Mighty Joe raised his eyebrows. Another change in attitude; Honest Yuri usually never invited first-time visitors into his studio. Either it had skipped his mind that Joe had brought a stranger with him, or Yuri was getting a little more mellow with age. Or maybe the isolation is finally getting to him, Joe thought as he laid his helmet and gloves down on top of a pile of oversized art books. He might be hungry for company, just for once. . . .

They ducked their heads and Joe led Annie through the connector sleeve into the second module. Once it had been a lab module, but Yuri had removed most of the fixtures and even a few bulkheads to transform it into a combination garage and studio. One end was dominated by scrap metal, bits and pieces of half-assembled electronics, tools, and torches; the other half was covered with paint-splattered tarps on which lay dozens of cans of oil paint, all imported at considerable expense from Earth. Parked on a large easel at the rear end of the room was a half-finished moonscape; it looked like a view of a sunrise over the Night Gallery. More paintings were stacked upright in the corner: astronomical art which, one day, would grace the walls of the private galleries in Leningrad and New York, where Yuri's work was sold at outrageous prices.

A tall, gaunt figure in a soiled white smock was bent over a workbench in the garage half of the room, back turned to them as they entered. A welder's mask was pulled down over his face, and white-hot sparks shot from an unseen object on which a mini-torch was being directed, emitting a harsh high whine as acetylene coaxed metal into place. The figure was concentrating wholly on his work; he didn't turn until Mighty Joe, grinning hugely, cupped his hands to his mouth and shouted, "Yuri!"

Honest Yuri jerked erect, half-turned to peer at them through the opaque visor, then quickly shut down the torch and ripped off his gloves. "Joe!" he yelled heartily as he shoved back his mask and stalked across the room to greet them. "Good to see you again!"

Before Mighty Joe could react, Yuri grabbed him in a Russian-style bear hug, kissing both cheeks and slapping his back with his big, callused hands . . . and then, as Annie tentatively raised her hand to offer him a courteous, conventional handshake, Yuri pounced on her in the same way, including the kisses and the back slaps, as if she were an old friend whom he had not seen in months. If Honest Yuri had cleaned up his living quarters, he had certainly not extended the same care to his appearance. He had let his hair and beard grow out again, and it was difficult to tell which was more filthy, his hands or his teeth. The last time Joe had seen him, Yuri had resembled Peter the Great; now he looked like Rasputin the Mad Monk.

Noonan looked as if she had just been licked by an over-friendly stray dog. Although she turned a little green, she didn't say anything, much to Joe's relief. He had forgotten to tell her how mercurial Honest Yuri's moods could be. Mighty Joe grinned. He wondered how many eccentrics like Honest Yuri she had encountered before.

"Come over here!" Yuri said, backing away from Noonan and excitedly waving them to the workbench. "Something for you to take back to the base with you when you return! A gift!" As Yuri whirled around, Joe shot a querying glance at Annie. She gave him a completely blank look, although her mouth was twitching at the corners.

A life-size bust, cast from pieces of scrap steel, rested on a polished aluminum pedestal. The sculpture was abstract enough that it lacked fine details, but it was apparently of an elderly, bearded man. It was beautiful, and entirely meaningless to both Joe and Annie. Yuri posed next to it proudly, hands tucked into the pockets of his smock, head smugly tilted back. He raised an eyebrow and waited expectantly for a response.

"Umm . . . pretty neat, Yuri," Joe said. Still Yuri waited. "Looks great," he added. Yuri's eyebrow arched just a little higher, but he said nothing. The pilot shrugged. "Who is it?" he asked.

Suddenly, Yuri's temperament changed entirely. The smile left his face, the twinkle escaped from his eyes; he hunched his shoulders slightly and glowered at Joe; then his dark eyes swept to Noonan. "Surely your companion has a better eye than you," he said, fixing Annie with his baleful gaze.

"Uhhh . . ." Noonan glanced anxiously at the bust, then at Yuri, then at the bust again. "You? A self-portrait?"

Yuri's eyes clamped shut. His hands wadded into fists inside his pockets and he muttered something in Russian under his breath which was undoubtedly obscene. Then he took a slow breath and looked back up at them. "René Descartes," he said with slow, drawling contempt. "The French philosopher-scientist after whom your base has been named." He turned his head and looked at the sculpture. "I thought it might decorate your miserable rec room . . . but for all I know, the idiots there might think it's some movie star."

There was a long moment of uncomfortable silence. "Sorry, Yuri," Joe said apologetically. "Didn't mean to insult you." Annie looked suitably chastened.

Yuri sighed. "I'll get over it. I suppose you're here for the fuel pump." He picked up the bust and carelessly shoved it into Mighty Joe's hands, then walked past him and Noonan to the connector sleeve. "It's out back. I'll get one of the robots to load it onto your truck for you."

Before he ducked through the sleeve, he peered over his shoulder and added, "That brewery system you ordered is ready, too. I'll have it loaded as well." Then he disappeared into the adjacent module, leaving Joe red-faced and Annie gaping at him.

"The *brewery system* you ordered?" she repeated. "Did I hear that right? A *brewery system*? As in . . . ?"

"As in homemade beer," Joe quietly admitted. "Yeah, you heard right. I asked him a couple of months ago to put one together to replace the still that the company tore out of here." He grinned sheepishly and shrugged. "They don't call it moonshine for nothing, sweetheart."

He started walking toward the sleeve, but Noonan planted herself in front of him, throwing up her hands to stop him. "No no no no no no," she said, shaking her head vigorously. "René Descartes' head, yes, but you're not bringing back a still. You know the new rules. . . ."

"New rules are just the same as the old rules. Just a matter of hiding it a little better this time, that's all." He looked down at her and let out his breath. "Look, darlin', it's already bought and paid for. I'm not about to just leave it out here, for chrissakes!"

"Uh-huh. And I expect we're just going to wheel into the base and unload it in front of Lester's and Quick-Draw's noses." Her eyes widened in mock innocence. "Still? What still? It's one of Yuri's weird sculptures . . . 'Ode to a Shot Liver.' "

"Well, actually, I was planning to drop it off at the massdriver on the way in. Tycho said he'd hide it in an equipment locker till we found a place in the base to set it up."

"Ohhhh . . ." Annie nodded her head in cynical agreement. "So now we have to trust our jobs to Tycho. Listen, Joe, I don't think . . ."

"That's right. You don't think." Joe angrily pushed past her, carrying the heavy bust toward the hatch. "Listen. It goes back with us and that's the end of it. Now let's get going. This fucking thing weighs a ton and a half."

"Good. I hope you drop it on your foot." She fell into step behind him, adding under her breath, "I'm going to cold-cock you for this, I swear to God."

In the next compartment, Honest Yuri had pushed some art books out of a chair and was seated in front of a computer terminal, typing instructions into the AI system that controlled the cargo robot. "The pump and the brewery gear will be on your truck by the time you get outside," he said without looking up. "I'd invite you to have some coffee, but I have to get back to my work now. I have a new painting to complete before Uchu-Hiko buys this place and kicks me out."

Mighty Joe carefully placed René Descartes on the floor by the airlock hatch and picked up his gloves. "That's not a fore-gone conclusion, Yuri," he said as he shoved his left hand into a gauntlet and locked down the wrist joint. "We're getting the production quota up again. The Korean project is right on sched-ule. I don't think . . ."

"That's correct," Yuri shot back impatiently. "You don't think." Joe winced, remembering that he'd just leveled this same unkind comment at Annie. "If the Japanese want something," Yuri continued in a condescending tone, "they're going to get it. That includes this base. Skycorp's going to sell you and me and your girlfriend, too, and there's nothing you can do about it."

He looked up from his keyboard. "Did I tell you that a wealthy art collector in Nagasaki has offered to buy the Night Gallery? Hmm? Five million dollars. He wants to place it in the rock garden behind his country retreat."

Annie paused in putting on her own gloves. "Are you going to sell it to him?"

Yuri's eyes went to her face. All of a sudden, he looked less like Peter the Great or Rasputin than an insecure artist, salvaging space junk while trying to pursue his vision in a lonely land. "What do you think I should do?" he said softly. "Five million dollars could buy me a lot of bronze instead of some beat-up pieces of aluminum. And I can't stay here forever."

Yuri looked away again, staring at the Renoir poster tacked above the work station. "I'll have to go home sooner or later." He closed his eyes for a second, then looked at Annie again. "Did you like my Night Gallery?"

Annie thought about it for a few seconds. "Yes," she said at last, with utter sincerity. "It frightened me . . . but it's the most beautiful thing I've seen on the Moon."

Then, impulsively, she walked to him, bent over, and kissed him on the cheek. "Thank you," she whispered in his ear.

He nodded his head gravely as she backed away. There was

another long moment of silence. "Yuri," Joe asked quietly, "when was the last time you sent your dosimeter to Monk for a check?"

Yuri said nothing for a minute. He stared straight ahead at the green type on his computer screen. "Take Mr. Descartes back to the base," he said finally. "Find a good place for him. It's a gift . . . and so is the brewer. No charge."

Mighty Joe looked down at the floor. "Thanks, Yuri," he mumbled. Then he suddenly looked up as a suspicious thought crossed his mind. "Hey, that pump works okay, doesn't it?"

Yuri's head whipped around. Yuri the tortured artist was gone and Rasputin was back. "Yes!" he yelled. "It *works*! Now go! I have art to make!"

They were in the truck again, driving back through the Night Gallery, with the fuel pump and other gear lashed down on the tandem-trailer, before Annie put forth the thought that had been bothering her. "Joe," she asked, "what did you mean about the dosimeter?"

Mighty Joe didn't answer at once. His hands gripped the steering column as he gazed straight ahead, ignoring the Night Gallery statues on either side of the trail. "Think about it a second," he said at last. "Look at this place and ask yourself how much time he's spent out on EVA, building these things."

Noonan glanced through the window at the statues of the phantom army. "Out here?" she asked. "Well, wouldn't he bring them into the studio and assemble them there?"

"Did you see an airlock big enough for any of this stuff?" he snarled. Annie jerked back, startled by the force of his question. "They weren't made in there! Do you think he just putters around in his studio all day? Chrissakes, Annie, he—!"

Joe stopped himself. He sighed and waited a few seconds for his rage to pass. "The Night Gallery was built right where you see it," he continued in a calmer tone of voice. "That's the only way he could do it. And not just during the night, either, and not just for a few hours at a time. Now think about it. How much radiation exposure do you think he's received over the last couple of years, working like this? How many REMs you think Yuri's collected?"

She didn't have to think about it for very long. At Descartes Station, at least, there was Monk Walker to keep track of everyone's suit dosimeters, to make certain that no one exceeded

OSHA standards for beta and gamma-ray exposure. At Descartes, at least, moondogs on EVA went straight from the ready-room to the vehicles or the Dirt Factory or the mass-driver plant; no one stayed out on the surface, with only their hardsuits between them and the radiation, for very long. But you can't do that if you're assembling the Crucifixion from pieces of scrap metal. The hours, the long hours . . .

She buried her face in her hands. "Oh, my God . . ." she whispered. "Cancer."

"If he doesn't have it now," Joe said, "he'll have it soon. And he won't do a thing about it either. If he tells anyone . . . if he shows Monk his dosimeter . . . they'll make him leave."

He was silent for a few moments. He listened to Annie quietly sobbing in the seat next to him; then he angrily slapped his fist against the dashboard. "God damn you," he said. "Stubborn son of a bitch."

They said very little to each other during the long ride home.

o
o
o
o
o
o
o
o
o
o
o

The Importance of Ice (Video.2)

(From High Enterprise: A History of the Private Space Industry*; Simon & Schuster Hypertextbooks (version 3.1), New York, 2031).*

(SCREEN: a Japanese rocket lifting off from a launch pad; a mock-up of a small space probe; images of the first American and Soviet lunar probes; an animated schematic diagram of the trajectory of Japan's first lunar probe on its way to the Moon.)

SCROLL: The second era of lunar exploration began on January 24, 1990, when Japan's Institute of Space and Aeronautical Sciences launched its Hiten spacecraft to the Moon from the Kagoshima Space Center on the island of Kyushu *(see Chap.1).* The launch of the small, unmanned probe was only barely noticed by the general public of the United States and the Soviet Union, the two global superpowers which had formerly been the only nations to send men and machines to the Moon. Yet the importance of the event was distinctly felt by the space community of the U.S., the U.S.S.R., and the European Common Market, all of whom thought that the Moon somehow belonged to them, yet were uncomfortably aware of the rapid strides Japan was making in space exploration. Suddenly, this complacency was disturbed; the idea that the world's largest economic per-capita nation was sending its first probe to the Moon was unsettling, at the very least. *Press "enter," please.*

(SCREEN: Neil Armstrong climbing down the ladder of the Apollo 11 LEM; President George Bush making a speech at the Smithsonian Institution; a session of the U.S. House of Representatives; a session of the Japanese Diet.)

SCROLL: Yet the launch of the Hiten probe, as seminal as it was at the time, was only the third-most important event of the era. Six months earlier—on July 20, 1989, the twentieth anniversary of the Apollo 11 landing—U.S. President George Bush announced during a ceremony on the steps of the National Air and Space Museum that the long-range goal of the revived United States space program would be to establish bases on the Moon and, eventually, on Mars *(See Chap.2)*. Despite criticism that the new Space Exploration Initiative ignored fiscal practicality— at a time when the United States was dealing with a staggering fiscal deficit, it was estimated that such a program would cost more than five hundred billion dollars over the next thirty-five years—the realization was dawning on governmental and private-enterprise decision makers in the West that space exploration was necessary to maintain a technological lead over its rivals in the East, as well as a means of developing alternate energy sources to free the U.S. from dependence on foreign oil. The first era of lunar exploration had been brought about as the result of a political "cold war" between the U.S. and the Soviet Union; the second era was begun by economic friction between the West and the East, and by the harsh lessons driven home by Gulf War I in 1991. *Press "enter," please.*

(SCREEN: a meeting during one of the "Case For Mars" conferences in Boulder, Colorado; diagrams and sketches of advanced rocket engines, space shuttles, spacesuits, lunar landers; pictures of science fiction writers; movie stills; the huckster room of a World Science Fiction Convention; the exterior of the Arthur D. Little Company headquarters in Cambridge, Massachusetts.)

SCROLL: Yet even the Bush Administration's recommitment of the United States to manned interplanetary exploration, in the long run, was overshadowed by theoretical work being done by space scientists around the world. In labs and offices, new technologies were being quietly explored by the next generation of dreamers, both in public and private circles. A whole new batch of basic-research scientists and rocket engineers and policy analysts—the kids who knew Peenemunde only as an item of interest from history texts, who had been weaned on *Star Trek* and who had read science fiction novels by flashlight under the bedcovers—were now huddled together in places as diverse as SF fan conventions *(See Appendix.1)*, campus beer-and-burger hangouts, and the industrial think-tanks of the Rand Corporation and the Arthur D. Little Company. There were looking for ways, by hook or by crook, to get people back to the Moon. *Press "enter," please.*

(SCREEN: a chunk of ice; a frosted glass beer stein; still-photos of Watson, Murray, and Brown; an animated map of the Moon, rotating to display first the north, then the south, lunar poles; simulation of a comet striking the Moon.)

SCROLL: In time, they found just what they needed: ice. When they located, in the dry depths of space, that same substance which encrusted the outsides of their beer mugs, they also found one of the most important resources of the reconquest of the Moon. The possible prescence of permaice in the Moon's polar regions was first postulated in 1961 by scientists Kenneth Watson, Bruce C. Murray, and Harrison Brown *(See Chap.1)*. They realized that the deep craters at the ''top'' and ''bottom'' of the Moon were never exposed to daylight. These permanently shadowed regions, therefore, could function as cold traps, collecting frozen water and carbon dioxide which might accumulate there. Thus, scientists theorized, if ancient comets had indeed collided with the Moon in its prehistory, ice sprayed out from the comets might have been buried deep beneath the regolith at the poles, never to have been evaporated by sunlight. *Press ''enter,''* please.

(SCREEN: Apollo astronauts walking on the lunar surface; Surveyor and Lukod probes in orbit above the Moon; spectrographic maps of the Moon; the outside of the SSI's offices in Princeton, New Jersey; artist's depictions of lunar mining operations; animation of comets moving through the Oort cloud.)

SCROLL: The polar-permaice theory, though, remained largely ignored during the Apollo explorations. Spectrographic and geological mapping of the poles was never accomplished by the American and Soviet probes that visited the Moon in the 1960's and early 1970's. Indeed, the question might have lain dormant except as an item of arcane astrophysical interest had it not been for the research of the nonprofit space research group, the Space Studies Institute *(See Chap.2)*. SSI researchers realized that a need for water had to be satisfied before large-scale lunar mining could be started, and although harvesting comets from the Oort cloud which passed through the inner solar system was the obvious solution, the technological capability of rendezvousing with these relatively rare comets was impractical, at least for the near-term. On the other hand, transporting vast amounts of water from Earth was economically daunting. SSI began to look elsewhere and, in the late 1980's, it rediscovered the old Watson-Murray-Brown theory of lunar permaice. *Press "enter," please.*

(SCREEN: a model of the SSI Lunar Prospector; footage of its launch from the Baikonur cosmodrome; model of the NASA Lunar Observer; footage of its launch aboard a rocket from Cape Canaveral; diagram of the Moon's north pole; orbital footage of Byrd Crater; Admiral Richard Byrd at the North Pole; diagram of subsurface permaice deposits at Byrd Crater.)

SCROLL: in the 1990's, two unmanned missions were sent to the Moon. First, the SSI's Lunar Prospector—a low-cost package containing a spare Apollo spectrometer donated by NASA and funded by several American companies—was launched from the U.S.S.R. by a Molniya rocket. The SSI's lunar probe became the first private-industry extraterrestrial probe in history (although Japan's Hiten was privately funded, it was conducted under the aegis of a government science agency). Three years later, NASA's more sophisticated Lunar Observer was launched by a Delta rocket from Cape Canaveral, but by then its most interesting mission was to confirm the findings of the cut-rate SSI probe. The Watson-Murray-Brown theory was correct; permaice existed within the regolith of the Moon's northern polar region—ironically enough, within the crater named after the legendary polar explorer, Admiral Richard Byrd. No such wellspring was found on the south pole, but one was enough: a source of lunar water had been located. *Press "enter," please.*

(SCREEN: animated diagram of the lunar north pole; NASA's first base in the Descartes highlands: the digging of the first well at Byrd Station; orbital photos of the Skycorp permaice extraction facility.)

SCROLL: This was the most important event of the 1990's in regard to the industrial development of the Moon. It meant that if a well could be established at Byrd Crater, the moonbase would have a relatively inexpensive source of water. Nature had made a nice deal with mankind, but as is the case in any deal, there was some fine print at the bottom of the contract: no one knew exactly how much permaice existed in Byrd Crater, or how long the supply would last. The answer to that tricky question was not answered until 2024, long after Skycorp had established its Byrd Crater Permaice Extraction Facility. *Key next chapter, please.*

15. Mighty Joe's Jinx

The lights on the airlock's status panel turned green; Lester shoved down the lockbar and pushed open the heavy steel hatch. As he removed his helmet in the antechamber, he heard the metronomic *clicka-click-click* of Butch Peterson's fingers on the computer keyboard in the lab module. "Find anything yet?" he called out.

"Maybe," she murmured distractedly as she continued working at the computer. Riddell was about to ask if she could help him out of his suit, but noticed that her own hardsuit was buckled into one of the racks. Nobody had been in the ice station's control module to help *her* out, so why should he demand assistance? This was a matter of professional pride. Lester backed into the second rack, buckled the shoulder grommets, then slid back the recessed cover on his chestplate and flipped the toggles which popped the rear access hatch. Can't be that difficult, he thought, as he ducked his head through the neck collar and began to pull his arms out of the suit's sleeves. Just a simple matter of co-ordination . . .

Nonetheless, it took fifteen minutes of sweating, tugging, and heaving to extract himself from the hardsuit. It was rather like trying to squirm out of a full-body cast; by the time he was done, Lester had pulled a muscle in the back of his neck and had banged the top of his skull on a bulkhead. Finally, though, he was standing in his nylon long johns in the antechamber, freezing his ass off in the unanticipated cold while he disconnected his coolant and urine-collection tubes.

Byrd Station's habitat modules were unoccupied most of the time; although the control and lab modules remained pressurized for the benefit of supply crews from Descartes, the thermostat was kept at 45°F. to keep the instruments inside from freezing. And there wasn't even any clothing in the anteroom for visitors to slip on over their hardsuit undergarments. Rubbing his arms and blowing little puffs of steam, Lester made a mental note to have the next resupply team bring a couple of pullovers up here; the joint was cold as hell, and neither he nor Butch was wearing enough clothing.

He walked into the next room, and suddenly he didn't mind that little annoyance anymore. Butch Peterson was seated cross-legged in a chair in front of the main computer station, intently studying the flatscreen through her glasses. She, too, was wearing only her long johns, but on her they fitted like a second skin. Her long black hair, braided into beaded corn rows, fell exotically around her slender shoulders. For the past few weeks, Riddell had tried to distance himself from Peterson's good looks; this time, though, she unconsciously exuded the sensuality of a nubile teenager in a string bikini.

"Have a little trouble there?" she asked, not looking away from the screen but faintly smiling just the same.

"Umm?" he said, trying to unstick his tongue from the roof of his mouth. "Oh, *that*! No, no, no. None at all. No problem."

Butch glanced around at him, giving him a look of don't-kid-me amusement. "Well, maybe a little," he admitted. "How did you manage to . . . ?"

"Get out of my suit? Try working as a fashion model for ten years. You learn to do stuff with your body that makes limbo-dancing look easy." Then, as if the long johns weren't enough, she swiveled around in her chair and, with the exhausted sigh of someone who had been staring at a screen for a couple of hours, stood up, reached back with her arms, and stretched until it looked as if her lithe body were about to rip through the seams of the undergarment.

Lester wondered if he was going to start drooling. Cut that out, he reprimanded himself. He swallowed and quickly looked away, focusing on the lab bench behind the computer station. A rack of test tubes held thawed specimens from the deep-core samples she had taken shortly after they had arrived at Byrd Station. While he and Mighty Joe had made themselves busy outside, pumping ice water from Byrd Station's holding tanks into the LRLT's cargo module, Butch had been in here, checking the satellite data she had collected at Descartes Station against the raw data Byrd Station's computers had automatically collated and her own core samples from the underground permaice deposits. He gently picked up one of the tubes at random and peered at it; the water in the tube was cloudy, with fine sediment floating in the water and more lying on the bottom. "Did you get this before it went through the filtration system?" he asked.

Peterson glanced at the tube in his hand. "No," she said quietly. "That's what came through the filters." She paused, then added unnecessarily, "It's what we're taking back to Descartes with us."

At once, all the horny thoughts fled from Riddell's mind. The well at the Byrd Station Permaice Extraction Facility worked on a fairly simple set of mechanics. The permaice which the artesian-style well penetrated was melted *in situ*, a little at a time to prevent vacuum boil-off and evaporation, and pumped into a heated holding tank, drawing it through a series of porous filters which sifted out the contaminants. Of course, the filters couldn't separate all the dirt; microscopic particles were expected to seep through, and they were later distilled from the water back at Descartes Station. But *this* water looked as if it had come out of a roadside ditch, not from the filtered water normally brought home by the long-range crop dusters.

"Before you ask," Peterson said, "I checked the filters and the pumps. The pumps are up to par. The filters are ready to be changed again, sure, but they shouldn't be, because according to the logbook they were replaced by the last supply crew which came up here."

Riddell shot her a disbelieving look. "They were changed last *month*?" The filters had a combined efficiency of at least four months. "But this stuff . . ."

"That's the stuff which came through the filtration system," Butch insisted, pointing at the tube. "And this . . ." She picked up another test tube from the rack and held it before his face. "This is the stuff that comes straight from the permaice pack itself."

The liquid in the second tube looked as if it had come from a sewer; matte-black, almost brackish with heavy particulate, it resembled swamp water from the Okefenokee. Lester took the second tube, uncorked the stopper and passed it under his nose; a pungent odor like discharged gunpowder made his nostril hairs want to curl up and die. He made a face and held the tube away. "Uh-oh," he said softly.

"Uh-oh is right." Peterson took the tubes from his hands and placed them back in the rack. "If it makes you feel any better,

I took a second batch from the secondary ice pack. The particle concentration and turbulence came out close to normal standard. But that second pack, as you know, has nowhere the volume of the primary pack. It's been treated only as a reserve supply. Are you catching my drift so far?''

"I'm afraid I am." Riddell turned and looked at the bar-graphs displayed on the computer screen. "What do the monitors have to say?"

Butch leaned against the back of the chair, looking down at the floor as she absently reached under her braids and kneaded her neck with her hands. Again, it was an undeliberately sexy pose on her part, but right now Lester was hardly in the mood. "I could go into gross detail," she continued, "but I'll cut right to the chase and spare you the geophysical gobbledy-gook. The computer confirms everything that's in those tubes. The permaice is drying up, Les. In fact, we're close to rock bottom."

"Oh, shit."

"Tell me about it." She sighed, shook out her hair, and looked straight at him. "The primary well . . . my best guess is that we'll be able to come up here one more time for some of this dishwater. Maybe two trips if we stretch our consumption. If we open the second well and start using the reserves, we've got somewhere between eight and twelve months' supply. Fourteen or fifteen months max if we tightly ration it. Then we're bone dry. Kaput."

Riddell took a deep breath and let it out. He looked down and found himself gazing at her breasts, which seemed to surge against the tight fabric of her undergarment; he could see the coffee-colored areolae of her nipples through the cloth, and he felt his face growing warm. Hell of a time to be noticing *that*. He glanced away from her again. "Are you sure?" he asked, then quickly shook his head. "No, no . . . if you say you're certain . . ."

"I'm going to dump all the files onto a disk and take them back to Descartes for analysis," Butch said. "Maybe I'll come up with something different, but I wouldn't bet on it if I were you." She hesitated. "To give you a straight answer, though . . . yeah, I'm pretty certain. And I might even be sugar-coating my last guesstimate. Counting the reserves, I'd realistically give it eight or nine months, tops."

"Terrific." Lester watched as she sat down in the chair again and began to save the files on a CD-ROM diskette. This was a potential disaster; he should be more upset than he already was. Besides that, he had more things to do outside before they left Byrd Station.

Yet, in spite of all that, he found that the thing he wanted to do most of all was to linger in the control module with Butch Peterson. Great. Makes a lot of sense. Here's a man crawling out of the Gobi desert on his hands and knees, deliriously gasping through his parched throat, "Sex . . . sex . . . sex. . . ."

"When you go out there," she continued, not looking away from her work, "you better tell Joe to top off the water tanks in the cargo module. We're going to need every drop we can get. Once the well starts going empty, there's going to be some boil-off, so we might as well grab it while we can."

"Okay. Sure." Lester hesitantly laid his hands on the back of her chair, looking over her shoulder at the screen and fighting the urge to take one of her soft braids and gently unravel it between his fingers. "Uh . . . you need any help in here?"

She shook her head. "No, that's okay. I'm just going to do this and download the current data from Hawking, then . . ." She stopped, and then half-looked over her shoulder at him. "What's the matter, Lester? Never seen a woman in her BVD's before?"

Lester felt all the blood in his face rush down to his feet. He coughed uncomfortably. "Sorry," he murmured. "Guess it was kinda obvious, wasn't it?"

Butch favored him with a sultry half-smile. "Doesn't matter to me. Not as long as you don't get any funny ideas."

Lester laughed . . . then, impulsively, he extended his forefinger and stroked the back of her neck. Peterson moved her neck out of the way, the smile disappearing from her face. "Like that one," she said. "If there was a cold shower available, I'd suggest that you go take one."

Riddell hurriedly removed his hand. *What the hell's gotten into you, pal?* he admonished himself. *The lady doesn't want or need this.* "I'll . . . um, go help Mighty Joe with the rest of the, um . . ."

"I'll be out in a few minutes." Her tone suggested that she had already forgiven and forgotten—at least for the time being. Lester turned and headed for the anteroom. Damn, he thought. *And I would have loved to see how she gets back into her suit. . . .*

• • •

"Okay, boys and girls, strap yourselves in and we'll be getting out of here." Still wearing his hardsuit, although he had removed the helmet and gloves, Mighty Joe Young gave his seat harness a final cinch, then reached out to the dashboard to power up the LRLT. Next to him in the co-pilot's chair, Lester automatically picked up the clipboard and pushed back a couple of pages on the checklist. "Don't need to worry about that," Joe said. "We've only been here a couple of hours, so everything's still configured for flight."

Lester raised an eyebrow as he replaced the clipboard in its slot. "Not exactly regulation, is it?"

Joe shrugged as he ran through the prelaunch routine of pressurizing the fuel tanks and arming the engines. "Maybe not, but it gets the job done just the same." He scratched at his beard and grinned at the general manager. "Don't fret. When you fly with me, you're flying with the best. But if you want to be helpful, you can double-check the cargo module to make sure she's clamped on nice and tight."

"Oh, Lester *always* wants to helpful," Butch Peterson said from the passenger seat behind Joe. "Isn't that right, Les?"

Lester shot a wary glance at her, which made Peterson giggle; Mighty Joe looked first at Riddell, then glanced at Peterson's reflection in the Plexiglas canopy in front of him. The scientist was hiding a wicked smile behind her hand, and the GM was pretending to study a status board on the right side of his seat. The flight compartment of the LRLT was about the size of a two-door economy car; very little of what went on inside could be kept a secret. Joe was about to make a comment, but decided to let it pass. Something had happened between the two of them while he had been loading the rest of the water into the LRLT's tanks . . . but whatever might or might not have occurred, it was none of his business.

"The module's secure," Lester said, ignoring Butch's jab. "Pressure nominal. No leakage."

"Okay then." Mighty Joe switched the electrical system from BATT. to MAIN, reset the guidance computer to MAN., toggled on the auto-sequence launch program and watched as idiot lights on the fuel tanks flashed from red to green. A low hum swept through the tiny cabin, signaling that the fuel tanks were pressurized; the VTOL thrusters and main engines were armed and ready. Through the windows, he could see the lights of the station reflecting off the modules and the tall, cylindrical tower of the well pump; around them rose the steep, dark walls of Byrd Crater. Joe couldn't wait to get out of there; despite the lights and the man-made artifacts, this had to be one of the most depressing places on the Moon.

He studied the flatscreen between him and Lester, then put his left hand on the attitude-control yoke and his right hand on the parallel throttles. "We're going for a ten-second countdown on my mark. Y'all set? Okay. Mark . . . ten . . . nine . . . eight . . ."

The Grumman LRLT-105 was a hybrid vehicle, a mutant among spacecraft. Too unstreamlined for effective use on Earth or Mars, not powerful enough for translunar orbital operations yet too powerful for short-range missions, it was principally designed for long-range operations which would take its four-person crew from one side of the Moon to the other. Long, slender and flat, the LRLT had a pressurized crew compartment in the front—including an aft-deck compartment containing four bunks and a miniature lab for extended missions—a double-truss strongback in the center which contained the separable, multifunction cargo module, and an oversized engine compartment in the stern, all of which was perched on four extendable landing legs. In short, it was a lunar version of the standard space shuttle design; although fuel-hungry, it was capable of transporting people and equipment on extended sorties into the hinterlands.

Normally, the LRLT flew above the lunar surface, skimming the tops of craters and mountains alike; hence its nickname "crop-duster." For supply missions between Descartes Station and Byrd Station, though, the standard flight profile was more exotic. The LRLT rose into vertical ascent, using the VTOL launch thrusters on the underside of its hull; when the craft had climbed to proper altitude, the pilot would tilt the nose slightly upwards, then simultaneously disengage the VTOL's and kick in the main engines. It was a difficult maneuver, but it would boost the LRLT into a suborbital arc which would take it thirty miles above the lunar surface and sling it around the limb of the Moon, matching gravitational pull against engine-thrust to send the crop-duster toward its targeted destination. It wasn't the smoothest of rides, either—those who experienced an LRLT slingshot often compared it to a ride on an amusement park tilt-a-whirl—but it effectively reduced the flight time for translunar missions from several days to a handful of hours. So a return trip from Byrd

Crater to the Descartes plateau was a relatively quick journey, if all went well.

From the instant that the red warning lights flashed across the engine status board, less than a minute after the VTOL thrusters were cut and the big Pratt & Whitney main engines were engaged, Mighty Joe knew that everything wasn't going to go well.

"Heads up," Young said as the spacecraft lurched and the lights went from green to red. "We've got a problem."

"Hmm?" Riddell had been looking out the window during the takeoff and ascent, admiring the crescent Earth rising above the curving horizon. As an annunciator sharply buzzed, his eyes darted to the co-pilot's station. "What's going on?"

"We're losing velocity," Joe snapped, "Damn if I know why, but we are." He hurriedly slapped off the alarm, disengaged the autopilot, and grabbed the yoke. He glanced at the digital altimeter and felt his heart freeze. The LRLT's ascent had stopped at 27.4 nautical miles; as he watched, the numbers suddenly switched to 27.3, then 27.2, then 27.1.

"Losing altitude, too," he said, more calmly than he himself could believe. His eyes swept across the gauges, searching for the problem. "What the hell is . . . ?"

"We're *falling*?" From the back seat, Butch Peterson's voice rose on a high-pitched note of panic. Looking past their shoulders, she could see the horizon slowly climbing into view again. "You mean we're going *down*?"

"No shit, lady. I gotta be jinxed or something, I dunno." Mighty Joe's gaze landed on the flatscreen above the engine throttles, where a red warning bar was strobing above a line of cryptic numbers. "Aw, damn," he hissed as he checked the readout. "I was afraid of that. Loss of IPS ratio from the mains. We're overloaded in the cargo module."

"What does that mean?" Peterson demanded.

"Means we shouldn't have topped off the water tanks," Lester said. "Too much mass aboard for us to reach escape velocity. The mains can't handle the extra load." He immediately reached for his panel and flipped back the candy-striped cover above the emergency cargo-module jettison. "Okay, let's fire the pyros and . . ."

"*Cut it out!*" Mighty Joe's right hand slapped Lester's hand away from the switch. "This is my ship and nobody touches a thing without my say-so!"

"But if we ditch the load . . ."

Mighty Joe shot an angry look at Riddell. "The water's too valuable for us to dump," he snapped. "You said that yourself. And we're not out of options yet." He snapped a set of toggles on the engine board. "Brace yourselves," he commanded, grabbing a smaller pair of throttles below the main engine sticks. "I'm cutting in the auxiliary thrusters. Three . . . two . . . one . . ."

Lester and Butch barely had time to grab the armrests of their seats before Mighty Joe yanked down on the auxiliary thruster bar. The spacecraft shuddered like a drenched dog shaking off water. The altimeter stopped at 25.2 and the horizon steadied in the windows . . . then, slowly, the LRLT began to ascend again. "Okay, there we go," Joe whispered. "Climb, baby, climb. *Climb—*!"

There was a loud *bang*! and a violent impact which felt as if they were in a car that had been rear-ended by a Mack truck; several alarms went off at once as the LRLT suddenly careened sideways. "Sweet fucking Jesus!" Joe shouted. "Not *again*!"

His hands were all over the controls, simultaneously cutting off the auxiliary thrusters, silencing the alarms, grabbing the yoke and struggling it back into trim. Lester heard Butch scream behind them. He didn't look back because he couldn't; he was transfixed by the sight of the lunar landscape, which had now tilted sideways and was rushing up at them. "What happened?" he shouted.

"That fuckin' asshole Yuri gave me a fuckin' piece of bullshit auxiliary fuel pump, that's what happened!" Mighty Joe was fighting the yoke. "Look at the fuckin' board! The bastard blew and took out one of the fuckin' main fuel cells with it. Fuck, fuck, *fuck—*!"

Lester glanced at the console. Yep. Everything that Joe had interpreted from the myriad dials and readouts was true. "I guess that means we're fucked," he murmured.

"Couldn't have said it better myself, pal." Mighty Joe glanced again at Lester. "Don't even think about jettisoning the cargo module now. Won't do us any good. The angle is all wrong, and I don't want to risk the chance of that thing taking out the engine pod altogether."

Lester glanced at the altimeter—14.5 nautical miles and falling like a rock. "But if we lose the module . . ."

"And I'm telling you, it won't make any difference." Joe was hauling back on the yoke; his words came out as a taut growl. "We could get screwed even worse, 'cause the sucker could whiplash back and nail the tanks. Trust me on this one, man. We're going down, with or without the module. . . . " He had both hands wrapped around the yoke now. "I'm not out of tricks yet. I can still use the VTOL thrusters to put us down easy."

"Easy?" Lester shook his head. "Don't shit me, Joe. I used to be a pilot, too. I can tell you right now . . ."

"You want to try flying this thing, Les? Huh? You want me to hand this ugly fuck over to you?" Mighty Joe didn't look at him; his eyes were locked on the controls. "Tell me now, 'cause we're about to make a ditch."

Riddell didn't say anything. It had been many years since he had piloted a moonship down on his own . . . and, he had to admit to himself, he had never brought in a wounded bird, not even in his military career. And he had seen Mighty Joe bring home a crippled tug, just a few weeks ago. . . .

"I guess I'm going to have to trust you," Lester said reluctantly.

"Damn straight, bubba." Joe didn't move his eyes from the console. "Now make yourself useful and give us a Mayday."

Riddell could hear Peterson crying in the rear seat. Poor woman thought she was about to be splattered across a mile of the Moon. There was nothing he could do for her now, though. Lester pulled forward against his harness to reach across Mighty Joe's arms to the communications board; he switched on the radio as he tugged the neglected communications headset up from his neck. "Mayday! Mayday! This is LRLT One-Three-Zero. Mayday! LRLT One-Three-Zero from Byrd to Descartes, we're going down at . . ."

He quickly checked the little screen on the navaids computer. "Fifty-eight degrees north by nineteen degrees west, estimated crash point . . ."

"Don't say crash!" Mighty Joe snarled.

The superstition of pilots. Lester wasn't about to argue. "Estimated touchdown north-northwest of Aristotle Crater." Even as he said that, Riddell was counting their blessings; at least they were over a flat mare region, the Sea of Cold. If they were going down near the lunar north pole, this was the best place; better, certainly, than having to ditch in either the heavily cratered region north of Aristotle or in the Caucasus Mountain chain to the south. "This is LRLT One-Three-Zero, Mayday. Do you copy? Over."

Through the canopy windows, he could see the darkened moonscape looming closer. The gyroscope ball on the main console had steadied evenly between the white and black hemispheres, showing that Joe had flattened out the LRLT's angle of descent, but the altimeter said that they were a little less than a mile above the Moon. The black pit of a giant crater swam past them, looking like a shark's mouth reaching up to snap off their legs. Then, as a stretch of rugged hills was passed, the low flatlands of the Sea of Cold appeared before them. Christ, he thought, if the relay comsats are down . . .

LRLT One-Three-Zero, this is Descartes Traffic. The unruffled voice of the traffic control officer sounded like that of an angel. *Mayday received and understood. Crash point at fifty-eight north by nineteen west. Have you landed? Over.*

Lester almost broke into laughter. "No, dammit, we haven't landed!" he shouted. "We're going *down*!" He caught himself. Don't lose your shit, pal. "Acknowledged, Descartes," he said as calmly as he could. "We haven't landed yet. Bring emergency assistance to . . ."

Riddell was suddenly thrown back in his seat as Mighty Joe kicked in the VTOL thrusters. The LRLT's nose pitched upwards and Peterson screamed again; she was past the point of panic.

"Hang on kids!" Mighty Joe shouted. "It's going to be a bitch!"

Through the windows, Riddell could see the dark maw of Aristotle Crater in the far distance, across the gray volcanic plains of the Sea of Cold. He thought to look at the altimeter again, but all of a sudden he didn't want to know. What the fuck did it matter? They were going down hard and fast; who cared about the specifics at this point? In his ears, static was breaking up the comlink: *One-Three-Zero, do you . . . krrk . . . repeat, this is Descartes . . . krrrrkk . . . do you copy? . . .*

Mighty Joe was snapping more toggles as he held the yoke tight in his left fist. "Landing gear extended!" he hollered. "Lights on!" A bright swath of light swept out before the cockpit; gray dust, unsettled by the thrusters, swam before the cockpit. "Emergency beacon on! Hang on . . . hang on . . . *okay, here we go!*"

Lester stiffened in his seat, grabbed the armrest with all his strength, and sucked in his breath . . . and still it felt as if the crash would never happen. Hey, he thought, maybe it'll be a soft landing after all. Maybe we'll just . . .

The LRLT hit the ground and he was thrown forward against his harness, the wind knocked out of his lungs, as the cropduster skidded along the hard, ancient pumice. It felt as if the current Golden Gloves champ had nailed him in the solar plexus. As a tunnel of darkness closed in around him, the last thing he heard was the sound of alarms, rending metal, Butch screaming, Mighty Joe howling *"Fuuuuuuuuuuuccccck . . . !*

And that was it. He didn't have a chance to know whether he had lived or if he had died.

The Moon Moths
(Interview.5)

E. Quackenbush "Quack" Lippincott II; former Skycorp Chief of Lunar Rescue Operations.

Look, son, let me tell you . . . if there was a group which was more maligned and neglected up there, it was the LSR team. You know what they used to call us?

(Nods) Yeah, that's right. The Moon Moths. Because we were supposed to be uselessly flying around, doing nothing at all. That used to piss me off. It even got on our official mission patch. *(points to a framed embroidered patch on his office wall)* See that? A stupid-looking moth circling the Moon. I mean, I got used to people quacking around me when I was a kid, only because that was my name and my granddaddy's name and because I kinda think it's cute and so does my wife . . . but you know how much shit we used to get about having mothballs?

'Course you don't. But I'll tell you right now, Al, nobody ever called us moon moths to our faces when we came out to save their low-rent behinds from the middle of nowhere. We got our share of respect when the time came. But that still didn't make up for the fact that the LSR team was the most underrated operation on the Moon . . . and if not by the other moondogs, then at least by the goddamned company.

Let me give you some background first, okay? Skycorp didn't have an LSR team in place at Descartes until pretty late in the game, well after Byrd Station and Hawking Observatory were established. Nobody in Huntsville thought there was any real need for search-and-rescue operations. The logic—if you want to call it that—was that since most surface EVA's took place within a short distance of the base, if someone got into trouble all anyone had to do was radio a distress call back to MainOps and they could send out a rescue team. And since there were

217

emergency solar-flare shelters scattered within ten miles of the base, complete with transmitters and foodsticks and all that stuff, all anyone had to do was duck into one of those things. So Skycorp thought they had it covered. *(imitating a stuffy executive voice)* "Lost? Nobody gets lost on the Moon. They just get misplaced."

(Laughs) Now that's your typical brand of Huntsville logic, because anyone who's actually been on the Moon can tell you that search-and-rescue up there is no easy matter. But Skycorp managed to get away with it for a few years, and even though a couple of people actually died while lost close to the base . . . like that that writer-guy, Sam Sloane, back in '16 . . . just because there were no Donner expeditions the company thought they could get away without a permanent search-and-rescue operation. They claimed it wasn't necessary, but the fact of the matter is they just didn't want to spend any money on search-and-rescue.

Then Hawking Observatory was built out on the farside and, sure enough, it was only a matter of time before people got lost out in the sticks where there weren't any convenient shelters. As it happened, one of the construction teams which was establishing the VLF array got stranded all the way over on the back one-eighty. Their LRLT broke down . . . it had a major computer breakdown and it just wouldn't leave the ground . . . and seven men and women were almost asphyxiated before anyone found them. Kinda like a ran-low-on-the-air sort of thing, y'know what I mean? A couple of them lost fingers and toes to frostbite when the cabin heater died, but at least they managed to get out of there alive. The company might have ignored that incident as a fluke, but then the survivors had the gall to sue Skycorp for negligence. And it *was* negligence, I can tell you that for a fact. I was on the volunteer team that went out to rescue them, and we had to play it entirely by ear because there were no company procedures for us to follow.

Anyway, after these guys won a few million dollars in court, the bright lads in Huntsville decided that it was time to establish an LSR team at Descartes. Not full time, mind you . . . we still had other jobs to do at the base . . . but it became part of our contracted job descriptions that we were on-call for search-and-rescue missions. So every year, the company was obligated to have at least five persons on permanent standby at Descartes

Station as an LSR team . . . four with Air Force, Navy or Coast Guard training, along with the chief physician.

Even then, we had to fight every fiscal year for continued funding. Practically on our own, too, because that goddamn useless union of ours wouldn't back us up. I mean, it's no secret that ASWI was in the back pocket of the space companies, and since Skycorp considered lunar search-and-rescue to be "non-cost-effective," we had to take it upon ourselves to beg for the stuff we needed. Extra medical supplies and specialized computer software wasn't any real problem, but do you know what a hassle it was to get Skycorp to send up a third LRLT and a dedicated ambulance module? We almost had to threaten to sic the Vacuum Suckers on the company's board of directors before Huntsville finally contracted Boeing to build the third LRLT and the module. I swear, we had to make veiled threats about slashing the tires of Rock Chapman's Porsche to get us everything we wanted, that's how bad it was. *(laughs)* It was a good thing he didn't drive a Ford or we might not have had a bargaining chip.

Seriously, though, it was almost as difficult to get the company to install emergency long-range homing beacons on the rovers and LRLT's until we pointed out to them that, without such equipment, it was difficult as hell to find a craft which had gone down in the boonies. I mean, even if the lost crew is in radio contact with the LSR team, you can't count on someone among them knowing enough about basic astronomy to give you a stellar fix on their location . . . and don't talk to me about following tire-tracks, because that might work only if they're close enough to the base that they've taken a rover or a truck. And if the vehicle got lost in a place where there's lots of tracks, forget it pal, you'll never find 'em that way.

How often did we . . . ? *(laughs)* Mr. Steele, I won't try to con you about how frequently we had to go out. We were fortunate on that score. Search-and-rescue operations were rare enough that we often went for months before we got the call to go beat the bushes. When it happened, though, all you could do was hope that the lost party had enough air and battery power to last them until you showed, that their homing beacon was switched on, and that maybe—just maybe—they had sent out a reasonably accurate fix on their proximity, such as their geographic landmarks so that we could find them. Every time, man, it was touch-and-go. Touch-and-go all the way. You just made it up as you went along, that's all, no space hero stuff. Each time we went up we made sure we had enough coffee and sandwiches to keep us going, because it was rarely a matter of just flying out to Butthole Crater and finding someone on the first try. I mean, I used to be in the Coast Guard, and tracking down someone on the Moon was almost as bad as trying to locate a life raft on the high seas.

The big difference is, shipwreck victims on a life raft in the Atlantic have an unlimited supply of oxygen. Nobody in a wrecked spacecraft on the Moon has that sort of resource. Each time we went on a mission, I was always scared that we would get there *(holding up a thumb and forefinger just slightly apart)* . . . just a little too late.

But it never happened to us. Not once. Somehow, by God's grace, we always managed to find our people. *(chuckles)* At least before they started losing their fingers and toes, at any rate.

16. Specter

Lester unfolded the tripod of the last of the three portable lamps, knelt, and carefully placed its legs on the ground. Standing up again, he extended the three-foot bar, made sure that the lamp was balanced on the rocky soil so that it wouldn't tip over, and gave the Plexiglas dome on top a clockwise half-turn. Bright light sprang from the lamp, illuminating a circle about fifty feet in diameter; the cone of light almost reached that cast by the second lamp, placed near the port bow of the LRLT, and the first lamp, which was on the other side of the main engines.

He stepped back and looked over his work. The lunar transport was now encircled by a ring of lights that could not be mistaken by the Moon Moths for subsurface outgassing, the transient phenomenon that sometimes provided natural sources of illumination on the lunar surface. As long as night prevailed on the Sea of Cold, the lamps—which were carried in the equipment bay for routine EVA work and now served as the equivalent of highway flares—could be clearly seen by another LRLT which might fly over the crash site.

Darkness would not remain in this area for very much longer. Lester turned and looked south, past the nose of the LRLT where it had buried itself in the ground. Beyond the horizon, the first light of the rising Earth was just appearing; the distant rim of Aristotle Crater was already touched by a thin silver glow. Aristotle was only a few miles away. Looking at it, Riddell again felt relief. The crash had been rough—both he and Mighty Joe had been knocked cold by the impact—but at least they hadn't slammed into the crater wall. Such a crash would have surely destroyed the LRLT; all three of them would be crushed, burned corpses by now if that had happened.

"Any landing you can walk away from is a good one," he murmured to himself.

Pardon? Butch Peterson's voice said in his earphones. *What was that?*

"Nothing. Just thinking aloud." Butch didn't say anything, and Lester added, "Something they always say to you in flight school, usually just before you make your first solo. How are you making out in there?"

Well . . . He heard her sigh over the comlink. *Joe says the left side of his chest still hurts, so I think he's definitely got a cracked rib or two. I've given him some Demerol and made him lie down in back, but he keeps wanting to come up here.*

"Tell him to lie down and shut up," Lester said. It appeared that Mighty Joe had been the only one of them to suffer serious injury. The pilot had been wheezing and complaining of stabbing chest pains from the moment he had regained consciousness, but if it had been anything worse than broken ribs, they would have known by now. If Butch had shot him up with Demerol and put him in one of the bunks in the aft cabin, that was the best they could do for the time being. "What about the radio?" he asked.

Negative. I've tried the voice bands and also the data-relay frequency, to shoot back the stuff I got from the station just in case we— She stopped herself abruptly.

"Don't even think about it, kiddo," Lester said. "We're gonna get out of this, don't worry." He thought for a moment. "Ummm . . . keep working the frequencies, and if that doesn't work, see if you can get Joe to tell you where the circuit-breaker panel is located. Maybe the transponder augered out when we hit. Ask Joe, he'll tell you what to do."

Sure, Les. Butch didn't sound very encouraged. At least she was over the hysterical fit she had thrown on the way down. *When are you coming back in?*

"Gimme a few minutes," he replied. "I want to check the cargo module and make sure it survived. Keep the channel open if it makes you feel better. Okay?"

All right. Sure. There was another pause. *Ahh . . . just one more thing,* she said hesitantly. *I gotta go.*

"Huh? You want to go EVA?"

No, no, I don't want to do that. More hesitation. *I mean . . . I gotta go. You copy?*

"Aw, hell." Lester shook his head in his helmet. There was

a standard-issue spacecraft head located in the aft cabin, just beyond the bunks where Joe was lying. Like all zero g toilets, it operated by univalve suction attachments which drew urine and feces back into a septic tank; normal gravity-dependent toilets didn't function in spacecraft. However, in hopes of preserving the life of the batteries, Lester had shut down all the noncritical functions of the LRLT. That included the toilet, which depended upon a power supply just as much as the computers. Funny how certain bodily functions tend to creep up on you at inopportune times, he reflected.

"Uh-huh," he said. "Okay, listen. There should be some sample-collection bags stowed back there. I know it's messy, but you'll have to use them. Tell Joe to turn his head and . . ."

Right, she said tersely. *I guess. Over and out.*

He heard a soft click as the comlink was shut off. The old Butch Peterson was back among them. Lester chuckled despite himself; he could just imagine the exchange between Butch and Mighty Joe which was going on right now in the crew cabin. For the moment, it was better to be out here.

In more ways than one, Lester was glad he was out of the crew cabin. It had been many years since he had been out on the surface of the Moon by himself. Here was darkness, peaceful and everlasting, and now that Butch was attempting to pee in a plastic bag there was only silence, unbroken except for the thin hiss of his air regulator.

Hell of a time to be enjoying himself. Yet, despite the criticality of their situation, he found within himself a certain elation. *I haven't felt this way in twenty years,* he thought . . .

Cut it out, he reprimanded himself. Time to look over the ship. Not that there was much left of the LRLT to be examined. The hull had remained intact, but on the whole, the spacecraft was totalled. They had come down in a shallow dive which had dug a furrow a quarter-mile long across the mare, leaving behind bits and pieces of the landing gear in a deep trench. Joe had accomplished a nose-up belly landing which would have done a carrier pilot proud; the destruction of the landing gear had helped to brake the LRLT and save the fuselage from the worst damage. Still and all, it didn't take an expert to see that the spacecraft would never move from this spot again. The trusses which comprised the midsection strongback above the cargo module were bent in the center; his helmet lamps shined across the buckled framework as he walked closer for another look. Out here in the boonies, there was no way this craft could be salvaged.

Lester bounced away from the lights, hop-skipping around the rock-battered cones of the main engines toward the starboard side. He rounded the aft end of the craft, and as he did, his helmet lamps captured a lone figure in a spacesuit, standing just outside the cone of light cast by the lamps. . . .

"Whaaa . . . ?" Lester yelped in mid-leap. His knees turned to jelly; his jump took him a few more feet; then he sprawled on his butt on the hard, stony ground, legs outstretched and arms cast back to catch his fall. Dirt kicked up around him, falling back around his feet and legs like soft gray rain.

He felt the impact even through the rigid carapace of the hard-suit, but it hardly mattered. Lester stared straight ahead, his helmet lamps again finding the spacesuited figure. The suit design was obsolete; Skycorp had stopped using that type at least five years ago. The overgarment was caked and soiled with dirt, as if the wearer had crossed—impossibly—hundreds of miles of lunar terrain; dust clung to every crease and fold as if it had been stamped in. The helmet's faceplate was scoured; Lester could see eyes, a nose, and a mouth, but nothing that suggested a personality, except . . .

His heart thumped loudly in his ears. His breath came as a harsh rasp. There was a warm jet of fluid in his crotch; he was pissing in his urine-cup, but it barely registered on him, for at that moment his helmet lamps captured, for the briefest of instants, the faded black-nylon name patch sewn on the suit's overgarment. . . .

Sloane, S.K.

"Sam," he whispered.

Very slowly, the figure's right arm rose, forefinger thrust out as if in accusation, pointing at Riddell. . . . Then, after hovering for a moment, it rose to point again, beyond Riddell, toward the wrecked spacecraft behind him.

Then, before Lester could force another word through his parched throat, the specter stepped backward. One step, two steps, three . . .

As, at that very moment, the sun rose above the far eastern horizon, casting a bright silvery haze above the terrain, extending long shadows from the rock and boulders of the mare and the wall of the giant crater in the distance. The first rays touched the figure . . .

And it faded, dissipating like smoke in a place where there had never been air. Gone, forever gone.

Heart still pounding in his ears, Lester sat up on the ground and slowly turned around to look in the direction the specter had pointed, at the LRLT. At the top of the forward fuselage where, for the first time since he had gone EVA, Lester noticed the bent-over mast of the high-gain radio antenna. The antenna had been broken by the crash. All he had to do was climb up there and fix the thing with duct tape, and they had telemetry again. The Moon Moths would find them once radio contact was established.

Lester looked around again. Nothing. Not so much as a footprint.

"Sam . . ." he breathed.

Mighty Joe's snores rumbled from the aft cabin, a counterpoint to the electronic crackle of the radio in the flight compartment: *hronnk! . . . hrronnnnk! . . . hrronnnnnnk!* Butch had gone back twice already, once to prod him and tell him to shut up, the second time to attempt to roll him over on his stomach. The first time, Joe had muttered something obscene and had quit snoring for all of two minutes; the second attempt had been futile, since he was too big and the fold-down bunk was too small. Finally she had given up and resigned herself to enduring the nasal foghorn.

"What do you want me to say?" Butch asked quietly as she finished typing the last instructions into the computer keyboard in front of the co-pilot's seat and tapped the ENTER button. The LCD readout flashed as the data she had collected at Byrd Crater were transmitted via satellite comlink with Descartes Station. As soon as Lester had repaired the high-gain antenna on top of the spacecraft, she had insisted on relaying the all-important data back to the base for safekeeping. "You saw a ghost? Okay. You saw a ghost."

"I don't know," Lester said. "Maybe I just want you to say that you believe me."

"Oh, I believe you, all right." Butch sat back on the couch and propped her sneakered feet up on the dashboard. The cabin was dark except for a few instrument lights and the half-light of the rising run, filtering through the polarized canopy windows. "I mean, I don't think you're making this up," she added as she sipped from the straw in the water bottle in her lap, "but I don't believe in ghosts, either."

Lester was looking out the window. "Neither do I," he admitted. "At least I didn't until . . ." He stopped and shrugged. "I saw what I saw, Susie."

"Susie." Butch grinned. "Nobody's called me that since I was a little girl. Thanks." The smile left her face. "Did you check your suit's air feed? Maybe the mixture was a little . . ."

"I already covered that," Lester replied. "No, the oxygen-nitrogen ratio was copacetic. Right by the manual. Of course, I had been working out there, and then was jumping around a bit, and maybe I hyperventilated, so it's feasible that I could have . . ."

He paused, then shook his head. "No. It's conceivable, but I know what I saw. That was no hallucination. That was Sam Sloane out there."

They were both silent for a minute. Once the antenna had been fixed, they had been able to reestablish contact with Descartes Station, which in turn passed the information to the Moon Moths. The search-and-rescue team had the crash-site pinpointed now; it was just a matter of waiting until they arrived. With Mighty Joe doped-up and asleep in the back, they had plenty of time to kill. *Time for a few ghost stories,* Lester reflected. *All we're missing now is a campfire and some marshmallows. . . .*

"You knew Sam personally, didn't you?" Peterson asked, interrupting his train of thought. Lester nodded his head. "Were you here when he . . . ?"

She didn't finish the question. "Uh-huh," Lester said. He propped a foot up on the instrument panel and clasped his hands around his raised knee. He hesitated, then added, "You could even say that I was responsible for his death."

"Umm." Butch put down the water bottle and laid her head back against the headrest of the upholstered couch. "I heard part of the story. He got stranded in a crevasse and a rescue party didn't go out for him until it was too late. That was when you were in charge of the first base, wasn't it?"

"Yeah. In a nutshell, that's what happened." Lester cleared his throat. "There were twenty-five of us back then. It was a much smaller base and the workload wasn't that heavy, so we had a lot of time on our hands. We had a good pipeline for getting dope shipped up to us from the Cape, so we had all the drugs we wanted. Uppers, downers, Ecstasy, crank, coke . . . we were always ripped to the tits on something or another.''

''Sounds like fun,'' Peterson said drily.

Lester shook his head. ''Naw. Not really. I've listened to a lot of so-called drug experts in my life, heard them yap on about how people get into dope because of . . . y'know, social pressures or media influences or all those theories about an innate human need to expand their consciousness. But they're full of shit, when it comes right down to it. Any doper can tell you that. You get into the stuff because you're bored with life.'' He waved a hand at the bleak landscape beyond the windows. ''I mean, look at this place. How boring can you get? A quarter of a million miles to the nearest decent cheeseburger.''

Butch cracked up. ''Never heard it put that way before. Two hundred and forty thousand miles to the nearest dill pickle.'' She shook her head and rubbed her eyes, still giggling, then regained her composure and looked back at him again. ''So you were high all the time,'' she asked in a more somber tone.

He blew out his breath. ''High. Wasted. Fucking cross-eyed. Spent hours lying on my back in my office with a pair of headphones on my head, listening to old punk-rock tapes. Everyone else was in the same condition.''

Lester stopped, remembering eight years gone by. ''Except Sam,'' he added. ''He didn't want any part of that shit, so he went out exploring by himself.'' He sighed. ''Must have been fun. More entertaining than frying your brain. But we thought he was a dink. I mean, I didn't care what he did. Not as long as I had enough pills and coke to get me through another day . . .''

He reached over and picked up Butch's water bottle. ''Then one day he didn't come back on time.'' He took a sip from the bottle and went on. ''We had just gotten another load of dope from our ever-friendly source at the Cape, so we didn't notice. *I* didn't notice . . . until someone bothered to check the EVA logbook and noticed that Sam had left the base twenty hours earlier.''

Remembering, Lester put down the water bottle; he bent forward, closed his eyes and placed his forehead in his hands. ''Twenty . . . goddamn . . . hours,'' he said slowly. ''Christ, he was down in that crevasse long enough to dictate his memoirs. And he *knew* we weren't coming to rescue him. He *knew* the general manager was a junkie who couldn't see straight. And you know all that he said on that tape that he dictated? 'You sons of bitches, I'm going to get you for this.' That was the worst thing he said about us.''

Lester lifted his head again. He steepled his fingers together and peered over them at the rising sun. ''I could have saved him, Butch,'' he said almost inaudibly. ''I could have gotten to him before his air ran out, but I was too late.''

He smiled with grim humor. ''And then his ghost comes back to save my ass. Talk about your classic fucking irony.''

There was another long silence between them. Mighty Joe snorted and grunted in his sleep, the radio made a constant static noise, the cabin air regulator made a soft hiss. ''So,'' Peterson said at last. ''That's why you've been riding everyone so hard at the base. Why you've tried to straighten up the base.'' Lester looked sideways at her and nodded. She sighed and looked down at her hands. ''And I thought you were just a regular company asshole.''

Lester smiled and shrugged. ''Maybe I am just a regular company asshole. But I've been the opposite, and believe me when I tell you that it sucks.'' He looked out the window again. ''So let me ask you a question.''

Butch hesitated. ''Do I think you saw a ghost? The answer is, maybe you did . . . although perhaps not quite the way you think.'' She stopped, then added, ''And I don't think you were directly responsible for Sam's death either. You didn't get him into that crevasse. He did that himself. But it's still something you and your conscience are going to have to settle between yourselves. I can't help you with that.''

''Uh-huh.'' He tapped his fingers nervously on the seat's armrests. ''I appreciate that . . . but that wasn't the question I was going to ask.''

He didn't say anything. After a moment she looked back at him. Neither of them spoke; they didn't have to, because the question didn't need to be spoken aloud. The long seconds stretched on endlessly. After a while, Butch sighed and looked away from him. ''That's certainly a change of subject,'' she said. ''Should have known what was on your mind, the way you were checking me out in the lab.''

Lester winced. ''Changing the subject seemed like a good idea.'' He glanced over his shoulder to make sure Mighty Joe was still asleep. ''Sex and death seem to go together, for some reason. I dunno.''

"Maybe so." She sighed and dropped her legs from the dash-board, primly folding her hands in her lap. "I'm going to have to think about it, Les. But whatever I decide, it's not here, and not now."

"Why not?" he murmured smoothly. "The kid's asleep, the cat's been put out for the night. . . . " She chuckled and shook her head. "And hey, at least it's something you can put in your memoirs. I mean, everyone's done it in the back seat of a car, but how many folks can say they've done it on the floor of a crashed spaceship?"

She blushed and fought to stifle a grin. "Not so fast. You're rushing me."

"Sorry. I didn't know I . . ."

"Look," she said, cocking her head toward the window.

At that moment a small set of bright lights rose above the southern horizon. As the searchlights of the Moon Moths' LRLT stroked across Aristotle Crater, beelining their way toward the crash site, a voice came over the radio. *LRLT One-Three-Zero, this is LSR Flight Alpha-Zero-One. We've got your lights, do you copy? Over.*

"Damn. Just when it was getting interesting." Lester pulled the headset up from his neck and placed the bone-phone against his jaw. "We copy, Alpha-Zero-One. Riddell here. How'ya doing, Quack? Over."

We're tired and we wanna go home, Quack Lippincott replied. *How are y'all doing? That's the important question.*

"Joe's got a couple of cracked ribs, but I think we'll be able to put him in a suit for the walk over. Have you got a stretcher in there for him?"

That's affirmative. Monk's here with us, so he can tend to those dinged ribs. Hell of a place for you to park that vehicle of yours, boss. What do you think this is, a goddamn airport?

Lester chuckled. It was the typical refried bullshit from Descartes' resident Texan good ol' boy. "I'll let you take it up with Mighty Joe, once he wakes up from his snooze. You've got good landing clearance on either side of us. We'll suit up and be ready for you by the time you touch down."

Good 'nuff, Quack replied. *We'll keep the engines warm. Make sure you leave nothing behind you might want, ya hear?*

The Moon Moths' chief meant any small equipment that needed to be salvaged from the wrecked LRLT. Lester glanced over at Butch, who was monitoring the conversation, and grinned at her. "We copy that, Quack. I've got everything I want right here."

Butch Peterson closed her eyes and looked away. But she was smiling. That was the important thing.

PART FOUR

The Great Space Swindle

Black Friday
(Video.3)

From "The CBS Evening News With Michelle Woodward"; Friday, August 16, 2024.

(THEME UP and FADE. Michelle Woodward is seated at studio desk.)

WOODWARD: Good evening, I'm Michelle Woodward, sitting in for Don Houston, who is on vacation this week. There was trouble in space today, as three astronauts were rescued from a remote region of the Moon after their spacecraft crash-landed following engine failure. Yet even more disturbing than that news was the revelation that lunar operations may be endangered by an impending shortage of a scarce, valuable resource—water. Garrett Logan reports from Huntsville, Alabama. . . .

(FILE FOOTAGE of an LRLT lifting off from a landing pad at Descartes Station. This is replaced by COMPUTER ANIMATION of the same vehicle plummeting to the lunar surface and making a crash landing, followed by a MAP of the polar region with the crash site highlighted.)

LOGAN (V.O.): A Skycorp long-range lunar transport, on its way back to Descartes Station following a routine supply and inspection mission to the company's Byrd Crater Permaice Extraction Facility at the Moon's north pole, went down soon after takeoff from the automated base. The accident occurred shortly after midnight on Earth, Eastern Standard Time. Although the craft was totaled, none of the three crewmembers aboard was seriously injured. The LRLT crashed in the Sea of Cold, about two hundred miles south of Byrd Crater. . . .

(FILE FOOTAGE of Skycorp's giant A-frame headquarters building in Huntsville, the installation at Byrd Crater, and Des-

cartes Station. This is replaced by COMPUTER ANIMATED diagram of the permaice wells at Byrd Crater.)

LOGAN (V.O.): Yet even as Skycorp spokespersons confirmed that the LRLT's crew had been found and safely rescued by a team from Descartes Station, they announced more bad news. Before leaving Byrd Crater, the same team had discovered that the ancient deposits of permaice—a valuable water resource which lies beneath the bottom of Byrd Crater and is mined for rocket propellant and drinking water for the one hundred and ten-person crew of the industrial moonbase—is rapidly drying up. . . .

(FILM CLIP of a Skycorp spokesperson, identified as Holly D'Amato, at a news conference in Huntsville.)

D'AMATO: We have received news from the base that the . . . uh, limited natural ice resource at the lunar north pole is in danger of being exhausted within a matter of . . . ah, some months.

LOGAN (V.O.): And that has some people worried. . . .

(FILM CLIP with space industry market analyst, identified as Clifford Brandenstein).

BRANDENSTEIN: If this is indeed the case, then it's bad news for Skycorp, because if they can no longer extract water directly from the Moon, it means they will have to import all their water from Earth. That means the overhead costs of operating the base could reach beyond the point of profitability. It's no big secret that Skycorp has been considering selling the base to the Japanese. The chief executives at Uchu-Hiko are probably doing handsprings right now . . . but it's a black day for the American space industry. . . .

(CUT TO Garrett Logan, standing in front of Skycorp headquarters.)

LOGAN: Corporate officials at Skycorp have refused to comment on what this development means for the future of Descartes Station, other than to say that the company is still studying its options. Spokespersons for Uchu-Hiko in Tokyo have likewise declined comment. However, Skycorp's price-per-share on the New York Stock Exchange fell by 15.2 points just before closing today, which may be a harbinger of worse things to come. As one market analyst told us, "Just wait till the market reopens on Monday, and you're going to see some big changes." This is Garrett Logan in Huntsville, Alabama. . . .

17. The Birth of a Scam

Elizabeth Sawyer slipped her keycard into the slot next to the greenhouse hatch and shifted her slender body so that Willard DeWitt couldn't read the six-digit string which she tapped into the lock's keypad. With a metallic grinding sound, the hatch irised open. "Harry's waiting for you," the middle-aged hydroponics chief said stiffly as she stepped out of the way. "Fifteen minutes . . . and you better think twice about pilfering any veggies while you're in there."

"Thank you, ma'am." DeWitt flashed her his most winning smile, but Sawyer wasn't having any of his sweet-talk. Folding her arms across the front of her grimy jumpsuit, she gave him a sour look which suggested she would just as soon go after him with a pair of gardening shears.

"Wipe your feet," she added as DeWitt stepped through the hatchway. There was a disinfectant mat on the floor just inside the hatch; DeWitt stopped and briskly wiped the soles of his sneakers across the mat and smiled again at Sawyer. She absently brushed back a lock of her graying red hair, pursed her lips distrustingly, and touched the button that closed the hatch behind him. "Fifteen minutes," she said again just before the hatch resealed.

"Ornery old biddy, aren't you?" DeWitt murmured. On the other hand, he reflected, as he turned and gazed upon the vast greenhouse that lay before him, she had every right to be protective about this place.

Descartes Station's greenhouse was a separate structure, adjacent to Subcomp A and almost as large as one of the dorms. Made of dense, inflated Kevlar and buttressed by hemispherical aluminum struts, its domed roof rose thirty feet above the floor, easily making the greenhouse the largest interior space anywhere on the base. The outer shell of the dome was covered with a thin shell of regolith fines, salvaged from the mining operations, which protected the crops from cosmic radiation. Suspended from the rafters were racks of track-lights and nutrient bottles whose feedlines dangled down into the long rows of waist-level hydroponics tanks on the floor. More than half of the tanks were given over to the farming of wheat—an efficient oxygen producer which also doubled as a good source of raw grain, which meant that one thing the moondogs' diet never lacked was wheat bread—with the back rows devoted to the cultivation of tomatoes, celery, bean sprouts, and an exquisitively small and precious (albeit experimental) crop of strawberries.

DeWitt walked slowly down the central aisle, relishing the enormous space, the warm humid air which smelled of green and growing things, the vague heat of the overhead lights. The greenhouse was like a Kansas farm field which had been miraculously transplanted to the Moon. It was no wonder that the greenhouse was closed to most of the moondogs; prolonged exposure to this much simple beauty could make anyone homesick in hurry. And besides, the greenhouse was a delicately balanced ecosystem of its own; to have people constantly tramping through the dome would invite damage to this miniature biosphere. *But,* DeWitt mused as he paused to run his hand through the high stalks of wheat thrusting up from a tank, *I could easily move my bunk in here*. . . .

"Enjoying yourself?" Harry Drinkwater's voice said from behind him.

DeWitt turned to see Drinkwater strolling toward him down the central aisle, his hands shoved in his pockets and a rare uncynical smile on his face. "Thought you might like this," he added. "Liz lets me in here from time to time, as long as I play an occasional k.d. lang or Randy Travis oldie for her at the station." He nodded meaningfully at the wheat stalks DeWitt had been stroking. "And as long as I don't touch her crops."

"It's nice," DeWitt said softly. He reluctantly withdrew his hand. "You got a good deal . . . but aren't you supposed to be on the air right now?"

"Lunch break. I've got a prerecorded tape and the CD racks playing DJ for me right now." He glanced at his watch. "I'm due back on the air in a half-hour, and you can bet Liz will kick us out long before that. As long as we've got privacy, we ought to make the most of it. You said you had something for me?"

"Umm-hmm." DeWitt started to lean against a hydroponics tank, felt it shudder, and quickly stepped forward again. "You know about what they discovered at Byrd Crater?"

Drinkwater's smile faded into a frown. He nodded his head slightly. "And you know what the stock market's doing?" DeWitt continued. "That Skycorp's price-per-share on the New York exchange went down yesterday by . . . ?"

"Fifteen-point-two points at closing," Drinkwater finished, pulling a hand out of a pocket and whirling it impatiently. "And probably down more when it opens again Monday. I've got an AP teleprinter in the studio, remember? Nobody here gets the news faster than I do. So what are you . . . ?"

"Bear with me a second," DeWitt interrupted. "Skycorp's stock is taking a power dive because the permaice well at Byrd Crater is drying up. That means that within a year at best, one of the two or three most valuable consumables at the base—plain, ordinary water—is going to have to be exported from Earth, increasing the cost by tenfold at the very least. Thus, the cost of operating Descartes goes up. . . ."

DeWitt raised his thumb toward the ceiling. "And the interest of the short-term floating investors goes down." His thumb cocked downwards. "And that drives the value of Skycorp's stock down in New York, similarly influencing the Tokyo and London exchanges. At this rate, it means the company might suffer third-quarter losses. Clear so far?"

"Crystal," Drinkwater said drily. "And you don't need to tell me the rest. Uchu-Hiko's been interested in acquiring Descartes from Skycorp for a long time now. If Skycorp's price-per-share softens too much, the company will cut its losses before it gets critical. The boys in Huntsville will dump this joint on the market, and guess who's waiting to acquire a tasty piece of developed lunar real estate?"

"Good prognosis," DeWitt said. "I'd say that it'll happen in less than a week. In fact, I'll bet my next paycheck that Skycorp entertains a bid for the base from Uchu-Hiko by the time Wall Street closes next Friday. Even by Wednesday if it goes sour too fast." He smiled and raised an expectant eyebrow.

Drinkwater shook his head. "I'm not going to take that bet." He shoved his hands back in his pockets and half-turned to gaze at the hydroponic farm surrounding them. "So what? You've deduced something any Harvard MBA could figure out in a minute. What's your point, Willard?"

DeWitt looked down at his shoes to hide his smug grin. He took a couple of steps closer to Drinkwater until he was standing next to his shoulder. "What if I told you," he said in a soft, slow voice, "that there's another source of water that's readily available?" He paused, then added, "Up here. In space. And you and I are the only ones who know about it."

Harry Drinkwater slowly turned around and stared straight into Willard DeWitt's eyes. "If you're trying to bullshit me . . ."

Unable to help himself now, DeWitt shook his head. "Let's go to my niche," he said. He brushed past Drinkwater and started walking down the aisle. When the DJ hesitated, DeWitt twisted around on his heels and tipped his head toward the hatch. "C'mon," he prodded. "Trust me. I've got something I want to show you. You're going to love it."

The rock was roughly shaped like a potato. It was about one mile in length and a half-mile in width, and its former neighborhood had been the asteroid belt between Mars and Jupiter until, over the course of several millennia, the Sun's gravity had gradually coaxed it out of its orbit and brought it spiraling toward the inner solar system. Because it had a medium-low albedo, it reflected light poorly; the optical telescopes at the Hawking Observatory on the lunar farside had noticed the rock only because it happened to occult a stellar cluster which was currently under observation.

The AI system which controlled the lunar observatory routinely logged the discovery of the new Apollo asteroid. Following a preset program, one of the optical telescopes tracked the asteroid for a couple of days, making the usual spectrographic analysis and estimate of its probable trajectory before the master computer filed the information in its memory, which in turn was transmitted to the computers at Byrd Station for eventual downloading by human hands. The discovery of a new Apollo asteroid, after all, was an item of little interest and low priority. Thousands of new asteroids that crossed Earth-orbit had been found since the first Hubble space telescope had been launched in 1990, and as long as asteroids didn't threaten to collide with Earth or the Moon, there was hardly any reason to red-flag it for anyone's immediate attention. The Hawking computer had even been free to give it a name; it designated the rock 2024 Garbo—it was currently working its way through a list of classic film stars; the last Apollo asteroid it had found had been named

2024 Fairbanks—and returned its attention to more important
things.

Willard DeWitt pointed at the dotted line which was slowly
inching along his computer screen. "And there it is," he said
proudly. "Now look where it ends up. . . ."

He waited until 2024 Garbo's trajectory crossed the ellipse of
the Earth-Moon system, then tapped the PAUSE key on his keyboard. He had loaded the data he had hacked from the science
lab's mainframe into his own computer, merging it with a simple
astronomical program he had also filched from Butch Peterson's
computers. As the trajectory froze, he typed in another command, and a red line lanced between the Apollo asteroid and
the Moon; at the bottom of the LCD, a set of numbers appeared.
DeWitt sat back in his seat and looked up at Harry Drinkwater.

"See?" he said with just a trace of smugness.

Drinkwater leaned over the back of DeWitt's chair and looked
at the screen. "Okay. It makes a close approach at six hundred
twenty-seven thousand miles on January 3, 2025." He shrugged.
"So what? Five months from now a big dumb rock comes sail-
ing past us." He glanced at his watch and eyed the closed door
of DeWitt's niche. "Listen, I gotta be back on the air in about
fifteen minutes, so if you've got a point to make . . ."

"Cool your jets a minute and check this out, okay?" DeWitt
hastily punched in a new set of commands; the screen split in
half, displaying a computer-generated image of 2024 Garbo and
a column of specific information which had been collated by the
Hawking computer from the raw data its telescopes had collected. He ran the cursor down to one line in particular and
highlighted it. "See that? Type-C carbonaceous chondrite . . ."

"Big deal . . ."

". . . with an estimated H_2O content of nine-point-three percent." DeWitt jabbed the screen with his forefinger and stared
straight at Drinkwater. "Run that through your noodle for a
minute. That baby's almost *ten percent ice*!"

Drinkwater, who was about to protest that he had a zillion
requests to deal with once he got back on the mike, found himself gaping at the screen. The pixel-silhouette of 2024 Garbo
slowly rotated on its long axis; he rested his hands on DeWitt's
fold-down desk and bent closer to study the screen. The numbers did not lie.

"Ten percent . . . *ice*?" he said slowly. "Hell, that's almost as much as they found at Byrd Crater in the first place." He looked at DeWitt. "How did you know about this?"

DeWitt grinned. "I didn't. I was just taking a shot in the dark." He coughed into his fist and turned away from the screen. "I was on my watch in MainOps when Peterson transmitted the data back from the LRLT crash site. I figured that given the situation they were in, it must have been something important. So after I downloaded it all in her computer, I came back here after my shift was over, sneaked into her system and took a peek. The data from Byrd Station was the most important stuff, of course, but once I had seen that, I decided to run through the latest from Hawking. Just for the hell of it, really." He snapped his fingers at the screen. "Jackpot . . . that's when I found our friend Garbo here."

Drinkwater nodded his head. He straightened up and thrust his hands into his back pockets. "All right. You've found an Apollo asteroid that's loaded with ice and it'll be swinging by in a few months. Sure, they've talked about asteroid retrieval missions before, but . . ."

"Who's they?" DeWitt asked, blinking but otherwise keeping a completely straight face.

"Skycorp," Drinkwater replied. "Uchu-Hiko. Arianespace, NASA, Glavkosmos, and all the rest. Everyone. It's an old idea, but nobody's ever really . . ."

"Nobody's done it because they didn't need to," DeWitt finished. "When they found the ice deposits at Byrd Crater, it wasn't necessary to talk about farming asteroids anymore. But now Byrd Crater's drying up. And, just in the nick of time, here's pretty Ms. Garbo, making her lonely way past the Moon. . . ."

Harry was shuffling his feet. "Yeah, well, okay, maybe Skycorp can send out a tug or two to . . ."

"Who said anything about Skycorp?"

The DJ stopped and looked at Dewitt. "I did. Skycorp's the only one that's got the boats up here that can do it."

DeWitt shook his head, but said nothing. "Listen," Drinkwater insisted, "they're the only company that can . . ."

Grinning now, DeWitt shook his head again. Drinkwater was feeling confused now. "But they own the tugs, so . . ."

"Who owns the tugs?" DeWitt asked teasingly.

"Skycorp!" Drinkwater said in exasperation. "I just said that!"

"What about Lunar Associates, Ltd.?"

"I never heard of . . . Who?"

"Lunar Associates Ltd." DeWitt was still smiling. "You know. The small start-up space company affiliated with Gamble, Hutton & Schwartzchilde, which has a seat on the New York Stock Exchange. When the bell rings on Wall Street Monday morning, they'll be tendering their first stock."

He looked at the computer screen again, then slowly turned his eyes back to Harry Drinkwater. "An incredible new investment opportunity which only a few select insiders in the space-futures market will know about. Gives a whole new meaning to the phrase 'owning a piece of the rock,' if you know what I mean."

"But the tugs . . ."

"Screw the tugs," DeWitt replied. He had the serene confidence of a man who had just tied a string around Wall Street's testicles and was ready to give the line a good, hard yank. "Listen to me, my friend. There are only two kinds of reality. Money . . . and everything else."

Harry Drinkwater felt his heart skip a beat. He glanced at the screen, then at Willard DeWitt, then at the screen again. "Are you seriously saying you're going to use this asteroid to . . . ?"

"That," DeWitt replied evenly, "and so much more. I think I found a way to do what you want to do. Come back when you're off the air. I'll have something to show you by then."

He sighed with blissful anticipation, like a high-school kid who was about to take the local beauty queen out for a ride in the park, and turned back to his keyboard. "Oh, boy," he said softly, more to himself than to his new partner, "will I have something to show you."

18. The Hidden Agenda

Lester assumed that he would be hearing from Skycorp before Monday morning. He was both right and wrong.

When the call came, he was in MainOps, putting in a few extra hours during the Saturday second-shift. For the sake of privacy, he had the communications officer patch the call through to his office; then he left the tower and trotted down the spiral stairs to the second level. By chance, Butch Peterson happened to be in the central corridor as he was approaching his office. "C'mon with me," he said without breaking stride. "This is something you ought to hear." Peterson didn't question him; she simply turned and followed him into his office, carefully shutting the door behind her.

Lester wasn't surprised to find that it was Arnie Moss who was waiting for him on the phone. The only surprise was that the vice-president of lunar operations wasn't calling from the Huntsville headquarters. Judging from the background on the phone's TV screen, his old NASA buddy was calling from home; Moss's open-necked golf shirt suggested that he had just come from spending Saturday morning on the links. Perhaps Moss had suffered a sudden attack of conscience on the 18th hole at the Huntsville Country Club.

Hiya, Les, Moss began. *Good to see you again.* He paused, then asked, *Are you alone right now?*

Before he had picked up the phone, Riddell had carefully rotated the screen toward his desk chair so that the rest of the office couldn't be seen through the lens. Peterson was standing silently near the door, where she couldn't be picked up by the camera but could still hear everything that was being said. "Sure, I'm alone," Lester replied easily. "Sorry for the delay, but I decided not to take this in MainOps. What's on your mind?"

You and your boys, for one thing. Moss sighed. *I shouldn't be calling you like this, you know. There's a lot of paranoia right now at the office. Some of the top people would just as soon keep you guys in the dark. I hope that whatever's said stays just between you and me. You copy me on that?*

"Paranoia?" Lester kept a poker-face; he laced his hands together and gazed innocently back at the screen. "What are you talking about?"

Moss shook his head impatiently. *C'mon, Les, don't do the dumb routine on me. What your chief scientist found at Byrd Crater was like dropping a nuke on this place, and you know it.*

Peterson had to cover her mouth to muffle her snicker. "Hey hey, whoa there!" Lester held up his hands defensively. "It wasn't my idea to leak the info to the news media. If you can't get your PR department to keep a lid on something like that, don't go blaming me. I'm a quarter of a goddamn million miles away, so I can't run your show for you."

If your pilot hadn't crashed you in the middle of nowhere . . . Moss stopped, took another breath and raised a glass of iced tea to take a sip. Lester would have killed and cannibalized his grandmother for a tall, cold glass of tea right then. *Never mind. It's over and done, anyway.* He grimaced. *Although you're right about the PR department dropping the ball. Some squirrelly kid on the third floor heard about it and got it in his head to contact the local spacehounds. He had some stupid journalism-school notion about any news being good news. If I know Ken Crespin, the kid's going to be carrying his stuff out in a cardboard box before lunchtime tomorrow.*

"You guys are so merciful with the entry-level types," Lester said drily, still eyeing the glass of tea cradled in Moss's hands. "Spit it out, Arnie. You aren't racking up your phone bill just to commiserate with me."

Moss frowned silently at the camera for a moment. *You guys are up shit creek.*

"Tell me about it."

Skycorp's been looking for an excuse to dump Descartes for months, Moss continued. *It's even worse than what I told you before we sent you up there. Trust me on this one, because I've seen the internal memos. The powersat operations have been making a mint, but the profit margin's being eaten away by the overhead costs of maintaining an expanded operation up there.*

The sale of lunar-oxygen to the other companies isn't making up for the losses, and . . .

"Hey, hold on a minute there." Impatient with the two-second delay, Lester inched forward in his chair. "Since I've been here, we've had three shifts working twenty-four hours, seven days a week. It's Saturday and I've got a full second-shift busting their humps out there right this minute. Overall production's up twenty-three percent, and the lunar-oxygen factory alone is up almost thirty percent. You can't tell me the company's sustaining a loss from this base, sport."

Okay, okay! Chill out, willya? Moss was visibly backing away from the screen, as if he were afraid that Riddell might somehow jump through the tube and grab the collar of his Izod shirt. *I know you've been meeting the new quotas. Shit, old buddy, I'm impressed. I told you that the other day. They didn't think you could do the job when they—*

He halted abruptly. His eyes widened a little and, even across hundreds of thousands of miles of space, his face could be seen turning deep-red. Lester noted, from the corner of his eye, that Butch, too, had caught the slip. "If they didn't think I could do the job," he said slowly, "then why did they rehire me?"

Arnie looked away from the screen; he nervously picked up his glass and took another sip of tea. Lester wasn't about to let him off the hook. "Answer me, Arnie," he continued. "If Sky-corp didn't think I could get this base to meet its production schedules, why did they send me up here to run the place?"

Forget it, Moss muttered. *Just forget I said anything. It doesn't matter.*

"I'm not forgetting shit!" Lester snapped. "Answer the question!"

Moss's arm moved forward toward the phone, as if to break the connection. "If you hang up on me again," Lester warned, "the very next thing I do is to call Crespin and pop that same question to him, letting him know that I just talked to you. So if you don't want to be emptying your own desk tomorrow, you better start playing straight with me . . . old buddy."

Moss glowered at the screen. He slammed the empty glass down on the desk in front of the phone—Lester could hear the rattle of the ice cubes—and leaned forward as if to huddle with his former NASA crewmate. *Okay, listen,* he said quietly. *It wasn't my idea, but there was this plan . . .*

"Skycorp sent me up here to fuck up," Lester finished. "That's the plan, wasn't it?"

Closing his eyes, Moss shamefully nodded his head. *You gotta believe me when I tell you that I didn't know the score when they sent me to recruit you. But I've seen the memos and I've heard the talk. You had enough experience to run the base, but you'd had your problems with pills, you had been out of the loop for eight years. . . .*

He let out his breath. *They figured that you couldn't make the base operate up to par. Especially not with a demoralized team and over fifty new guys on your payroll. They thought you'd screw the pooch, blow the probation period, the quotas, the works. In fact, they were counting on it. That way, they would have an excuse to lay off everyone without ASWI getting in their way.*

"And sell the capital assets to the Japanese with only a minimal loss." Lester sighed and rubbed his eyes. "Un-fucking-believable." Then he grinned. "But then I really screwed up, didn't I?"

Moss self-consciously grinned back at him. *That you did. You did what they thought you couldn't do. You got the place to run like a top. Production quotas being met, people working their asses off . . .* He laughed and shook his head. *And you know that new security chief they sent you? Tina McGraw? They deliberately found the most antisocial hard-ass NASA would lend them, hoping that she'd piss off your guys to the point where they flat-out wouldn't cooperate with you and make matters worse. But the whole thing backfired on them. It's almost funny.*

Lester was almost sorry he hadn't thought to tape this conversation. He would have loved for Quick-Draw to hear this assessment of her character. Yet there was little consolation in the knowledge that she had been set up for a fall just as he had. "You hear me laughing?" he asked Moss.

No. Sorry. It can't be funny, not where you're sitting. Moss collapsed back in his chair. *But you're still not making enough money to satisfy these characters. Gross revenues are fine, but the profits aren't high enough for them. It's not like the old days when the space business was just getting started. Remember that? That was when guys like Deke Slayton and George Koopman were willing to endure quarterly losses for years before their companies turned a meager profit, and their employees volunteered to go on working without getting a paycheck, even for months. It's a whole new breed in there now, man. These guys, they don't know the difference between a rocket and a refrigerator, and they don't give a shit either. They don't have any dreams except being able to buy a gold-plated Lamborghini and* . . .

"Yeah yeah yeah," Lester grumbled. *And I bet you're living in a garage yourself,* he thought, although he restrained himself from voicing that particular opinion. "Spare me the philosophy, Arnie. I want facts. They want to use the permaice shortage as an excuse to unload Descartes, is that it?"

Moss slowly nodded. *I just got word that Crespin took a flight out of Atlanta this morning to Tokyo. They may not wait until the stock market bottoms out during the week . . . and you can bet your old campground that's exactly what it's going to do.* Then he smiled and wagged a finger at the screen. *But you can also bet that Uchu-Hiko is going to drive a hard bargain. The Japs want the base, but they're not going to make a lousy deal with Skycorp. I mean, the fact that Byrd Crater's drying up is bad enough, but'* . . .

His voice trailed off again, yet this time deliberately. Moss continued to stare at the screen. "But what?" Lester asked.

If something . . . y'know, unforeseen were to occur. Moss's face was a mask now. *Something weird. Something beyond their control. You know what I'm saying?*

Riddell darted a look at Butch Peterson. She shrugged and held up her hands; she didn't know what Arnie Moss was hinting at, either. Lester looked back at the camera. "No, I don't," he answered. "What are you trying to tell me?"

All at once, Moss's disposition changed. *Well, Les, it sure has been nice talking to you,* he said breezily, as if the two of them had been chinning about their old flight-school days. *Gotta be signing off now. I think the old lady wants to get me in for lunch and* . . .

"Goddammit, Arnie, what are you trying to tell me?"

There was a very long pause from Moss's end. *The debt's settled,* he said at last. His face was expressionless, his thoughts unreadable. *You're on your own now. Let's see how you manage this one, buck.*

He reached forward again. *See you around. Good luck.* . . .

"Arnie! What are you . . . ?" And then the screen blanked, replaced an instant later by the comsat test-pattern.

• • •

Lester studied the abstract image on the screen for a moment before he reached forward and switched off the phone. Butch Peterson exhaled and leaned against the closed door. "Nice friend you have there," she said. "What was he talking about?"

Riddell raised his legs, propped his feet up on the desk, steepled his fingers together and slowly shook his head. "Kiddo," he murmured, "I haven't the foggiest. But I don't think he was fooling when he . . ."

There was a buzz just then; Lester automatically reached for the desk phone before he realized that it was his portable beltphone which had sounded. Never a dull moment, he thought as he unclipped the smaller unit and flipped it open. "Riddell here," he said into the mouthpiece.

Lester, it's Tina. He winced at the sound of the security chief's voice. *There's a situation in Storage Two which looks a little fishy. I'm going to check it out, but I think you ought to be with me when I—*

"Look, Tina, I'm in a meeting right now," Riddell interrupted. "Can you handle this by yourself? I'll be down there soon as I'm free. Okay?"

Yes sir, she said stuffily, obviously miffed. *Security out.*

Peterson was gazing idly at the picture of the old Descartes Station. "Quick-Draw?" she asked as he switched off the phone. He nodded. "What did she want?"

"More of the same," he said. "Every time there's some petty theft or a fight that has to be broken up, she thinks I have to be there. I wish she would be a little more independent and handle these things by herself." He self-consciously cleared his throat and settled back in his chair. "Never mind that now. I want to know what you thought of that conversation."

Butch smiled, folded her arms across her plaid shirt, and gently shook her head. "No, you don't," she said. She slowly walked across the room until she reached his desk. "I mean, I listened to everything that was said, but . . ."

Unexpectedly, she slid onto the edge of his desk, perching there on one thigh. "You're the GM, after all," she continued. "You don't need my two cents, any more than Quick-Draw needs to have you backing up everything she does." She smiled mischievously at him. "C'mon, Les. What's *really* on your mind?"

Looking at her close up, Lester thought he might go into cardiac arrest. *Good grief, woman, you don't want to know . . .* "No," he stammered. "Honestly. What did you think of what

Moss just said? I mean, they set me up. The company thought I was incompetent enough to drive this base into the ground. They . . .''

"And they were wrong, weren't they?" Her smile grew broader; she tossed back her braided hair in a fetchingly absent-minded way. "What do you want me to say? Do I think you're incompetent? No. Did I ever think you were going to wreck this operation? It was already wrecked by the time you got here. Everything you've done in the last two months has helped to make it run better. Do I like the fact that Uchu-Hiko is probably going to buy Descartes and get rid of everyone here? No, but there's not much we can do about it, is there?"

"No!" he snapped. He was pissed off. "For Christ's sake, Susie! Arnie was trying to tell me something. There's got to be some way out of this mess. We've gone too far just to give up because some corporate greedheads want a few more bucks. We've got to . . .''

His train of thought wandered. "We've got to what?" Butch insisted. "Petition the board of directors? Quit in mass-protest? Take it up with that useless union of ours?"

She bent over the desk a little closer to him. "C'mon, Les," she said gently, looking into his eyes. "It's *over*. You did the best you could, but they had the deck stacked against you before you got here. If we're fired, you can go back to running your campground and I can find some teaching job somewhere." She shook her head. "Sometimes you can't win," she added.

Lester slowly nodded his head. "I know," he said quietly. "It's just that . . . losing like this, it sticks in my craw."

He turned his head and gazed out the window next to his desk. The three-quarter Earth hung above the distant, silver-gray slopes of Stone Mountain, casting narrow shadows from the long rails of the mass-driver stretching to the horizon. In the closer distance, the lights of the regolith combines and 'dozers prowled the worked-over gray-brown lunar soil. Second-shift would be coming in soon, he thought, and the third-shift team would be going out.

Even now, on a Saturday when most of America was enjoying a late summer afternoon—grilling hamburgers, drinking beer, dozing on the couch, catching a baseball game on TV—there were men and women going to work on the Moon, breathing bottled air and pushing around moonrocks. Maybe those on Earth would look up at the light-purple Moon hanging in the sky and think of a time when it was a place that Americans had once visited and abandoned. Perhaps they wouldn't think of it at all; take its colonization as a given part of life, just as many turned on their lights and computers and TV's without considering that the electricity powering these appliances was made possible by a network of solar-power satellites, which, in turn, had been built from the stuff of moondust. Nobody ever thinks about the ones who do the dirty work. No one ever thinks about the sacrifices they have to make. . . .

"That's the way it is," Butch was saying, unaware of what he was thinking. "Life goes on. Some you win and some you lose. That's just the way it is." She paused. "You can't carry the weight by yourself all the time."

"It's just not fair." Lester was still looking out the window. "You come up here to get a job done, and the bastards won't let you do it. That's all. It's just not fair."

"Whoever said fairness had anything to do with it?" Butch asked. She was silent for a few moments; then, all of a sudden, she reached across the desk and placed her hand over his. "You know what you need, pal?" she said.

Lester looked away from the window, down at her soft brown hand covering his angry fist. He nodded his head wearily. "Yeah," he said. "I think I know what I need. . . ."

Withdrawing his hand, he pushed back the chair and stood up. "I think I want to go down to Storage Two."

The sultry expression on Butch's face abruptly changed to one of bewildered rejection. Riddell quickly shook his head. "No no no," he said. "Just come with me. I've got a sneaking suspicion I know what's going on down there. And if it's what I think it is, that's what we need a little bit of right now."

A confused smile appeared on her face. "I don't get it," she said, shaking her head. "What do you think is in a storeroom that we need?"

He smiled a little. "A party." He stepped around the desk and took her hand again. "Call it a date. Now c'mon. Let's go crash it."

19. Why Don't We Get Drunk and Screw?

The elaborate brewery system wasn't exactly a masterpiece of engineering. It was in fact, Mighty Joe had to admit, as ugly as anything you could expect to find stashed in the northern Florida woods.

Yet, despite its old Appalachian "hog" design, it did have a certain high-tech look about it. The fifty-gallon barrel was made of scrap spacecraft oxygen tanks which Honest Yuri had welded together, and instead of a firebox, the mash was cooked with heating elements pilfered from the galley. The rest of the rig—the cap and cap arm, the water tank, the spiral-shaped "worm," or feed tube, and the filters—had been pieced together from spare parts found or stolen from all over the base. It was big and cumbersome and a bitch to put together, but it would have done a Prohibition-era moonshiner proud. And when Quick-Draw McGraw found the thing, all that Joe or anyone else could do was to grin, stand aside, and let her admire their work.

In hindsight, they should have expected the security chief to find it. For one thing, the wheat that had been swiped from the greenhouse by clean-up crews would have been eventually noticed by Sawyer and reported to McGraw. Also, fifty gallons of water didn't vanish from the storage tanks without someone taking notice. And there weren't too many places in Descartes where such a contraption could be safely hidden—especially since McGraw had an all-access keycard which allowed her to open any door on the moonbase. As the chief *braumeister*, Mighty Joe had known that he was taking a considerable risk in a storeroom on the lower level of Subcomplex A, right underneath the galley. But it was hardly less risky than building the thing in the bunkhouse or in one of the adjacent radiation shelters on the same level; McGraw regularly checked these places, and would have found the contraption even before the first batch of beer had been brewed. And considering how word had leaked out among the crew that there was to be a little "tea party" going down Saturday night in Storage Two, they should have just sent her a written invitation. On the other hand, perhaps Quick-Draw had been watching all along, waiting for her chance to catch the Vacuum Suckers in the act. Nothing that happens in Descartes Station remains secret for very long.

As it was, when she finally raided the covert brewery, there were almost a dozen moondogs sitting around on crates of freeze-dried god-knows-what, holding foam cups of warm, high-potency moonbrew and grinning foolishly from various degrees of inebriation. Portable lamps had been set up for the drinking party, with a towel pushed against the crack at the bottom of the door to keep out the light, and admittance was gained by giving three staccato raps, then one slow knock, on the door. They knew it was a bust when the door opened without a single knock and the overhead ceiling lights were suddenly switched on. There was the unmistakable jangle and clank of her equipment belt, and as everyone winced in the abrupt glare of the lights, Quick-Draw McGraw stepped into the storeroom.

"All *right* . . ." she began.

For a moment or two, there was dead silence. Annie was the first to recover. "Surprise!" she shouted merrily. She stood up from her crate of freeze-dried eggs and, with the chutzpah only the seriously shitfaced are able to muster, raised her fourth cup of beer in a mock toast. "Happy birthday to you," she began to sing. ". . . Haaappy biiirthday to yooou . . ."

Everyone in the storeroom rose to their feet and, holding forth their cups of fifteen-proof home-brew, joined in: ". . . Haaaaappy biiirrthday, dear Quick-Draaaaw . . . Haaappy biiirthday to yooooooou. . . ."

"Blow out the candles," someone muttered.

"Yeah," someone else hiccuped, "and shut the friggin' door. You want the cops to find us or somethin'?"

They all laughed and sat down again. Mighty Joe, at his post next to the tap, watched Quick-Draw's face as it went through various states of apoplexy. Some of the best and brightest of Descartes Station's staff were in here: Tycho Samuels, Rusty Wright, Quack Lippincott, Casey Engel, Seki Koyama, Harry Drinkwater, and a dozen or so more—most of them already zoned beyond any thought of respect for law and order. Mc-

Graw's hand wavered on the butt of her Taser as her eyes swept across the crowd and the vat in the back of the storeroom.

"Okay," she said stiffly, taking a deep breath, spreading her feet wide, and thrusting her chest forward. "Party's over, ladies and gentlemen. By authority of the National Aeronautics and Space Administration, I'm shutting down this unlawful gathering and . . ."

"Aw, give it a rest, willya, Tina?" Mighty Joe said. He would have stood up, but the bandages around his ribs prohibited him from making sudden movements. He remained instead on the upended crate next to the hog. "What are you going to do?" he asked calmly. "Arrest us? Zap everyone in the room?"

Her eyes narrowed menacingly as her angry gaze shot to him. "I'm willing to forget everything I've just seen," she intoned sternly, "if you'll calmly disperse and . . ."

"What?" Quack interrupted. Lana Smith, the ready-room suit tech, was sitting in his lap; he had to look around her to see McGraw. "And break up a good party? You gotta be shitting me, lady."

Everyone laughed again. That only seemed to further infuriate McGraw. "It's within my authority," she said as her voice rose to a frustrated shrill, "to have the employment of everyone here terminated, with no possibility of appeal or . . ."

"Aw, bullshit," Harry replied in his sculpted disc-jockey voice. "There's not a thing you can do to us now."

"S'right," Annie slurred. "We're termi . . . terminationated . . . I mean, we're fucked already. So beat it, bitch."

McGraw looked as if she was about to use her Taser on Annie. "Try a little reality, Tina," Mighty Joe said reasonably. "If you haven't been paying attention to the news, Skycorp's about to sell out to Uchu-Hiko. The smart money says that by Friday that means this place belongs to the Nips. . . . ."

Seki Koyama haughtily cleared his throat. "Sorry, *Seki-san*," Joe quickly added, glancing at the combine operator. "Nothing personal intended."

"Apology accepted, *gaijin* asshole," Seki said, smiling a little and tipping his cup toward him.

"Anyway," Joe continued, looking back at McGraw, "by the end of the week we're all going to be laid off anyway. We're screwed and turned blue. Face it. Your authority and threats don't mean jack-shit to us anymore."

McGraw stiffened and laid her hand on the butt of her Taser, but Joe quickly shook his head. "Now, don't get all hot and bothered. Nobody's about to give you a necktie party or anything. But you might as well sit down and have a beer. Hell, there's nothing else you can do, right?"

At first it seemed as if Quick-Draw might actually heed his advice. Then her upper lip curled and she shook her head. "I've still got a job to do, even if it's only for a week."

"Aw, c'mon, Quick-Draw . . ."

Wrong thing to say; nothing irked McGraw more than having her hated nicknamed used in front of her. She pulled her baton out of her belt and, taking one step forward, patted it meaningfully in her left hand. "All right, Joe, stand up and get out of the way. I'm going to have to . . ."

"Hello?" someone said behind her. "Is this the right place?"

Startled, Quick-Draw spun around and raised her baton defensively, only to find Lester Riddell standing behind her. Just behind him was Butch Peterson; the senior scientist reflexively took a step back, but the general manager simply beamed at the security chief. "Tina!" he said in mock surprise. "How *nice* of you to come! Have you introduced yourself to everyone here?"

Annie Noonan looked over at Mighty Joe. "Great," she muttered, letting her eyes roll up. "There goes the goddamn neighborhood."

The storage room had gone quiet, but judging by their expressions most people had the same thought. Besides Quick-Draw McGraw, Les Riddell was probably the most disliked individual on the Moon; this was definitely the death of the party. Joe, however, shook his head. "Just wait," he whispered to Annie, not taking his eyes off the GM. "Let's just wait and see. . . ."

Quick-Draw had lowered her baton and relaxed a little. "Mr. Riddell," she said, formal as always when they were in the presence of other crew members. "As you can plainly see . . ."

"Yes, yes, yes," he interrupted, dismissively waving his hand. "There's a party going on and they've got a brewery." He looked over his shoulder at Mighty Joe. "Nice rig you've built there, Joe. What have you got in it? Moonshine?"

Everyone looked at Mighty Joe. The pilot grinned and patted the top of the makeshift brewer. "No sir," he replied. "Just a little home-brew beer. A little raw around the edges, but mighty tasty indeed." He paused, then casually added, "Care for a sip?"

"Well, I happen to be a teetotaler . . ." Lester began. Everyone except Joe seemed to sag a little: Aw, shit, here it comes. . . .

"But after the week I've just had," he finished, "I could use a beer."

And while every person in the storeroom was still trying to pick their jaws up off the floor and force their eyes back in their sockets, Les Riddell calmly pushed past Quick-Draw, walked down the center aisle, took the paper cup of warm, sudsy brew which the humongously beaming Mighty Joe held out to him, and took a long, slow sip.

The room was dead silent as Riddell swallowed, closed his eyes, and hissed between his teeth. *"Shiiiiit,"* he gasped. "That's strong!" Then he turned and looked back at Quick-Draw. "Tina, you gotta try this stuff," he urged, holding out his cup. "It'll put hair on your teeth."

Quick-Draw's face convulsed and went through various shades of purple; the fist holding the baton seemed to tremble with repressed fury. Her eyes traveled around the storeroom, and it seemed to dawn on her that every man and woman in the party was waiting for her next reaction. She took a deep sigh, resignedly shoved the baton back into her belt loop, and walked across the room to Lester.

"What the hell," she muttered. McGraw took the cup from the GM's hand and killed it one gulp. As a collective cheer rang out from the gathered moondogs, she thrust the cup back at Mighty Joe, pursing her lips and quickly nodding her head. Joe took the cup and began to refill it from the tap.

Amid the applause and whooping and howling, as everyone stood up to surround him—slapping his back, pushing more cups of beer at him, telling him that he was an all right kinda guy after all—Lester looked through the crowd at the door, raising his hand to coax Butch into the party.

But she had disappeared from the doorway, and was not to be seen anywhere in the storeroom. Sometime in the last couple of minutes, without his noticing, Butch had left.

It didn't take long for word to get out that an open-door beer bust was going on down in Storage Two and that even Quick-Draw McGraw had entered into the party spirit. Within an hour, everyone who wasn't working was in the lower level of Subcomp A, lined up with paper cups in hand. The party spilled out of the storeroom into the corridor and the central atrium, where people sat on the floors and the main stairwell: talking, joking, laughing, telling each other stupid stories, getting blasted on Mighty Joe's hellaciously potent home-brew.

Someone in MainOps informed the boys on the third shift that there was a party going down, and just when it seemed as if the party had reached a comfortable size, thirty more moondogs trooped through the nearby access tunnel from the EVA ready-room in Subcomplex B, still dressed in their hardsuit long johns and demanding their share of the beer. Even the non-drinkers among the crew—the handful of devout Mormons, Muslims, Buddhists and sundry health fanatics—decided to come down for the sociality, if not the booze. Quick-Draw soon had to open the door to the adjacent storm shelter just to make room for the spillover.

Mighty Joe's still had a fifty-gallon capacity; he had brewed that much moon-juice, yet it didn't last for very long with more than a hundred persons drinking from the tap. Shortly after 0100 hours he announced that the barrel was dry; by then, however, the party was already on its last, teetering legs. It had been a long, long time since most of the men and women of Descartes Station had drunk anything stronger than coffee, and Joe's fifteen-proof home-brew had hit most of them harder than a sack of lead. Within a half-hour of last call, almost everyone was gone from the party, having either staggered up the stairs to their dorms to sleep it off or—in the case of a few more inebriated folks—passing out cold on the floors of the corridor and the storm shelters. Quick-Draw might have rounded up those who had passed out, had she not been blitzed herself. Instead, she had last been seen struggling up the stairs, hanging on to the shoulder of some guy named Sid, to whom she'd become romantically attached. Of all the couples who had left the party together, those two would undoubtedly have the most privacy; after all, she had the keycard to the sacrosanct Descartes Hilton.

In Storage Two, a few of the last conscious carousers were left to stare dizzily at the debris: crumpled cartons of dehydrated crap, flattened paper cups, a few beer-soaked pieces of dis-carded clothing (including a pair of men's shorts and a woman's bra), and some indispensables like ankle-weights and keycards, which had been discarded and forgotten by their owners. The storeroom stank of booze and tobacco spit; the floor was slick and greasy with beer and puke.

Outside the storeroom and down the corridor, a couple of voices were singing: "This land is their land . . . it ain't our

land . . . from the Wall Street office . . . to the Cadillac car-
land. . . . ''

Mighty Joe, still maintaining his lonely post by the empty
vat, managed a perfectly disgusting belch which made him weave
a little on his perch. ''That's depressing,'' he grumbled to no
one in particular. After concentrating for a moment, he bawled:
''Well, standin' on the corner . . . with a dollar in my hand . . .
Lookin' for a woman who's lookin' for a man . . . Tell me how
long, do I have to wait? . . . Can I get you now, or must I
hesitate? . . .''

He stopped and slurped some more warm beer from his cup.
''That'll show 'em,'' he muttered.

Undeterred, and just a little louder now, the voices down the
hall continued singing in off-key *a capella*: ''If this is our land
. . . you'd never know it . . . so take your bullshit . . . and
kindly stow it. . . . ''

Listening to the distant voices, Lester, Annie, Quack, and
Tycho broke up laughing. Joe scowled and brayed: ''Well, the
eagle on the dollar . . . says in God we trust . . . Woman wants
a man, she wants to see a dollar first . . . Tell me, how
long . . .''

The discordant voices rose even louder, the bastardization of
Woody Guthrie's anthem drowning out Mighty Joe's attempt at
''Hesitation Blues'': ''So let's get together . . . and overthrow
it . . . then this land will be for you and me!''

The song ended with cheering and more laughter. ''Give it
up,'' Lester said, sitting on a collapsed crate of toilet paper.
''You'll never beat 'em.''

''Nyehh . . .'' Mighty Joe shook his head and sipped again
on his beer. Finding his cup near empty, he swiveled around
and pushed it underneath the spigot. He had lied about the beer
being tapped out. There was just enough left to make a few close
friends happy. Quack burped and held out his own paper cup,
and Joe managed to take it between the thumb and index finger
of his left hand while he refilled his own cup with his right hand.
''They got the right idea, anyway . . . I mean, anyway. I mean,
what the fuck's left?''

''No,'' Lester mumbled. ''We still . . . we still . . .''

Defiantly he held up a forefinger and shook it in the air as he
stared fixedly between his knees. Something was stirring in his
brain, weaving back and forth like a drunk driver trying to make
his way home without running into a police roadblock. He re-

membered something Arnie had said to him yesterday. Was it yesterday? A few hours ago—yep, that qualified as yesterday. . . .

"We've still got an option," he managed to say clearly.

"What are you talkin' about, man?" Tycho was zipped, too, but he was more coherent than anyone else in the room. He stroked the thick black beard he had cultivated over the past few weeks—his skull was still as bald as an eight ball—and peered straight at Lester. "The company? We're shit out of luck there. One week . . . two weeks tops . . . and we're all on the unemployment line." He shook his head dolefully. "Man, my father's gonna kill me. He told me not to come up to the Moon."

"Man's right." Mighty Joe passed Quack's cup back to him. "I mean, when he's right, he's right. The Japs'll have this place right in the pockets of their kimodos. . . . "

"Kimodo's a dragon," Quack said.

"Their saris . . ."

"That's what they wear in India."

"Well, their hibachis or their kamikazes or whatever the fuck they wear over there . . . Christ, where's Seki when I really need him?" Joe paused to belch noisily again. "Anyway, they'll have the base once Skycorp gets rid of it, and you know what's next? *Robots*, for the luvagod!" He swept his arm around to encompass the base. "Instead of a hundred hard-working American men and women, we've got twenty-five or fifty Japanese guys with VR helmets and wires coming outta their kazoos, sitting around teleoperating a buncha cheap-ass robots."

He leaned forward on his box, angrily jabbing a finger at them. "But you think a robot can tell if something's not right on a job? Hell, you think a *robot* has a sense of fucking *pride* in his work? Sure, maybe they'll save some bucks . . ."

"Yen."

"Go to hell, Quack. The point is . . ." He stopped as alcohol-fueled emotion overwhelmed his ability to form his thoughts into words. "Shit. The point is . . . the point is, people's what matters in the long run, not money or machines. And this is a place for people. We *made* this goddamn base, not some doohickey robot from Long Dong Electronics."

"Fuckin' A, bubba," Tycho said, holding up his cup in a toast. "Got that right in any language."

"Damn straight." Mighty Joe slumped back on his box and

took another sip. Then he looked over at Lester. "So what's our option there, Les? What've you got that can save us?"

Lester opened his mouth to speak. The others turned to listen attentively, and suddenly he stopped short of saying the first words. *Jesus Christ*, he thought, in the part of his mind that still retained a little sobriety. *What the hell am I doing? This shouldn't be discussed even when I'm not cross-eyed. This isn't the time, this isn't the place. . . .*

And yet, there was the realization that this *was* the time and the place. And more important, these were the people. More than a hundred people had trooped into this room tonight and gotten themselves rip-shit drunk. Two days ago, he wouldn't have believed that he could allow this to happen, let alone participate in it. He would have shut down the party the minute he walked through the door.

But he had been here, had gotten plowed with his crew—no, not his crew, his fellow workers—and what had he seen? Or rather, what had he *not* seen. Not one argument. Not a single fist fight. There was a sense of . . .

He sought for the right word, and found it: community. The moondogs of Descartes were, as a whole, loud and obnoxious and weirder than hell. Nonetheless, they were a community. They obviously felt it among themselves, even if it was never articulated. Lester felt it operating—and counted himself a part of it. And true communities don't take this kind of bullshit lying down. . . .

"Les?" Quack asked. "You've got something you want to say?"

Lester sucked in his breath. He knew what Moss had been suggesting; all evening he had been pondering the idea. And here it comes. . . .

"Yeah," he said. "One word . . ."

He stood up slowly, tottering on his feet, feeling the vile-smelling little storeroom tilt around him. Eight years on the wagon, pal, and look where it gets you: starting a goddamn worker's revolt.

"Strike," he said. "We're going on strike." Then he pitched forward and collapsed on the wet floor.

And just before he passed out, he heard Mighty Joe say, "Y'know, he might have something there. . . ."

20. Pressure Drop

Brain splitting, eyelids swollen and aching, stomach soured, bowels grumbling, tongue tasting like a rag that a sick dog had whizzed on, Lester awoke to the absolute, positively worst hangover of his life.

He lay still on the hard surface on which he had regained consciousness, rubbing his hands across his face. *Hands still work, and I've even got a face left. Doing great so far, kiddo.*

He began to size up his present condition. He was in a dark room, but it wasn't his niche in the bunkhouse. No, not quite so dark: There was pale silver-blue light streaming through a window just above him. Reggae music blared from somewhere nearby. He was lying on the floor of . . . *Oh, hey, I get it now. I'm on the floor of my office. Someone must have dragged me back here. Opened the door with my keycard and tossed me in. Good deal. Now, how long have I been out like this?*

He raised his right wrist in front of his face and touched a stud on his watch. The digital face lit up: 1306 hours. Good God, it was Sunday afternoon already. He should have been on his shift in MainOps hours ago. . . .

Lester started to sit up. His tender muscles betrayed him, though, and he collapsed back on the floor, his head striking the thin carpet. He hardly felt the impact. Perhaps he should just lie here for a few hours longer. It was dark, he was reasonably comfortable, and maybe the base could run itself without him for a day or two. *Why, sure it can*, he thought. *They don't need me upstairs. I mean, what could possibly require my attention . . . ?*

The get-happy calypso beat of "Pressure Drop" slowly faded from the speaker nearby, drowned out by Moondog McCloud's familiar voice. *Yeaaah now, The Maytals, rat-c'here on*

LDSM. . . '' Harry Drinkwater was sounding awful today, hoarse and rasping. *That's going out by special request of the strike committee, for all our brothers and sisters in the effort. . . .*

Strike committee? "Brothers and sisters in the effort?" he mumbled aloud. What kind of crazy shit was this?

Here's another reminder that there will be a special meeting of all station personnel . . . McCloud coughed raggedly. There was a noticeable lack of his usual hipster patter. *'Scuse me. There's going to be a meeting in the mess hall at exactly fourteen-hundred hours, for all those interested in participating in or supporting the strike. Till then, of course, work will be continuing as usual . . .* A dry chuckle. *For all you who are capable of working at all, that is. Just remember, now. Strike meeting at the mess hall in about an hour. Be seeing you. Now here's Wintermute and the Cowboys. . . .*

"What the hell?" Lester forced himself up on his elbows. Strike meeting? *Strike meeting?*

He suddenly recalled the last thing he had said last night—or rather, early this morning—just before the home-brew beer had won and he had plastered his face on the floor of Storage Two. Oh, no . . .

He struggled to his knees. Not that . . .

He lurched to his feet, retched and swallowed acidic bile, groped through the darkness for the door. *Don't tell me someone actually took me seriously. . . .*

At the exact same moment that he found the handle, he heard footsteps in the outside corridor and the door was abruptly opened from the other side. Standing in the shaft of bright light, Monk Walker was holding a steaming mug of hot coffee. "Lester?" he said. "Are you okay?"

One whiff of the coffee was all it took for his stomach to make one mighty, volcanic surge. "Sure," Lester managed to croak. "Just super . . ."

Then he doubled over and vomited on the floor.

Monk got Lester cleaned up and into some fresh clothes, and even managed to get some fresh coffee into his stomach, but there was nothing he could do for his hangover. "At least you got the rest of the booze out of your system by vomiting," the chief physician commented as they walked down the corridor to the mess hall. "I've been treating people like you all morning. Guess we should consider ourselves lucky that nobody came down with acute alcohol poisoning, considering the way you guys were drinking last night.''

''Yeah. Thanks.'' Lester still felt fatigued—why was it that getting drunk required so much work?—and even though the shower and the coffee had helped somewhat, the hangover was still very much with him. ''I appreciate it, Doc,'' he added, for lack of anything else to say.

They rounded a corner; the mess hall was straight ahead. The door was closed and Tycho was standing in front of it. ''It was worse for you because you've been on the wagon for so long,'' Monk added quietly.

Lester shot a look at him, and Monk nodded. ''Butch told me, and I checked your medical records. For recovered substance-abusers, a lost night in an eight-year period isn't all that uncommon.'' He paused. ''As long as you don't make a regular habit of it, that is. If it happens again, I might get seriously worried about you.''

''*Nggh.*'' Lester slowly shook his throbbing head. ''Don't worry. I think I just remembered all the reasons why I stopped drinking.'' Something else Monk had just said occurred to him; he stopped walking and turned to face him. ''Butch . . . Susan left shortly after we got to the party. Is she . . . ?''

''Mad at you?'' Monk stopped walking and folded his arms across his brown tunic. ''Sort of. More like disappointed, though.'' The string of wooden beads in his right hand clicked a couple of times. ''She cares for you,'' Monk added softly. ''Maybe a little more than you know. You let her down last night. If she wants to talk to you, though, it's going to have to be something she'll decide. Butch is stubborn that way.''

''You know her pretty well, don't you?''

''Pretty well, yeah.'' Monk raised an eyebrow and frowned at him. ''If you're insinuating that we're . . .''

Lester shook his head. ''No, no, nothing like that. I know about . . . um, about your vow of celibacy. What I'm getting at is . . .'' He faltered. ''Hell, Monk, if she likes me that much, why didn't she do anything about last night?''

There was the faintest hint of a smile on Monk's face. ''We're close friends, Les,'' he said, ''but that doesn't mean she always confides in me. When she talks to you again—*if* she talks to you again—you're going to have to pose that question to her yourself.'' He tapped Lester on the arm and cocked his head toward the door. "Better hurry now. I think the meeting's about to start."

However, when they got to the door, Tycho stepped in front of them to block their way. "You with the company?" he asked stonily. The question was directed more at Lester than at Monk; Tycho folded his arms across his chest and looked down at the general manager from his formidable height.

Lester sighed. "C'mon, Tycho, I run the joint. Lemme in." Tycho didn't budge, and Riddell tried again. "Remember who brought the subject up in the first place? Now let us in . . ."

He started to move past the huge moondog, but Tycho put out a hand and, firmly but gently, pushed Riddell back. "Question's still the same, man. I've already thrown Quick-Draw out of here. What's your excuse?"

It was, Riddell had to admit, a damn good question, at least for himself. However, he was also getting fed up. He was beginning to consider his chances of sucker-punching Tycho—which were not very good, at least in terms of getting away with it, let alone surviving Tycho's likely reaction—when Monk intervened. "We're here as nonpartisan observers," Monk said. "We won't interfere and we'll respect whatever decision is made in there."

Lester looked first at Monk, then back at Tycho. Monk shot him a warning glance; Tycho nodded once at Monk, then waited for Riddell's response. Obviously even Descartes' general manager—*especially* the GM—wasn't getting through the door unless his loyalties were made clear. "Okay, okay," Lester said reluctantly. "Nonpartisan observer."

Tycho didn't say anything, but his gaze never left Lester's face as he stepped out of the way. "Thanks," Lester said as he opened the door and walked into the mess hall. Again, Tycho said nothing, yet there was an amused glint in his eyes as he admitted them to the meeting.

The meeting was just starting as Lester and Monk entered, yet the moment they walked in, all eyes turned toward them and a mean silence descended upon the mess hall. Mighty Joe Young was standing at the head of the room; the pilot looked as if he was just about to bring the meeting to order, but Lester's entrance had stopped the proceedings cold. It was much like the general station meeting that Riddell had called upon his arrival almost seven weeks ago, yet this time Lester was clearly not in charge. Some things had not changed, though. He was no more welcome now than he was then.

There were two empty chairs at a table in the back of the room. Monk led the way through the uncomfortable silence to the table. The five moondogs already seated there said nothing as Lester sat down, but Riddell sensed that they would have moved had there been any other vacant seats. *Now I know what a leper feels like,* he thought.

"Okay . . ." Mighty Joe began, and the attention moved to him once again. "Thank you all for coming . . . uh, and I don't think I need to explain what this is all about. We're here to talk about a general walkout against the company. If our gatekeeper let you in the door, that means you're at least willing to discuss this without automatically taking sides with the company. Now let's . . ."

"What about *him*?" someone across the room shouted.

Similar grumbles swept through the room and Lester swallowed a hard stone in his throat. There was no doubt whom the unseen moondog meant. He glanced at the door and weighed his chances of making it outside before someone thrust a noose around his neck.

Mighty Joe held up his hands. "If Mr. Riddell is with us right now," he said, "it means he's at least willing to listen. That right, Les?"

Once again, every face in the room turned toward the back of the room. Lester quickly nodded his head and gave Mighty Joe the thumbs-up. Again there was discontented muttering, but no one moved to eject Riddell from the mess hall. Joe nodded back at him. "If the truth is to be told," he went on, "and I'm sure you'll agree with me that the time for bullshit is over"—he grinned like a pirate—"well, it was Lester himself who suggested a strike. Last night, when we were engaged in . . . uh, call it an executive-level meeting if you want."

Knowing laughter from around the mess hall. The temperature of the room seemed to warm just a degree or two. Lester guessed that most of the people at the meeting were suffering from hangovers of their own. He didn't have to wonder, though, about how fast the word of a general strike had moved among the crew. Nothing remained secret in Descartes Station for very long. Except maybe the facts . . .

The laughter died out. "Moving right along . . ." Mighty Joe continued.

"If it's *his* idea," the same voice from across the room demanded, "why don't we get *him* to speak?"

There was an abrupt silence . . . then, all at once, everyone began making noises of approval. Joe seemed unprepared for the suggestion; his eyes danced back and forth as he held up his hands in an attempt to restore order. "Hey, hey, *hey*—!" he yelled.

Monk laid a hand on Lester's shoulder. "If you want to get out of here . . ." he whispered. Lester shook off his hand. Moment of truth. If you want a chance to be heard, he thought, it's right this second. . . .

"All right!" he shouted as he stood up. "Okay! *Shut up!*"

If Lester had claimed that he had a grenade in his hand and was about to pull the pin, he couldn't have attracted more attention. Suddenly, the mess hall went still. In some sense, he was still the boss. Even if they didn't respect his opinion, at least they wanted to hear it. *Better make it good, because you're not going to get this break again.* . . .

"Joe's right," he said, addressing the faces around him. "It *was* my idea to go on strike, even if I was drunk when I said it. . . . " Precious few laughs. "And even if I am a bit hungover, I still support the idea. . . ."

Loud applause and yells started up. "Hold it!" he shouted, raising his arms. "Just *hold everything!*"

The noise died away again. Nervous, yet managing to hide his trembling hands, Riddell slowly walked down the center aisle between the tables, gradually making his way toward the front of the room.

"I'm in a favor of a strike," he continued, "but you've got to know what you're up against. . . . "

"Don't try to bullshit us," someone behind him said.

Lester didn't look around. "No bullshit. I'm not trying to talk you out of anything. You just need to know the odds before you start."

He held up a finger. "One. ASWI's not going to support us. The last union agreement with Skycorp specifically rules out a strike by any off-Earth employees for the life of the current contract, and that doesn't expire for another seventeen months. That means any strike we call is going to be illegal, and neither ASWI nor the AFL-CIO is going to be there to back us up. We'll be on our own. . . . "

A woman at a nearby table spoke up. "So what? If it's illegal, who gives a damn? What can Skycorp do about it?"

"That's a good question," Riddell replied. "What it means is that Skycorp can legally fire everyone on this base, whether they were participating in the strike or not. Since you're—since we're all union members, that makes us all culpable in the eyes of the law. Look it up in your union book if you don't believe me."

Again, there were murmurs from the crowd. Lester held up a second finger. "Two. The reason ASWI made that agreement with the company is because of the nature of what we do here. Now, maybe the Korean SPS project will be held up because we're not shipping them aluminum-roll or solar cells anymore, but that's not what's going to get to them. It's *oxygen*! If we won't ship oxygen to Skycan or any other orbital operations . . ."

He snapped his fingers. "They'll have to shut everything down. Or go seriously into the red. What I mean is that, within two or three weeks, Skycorp and Uchu-Hiko and NASA and all the other companies that use lunar oh-two for life-support and propellant will either have to ship up LOX from Earth or start bringing people back to the ground because they don't have anything for them to breathe. Either way, it'll will cost 'em some serious money."

"Then that's good leverage to use against them," Quack Lippincott said. "They don't give in, we don't send 'em any more air. Isn't that the general idea?"

"Yes and no." Riddell held up his hands to quell the noise before it could start again. "In theory, yeah, it's a great bargaining tool . . . but only if the other guy's playing clean."

He turned around slowly, pivoting on his feet to search out every eye he could find. "It's leverage, sure, but it also means they have the legal right to play dirty," he continued. "If you don't know it already, there's a special hangar at Phoenix Station for a military lander. It belongs to the 1st Space Infantry of the U.S. Marines. They built that lander just in case the Russians or the Japanese or someone else got nasty ideas about taking over Descartes by force. That's the whole reason why the 1st Space was formed, to protect American space installations against hostile takeovers. So you know, and I know, that the First could easily deploy troops on the Moon. . . ."

"You're lying!" someone yelled. "Siddown and shaddup!"

This time, though, there was no support for that lone opinion.

"You know it's true," Lester went on without raising his voice. "There's nothing secret about any of that. Now look at it from their point of view. An illegal strike. Critical supplies threatened, not to mention a precious trade agreement between the U.S. and Japan."

He stopped and looked at the hesitant faces arrayed around him. "We could have the posse coming down on us in a matter of days. And I shouldn't have to remind you that there isn't a single firearm on this base. A rapid-deployment force could overrun Descartes in a few hours, and all we could do is chuck a few rocks at them and use bad language."

Scattered coughs. Some mumbling. Everyone present knew that what Riddell had explained was true. Descartes Station was a mining operation, not a fortress. There had been no need to arm the base; any conceivable outside threat was supposed to be handled by the 1st Space. Yet no one had ever envisioned a day in which the cavalry itself would be the invaders.

"So what are you saying?" asked Casey Engel. "Give it up? Don't go on strike?"

"I don't much like that option," Joe said.

Lester glanced at him and nodded his head. "I don't either," he agreed, "but you have to know the risks involved before you—before we commit ourselves." He faced the room again. "Okay, those are the drawbacks. Now here's what we stand to gain."

Once more, he began to tick off points on his fingers. "One, if Uchu-Hiko buys Descartes from the company—and I received word yesterday that Skycorp's already working on just that kind of deal—we're all going to lose our jobs anyway. So it really doesn't matter if Skycorp fires us for calling an illegal strike. We're screwed if we do and screwed if we don't."

Scattered laughter. Riddell grinned and held up another finger. "Two, if we make sure that this is publicized, it means that Skycorp can't screw us without attracting public attention . . . and believe me, the first labor strike on the Moon is bound to make major headlines back on Earth. The Japanese like to conduct their business quietly. If they think acquiring Descartes is more trouble than it's worth, they may not decide to sign the deal."

He shrugged. "Who knows? It's a long shot, but if Uchu-Hiko decides to drop the ball because of a strike, then Skycorp doesn't have a ready and willing buyer for the base. And if that's the case, then we . . ."

His eyes, still wandering around the mess hall as he spoke, lit on a corner of the room where he hadn't looked before, and he saw Butch, her elbows propped up on the table, her face resting in her hands. She was gazing directly at him. The expression on her face was unreadable.

Don't think about that right now, he told himself. He deliberately turned his back to her. "Then we . . . then we've got a chance of keeping our jobs," he finished. "Maybe. Like I said, it's a long shot."

Whispers and murmurs coursed through the mess hall. "I don't know about all this 'long shot' stuff," Quack interrupted. "Let's say Uchu-Hiko decides not to buy the base and Skycorp has to keep us. We've still staged an illegal strike. That's bound to make the boys in Huntsville madder'n hornets. Who's to say they won't fire us anyway?"

"Nothing," Lester admitted, "except that they've staged one purge this year already. It cost them a lot of money to hire, train, and ship out new personnel to replace those they canned last April. Half of you guys represent a considerable dollar-investment for Huntsville. Somehow I have a hard time believing that they'll dump all of us, because it'll only mean that they have to replace us. That's a lot for any company to absorb in one fiscal year. And they've got to keep Descartes operational in order to complete the Korean SPS."

"Then we can't lose," Rusty Wright said.

Lester shook his head. "Oh, no, we can lose all right. I can think of a half-dozen things even a successful illegal strike can do to our benefits and bonuses. . . ."

"What hasn't the company done to our benefits and bonuses already?" another moondog yelled. "We've met the six-week quota and they still haven't kept their part of the bargain! If it was any worse, we'd qualify as slave labor!"

Once again, there were murmurs of agreement. Lester held up his hands for quiet. "Look," he said once the room had settled down, "it's not a black-and-white situation, calling an illegal strike like this. It can swing any which way. But we're already in a no-win situation, so I can't imagine how it can get much worse. . . ."

"An RDF squad from the 1st Space landing here and shooting

up the place could make it a whole lot worse,'' Quack pointed out.

Lester smiled and, looking over at the search-and-rescue chief, held up a finger. ''Maybe so, but I've got some ideas of my own in that contingency—some things we could do to defend ourselves. We could—''

He started to elaborate, then thought better of it. The last thing he wanted to do was give anyone a false sense of security. He stopped, and thrust his hands into his pockets. ''Look,'' he murmured, looking down at his shoes, ''I've gone on too long already. Mighty Joe's your strike leader, so maybe I ought to give the floor back to him. But I just want to say . . .''

Suddenly, he found himself without words, even though he knew what he wanted to say: *Whatever you do, please, don't let yourselves get hurt, because I can't bear to have another death on my conscience. I'll do whatever I can to help, but I won't permit any of you to get killed, because I've done that once already. . . .*

He looked around the mess hall, at the men and women whom he had bossed for the past six weeks. He couldn't tell them about a ghost he had met only a few days earlier.

''I'll help you in whatever way I can,'' he stammered. ''Maybe I'm the bastard you love to hate. Maybe I'm still the enemy to some of you guys, but I'm on your side, just as long as you don't . . .''

He couldn't say anything further. ''That's all,'' he finished. ''Thanks for listening.''

He ducked his head again and began walking back to his chair.

There was utter silence until he sat down again. He barely felt Monk Walker patting him on the shoulder, and he didn't look up when Mighty Joe Young called for a show of hands for those in favor of a strike. It wasn't until he raised his own arm and heard the whooping and howling that he looked up again and saw that, with the sole exception of Monk Walker, every man and woman in the room had raised their hands.

It was nearly unanimous. He let out his breath and slowly shook his head, feeling elated and frightened at the same time.

God help them, they were going on strike.

Front Page News
(Pressclips.5)

Excerpted from The New York Times *(on-line edition); August 19, 2024; headline: "LUNAR BASE WORKERS VOTE FOR STRIKE"*

HUNTSVILLE, Ala., Aug. 18—Skycorp workers employed at the Descartes Station mining facility on the Moon voted today to hold an illegal strike, sources at the space company's headquarters confirmed today. The strike, which became effective as of 6 P.M. Greenwich mean time, is in protest over Skycorp's alleged plans to sell the lunar base's capital assets to the Japanese space firm Uchu-Hiko Kabushiki-Gaisha, according to a statement issued directly to several news organizations, including the Times, from the striking workers.

According to the unsigned statement, which was faxed from Descartes Station via satellite, the vote to strike was "nearly unanimous" by the base's 110-person work force. In part, the statement reads: "Until Skycorp, ASWI, and Uchu-Hiko are ready to negotiate directly with us regarding the continuance of our employment on the Moon and overall future of the base, we have no choice but to shut down the mining, processing, manufacturing and exportation of all lunar-derived materials."

The statement claims that the strikers have "lost all faith in the ability of our union to fairly represent our interests in these matters." It also accused the union, the Amalgamated Space Workers International (ASWI), of "conspiring" with Skycorp to "undermine the members of Local 7 in order to fatten their own pockets and meet the union's own short-term interests."

Spokespersons from both Skycorp and ASWI deny charges of collusion against the members of ASWI Local 7 and claim that the strike is illegal because it violates a "no-strike" clause in the current union contract reached two years ago between the company and ASWI Local 7, which is Descartes Station's local board of the spaceworkers union.

"We cannot negotiate in good faith with the strikers because they haven't acted in similar good faith with us," said Holly D'Amato, a spokesperson for Skycorp at the press conference at which the strike was officially confirmed by the company. "When they're ready to call off their strike and be legally represented again by ASWI, then we'll discuss their real or imagined grievances."

Ms. D'Amato would not comment on the strikers' allegation that Skycorp was planning to sell Descartes Station to Uchu-Hiko, other than to say that the lunar base's future "is currently under review by the corporation's board of directors and its major stockholders." It was disclosed last Friday that the lunar base's permaice reserves, located at Byrd Crater at the Moon's north pole, had fallen critically short. This in turn caused Skycorp's price-per-share on the New York Stock Exchange to plummet by an average of 15 points. It has sparked rumors that Skycorp might divest itself of its capital assets on the Moon *[see related story, page D-1]*.

William Alstead, a spokesperson for ASWI's headquarters in Washington D.C., said that the strikers' accusation of collusion between Skycorp and the union was "absolute, unmitigated nonsense." He said that, because the strike is in violation of the current agreement, "we can't help but take sides with Skycorp in order to protect the current contracts between other union locals and Skycorp."

In the last fiscal year, Descartes Station produced and exported 90,000 tons of finished material, including aluminum, glass, oxygen, and silicon-based solar cells. Ms. D'Amato said that this figure fell short of the base's expected output of at least 115,000 tons, and that the base's personnel had been "placed on probation" until a larger quota was delivered from them in the six-week period which ended on August 13, last Tuesday. She would not comment on whether the workers had met this quota by the deadline.

"Much of that quota is oxygen, which is necessary to support manned operations in Earth-orbital space," Ms. D'Amato said, adding that much of that was sold by Skycorp to the U.S. government for its own operations. "The strikers should be warned that cutting off such a life-critical resource may not be tolerated by NASA."

Public affairs officials of the National Aeronautics and Space Administration's headquarters in Washington D.C. had no immediate comment on the strike. . . .

From The New York Times *(on-line edition); August 19, 2024. Sidebar headline: "Space Marines Placed on Alert"*

VANDENBERG AFB, Calif., Aug. 18 (Associated Press)— Unofficial sources at the U.S. Air Force Space Command here stated today that the 1st Space Infantry, U.S. Marine Corps., has been placed on full alert in connection with the work-stoppage at Descartes Station on the Moon. Eyewitnesses at the military space shuttle launch facility here say that the USAF shuttle *Concord* has been rolled out for launch.

The same unofficial sources also say that the U.S.S. lunar transport *Valley Forge* is being prepared for launch from Earth orbit in the event that "military intercession becomes necessary." Official sources at Vandenberg AFB and the Pentagon would neither confirm nor deny the reports.

21. Full Moon

"Okay, whoa!" Mighty Joe snapped into his headset mike. "Swing left, left . . . a little more, just a little . . . "

Wanna be a little more specific? Seki Koyama's voice said in his headset. *I mean, a "little" can be a foot, or two feet, or a yard or . . .*

"Just hold it. You're doing fine." Mighty Joe glanced down at a hand-sketched diagram lying on top of the console, then peered through the windows of the traffic control cupola. Out beyond the landing pads, the bulldozers were slowly shoving mounds of regolith into place, gradually forming steep, narrow berms of rock and soil. "Just push it in now. Make it as high as you can . . . ."

Okay. Roger that. The blade of the nearest 'dozer dipped to the ground and began to inch forward, shoving more gravel and dirt in front of it. Koyama, riding Dozer Three, was building barriers to block the hangar doors of the spacecraft maintenance building; the three landing pads themselves were presently occupied by the two tugs and one of the LRLT's, effectively preventing the pads from being used by the 1st Space. Koyama stopped about fifty yards from the edge of Pad Two and the eastern corner of Subcomp B, just below the vehicle ramps of the garage. *How's that?*

Joe looked again at the defense plan he and Lester had drawn last night. "Close enough," he replied. "Keep working on it. When you're done there, go down and do the same thing between Pad One and Pad Two. Be careful of the storage tanks, though. I don't want . . . "

You don't want me to hit 'em. Right. Koyama was beginning to sound exhausted. No wonder; he had been out on EVA for the past four hours. Operating a 'dozer was a bitch even out in the regolith field; working in the close confines of the base itself, surrounded by equipment and buildings, was enough to make anyone gripe. Mighty Joe made a mental note to get a replacement for Seki; perhaps he could get another heavy-metal pusher out there soon to spell him . . . .

Yeah. Fat chance of that. It was 2100 hours Monday; almost everyone had spent the last couple of days fortifying the base. Anyone who was still conscious was busy with something else. Mighty Joe Young stretched his aching back, feeling the hours he himself had spent in the cupola, bent over the diagram while supervising the erection of the barricades. Once again, he gazed around the southern perimeter of the base from his vantage point on top of Subcomp B. One 'dozer was building a long berm to block Airlocks One and Two; on the opposite side of the sub-complex, beyond Pad Three, another 'dozer was doing the same for Airlocks Five and Six. Once another berm was built between Pad One and Pad Three, the interior airlocks from the unpressurized spacecraft hangars, Three and Four, would be effectively barricaded.

Okay. So much for the main entrances to the base. But that still made the nukes vulnerable. The SP-100 nuclear power plants, located in the bottom of the crater at the southwestern periphery of the base, simply could not be adequately protected; their high radioactivity prevented anyone from approaching them in a hurry. Maybe the Marines could try shutting them down as a last resort . . . .

Naw, Joe thought, shaking his head. Even if they wanted to chance it, the nukes were at their lowest output right now. Since Descartes was in full-daylight at this time, the base was drawing most of its power from the solar farm, so shutting down the SP-100's would not cause a critical loss of power. Even so, the seldom-used underground access tunnel which led from the base to the crater was being blocked from within, just in case the Marines tried to use that as a means of getting into the base. The grunts would have a hard time taking Descartes.

"Who are you kidding?" he muttered to himself, tiredly massaging his eyes with his fingertips. If and when the 1st Space landed—and Joe had no doubt that it was more of a matter of *when* than *if*—the barricades and blocked airlocks wouldn't do much more than slow them down. Maybe it's only going to be a small handful of them, he thought, and maybe we've got a few more cards up our sleeves . . . but if they want to shoot their way into the place, I don't see how in the hell we're going to stop 'em unless we shoot back. And there's not so much as a slingshot in the whole goddamn—

His beltphone buzzed; Joe unclipped it and spoke into the mouthpiece. "Young here," he muttered.

It's Lester. The GM's voice sounded snappish; it was vaguely comforting to know that Riddell was feeling the pressure as well. *Did you get in touch with that crazy hermit pal of yours? Umm . . . Honest Yuri, or whatever he calls himself.*

Young nodded despite the fact that Riddell couldn't see him. "Yeah, I called him last night and told him what's going on. I thought he should be filled in."

What did he say?

"Not much of anything," Joe replied, "but that's typical of Yuri. Why, did he just get back to you?"

Yeah. He's in a truck about a mile and a half north of here, coming in. Says he's got something for us and wants you to meet him outside Airlock Five. You know what's going on with him?

"No, I don't." Mighty Joe turned and peered to the north. Between the low hills, he could make out a distant pair of headlights moving toward the base. "He's weird, but he's okay. What did he say he had?"

Something about bringing us the Night Gallery, Lester replied, and Joe suddenly found himself grinning. *Whatever that is. Do you have the foggiest notion what he's . . . ?*

Joe laughed out loud. "I think I do," he said. "Get Quack or somebody up here to run the show. I'm going below to put on a suit and go see him . . . um, and try to find Annie Noonan for me, okay? Get her to meet me in the ready-room for suit-up. I think I know what Yuri's got in mind."

Sure, but your girlfriend's already on EVA, over in the north quadrant. Several moondogs in the north quad were working to place shields over the few exposed windows in Subcomp D. Joe wasn't aware that Annie had volunteered for the job. *I'll get her to skip over and . . .*

There was a pause. Joe heard background voices from Main-Ops. Looking over his shoulder, he could see indistinct figures moving through the windows of the control center. Lester's voice returned a few moments later. *Gotta run. Huntsville just came on the horn, and TRAFCO just said that something's happening in cislunar space. . . .*

"Shit!"

You got it, ace. I think it's starting. Riddell's voice had taken on an urgent tone. *I'll get Quack up there, but don't waste any more time with this Yuri character than you have to. I think the countdown just started.*

"Got it," Mighty Joe said, but Lester had already clicked off. Joe hastily clipped the phone back on his belt, turned around and headed for the passageway leading to the EVA ready-room. Perhaps he shouldn't be bothering with Honest Yuri, just when all hell was beginning to break loose. But he also had the sneaking suspicion that Yuri had something useful to offer them.

Okay, so he's a mad genius, he thought as he ducked into the passageway. But right now, any kind of genius is better than none at all.

It wasn't Arnie Moss who was on the phone from Huntsville this time. Nor was it Skycorp's CEO, Dallas "Rock" Chapman, as Lester had anticipated. And that was definitely a bad sign.

You were, perhaps, expecting your friend Mr. Moss. Kenneth Crespin—polished and proper, neatly dressed in his habitual dark blue pinstripe suit—gazed calmly out of the screen on Riddell's desk in MainOps. *I regret to inform you that Mr. Moss's employment with this company has been terminated. For the time being, I will be assuming his duties as vice-president of lunar operations.*

Riddell tried not to let his anger show. Arnie had been fired, no doubt because of their phone conversation two days ago. Skycorp had a knack for finding out what their execs did behind the company's back; the company's internal security division had probably tapped his telephone at home. In hindsight, Lester should have expected Skycorp to do something like that. Crespin must be enjoying this, he thought. It gets him one seat closer to the president's office. But he immediately tried to put Arnie out of his mind; it wouldn't do any good for Crespin to see that he was irritated.

"Sorry to hear that, Kenneth," he said, absently juggling a pen between his fingers. "But I was rather expecting to be hearing from Rock. Will he be joining us on a conference line?"

Crespin smiled with irritating smugness. *No, he will not. Mr. Chapman has delegated the matter at hand to me. I'm to make sure that this nasty piece of business is brought to a satisfactory conclusion.* He paused, then added, *Without its getting nastier, of course.*

Lester wondered about that. Dallas Chapman was a former NASA astronaut; in fact, he had commanded the second lunar expedition, following the one that Riddell himself had piloted in '05. Lester knew "Rock" Chapman well; he was very much a hands-on sort of executive, who normally would not have relinquished the responsibility of an in-space crisis such as this to a desk jockey like Ken Crespin. Some sort of a power struggle might be taking place in Huntsville. The board of directors could have taken the matter out of Rock's hands and put Crespin in charge.

It made a certain kind of sense. Kenneth Crespin had been one of the few Skycorp senior executives who had weathered the Big Ear crisis of eight years ago without his reputation being tarnished, even though the spysat system had been largely his project. It was fairly common knowledge within the company that Crespin had survived because he had put lower-level associates on the front lines to take the bullets meant for himself. Perhaps the board was hoping that Crespin could handle the strike just as smoothly.

All of this was conjecture, though, and not doing Lester a damn bit of good right now. Below the dais, several people were clustered around the TRACFO and TELMU stations trying to track and identify the spacecraft which Descartes' long-range radar had picked up in cislunar space at the same time that Crespin had called. Riddell was careful not to look in their direction.

"Getting nasty?" he replied smoothly. "Going on strike is a fine old American tradition, Kenneth. It's not like a declaration of war, after all."

You might just as well have hoisted the Jolly Roger, Crespin replied. *Of course, some of your people are rather experienced at piracy, aren't they? I suppose you'll be taking hostages next.*

"Piracy?" Riddell blinked innocently. "Whatever are you talking about, Kenneth? And as far as hostages go, the few people here who did not vote in favor of the walkout are not being harassed or harmed in any way. That includes our chief physician and our security chief."

Dr. Walker's religious convictions are a matter of record. As a Buddhist monk, he wouldn't participate in a tawdry little labor strike like this unless lives were at stake. His reserve is admirable. I would have expected it of you as well. . . .

"Surprise, surprise," Lester drawled, barely able to hide his smile.

As for Ms. McGraw, Crespin continued, *her failure to contain this crisis . . . well, this affair might have led NASA to fire her on our recommendation if she had not acted first. She tendered her resignation in writing earlier this morning, in a letter faxed directly to us.*

This time, Lester was unable to conceal his shock. "Quick-Draw . . . I mean, Tina resigned?" He shook his head. "I . . . she hadn't told me about this before."

She quit before she was fired, Crespin said haughtily. *Personally, that seems to be a prudent course of action. You and others up there might well consider doing the same thing before things get a little rough.*

Here we go . . . "Let's cut out the double-talk, okay?" Lester leaned back in his seat and clasped his hands together in his lap. "What have you got on your mind?"

Crespin glowered at him from the screen. *It wouldn't do much good for me to claim now that Skycorp isn't planning to sell Descartes to Uchu-Hiko,* he said. *I have to hand it to you, your ability to foresee coming events has been rather sharp. In fact, Rock is at this moment engaged in negotiations with the Japanese regarding the sale of the facilities. . . .*

"I figured as much. Go on."

You should also know by now that ASWI is opposed to this illegal strike, he continued. *And the AFL-CIO has just issued a statement that it won't support your strike either. However, our business partners in Tokyo are a little more understanding. They realize that there will be a need for certain in-place expertise once they've acquired Descartes. After all, you can put people through simulators until hell freezes over and you still won't have that necessary core of experience to . . .*

"I hear the Japanese make great simulators," Lester said briskly. "What are you driving at?"

Leniency. If you and the other leaders of this strike will convince the rest to drop the action and resume work, management and foremen may be rehired by Uchu-Hiko once they've acquired the base. That is, your jobs will be continued without interruption. Kenneth smiled. *Just as if this . . . well, let's call it a philosophical disagreement . . . never occurred in the first place. Not a bad deal, considering.*

"Considering," Lester repeated. "But the key word here seems to be 'maybe.' "

Crespin shook his head. *I can't speak for the Japanese. I can only repeat what Uchu-Hiko's chairman, Mr. Hiyakawa, told me on the phone this morning.*

"Hmm. Interesting." Lester wasn't ready to trust Ken Crespin for a moment. Even if Uchu-Hiko's CEO had agreed to the outlined proposal, there was no way of knowing for sure. Not as long as Crespin was running the show. And this was even supposing that Riddell had the ability to stop the walkout all by himself, which he didn't. He was not about to confess to Crespin that a decision to strike had been put in motion while he himself had been passed-out on his office floor. It did tell him one more thing, though: Skycorp and Uchu-Hiko clearly believed that he was the chief instigator of the strike.

Pretending to be thinking things through, he casually looked away from the camera at the MainOps floor. The TELMU on duty, Doug Baker, seemed to perceive that the GM was looking his way. He looked over his shoulder, pointed at the blip on his screen, and nodded his head gravely. "Marines," he said very quietly.

Riddell nodded back in acknowledgment, covering the gesture by coughing into his fist. He looked back at the camera. "And if we don't take up your offer?"

That's not a wise idea, Lester. Riddell couldn't help but notice that this was the first time Crespin had addressed him by his first name. *There's good reasons why you should seriously consider our proposal.*

"I'm listening."

It doesn't matter very much if you've delayed the Korean SPS project. That's the sort of thing which tends to be self-correcting. But you've also bottlenecked the shipment of oxygen supplies to other orbital operations.

"Oh, really?"

Oh really. In fact, the U.S. government is rather upset with you and your little band of pirates. Losing a Spam-can or three is something which can be ignored over the long haul . . .

"Excuse me?" Lester interrupted. "I think we've got a little static here on the line. . . ."

Crespin continued undeterred. *But shutting down the flow of a vital resource is more than a few persons in power can bear.* He pointed a finger at the screen. *Get this straight, once and for all. If you and your compatriots continue cutting off key consumables . . .*

"Wonderful alliteration," Lester said, smiling. "Ever thought of working in dinner theater?"

. . . an RDF squad from the 1st Space Infantry will be launched at 1200 hours GMT tomorrow from Phoenix Station, Crespin went on. *They'll come down and swarm all over your gang like . . .*

He stopped and smiled gloatingly. *Well, I suppose you can imagine the results. I shouldn't have to remind you that you're unarmed and utterly defenseless.* He paused again. *Of course, if you're willing to negotiate a quick end to this strike . . .*

"Hmmm. Maybe we shouldn't rule out negotiation altogether." Lester looked away again to buy a few precious seconds, contemplatively stroking his chin while he looked at the image which was displayed on the TRAFCO screen. Crespin was telling only half the truth. The *Valley Forge* wasn't about to launch—it was already on its way. Since the military moonship had the new GE Pegasus nuclear rocket as its AOMV, at constant thrust it would make the trip in little less than half the time lunar transit usually took. They could be here by tomorrow. Yet Crespin had obviously underestimated not only the base's ability to track spacecraft in cislunar space, but also Riddell's own knowledge of the 1st Space.

Crespin isn't interested in negotiation of terms, he suddenly realized. *The only thing he or Skycorp will accept is complete surrender.*

And it was obvious that he wasn't the only one at Descartes who had hit upon that realization. Around him, MainOps had gone quiet. The command crew had been eavesdropping on their conversation, but now their interest was not quite so subtle. They openly watched their general manager, apparently wondering if he was going to sell out, now that the Marines were on the way and amnesty had been offered to strike leaders who bowed to pressure from the company.

Good Lord, he thought, *what am I going to have to do to earn these guys' trust? Put on a hardsuit and start walking around the outside of the base with a sign reading "On Strike"?*

"Okay," he said at last, looking back at the camera. "I'll take your proposal under advisement. Maybe we can . . . ah, reach some sort of accommodation."

"Bastard," he heard someone whisper.

Crespin's smile grew larger. *Very good. I take it you've seen my point.*

You son of a bitch, Lester thought. You think you've already won. . . . "Oh, you've made your point, all right," he said. *You've made your point that you can't be trusted,* he added silently. "We have three demands."

All right. Crespin picked up a pen from his desk and prepared to write; more theatrics, since Riddell had no doubt that the entire conversation was being taped and monitored by others. *Fire away.*

From around the command center, Lester felt everyone's eyes upon him. "First," he said, "I want amnesty extended to everyone participating in the strike, now and after the sale of the base. No firings, no layoffs, no reprisals in terms of salary or bonuses. We don't care if we work for Skycorp or for Uchu-Hiko, but everyone here keeps their job at the same rate of pay."

Crespin raised an eyebrow and his pen stopped moving. *Come now. After all this you can't possibly expect the company to . . .* He sighed. *Oh, all right, if you must. I'll at least bring it to their attention. Next?*

"Second," Lester continued, "an end to the embargo on nonessential supplies. We're not slave labor, and we don't like being treated as such. If we ask for something . . . books, films, underwear, chewing tobacco, a new Coke machine, whatever . . . we're going to get it as long as it doesn't violate company rules against contraband."

Oh, certainly. Certainly. Even as Crespin was writing, Riddell could tell from his face that there was no more chance of the second demand's being met than the first. Quarter of a million miles away, he reflected, and I can still tell the bastard's got his fingers crossed.

Crespin looked up from his notepad again. *Very well,* he said with a condescending smirk. *Your third demand?*

I'm going to enjoy this . . . "My third demand," Lester said slowly and carefully, "is that I want you to come up here personally and kiss my ass."

What? The VP's smile vanished. He shook his held in bewilderment. *Pardon me, but I'm not quite sure I understood what. . .*

From the looks on the faces of the MainOps crew, it didn't seem as if they believed that they'd heard him correctly either. "The way I figure it," Lester said, "you owe me a little something. You sent me up here, deliberately expecting me to run the base into the ground. I take that as a personal insult. Then you reneged on the terms of the six-week probation period and didn't give these guys their bonuses for meeting your own production quota, so that's an insult to them.''

Riddell shook his head. ''That wasn't very nice of you. But since I'm a nice guy, I'm willing to forgive and forget.'' He paused. ''All that you have to do is to kiss . . . my . . . ass.''

Crespin glared out of the screen at him. *Really, Lester,* he said with infinite condescension. *There's no reason to be crude about this.*

''Crude?'' Lester was already standing up. ''Looky here, Kenneth. Let me show you crude. . . .''

He then turned around, unbuckled his belt and unzipped his fly, pushed down his trousers and underwear, and bent over so that his buttocks were thrust straight at the camera lens.

As everyone in Main-Ops whistled and hooted, he added, ''No pun intended, Mr. Crespin, but this is called a full moon. Get it?''

No reply. By the time Lester had straightened up and pulled up his pants, Kenneth Crespin had already switched off. Amid the applause and cheers, Lester smirked as he rebuckled his belt. ''I think he got it,'' he said to no one in particular.

He then clapped his hands for attention. ''Okay, listen up!'' he shouted, and the uproar in MainOps gradually died away. ''That *was* crude . . . ''

''But effective,'' Baker added. More laughter.

Lester grinned and held up his hand for silence. ''But it doesn't get us off the hook. The ball's back in their court, and if you haven't heard already, we've got a 1st Space RDF squad breathing down on us. TRAFCO can work out the exact ETA, but my guess is that the *Valley Forge* will be here within twenty-four hours. You know the game-plan and you've received your assignments. We've still got a lot to do between now and then, so let's get to it.''

A few more yells and a smattering of applause, but now the show was over and everyone was heading back to work. Lester needed a cup of coffee badly. He walked away from his desk, stepped off the dais, and was turning to head for the stairs when he came face to face with Susan Peterson.

''Oh. Hi.'' He hadn't spotted her before now; she must have entered MainOps in the middle of his talk with Crespin. In fact, it was the first time he had been near her since just before he had found the party in Storage Two on Sunday night; it felt like a week had passed since then.

"Hi yourself," she said. There was a faint, coy smile on her face.

And the last time you saw me, he thought, I was about to get drunk. Embarrassed, he looked down at his feet. "What's up?" he asked, lacking anything else to say.

"Well, your bare tush, for one thing . . . "

"Oh, jeez," he murmured, "you caught that." The only thing hotter than his face was the lunar surface outside the windows. "I was just . . . I was trying to . . . "

"Make a point. Right." Still smiling, she shrugged her shoulders. "Nice ass, I've got to admit," she added softly, stepping a little closer.

"Uhhh, well . . . "

Before he could stop her, she reached around him, in a way so that no one else could see what was going on, and gave his butt a little squeeze. "I think," she whispered into his ear, "I know something better to do with that ass than show it off to a company vice-president, don't you think?"

Lester took a deep breath. "The strike . . . "

Butch took her hand from his ass and laid a finger across his lips. "Can get along without you for a little while. Now c'mon. We've got a little unfinished business, you and I."

She lowered her hand and gracefully stepped around him, brushing her fingers across the back of his left hand as she headed for the stairwell. Lester looked around the operations center once more. No one was paying attention to them. Then, without looking back, he followed Butch to the entrance to MainOps and down the spiral staircase.

Conjecture of a Time
(Montage.3)

Alone at last in the infirmary, Monk Walker meditates. The lights are dimmed, his surgical instruments, bandages, and anesthesia are laid out on sterile white cloths in readiness for the uncertain hours ahead, the hallway door is shut just for once to preserve the peace. Monk sits cross-legged on a gurney, rolling his string of wooden beads between his fingers. Alone, but not in silence. On the tape deck, a book-tape slowly spins, the crimson LED light sparking on and off as Kenneth Branagh recites from *Henry V*:

> *"Now entertain conjecture of a time*
> *When creeping murmur and the poring dark*
> *Fills the wide vessel of the universe. . . ."*

Across the hall and down the corridor, behind the closed door of the general manager's office, Lester Riddell slides Susan Peterson's open shirt from her shoulders. Weak blue earthlight shines through the window, touching the raised nipples of her breasts. Her shirt rustles gently as it drops to the floor, joining the rest of their clothes at their feet. He gently cups his hands around her breasts and, as she draws him closer, starts to say something, but she shakes her head and wordlessly shushes him as she stands on tiptoe and places her mouth over his. . . .

> *"From camp to camp, through the foul womb of night,*
> *The hum of either army stilly sounds,*
> *That the fixed sentinels almost receive*
> *The secret whispers of each other's watch. . . ."*

In the EVA ready-room, suit techs move from empty hardsuit to empty hardsuit, prepressurizing air tanks, cleaning helmet faceplates, double-checking radios. Tomorrow there will be no time for the usual checkout routine; it must all be done in advance of the landing of the 1st Space Infantry. Kneeling in front of Airlock Two, an electrician consults the manual on the floor, uses a tiny screwdriver to make a final unauthorized adjustment to the pin-plate of the delicate electronic circuitry within, then shuts the service panel, picks up his toolbox and book, and heads for Airlock Three. . . .

> *"Fire answers fire, and through their paly flames*
> *Each battle sees the other's umbered face.*
> *Steed threatens steed, in high and boastful neighs*
> *Piercing the night's dull ear; and from the tents*
> *The armourers, accomplishing the knights,*
> *With busy hammers closing rivets up,*
> *Give dreadful note of preparation. . . ."*

Out on the lunar surface, beyond the barricades of gray-brown sand and rock surrounding the main airlocks, the last of Honest Yuri's statues is gently unloaded from the bed of the truck on which it was carried from the Night Gallery. Six moondogs carefully haul the heavy, scowling demon down from the huge-tired vehicle, gasping as they collectively struggle to set the scrap-metal creature upright on the soil. Farther away, within the walls of the newly risen battlements, two more moondogs find a place within the curled forms of the welded-aluminum lovers to place a slender round cartridge. It fits neatly between their touching bellies; the moondogs grin lasciviously at each other, and then one touches a switch on the bottom of the cartridge, causing a red LED to light. Nearby, Honest Yuri watches; the expression on his face is unreadable behind the silver mask of his helmet faceplate, on which are reflected the lights of other vehicles moving past him in the distance. . . .

> *"The country cocks do crow, the clocks do toll,*
> *And the third hour of drowsy morning name . . ."*

Standing before a window in MainOps, Mighty Joe Young silently watches as the 'dozers and rovers, now freed from their other jobs, move into their strategic positions on the outskirts of the base. Around him, a skeleton crew of command personnel sit through their graveyard shift at their consoles, listening to their headphones, studying the rubric of code-numbers and code-letters scrolling up their flatscreens, occasionally glancing up—again—at the main screen on which the trajectory of the *Valley Forge* is displayed. Mighty Joe fights back a yawn. Almost as if by magic, a fresh mug of coffee appears in front of him, followed by the smooth touch of slender fingers at the nape of his neck. He looks around at Annie Noonan, smiles back at her, and takes the coffee mug from her hand. . . .

"Proud of their numbers and secure in soul,
The confident and overlusty French
Do the low-rated English play at dice;
And chide the cripple tardy-gaited night,
Who like a foul and ugly witch doth limp
So tediously away. . . ."

The rec room is vacant, the corridors empty, the mess hall deserted. Those who are not working are in the dorms. In some niches, tense games of gin and poker are being played, to while away the long hours. In others, men and women turn restlessly in their sleep—tossing their blankets, pounding their pillows—or don't sleep at all. In her bunk in 2-B, Tina McGraw stares up at the ceiling, feeling cool tears slide down her face as she silently weeps for a job lost, a career squandered. Above her, on level 1-B, Seki Koyama gazes at a postcard on his wall of Mount Fuji, hoping to gain courage from its formidable snow-capped cone, finding none except what little he can muster from within himself. Over in 1-A, Tycho dozes, wakes up, dozes, wakes up again to the sound of fingers tapping on a keyboard from somewhere down the row of niches. At first he thinks to get up, put on his shorts, stalk down there, and bang on some-one's door and tell him to cut-it-the-fuck-out. But then, just as impulsively, he decides that something important must be happening down the hall, so instead he rolls over and buries his shaved head beneath his pillow. . . .

"The poor condemned English,
Like sacrifices, by their watchful fires
Sit patiently and only ruminate
The morning's danger; and their gesture sad,
Investing lank-lean cheeks and war-worn coats,

Presented them unto the gazing moon
So many horrid ghosts. . . .''

Harry Drinkwater sits on the edge of Willard DeWitt's bunk
and watches as DeWitt scans the cryptic figures ceaselessly
winding up the screen of his laptop computer. The latest numbers from Wall Street, messages from brokerages in New York,
Chicago, Rio, Houston, Tokyo, London, Paris, the Hague, Atlanta . . . Willard alternately chuckles, sighs, snarls, mutters,
curses, and laughs again, all while his nimble fingers dance
across his keyboard and his eyes dart to the reams of printout
thrown across the desk, the floor, his lap, the bunk next to Harry.
Drinkwater is dog-tired; his eyes feel grainy, threatening to
squeeze shut for one last time. Yet, at the same time, he is
mesmerized by the high-stakes game being played. Financial
alchemy is being performed, and DeWitt, who has all but forgotten that someone is in his niche with him, is the sorcerer
stirring a cauldron of price-indices and market-quotes and a
dozen different currencies. Working within the nebulous network
of banks and brokerages, hidden behind a galaxy of cutouts and
false (and very real) accounts, Willard DeWitt is struggling to
make a miracle happen. This is something you don't snooze out
upon. . . .

''O now, who will behold
The royal captain of this ruined band
Walking from watch to watch, tent to tent,
Let him cry, 'Praise and glory to his head . . . !' ''

Monk lies back on his gurney, the beads still clicking between
his fingers. . . .

Butch gasps, arching backward, as the first wave of orgasm
reaches her; on the floor between her thighs, Lester shouts as
white-hot pleasure-pain rushes through his body. . . .

The electrician slaps shut the service panel of Airlock Five as
the last hardsuit in the ready-room passes inspection. . . .

Another cartridge is loaded by a moondog into a Night Gallery sculpture as Honest Yuri turns his back and slowly trudges
away. . . .

A rover is put in position, its driver climbing out of the saddle
to give the thumbs-up to MainOps. Mighty Joe returns the ges-

ture as he sips from his mug of now lukewarm coffee. Annie catches a few winks in an empty chair next to him. . . .

The last card game finally winds down. Quick-Draw, Seki, and Tycho finally find a way to go to sleep. . . .

"For forth he goes, and visits all his host,
Bids them good morrow with a modest smile,
And calls them brothers, friends, and countrymen. . . ."

And, through the long night-that-isn't, Willard DeWitt works the numbers, manipulating dollars and cents.

22. Shady Grove

Operation Shady Grove began at 1700 hours GMT on Tuesday, when the twin PBR nuclear engines of *Valley Forge*'s AOMV made a five-minute braking burn which placed the military spaceship in low orbit fifty miles above the Moon. Before retrofire, the five-person U.S. Marine Corps RDF squad had already crawled from the crew module, through five small hatches located laterally on top of the lander, the *Delaware*, directly into their combat armor suits in the belly of the remora vehicle. The *Delaware*'s pilot, wearing a normal hardsuit, climbed through his own hatch into the bubble-shaped cockpit in the bow of the lander. The five Marines sealed their CAS armor from within and the *Valley Forge*'s bosun's mate battened down the external hatches before returning to the flight deck.

As soon as the *Valley Forge*'s nuclear engines completed the burn, and its pilot, Lt. Commander Frank Jaffrey, told the *Delaware* that LLO had been successfully achieved, Captain Jacob "Lazy Jake" McAdams ran through the quick-start countdown, pressurizing the lander's liquid-fuel tanks, switching the electrical system to internal batteries, and detaching the umbilical. "All right, gentlemen," he said into his helmet mike, "we're on standby for depressurization. Two minutes to drop and counting. Sound off. Bleek. . . ."

Ready.

"Overby . . ."

Ready. This from Lt. Karen "Sweetheart" Overby, the team's only female Marine.

"Snodgrass . . ."

Rock 'n' roll!

"Just tell me if you're ready, Too-Tall."

Ready. Sorry, cap'n.

"DiPaula."

Ready and able, sir.

"I like your attitude. Colonel Rainman?"

Ready, Jake, replied the RDF team leader. *Let's take her down.*

"Yes sir. Depressurization cycle initiating. Ninety seconds to drop and counting." Lazy Jake ran his eyes across the board once more, making sure that all systems were enabled. Satisfied that the *Delaware* was ready for the drop, he moved his right hand to the dashboard and flipped the toggles which would depressurize both the crew compartment and the cockpit. This was done for two reasons; riding down in an unpressurized vehicle conserved fuel, and in the unlikely event that the *Delaware* was attacked during the descent, a hole in either the cockpit or the crew compartment would not cause an electrical fire or a fatal blowout. Since everyone aboard was already in their suits, it didn't matter if they made the drop in hard vacuum.

"Depressurization complete," the pilot reported. "Withdrawing shroud." He pushed down a pair of toggles, and the panels which had covered the upper fuselage of the *Delaware* during the trip from Earth orbit peeled back. The long, angular hull of the *Delaware* was now completely exposed to space. Lazy Jake could see the bright gray surface of the Moon slowly moving past; it looked as if he could step through the bubble canopy and take a long jump straight down into the Sea of Tranquillity. He sucked in his breath and deliberately moved his attention back to his job. "Shroud back, all systems green-for-go. T-minus thirty seconds and counting."

We copy, Delaware, Jaffrey responded from the *Valley Forge. You're on full internal. All systems A-OK for your drop. Detach at fifteen seconds on my mark. Mark, fifteen seconds . . .*

"Fifteen seconds," Lazy Jake echoed. He entered the appropriate program code-number on the computer keyboard, flipped the master launch-control toggle to AUTO, then let his left hand hover in weightlessness above the main console. "Fourteen . . . thirteen . . . twelve . . ."

When the countdown reached zero, Capt. McAdams stabbed the EXEC. key on the computer. The grips holding the lander to the underside of the *Valley Forge* snapped back; RCR's on the Delaware's forward and aft outboard engine nacelles fired in preprogrammed sequence. There was a gentle bump as the *Delaware* fell away from the mother ship, and the curving horizon of the Moon swam up in front of the cockpit bubble, the terminator line cutting through the Ocean of Storms clearly visible through the canopy. Pretty as hell, Lazy Jake thought. *Too bad I'm here under these circumstances. . . .*

Drop maneuver complete, Jaffrey's voice said in his earphones. *Looking good there, Delaware.*

"Roger that, *Valley Forge.*" He glanced up and saw the long underside of the AOMV rapidly receding. The *Valley Forge* would remain in orbit while the mission was being carried out. "Operation Shady Grave now in commencement. Observing code Delta Two on my mark." He waited a second, then said, "Mark."

There was no reply. Code Delta Two designated radio silence. It was entirely possible that hostile forces could be monitoring their radio transmissions, and even though it was unlikely that they would have missed the arrival of the *Valley Forge* or the deployment of the *Delaware,* there was no sense in tipping their hand more than necessary by chattering back and forth. From here on out, the *Delaware* and the RDF squad were completely on their own.

Lazy Jake pulled his helmet's VR visor down into place, attached its umbilical cord to the socket in the dashboard, and typed in the appropriate command-code on the keyboard. A curving three-dimensional grid instantly was laid over the real-life panorama of the moonscape spread before him; Descartes Station was clearly outlined by a glowing blue circle. Unlike the usual descent trajectory made by Skycorp's LTV landers, the *Delaware* would not orbit the Moon once before landing. Instead, the mission profile called for a direct lunar descent; it was less fuel-conservative, but also far more efficient for a military operation.

"ECM on," Lazy Jake said. "Lower main gun." The computer, now voice-activated, raised the *Delaware*'s electronic countermeasures pod; the ECM would block any bogus transmissions that Descartes might try to throw their way. The aft gun-bay doors simultaneously opened, and a line of type on the VR visor told him that the lander's 30 mm cannon was deployed from its bay within the lower fuselage of the lander.

"Test gun turret," he murmured, and a small red crosshatch appeared in his field of vision. He moved his eyes left, right, and focused directly upon the blue circle; the target accurately followed the sweep of his eyes. "End test gun turret." The target disappeared. "Arm gun." A small red spot appeared at the lower right side of his visor; the gun was locked and loaded.

Time to check on the grunts. Lazy Jake switched the comlink to the bay, using a shielded frequency, and asked, "How's it going back there, boys and girls?"

"Show me the way to go home . . . " The singing voice belonged unmistakably to Too-Tall Snodgrass, the squad's smartass-in-residence. *"I'm tired and I wanna go to bed. . . ."*

If you take much longer up there, I'm going for some Z treatment myself. Sweetheart Overby sounded impatient. Lazy Jake grinned; it was just like her to be overeager for action.

Chill out, Colonel Taylor Rainman snapped, and the others shut up. The squad leader was all business, as usual; a weird mix of Irish and Apache bloodlines made him a relentless s.o.b. *We're doing fine, Jake. Just let us know when we're down. We'll do the rest.*

"Got it, Colonel." Lazy Jake could easily empathize with the RDF squad. Behind him, separated by the bulkhead aft of the cockpit, each grunt was cocooned within his heavy CAS armor, held immobile by breakaway straps until he landed and threw the switch which would open the egress hatches on the lower fuselage. All they could see were the VR displays on the inside of their helmets. Until they landed, the grunts were blind, cramped, utterly helpless larvae in the womb of the insectile lander . . . and these were four men and one woman who did not *like* being helpless.

"You want it, you got it." Lazy Jake keyed the computer to switch from AUTO to MANUAL, armed the engines, and grasped the attitude-control stick between his legs. "Hang on now," hc said. "We're going in."

The pilot nudged the stick forward, and the main engines on the *Delaware*'s nacelles fired, sending the lander on its way down to the shadowed wasteland below, straight for the big blue circle on his visor.

"Semper fi," he muttered. Time to make some wicked voodoo.

As it turned out, though, the civilians were capable of making voodoo of their own. Ten miles up and fifteen miles downrange from Descartes, the weapons-board started bleeping, announcing that objects had been launched from the moonbase. At the same moment, Lazy Jake spotted five white spots shooting up

from the direction of the base. Ground-to-air missiles? No way
. . . Descartes Station was unarmed. "Track and identify incoming objects," he told the computer.

There was the briefest pause before the computer's androgynous voice spoke in his ears. *Objects identified as mass-driver
cargo canisters. Five in number. Velocity two-point-three-three
kilometers per second. Bearing due west, longitude eleven-two
degrees. Altitude thirty kilometers and holding, range twenty kilometers and decreasing.*

Damn! "Target missiles on best of the five bogies and prepare
for manual firing," he said. On his visor, the canisters showed
up as thin white crosses.

What's going on up there? Colonel Rainman asked.

McAdams was already arming the *Delaware*'s two smart-
rocks, located in separate bays just above the aft-engine nacelles. "They've shot up five mass-driver cans, sir," he said,
thumbing aside the covers of the twin firing switches. "They're
not heading our way, but I think I know what they're up to.
Firing missiles now."

There was a slight jar as the two Star Cobra missiles were
launched from their bays. They showed up on Lazy Jake's visor
as curving white lines, heading for the limb of the Moon. Within
a minute, he spotted their explosions high above the Sea of
Clouds. *Two targets destroyed*, the computer reported. *Remaining three targets passing beyond visible horizon.*

McAdams grimaced. "Shitfire," he muttered. He had already
figured out the opposition's strategy. "Sneaky. Very sneaky."

I don't get it, the squad leader said. *If they were launched
away from us . . .*

"That's the idea, Colonel," Lazy Jake replied. "I'm afraid
we haven't seen the last of 'em yet. I scratched two, but the
other three are heading around the Moon. If I've got it figured
right, in ten or maybe fifteen minutes they'll boomerang back
over the eastern horizon and nail the *Delaware* when it's on the
surface."

Damn! Any chance of hitting them with the cannon?

"When they come back? Not a prayer, Colonel. They'll be
coming in too fast for the gun to track 'em." Lazy Jake hesitated, then added, "Cute trick. They've got creativity, I'll give
'em that."

Too much creativity. There was a pause. *All right*, Rainman
announced, *change of plan. It's going to be a dustoff, ladies and*

gentlemen. Jake, put us down at the drop zone and get back upstairs to the Valley Forge *mucho pronto. . . .*

What about our lander backup, Colonel? This from Two-Tall Snodgrass.

Won't be any if one of the things socks the Delaware *while it's on the ground. I don't want us stranded down there. Jake, when we're dropped and you're safely upstairs again, break Delta Two and inform the* Valley Forge *of our situation. Maybe Frank can ECM the cans' guidance systems from orbit, but it's going to take more time than we've got during the drop. Copy that?*

"Loud and clear, sir," Lazy Jake said reluctantly. As much as Rainman had a point—it wouldn't do to risk getting the *Delaware* nailed by a mass-driver can—he didn't like the idea of abandoning the squad in Indian country either. The operation had called for the lander to back up the team with its onboard arsenal. "I'm going to write General Dynamics when we get home and tell 'em to put some more missiles on this hunk of tin."

You do that, Captain, and I'll sign it too. Okay, Marines, it's going to be a quick one, so let's lock and load.

The target was already visible through the cockpit bubble, even without the aid of the VR visor: Descartes Station, a white-on-gray jumble of rectangles and domes. Lazy Jake moved the attitude-control stick between his thighs, firing the descent engines to retard their velocity for landing. Okay, you bastards, he thought. You won the first round. But if you fuck with us any more, I'm coming back with the gun firing. And that's a promise you can take to the bank. . . .

As anticipated, the base's landing pads were blocked with tugs and LRLT's, the navigational beacons darkened. No surprises there. The *Delaware* set down two hundred yards east-northeast of the base, in a boulder field just beyond Pad Two. As soon as the lander was on the ground, Capt. McAdams released the crew bay hatches and extended the elevators.

One by one, the RDF squad descended through the open hatches the final eight feet to the ground, lowered on small platforms that vaguely resembled forklifts. The graphite-composite CAS exoskeletons were too cumbersome to allow them to jump straight down from the lander; vaguely egg-shaped, completely opaque except for thin eye-slits that curved around the smooth upper carapaces, with servomechanical arms and legs that increased their power tenfold, and three-fingered claw-manipulators for hands, they gave the Marines the appearance of robots.

Lt. Mike "Too-Tall" Snodgrass unbuckled his harness and stepped off his elevator. He felt the solid crunch of lunar soil through the six-inch soles of his armor's boots; inside his $2.5 million exoskeleton, he grinned happily. "Hot diggity shit," he said. "I'm on the Moon!"

One small step for man . . . he heard Sweetheart say reverently through the comlink.

And a big fuckin' deal for mankind, Carl "Lollypop" Bleek finished sourly.

Poetry, Lollypop, Sweetheart said. *Sheer poetry . . .*

Okay, cut the comedy, Rainman snapped. Through the wraparound eye-slit, Too-Tall could see the team leader already bounding forth into the boulder field, clearing the shadow of the *Delaware.* He turned around, clutching his assault rifle to his chest. *Penguin, get off the ramp and let the captain get out of here.*

Yes sir. Working on it sir. Alec DiPaula seemed to be having trouble with the restraints. He had ridden down in the cell just in front of Snodgrass. As Too-Tall watched, DiPaula gave up on trying to unbuckle the frozen snap of his chest harness; he grabbed both ends of the stubborn strap between his claw-manipulators and yanked. The exoskeleton's arm servomotors gave him the power to rip the webbed fabric apart like paper; the harness fell away and Penguin jumped free of the ramp. Typical Penguin maneuver, Too-Tall thought. If finesse defeats you, try brute force. . . .

Snodgrass took a couple of baby steps to get himself accustomed to one-sixth gravity—it wasn't much different or any more difficult than the practice sessions in the neutral-buoyancy tanks—then jumped clear of the *Delaware's* shadow. In the instant before the suit's coolers sensed the sudden change in the thermocline, he felt for a moment the searing heat of the unfiltered sun. Like a spacewalk, but somehow different. Then his suit began to cool off—he all but ignored the digital numbers on the bottom margin of his screen telling him that the coolant system was compensating for the abrupt temperature change—and he landed on his feet twelve feet away from his jump-off point, his knees bending just slightly as the leg servomotors took the brunt of the impact. He glanced at the heads-up display, saw no red numbers. *Jesus,* he thought. *If I jump high enough, I could put myself in low orbit with this suit.*

Lollypop had apparently discovered the same effect. *Faster than a speeding bullet,* he quipped. *More powerful than a locomotive. Able to leap tall women with a . . .*

Cut it out! Rainman took a couple of small steps backward; Too-Tall and the rest of the squad followed, leaving the *Delaware* behind them in a few short leaps. *Okay, Jake, get out of here.*

On my way, Colonel. Good luck. Snodgrass turned around in time to see the engines on the *Delaware*'s outboard nacelles flare, sending gray dust spewing in all directions, as the military lander silently lifted off and rose into the black sky. Behind it, he could see the half-Earth hovering high above the mountainous terrain. *You're a long way from Chattanooga now,* he thought. *You always wanted to get out of there. So how's this for distance . . . ?*

Colonel Rainman's voice brought Too-Tall's mind back to his job. *Sightsee later, Marines,* he snapped. *We've got work to do. Go!*

"Yes sir, sir." Too-Tall turned and began to run west-northwest, vaulting across the regolith. He eyed the darkened windows of the base as he leaped across the lunar turf, kicking up small sprays of gray sand with each ten-foot step. No movement, no sign of life. Descartes looked almost as if it had been abandoned, except . . .

He came upon a sheet of scrap aluminum, shoved upright into the ground and held up by a small cairn of rocks. Someone had written on it:

WELCOME TO DESCARTES STATION!
NOW GO HOME!

"Cute," Too-Tall murmured. "Real cute." He kicked over the sign, then continued running toward the domes of the Dirt Factory.

Operation Shady Grove's strategy for taking over Descartes Station was thought to be foolproof: perfect, flawless, a guaranteed success. And naturally, it fell apart virtually from the moment it began.

The key to penetrating the base was taking control of the

airlocks at the EVA ready-room in Subcomp B, since it had been rightfully assumed that the hangar and garage doors would be closed and the emergency hatches to the Dirt Factory domes and the power station would be sealed. Therefore, the assault phase of Operation Shady Grove was a three-prong attack. Rainman and Bleek took the most direct route to Subcomp B, heading straight west to Airlocks One and Two. DiPaula and Overby went south by southwest, skirting the edges of the landing pads and the spacecraft maintenance center to take Airlocks Five and Six on the opposite side of the subcomplex.

It fell to Snodgrass to handle the longest route, going northwest all the way around the Dirt Factory, cutting between the domes and the mass-driver and passing Subcomp A, to the emergency airlock located beneath Subcomp D, Dorm 3-A—the so-called Descartes Hilton. Taking the emergency airlock at Subcomp D was a backup maneuver; its only purpose was to prevent anyone in the base from escaping through the back door once the main airlocks at Subcomp B were penetrated.

It was an elegant plan, making the best use of the limited number of Marines in the squad. However, the strategists who had devised the tactics—Colonel Rainman among them—had made a crucial error in assuming that since the base was unarmed, it was therefore defenseless.

That was a bad mistake.

First, there were the statues. A crouching demon and a Christ figure set side by side were encountered by Rainman and Bleek as they moved in on Subcomp B. Similarly, a platoon of life-size soldiers were found by Overby and DiPaula as they circled the berms which had been bulldozed into place around the landing pads. Rainman and Bleek stopped to gaze warily at the demon and crucified martyr, which—inherently weird to begin with and, moreover, set so closely together—were more than a little unsettling.

At least Rainman and Bleek realized that they were looking at statues. Overby and DiPaula, on the other hand, got trigger-happy when they unexpectedly came upon the ghostly platoon and wasted several rounds of 13mm gyrojet ammo from their assault rifles on the statues (*Congratulations*, Too-Tall heard Sweetheart tell Penguin over the comlink, *we just murdered a mannequin.*) The statues outside the barriers were harmless, but they distracted the first four members of the RDF squad long enough for the 'dozers and rovers to move in.

They had all seen the lunar vehicles randomly parked just beyond the barricades, yet had thought little of it. If they hadn't been concerned with the eldritch shapes of demons and Christ-figures and phantom armies, they might have given the vehicles more serious consideration. But while Rainman was demanding a reason for the shooting and Penguin was trying to explain, the neglected 'dozers and rovers suddenly started to move toward them, guided by remote-control through the seldom-used teleoperation programs.

Again, the squad wasted more ammo by laying down suppressive fire before they realized that there were no drivers in the vehicles to either frighten or kill. On Rainman's order, they launched grenades from their rifles; two rovers and a 'dozer were destroyed before the remaining vehicles got too close for the grenades to be safely used. The squad was forced to evade them by leaping through the seemingly random breaks in the berm walls.

For a few moments, it seemed like a good idea, until Sweetheart and Penguin found another statue—a hunchback giving them the bird—positioned just in front of the entrances to Airlocks Five and Six; meanwhile, Rainman and Lollypop found two absurdly obscene figures fornicating in front of Airlocks One and Two. It appeared as if these statues were as harmless as the ones outside the barricades; yet, just as Bleek was wickedly remarking, "Now there's a slow, comfortable screw if I ever saw one . . . " the low-yield mining charges secreted within the statues went off.

The charges were normally used for breaking up especially large boulders in the regolith fields. They didn't have much of a punch, and although the grunts were knocked flat by the concussion, the charges were incapable of seriously damaging their exoskeletons. The only real damage sustained was caused by the hunchback's middle finger, which rendered the right leg of Penguin's exoskeleton immobile when it ripped through a primary electrical busline on the inside of the knee.

Despite Penguin's CAS being crippled, the four RDF members were able to make it to the airlocks. Because of the size of the exoskeletons, each Marine had to enter an airlock separately. As Rainman made hand-signals to Lollypop to cycle through Airlock Two, he had little doubt that they could still complete their mission. Once in the airlocks, there was little or nothing the strikers could do to keep them out of Descartes Station.

Wrong again.

Rainman, Sweetheart, Lollypop, and Penguin entered the airlocks, pressed the wall-mounted switches which would start the electromagnetic-sterilization and pressurization cycles in each little compartment, saw the overhead status lights switch to red, watched their own heads-up displays eventually indicate that pressure in the airlocks had become normal . . . yet the airlock status lights remained red. The hatches remained shut, coming *and* going.

Someone had tampered with the airlock controls. They could neither enter the base nor retreat through the outer hatches. Furthermore, since the electromagnetic scrubbers were still in operation, the comlink between the four grunts—and between Too-Tall Snodgrass, who by now had no idea what the hell was going on—was completely disrupted (*Snnnkk . . . sqrrrrkk . . . sqoonkkk* was all that Too-Tall could hear through his headset). Their assault rifles were useless; since the airlocks were cramped, the grenades were too dangerous to use, and because the gyrojet bullets required a firing range of at least three yards before their miniature solid-rockets could ignite and be propelled to their targets, firing at the doors was futile.

So here they were: four members of the elite 1st Space Infantry, trapped in airlocks, their weapons incapacitated, their lines of communication effectively severed. Yet Descartes Station had a neglected Achilles' heel. While the moondogs in MainOps were cheering and yelling and slapping each other's backs, congratulating each other on the fact that four Marines had been taken prisoner in Subcomp B, they were completely unaware that the fifth grunt, Too-Tall Snodgrass, had slipped past the berms, teleoperated vehicles, and exploding statuary, and even now was successfully cycling through the emergency airlock below the Descartes Hilton.

Ignored. Armed. And totally pissed off.

23. The End of the Strike

"Look," Lester said, "I'm going to ask you one more time. Are you going to come out of there peacefully?"

Once more, he waited for a reply and got none. Around the darkened operations center, command personnel listened to the faint hum of static from the ceiling speakers. Butch Peterson, standing behind Lester on the dais, gently laid her hand on his shoulder. He sighed and looked up at her; she nodded her head. He shook his head and sighed again.

"Hello?" he said. "Is there anybody in there? I mean, have you guys run out of air or something?" No, that was unlikely; the airlocks had been pressurized shortly before the locks were frozen. Yet there was still no response. "Look, this stubborn act isn't getting us anywhere," Lester prodded, "so why don't you . . . ?"

Rainman, Colonel Taylor M., a harsh voice suddenly spoke. Everyone in MainOps looked up. *United States Marine Corps, 1st Space Infantry. With whom am I speaking?*

About time you said something, Lester thought, leaning forward in his chair again. "Lester Riddell, general manager of Descartes Station," he said. "Thanks. I was wondering if you guys had been asphyxiated or something. Hey, are you all right?"

Another long pause. The airlock scrubbers had been temporarily switched off to allow Riddell to radio the occupant of Airlock One, whom he had figured from observing his behavior inside the barricades to be the squad leader. Rainman was probably using another, shielded frequency to check on the occupants of Airlocks Two, Five and Six. *I don't have to tell you anything except to identify myself,* he said at last. *Rules of war.*

"War?" Lester laughed out loud. "What do you think this is, Colonel, Nicaragua? I'm just trying to ask you if—"

I'm fine. So are my men. Is there something else you want from us, Mr. Riddell?

Lester blinked. He switched off his mike and looked over his shoulder at Butch again. "Am I getting through to the clown? I mean, should I try French or Latin or something?"

Peterson snickered. "It might help."

"Figures I would get some asshole. He probably wears a lead jockstrap." He shook his head in exasperation and toggled the bonephone again. "Listen, Colonel Rainman, this is not a war. We're a bunch of dumb Skycorp employees . . . well, maybe ex-employees by now . . . on strike. This isn't Central America or the Middle East, and we're not Islamic terrorists or Sandinista guerrillas or whatever you're used to fighting. If you've listened to a word I've said over the last few minutes, you'd know that we'll gladly let you and your team out of those airlocks if you'll just promise not to come out shooting. Now what do you say, huh?"

There was no hesitation this time. *I've got my orders to take control of this installation, Mr. Riddell. That is the beginning and the end of it. If I were you, I would have your forces surrender to us immediately.*

Lester couldn't believe what he was hearing. "Surrender?" he almost yelped. "Take a reality check, Colonel. You're the one stuck in an airlock, not me. You couldn't get out of there even if you had a can opener! You . . . "

"Calm down," Butch whispered.

Lester took a deep breath. "Listen, Colonel," he said slowly, "if you're worried about the safety of you and your men, I can personally assure you that nothing will happen to anyone. We'll unload your guns, recharge your life-support systems, even give you a bite to eat if you want. Then we'll escort you back out to the base periphery where your lander can pick you up again. No lynch parties, no abuse, no bullshit. We're all Americans here and Americans don't go shooting Americans. Except in Brooklyn, maybe."

He waited. No reply. "That's a joke, Colonel," he added. "No offense if you're from Brooklyn."

I repeat, Rainman replied. *I have my orders. You will surrender to us immediately or suffer the consequences.*

Riddell didn't bother to reply. "So rot in there, you dumb helmet-head," he muttered, switching off the mike. "Turn on the scrubbers again. Let the colonel stew for a while." He swiv eled around to look at Peterson, raising his hands in desperation. "I swear, you must have to flunk an IQ test to become a colonel in the . . ."

"Les, I've got a light on the emergency airlock in Subcomp D!" The duty officer at the environmental control station was staring at his status board. "It just opened up from inside! Someone's coming through!"

What the—? Lester turned back to his console and jabbed commands into the keyboard, calling up a schematic display of Subcomplex D on his screen. Sure enough, the emergency airlock beneath the Hilton had pressurized and the inside hatch had been opened. "Goddammit," he yelled, "who was supposed to be watching that fifth guy?"

No one answered. Everyone looked at him. Right, Lester thought. My plan, my strategy, my responsibility. He had been so proud of taking four Marines prisoner in the EVA airlocks that he had neglected the fifth grunt who was still roaming the surface. And now the sumbitch was inside the base. . . .

"Okay," he said, trying to muster some calm, "don't everyone fly off the handle. Steve, try to get a fix on him and . . ."

"Les, we've got the lander coming in again!" This from Doug Baker at the TELMU station. His hands were racing over his console as his eyes swept across his screens. "Forty miles up, twenty-seven miles east, and closing fast!" He tapped buttons on the keyboard in front of him, then glanced over his shoulder. "Loss of uplink with the canisters, too. They're still there, but they're not responding to my signals. I think they've been jammed, boss."

Riddell bit his lower lip. The canisters which the mass-driver had shot into low orbit had been their only hope of keeping the *Delaware* at bay. With them gone—as a not-so-wild guess, he figured that their guidance systems had probably been ECM'd by the *Valley Forge*—there was nothing to prevent the armed lander from attacking Descartes Station. The first two rounds had been too easy to win, he thought. Now it's the third round and the heavyweight champ is stepping back into the ring. . . .

"Oh, shit," he breathed. "We're in trouble."

There was a monster on the loose in the ladies' dorm.

Most of the women had managed to escape from Dorm 2-A before the armored Marine had come in through the tunnel from the Hilton, but a few were still trapped in the section when

Mighty Joe managed to bypass the emergency hatch controls of the tunnel leading into Dorm 1-A. He caught a glimpse of the mammoth CAS clunking purposively toward the tunnel just as the twin hatches, eight feet apart from each other, irised shut.

The hatches were designed to seal automatically in the event of a decompression accident, isolating the dorms from each other so that a blowout wouldn't affect the entire subcomplex. They weren't as sturdy as the airlock hatches, but they were airtight; they should be able to stop a Marine in a CAS. But Mighty Joe wasn't taking any chances. . . . "Liz, what's going on there?" he demanded, speaking into his headset mike. "Talk to me! You guys okay?"

Elizabeth Sawyer, the hydroponicist who was stranded in 2-A, was on the phone in her niche on the other side of the sealed tunnel. *We're fine. It . . . he could have fired at us when he came through, but I guess he's not going to unless we get in the way.* Static for a moment, then: *He's in front of the hatch now. He's raising his rifle and . . . Joe, I think he's going to fire a grenade!*

Holy shit! "Everybody, *duck!*" he shouted, almost tripping over his own feet in his haste to get away from the hatch. "Incoming! Down, down, *down!*"

Behind him, a dozen men and women scurried for cover, dodging behind niches, falling over each other to get through the adjacent tunnel into Subcomp A, even bolting into a nearby restroom. *Some goddamn great defense force we've got here,* Mighty Joe thought as he backed up against the door of a niche. . . .

Whammmm! There was a muffled explosion from the tunnel and the floor itself seemed to shake. *There goes the first emergency hatch,* Joe thought. The niche door behind him popped open. He glanced around and saw Harry Drinkwater peering through the cracked door. Over Drinkwater's shoulder, he glimpsed one of the communications officers—what's-his-name, Schneider—bent over the keyboard of a laptop computer, his desk and bunk covered with reams of printout. Schneider didn't even look up from his computer screen. "What's going on out here?" Drinkwater demanded.

"Where have you . . . ? Never mind that now, shut the goddamn—!"

WHHAAAAMM!

Mighty Joe ducked, throwing his arms over his head, but

looked up just in time to see the hatch cover being blown straight out of its frame. It hit the wall at the far end of the corridor with a loud *Clanngg!* "Hell's bells," he whispered. "I shoulda joined the Marines. . . ."

A new voice came through his headset. *Joe, what's going on down there?* Les Riddell snapped. *Is that Marine in the dorms?*

The niche door slammed shut behind Drinkwater. "No shit, Les!" Joe said, "And I think he's pissed off about something!"

The hulking CAS lurched through the destroyed hatch, the big muzzle of the assault rifle sweeping back and forth. The armored Marine half-turned toward Mighty Joe and the rifle pointed straight at the moondog's face. Joe instinctively raised his hands above his head. Just below the eye-slit was a tiny audio grille; Joe was surprised when a voice came out of it.

Where's MainOps? a harsh, distorted voice squawked.

Mighty Joe stared back at the rifle. "Point that thing somewhere else, egg-man," he growled. "Don't you have any fucking manners?"

The gun didn't move from his face. *I don't have time for bullshit, hairy. Tell me the way to MainOps or I'll shoot your nuts off.* The muzzle dipped a few inches until it was pointed straight at Young's groin. *One . . . two . . .*

Mighty Joe wasn't about to see whether or not the Marine was bluffing. "Take a left into the next tunnel and go straight until you reach the stairs," he said quickly, pointing with his right hand. "Can't miss it."

The Marine said nothing, but the assault rifle swung away from Joe. As the mammoth exoskeleton turned ponderously, Joe shouted, "Hey! Robby the Robot!" The hulk hesitated for a moment. "Don't shoot anybody, okay? It's just a goddamn strike, for chrissakes."

The Marine didn't reply, but the massive arm holding the gun rose and fired a single round at the ceiling. Mighty Joe flinched as a recessed light fixture shattered, spraying glass across the corridor. Then the gun came down and the juggernaut lurched toward the open tunnel to Subcomp A; someone on the other side must have realized that it was pointless to seal its hatches as well.

Mighty Joe took a deep breath, lowered his arms, and touched the lobe of his headset. "Les, this is Joe. He's coming your way." He closed his eyes and let out his breath. "Sorry, man, but you're on your own."

• • •

Harry Drinkwater instinctively ducked as he heard the muffled gunshot from the other side of the niche door. He half-expected to hear more shots, or even the door itself being ripped straight off its hinges. Instead, he heard Mighty Joe saying something indistinguishable, then the heavy *thunk-thunk-thunk* of the Marine's boots stomping through the dorm.

Behind him, the steady tapping of Willard DeWitt's fingers on the keyboard continued unabated, as if the con man were completely unaware of the sudden violence occurring just outside his niche. Drinkwater glanced over his shoulder and once more saw the incredible concentration on DeWitt's face. For almost twenty straight hours now, DeWitt had been hunched over the laptop computer, glued to the ever-shifting numbers on his screen, immersed in the separate reality of the high-stakes game he was playing. A game which was about to end . . .

The general-quarters alarm went off, a steady Klaxon which was meant to signal either a blowout or a solar storm. In this instance, Drinkwater knew what it meant. "We've run out of time, Willie," he said softly. He sagged against the niche door and, looking down at the floor, shook his head. "Nice try, pal, but we didn't make it. Might as well give up."

For a moment, it seemed as if DeWitt hadn't heard. Drinkwater was about to repeat himself, when DeWitt casually looked up from his screen—for the first time in many hours—and smiled beatifically.

"Skycorp's made an offer," he said with eerie calm. "Think we should take it?"

An instant was all it took for Tina McGraw to make her move.

Lana Smith and Casey Engel were in the EVA ready-room, standing watch on the airlocks; when the alarm went off, they both ran from the tunnel entrance toward the airlocks. The plan had been, in an emergency, to warn the Marines to seal their CAS armor, then to blow the outer hatches and jettison the RDF squad back out onto the surface.

McGraw wasn't about to let that happen. She had been lurking in the access tunnel to Subcomp B for several minutes now, from the time she had heard that a fifth Marine had made it through the emergency airlock in Subcomp D. As soon as the two moondogs were away from the open tunnel hatch, she rushed through the entrance, aimed her Taser at Smith and squeezed the trigger.

The 2,500-volt charge hit the suit tech smack in the back; she crumpled to the floor without a sound. Engel got a chance to turn and throw up his hands—yelling that hated nickname of hers—before Quick-Draw nailed him with the Taser's second dart.

"The name's Officer McGraw to you, buster," she muttered as she jumped over his unconscious body. Running from one airlock to the next, she engaged the manual overrides; one at a time, the inner hatches slid open, freeing each trapped Marine.

Like imprisoned giants from a pulp fantasy novel, the armored Marines stepped through the open airlocks. The one who came out of Airlock One half-raised his assault rifle to cover her. *Who are you?* a metallic voice barked from his suit's exterior speaker.

"Officer Tina McGraw, NASA Space Operations Enforcement Division," she snapped back. "I'm the one who just set you free." McGraw pointed toward the tunnel entrance. "Straight through the tunnel, down the corridor, and up the—"

We know the way. The massive CAS suits began moving toward the tunnel. *Thanks for being a fink, McGraw. We'll handle it from here.*

"Uh . . . sure." She watched as the four armored Marines tromped across the ready-room and moved in single file through the tunnel.

Where there had once been a heroic vision of herself leading the charge, retaking the base from the drunken, oafish rednecks who had humiliated her and dishonored her badge, there was now the abrupt sense of loneliness. A single word, from her own ally, had struck her with greater impact than a dart from her own Taser.

Fink . . .

The Taser dangled in her hand as she looked down at the still forms of her fellow moondogs.

"Track to target," Lazy Jake told the *Delaware*'s fire-control system. The red crosshatch on his VR visor followed the movements of his eyes, shifting two degrees to the left, ascending five degrees to the right, and falling into place on the MainOps tower.

"Lock on target," he murmured and the crosshatch pulsed twice, signaling that the fire-control system would remain targeted on MainOps. The *Delaware* was whipping across the lunar wasteland, flying low and bearing down on Descartes Station. McAdams was on full auto now except for the stick, which he controlled inside the fist of his right hand: five miles up, seven miles downrange from target, and closing in like a bat out of hell. Take out MainOps and there goes the ball game. . . .

"Arm cannon," he told the computer. An amber light flashed at the bottom of his visor. "Fire on my command." A double click in his headphones. Just aim 'em and waste 'em, as his combat instructor once said. We'll supply the body-bags.

He pushed the stick forward a little more. Altitude dropped to ten thousand feet, range to five miles. He checked the screen again. Classic. Coming in right out of the Sun. The last range of hills was coming up now. Descartes was now a big, easy bull's-eye in front of his eyes. . . .

DeWitt pointed at the message on his screen and *tsk*ed. "One-point-five billion over the next three years and an option for purchase of product over the next ten fiscal years at a twenty-five percent discount?" he complained. "Who do they think they're dealing with here?"

Drinkwater could barely hear him over the general-quarters alarm blaring through the ceiling speaker. "Just sign the deal already!" he shouted.

"You've got to be kidding me." DeWitt picked up his cold mug of coffee and took a sip. "I mean, the subsidiary stock option alone is worth . . . "

"I don't give a righteous goddamn!" Drinkwater screamed. "Just make the deal!"

Willard DeWitt sighed and picked up his lightpen. Then he stared at the screen, shook his head, and dropped the pen back on the desktop. He placed his fingers on the keyboard once more. "One-point-twenty-five over three and a fifteen percent discount," he murmured aloud as he typed in the new numbers. "And that's our final offer."

Harry started to yell at him again. Then he caught himself. It was their one last chance. . . .

"I'm heading for the radio station," he blurted, wrenching open the door and bolting out into the hallway. "Call me there when you get something!" He stopped in the doorway and yelled back, "And *forget* about the fucking discount!"

"Airlocks One, Two, Five, and Six are opening!"

"*Delaware* downrange two miles!" Baker called out. "Altitude three thousand feet and closing!"

He was intently watching the blip on his screen, but already they could see a white dot moving past the rim of Cyrillus Crater on the far horizon. From behind Lester's chair, Butch was watching the incoming lander. "I don't like the looks of this," she whispered.

"Neither do I." Riddell was already out of his seat. He intuitively realized what was about to happen; the *Delaware* was about to make a strafing run, and MainOps was the most vulnerable target at Descartes Station. . . . "All right, everybody, clear the deck," he said, trying to keep his voice calm.

The command crew looked up at him uncertainly, but one more glance through the window was enough to make Riddell more insistent. "C'mon, folks!" he yelled, jumping off the dais and clapping his hands. "Move, move, *move*!"

That was enough. All at once, the men and women in MainOps were out of their seats and stampeding for the stairwell hatch. Lester grabbed Butch's hand, yanked her in front of him, and shoved her headlong toward the hatch. "Get out of here!" he shouted at both her and the others. "Haul ass! Move!"

Butch grabbed his hand, but she was pulled away by the riptide of bodies. The next moment, she was swept out of sight through the stairwell hatch. In another few seconds, MainOps was deserted; Lester could hear the command team stampeding down the spiral stairs, yelling in confusion and fear at each other. He was the last to leave.

He headed for the hatch, then hesitated and glanced around the empty command center. One last look. . . .

"Goodbye," Lester said softly. It was like saying farewell to an old friend. Then he jumped through the hatch, catching himself upon the railing at the top step. He whirled around and yanked back the cover of the emergency hatch control panel.

At that moment the fusillade of 30 mm shells ripped through the eastern windows of MainOps; there was a roar as all the glass panels blew out at once. Lester screamed and stabbed the button to close the hatch. His hair was whipped around his head by the tornado-like force of the blow; deafened by the roar, shielding his eyes with his hand, he caught a glimpse of glass, printout, pens, and potted plants being torn loose by the fogged escaping air, until the hatch irised shut, closing off the noise and fury.

Lester sagged against the railing. *Christ almighty, that was too close. . . .*

He let out his breath and brushed his hair out of his face; little pieces of glass fell out of his scalp and tinkled on the metal steps around his feet. Looking down, he saw that the stairwell was empty. MainOps was destroyed, but everyone who had been in there was safe.

Okay. So far, so good. He staggered down the steps, heading for Level One. Get everyone he could find into the solar shelters in Level Two, he thought dizzily. We've got food in there, medical supplies, an independent oxygen supply. Seal the doors and make our stand. Not over yet, sport. Like they say, it's not over till the fat lady sings. . . .

He reached the bottom of the stairs, turned around and saw Butch, Tycho, Monk, Quack, Mighty Joe, the MainOps crew—hell, just about everyone he knew—crowded into the corridor in front of the rec room. At the far end of the corridor, he saw a Marine in CAS armor blocking the tunnel to Subcomp D, his assault rifle held in firing position.

And before Lester could say anything, the muzzle of another gun was jabbed into the base of his neck.

Freeze! an electronically filtered voice commanded.

"Like an ice cube," Lester replied. He dared not move a muscle.

A hard metal claw reached from behind and roughly patted his sides. *Okay,* the Marine snapped. *Turn around and put your hands on your head. Make it slow.*

First you want me to freeze, then you want me to make it slow, Lester thought. Our relationship is definitely thawing. . . . But he didn't voice his comments as he obediently clasped his hands on top of his skull and slowly turned to face the massive exoskeleton standing behind him.

"Greetings," he said as pleasantly as he could. "Anything I can do for you?"

A few chuckles from the crew, but it definitely wasn't a crowd-pleaser. The rifle didn't move; it was now aimed straight at his throat.

There was a soft hiss of escaping air, like a rattlesnake clearing its throat, and the top hatch of the exoskeleton unsealed and slowly rose on its hinge, exposing the man buried within the armor. From deep within the upholstered bulk of the suit, a grim face with a trim black mustache peered out at him.

"Mr. Riddell," the Marine said, "I'm Colonel Taylor Rainman, United States Marine Corps, 1st Space Infantry."

"Glad to meet you finally," Lester replied. "Hope you didn't find our airlocks too uncomfortable."

Rainman's face remained stoical. "Not in the slightest," he said drily, "but you should have taken my advice a few minutes ago. It would have saved us all a lot of grief."

Lester shrugged. "You shoot up our command center, fire a couple of grenades into a bunkhouse, hold my friends at gunpoint, stick a rifle in my face . . ." He shrugged. "Hey, what's a little violence between friends, right?"

The squad leader's mouth twitched. "As I said, it could have been avoided if you had—"

"Hey, man, *fuck* this shit!" Tycho's voice suddenly shouted out. "There's two of them and at least thirty or forty of us here! Let's take the fuckers and ream 'em with their own guns!"

Suddenly, there were shouts of assent, the rustle of people beginning to move. Quack grabbed Tycho from behind and pinned his arms back. Rainman's head jerked up. The rifle swerved away from Lester to cover the crowd, and Lester saw the colonel's forefinger dart back within the trigger guard. . . .

"*No!*" he shouted at the top of his lungs. Still keeping his hands on top of his head, he whirled around and faced the moondogs jammed into the corridor. "Nobody move! They've got us! Just give it up, okay?"

Once again, the crowd was shocked into still silence. Except for Tycho. "You're going to let these bullet-head . . . ?"

"Tycho, shut up," Lester demanded, finding the big black man's face in the mob. "You're not doing anyone any good, so just clam it. . . ."

Tycho's face remained defiant. "Where's the rest of 'em, huh, Les?" he said. "I only see two of these robo-muthafuckers. What's going on with the other three?"

"We've got the other three units sweeping the rest of the base," Rainman said loudly, addressing the crowd. "Right now we've got another Marine standing watch on a group in the mess hall down the corridor behind us. The other two are working their way through the base, rounding up everyone else. The *Delaware* has landed outside the base and is backing us up. Your boss is right, ladies and gentlemen. Further resistance is pointless. We've assumed control, and nobody will be hurt if you—"

All at once, the sound of a blues saxophone jumped through the ceiling speakers: Noble "Thin Man" Watts yelling out the sassy first bars of ''Skunky.'' Every single person in the corridor jerked and stared up at the ceiling, as if expecting the bluesman himself to come down out of the rafters.

Hollllld everything! the voice of Moondog McCloud shouted from the speakers.

Rainman stared at Riddell. ''What are you trying to pull now?'' he demanded. Mouth agape, Riddell stared back at the colonel over the rifle barrel and shrugged helplessly.

Before things get a little too rough out there, McCloud went on, *there's an important announcement y'all ought to take into consideration, if you'll just bear with me. . . .*

Tycho, held back by Quack, stopped in mid-struggle as they both listened.

This station has just received news . . . and, make no mistake, this is the real, authentic, no-bullshit deal here . . .

Cringing within the crowd, head instinctively covered with her arms, Butch Peterson gradually raised her eyes as Monk Walker, who had thrown himself protectively around her, slowly extricated himself.

. . . that Skycorp, our former employer, has just reached a tentative agreement for the sale of Descartes Station . . .

Quack Lippincott sighed and closed his eyes. All this, and the goddamn Japanese win anyway.

. . . with the newly established firm of Lunar Associates Ltd. . . .

Lester blinked. Who? What?

. . . which is, for your information, completely and wholly owned by the only stockholders who really matter . . .

''Gotta be the Japanese,'' someone murmured.

''Naw,'' someone else sighed. ''Arabs.''

''Europeans.''

''What do you wanna bet it's the Aussies?''

. . . and that is you!

''What the fuck?'' Lester heard himself say.

. . . That is correct! This is the truth! Absolutely no bullshit! You heard it here first! Lunar Associates Ltd. is solely owned and operated by the employees . . . whoops, I mean former employees . . . of Descartes Station! We are now its principal shareholders, its management, its work force. . . .

Lester glanced at Rainman. The Marines Corps colonel had his left hand cupped around the earpiece of his headset. He listened, silently nodded his head, listened some more. Then he looked straight at Lester and made a slow, definite nod.

We are now in control of this mining facility, by the terms of an exclusive agreement reached today between the New York firm of Gamble, Hutton & Schwartzchilde and the majority share-holders of Skycorp and its management. . . .

The squad leader appeared stunned, but he was already lowering his gun. Through the corridor, moondogs were transfixed upon the ceiling speakers. Quack was relaxing his grip on Tycho; Monk was giving Butch an uncharacteristic hug and kiss.

. . . Now, once y'all are through changing your underwear, if you know what I mean, the first stockholders meeting of Lunar Associates Ltd. will be held, as customary, in the mess hall at . . .

From the mess hall behind him, Lester could hear shouting, yelling, whooping. Maybe it was bullshit, and maybe it wasn't. He grinned, and was startled to see that Rainman was grinning back at him.

. . . well, when everyone gets there, I guess. At this time we'll be hearing the details of this deal from our new CEO, Mr. Willard . . . 'scuse me, Mr. Jeremy Schneider. . . .

"What?" Lester's eyes darted to the ceiling again. Schneider? The communications officer? What the holy hell was going on here?

. . . And that, boys and girls, means this strike is unofficially ended. Now back to more music from LDSM.

Lester brushed past Rainman, who was no longer holding him at the business end of his rifle, and began pushing his way through the yelling, deliriously happy crowd. He was halfway to the radio station when he was suddenly tackled by Butch Peterson. She silently held him in a hug, her face pressed against his chest. Lester gasped, thought again about finding Moondog McCloud or Jeremy Schneider to get some straight answers, then surrendered himself and hugged her in return.

It beat the hell of catching a bullet, even if he had absolutely no comprehension of what had just happened. "What the fuck," he murmured into the nape of Butch's neck. "We'll figure it out sooner or later."

"Later," Butch whispered back to him.

Big Deal
(Video.4)

*From "The CBS Evening News With Don Houston"; Wednesday,
August 21, 2024:*

(THEME UP and FADE. Don Houston at studio desk.)

HOUSTON: Good evening, I'm Don Houston. The three-day
strike by workers at Descartes Station on the Moon ended early
this morning when a five-person assault team from the United
States Marine Corps raided the industrial lunar base. Then, just
when the elite cadre stormed the base and had taken the strikers
captive, there was an unexpected twist. The corporation owning
the base agreed to *sell* Descartes Station to a new company . .
one apparently controlled by the miners themselves. Garrett Lo
gan reports from Huntsville, Alabama, on this strange, fast
moving story. . . .

(FILE FOOTAGE of the U.S.S. Valley Forge *in its orbital
hangar, followed by COMPUTER ANIMATION of the space
craft's flight to the Moon, FILE FOOTAGE of Descartes Station
and a DIAGRAM of the deployment of the RDF squad at Des
cartes Station.)*

LOGAN *(V.O.)*: Following a one-day sprint to the Moon . .
the fastest manned lunar flight yet on record, thanks to an ex
perimental nuclear engine . . . the U.S.S. *Valley Forge* arrived
at the Moon early this morning, bringing with it a five-member
rapid-deployment force from the elite 1st Spacc Infantry of th
United States Marines. The mission, which Pentagon source
say was code-named Operation Shady Grove, was to break th
illegal strike begun on Monday by employees of Skycorp at th
Descartes Station lunar mining facility and to take control c
the base. The *Valley Forge's* military lander, the U.S.S. *Dela
ware*, landed just outside the base. The Marines then rushed th
base's airlocks and, according to spokesmen from the Depart

ment of Defense, made it into the base without encountering much resistance. . . .

(FILM CLIP of a uniformed Marine officer, identified as COL. LUCAS BAYLOR, at a Pentagon news conference.)

BAYLOR: We are pleased to report that the . . . uh, operation went off without too much . . . uh, undue difficulty and that the lunar facility was captured . . . ah, that is secured . . . um, without casualties being reported by either our RDF team or the . . . uh, opposing forces . . . that is, um, the strikers. The mission went by the numbers.

(FILE FOOTAGE of the floor of the New York Stock Exchange: traders crowding the floor, numbers flashing on the Big Board, etc. This is followed by COMPUTER ANIMATION of a large asteroid tumbling through deep space, heading toward the distant Earth, and FILE FOOTAGE of Skycorp's Byrd Crater permaice facility at the lunar north pole.)

LOGAN (V.O.): Yet even while this was happening, another story was being played out on Wall Street and on other stock exchanges across the world. Investors had been alerted by computer network of a new stock offering by a heretofore unknown company, called Lunar Associates Ltd., in connection with the planned launch of an industrial mission to a newly discovered asteroid, 2024 Garbo. The importance of this mission was obvious to quick-minded investors, since Skycorp had just announced that permaice resources at Byrd Crater were rapidly diminishing, which would make the operation of Descartes Station much more expensive in the future. Lunar Associates Ltd. has proposed a rendezvous with 2024 Garbo when it nears the Moon later this year to extract water trapped within the asteroid at considerably less cost than having it shipped up from Earth. Word of this spread quickly through the international finance community, and over the past two days investors have been snatching up stock in Lunar Associates. So much so, that even as the Marines were launching their raid on the moonbase, Lunar Associates was striking a deal with Skycorp. . . .

(FILM CLIP of a Skycorp spokesperson—identified as Holly D'Amato—at a news conference in Huntsville.)

D'AMATO: The company has received today a worthwhile offer from a new company, Lunar Associates Ltd., for the purchase of the capital assets and financial liabilities of our mining facility at Descartes Station. Given the . . . um, recent difficulties that we have encountered with the . . . ah, continued operation of Descartes Station, we have decided to accept their offer.

REPORTER (offscreen): What about reports that the majority of the investors in Lunar Associates are, themselves, striking workers at the lunar base?

D'AMATO: We've . . . um, received the same reports and have been unable to confirm them, but even if it's true . . . ah, it doesn't affect the deal we've made with Lunar Associates. We will sign with the company under the present terms of our tentative agreement.

(FILM CLIP of a space industry market analyst, identified as Clifford Brandenstein.)

BRANDENSTEIN: If it's the strikers who are behind Lunar Associates, well then . . . *(shrugs)* Who cares, really? Uchu-Hiko was negotiating for the purchase of the base, but I've been told that it's been losing interest in the deal since the strike started. I'm sure that the Japanese were seriously reconsidering their bid even before the Marines were sent in. If the miners can come in through the back door and make an equitable deal with Skycorp, the company would be all too happy to get rid of the base. The whole thing has been a disaster for them . . . for Skycorp . . . from the word go, if only in terms of public image, if not labor relations and all the rest. They're probably happy to sell Descartes Station to the miners, and good riddance. The name of the game here is money, not settling scores. . . .

(CUT TO LIVE FOOTAGE of Garrett Logan, standing in front of Skycorp's corporate headquarters in Huntsville.)

LOGAN: At this time, the Pentagon has announced that Operation Shady Grove is over and that the Marines will be withdrawn from the Moon, in light of the peaceful—if wildly unexpected—resolution of the crisis. Back to you, Don . . .

(CUT TO studio shot of Don Houston. Garrett Logan shrinks into a WINDOW in the upper-right corner of the screen.)

HOUSTON: Garrett, there's still a nagging question. If Lunar Associates Ltd. is largely backed by the miners themselves . . . or actually, I understand, by investment firms that handle funds for the lunar workers . . .

LOGAN: That is correct. Those investments count for just over fifty-five percent of the total stock, which gives the miners a controlling interest. . . .

HOUSTON: If that is the case, then why didn't Lunar Associates simply make their bid for the purchase of the base withou

oing on strike first? Wouldn't it have been easier for them to
ammer out this agreement with Skycorp without first taking the
rastic measure of going on strike?

LOGAN (coming back into full-frame): You're right, Logan.
his is still an open question, and one which the Federal Trade
ommission will undoubtedly investigate before it makes final
pproval of the deal between Lunar Associates and Skycorp. At
is point, there is a general theory that there were two factions
mong the workers on the Moon . . . one which openly went on
rike, in opposition to Skycorp's plans to sell the base to Uchu-
iko, and one which was quietly working behind the scenes to
se financial leverage in negotiating with the company. Again,
e government will be investigating, yet FTC officials with
hom I've spoken privately say that there's no hard evidence so
r to suggest unfair trade. Since neither Skycorp nor Uchu-Hiko
ve objected to the agreement, the deal will probably go
rough. Everyone's interested in keeping that base in operation.

HOUSTON (V.O.): And the miners themselves? What have
ey had to say about all this?

LOGAN: As usual, Don, the workers at Descartes Station
en't saying anything. They're a quarter of a million miles away,
ter all, so it's a little difficult for them to hold press confer-
ces. This is Garrett Logan, live from Skycorp headquarters in
untsville, Alabama.

HOUSTON (full-screen): Thank you, Garrett. Next up . . .
w concerns over genetic engineering among New York City
eschool children. Is it ever too early to learn quantum physics?
nd Mindy Oliver at the Great Neck Chicken Ranch, where the
ns are being taught a new song to cluck. . . .

*(THEME UP. FILM CLIP of a farmer with a baton leading
ickens through "The Star-Spangled Banner." FADE OUT.)*

24. The Last General Manager

Descartes Traffic, this is the Collins, Alli James' voice r͏ ported. *We're standing by for tank pressurization and fin͏ countdown. If you can . . . ah, remind our last passenger th͏ we've got a schedule to meet here, we'll load 'em up and be ͏ our way.*

Casey Engel looked over his shoulder at Lester. The form͏ general manager was standing at the window of the traffic co͏ trol cupola; he was wearing a headset, but he was apparent͏ lost in thought, staring out at the lunar landscape. The *Collin͏* lander was squatting on Pad Two, with the launch crew standi͏ nearby, ready to connect the fuel lines and disconnect the u͏ bilicals. Another group of pad rats were gathered around t͏ *Beautiful Dreamer*, unloading the last of the Spam-cans whi͏ the tug had ferried down from the orbiting LTV late yesterda͏ But Lester wasn't watching the activity on the pads; Casey co͏ tell that his gaze was fixed on the distant slopes of Stone Mou͏ tain, apparently lost in his own thoughts.

Engel was about to clear his throat when Riddell touched ͏ headset lobe, as if he had been paying attention the whole tin͏ "We copy that, Alli. I just need to go grab my bags from ͏ office and we're out of here."

Take your time, Alli replied. *Just don't take too much of ͏ know what I mean? I got two other people out here who want ͏ go home. Over.*

"Affirmatory on that, ace. I'll be out on the pad before ͏ finish your checks. I'll give you back to Casey now. Over ͏ out." Lester pulled the headset off, disconnected it from his ͏ unit, and dropped it on the counter. He gazed down at it fo͏ moment. "Guess I won't be needing that anymore, huh?"

"Not where you're going, you won't." Casey switched off

omlink for a moment and swiveled around in his chair. This
me, he did clear his throat before speaking. "Listen, boss,
efore you skedaddle out of here, I just want to tell you . . . "

Riddell smiled, shaking his head and holding up his hand.
'Aw, save it, willya please? I've been going through this long
oodbye stuff all day." He looked away from Casey and grinned.
I mean, thanks for whatever you were going to say, but enough
enough already. . . ."

Engel pretended to be affronted. "I was just going to tell you
at you're a heartless son of a bitch and we're really glad to be
etting rid of you so we can start having fun again. That's all."

Lester shot a baffled look at the traffic control manager. Casey
anaged to keep a sour expression on his face for another sec-
nd before he cracked a grin. "Or words to that effect," he
ded.

Lester grimaced and shook his head again. "And fuck you,
o," he said. Engel laughed and put out his hand; Riddell
abbed it in a thumbs-up shake. "Take it easy, sport. Don't let
y of these assholes crash, okay?"

"Not on my shift, at least." Engel released Lester's hand and
atched as he turned and walked to the exit hatch. Just as Lester
nt to climb down the ladder into the access tunnel, Engel said,
Hey, one more thing . . . "

Lester stopped, his feet on the top rung, and looked up. "Are
u going to miss this place?" Casey asked.

"Are you kidding?" Lester continued climbing down the lad-
r. "I can't wait to get out of here. See you . . . "

"See ya." Casey waited until Lester had disappeared before
ietly adding, "You lying bastard."

This time he meant it. And if Lester had heard him at all,
ere was no comeback.

Lester made the trip through the tunnels to Subcomp A as
ickly as he could without jogging. He had heard Casey's last
mark, and he had been right; like it or not, he was going to
ss this place. And for that very reason, he wanted to make it
t to the *Collins* as fast as he could. He was leaving the Moon
the last and final time; no sense in farming it out any longer
n he needed.

There was hardly anyone in the tunnels or the corridors for
n to encounter. An off-shift moondog here and there slapped
arms, wished him farewell, good luck, godspccd, and all thc

usual platitudes, but the second shift was out in the regolith fie[l]
or in the Dirt Factory or at the mass-driver plant; first-shift wa[s]
catching zee's in the dorms and a large group of volunteers fro[m]
the third shift were on EVA on the roof of Subcomp A, repairin[g]
the damage to the MainOps tower.

It would still be weeks before the windows were complete[ly]
replaced and the equipment repaired or replaced. Only then coul[d]
the operations center be brought back to life. Still, he found [it]
hard to believe that persons from each off-shift were working—
on their own time—to restore MainOps from the beating it ha[d]
taken from the *Delaware*'s strafing run. Only three weeks ag[o]
he would have had to offer the same people triple-time pay, a[nd]
not without a lot of cussing and griping even then. Descart[es]
Station was changing. . . .

Right, he thought as he climbed the spiral stairs up throug[h]
Subcomp A's atrium to Level One and walked down the corrid[or]
to his former office. And that was one more good reason to b[e]
getting out. Arnie Moss had told him that Descartes needed [a]
mean son of a bitch to ramrod the place for Skycorp. But Sk[y]
corp was no longer in charge, and a ramrod was no longer ne[c]
essary. If Lunar Associates Ltd. was successful in operating t[he]
base at a profit . . . if they didn't fail to show a profit for t[he]
earthbound investors, if they managed to meet their supply-an[d]
demand agreement with Skycorp, and a thousand other *ifs* aft[er]
that . . . then pretty soon they'd be needing someone who cou[ld]
manage day-care services for the kids of the permanent settle[rs]

And you know they're coming, he thought. *It's inevitable*. Le[s]
ter imagined himself trying to diaper a squalling baby and winc[ed]
as he reached the office door. *Screw that. I'd rather be a me[an]
sumbitch any day.*

He was about to push open the door when he once aga[in]
glimpsed the white duct-tape pasted across the screw holes whi[ch]
had once held a plastic plaque reading GENERAL MANAGER. W[rit]
ten out firmly with a black marker was the new sign: PRESIDE[NT,]
LUNAR ASSOCIATES LTD. The tape had been there for a few da[ys]
now, but Riddell still couldn't get used to it. *I don't care wh[o's]
sitting in here now*, he thought as he rapped on the door a[nd]
pushed it open, *it's still* my *office*. . . .

Jeremy Schneider was working at his terminal when Les[ter]
stepped in. "Hang on," he murmured without looking aw[ay]
from his screen. "Be with you in a just a . . . ."

Then he glanced up and saw Riddell in the doorway, "Le[s]

he said, his look of intense concentration relaxing into a smile. He hurriedly tapped the HOLD key on the computer and stood up behind his desk, tucking his hands into the pockets of his shorts. Schneider looked uncomfortable; maybe he, too, felt that he was sitting in someone else's office. His eyes flitted to the airtight duffel bag and attaché case resting against the wall near the door. "You're . . . uh, here to pick up your stuff. . . ."

"My stuff, yeah. Sorry to bother you." Lester sauntered into the office, gazing around at the walls. Nothing had been changed since he had informally turned over his workplace to the new president of Lunar Associates. Same pictures of the first outpost; same framed newspaper clipping of the original Moondog. There had been almost nothing for him to clean out of his desk. At least there wasn't a spittoon behind the desk; Schneider refrained from chewing tobacco, thank God.

"You ought to get a real sign for that door," he murmured, his eyes absently fixed on the photo of the original base. "Lend some dignity to the place."

"Yeah, yeah . . . " Schneider grinned wryly and scratched at his blond beard. His eyes followed Riddell's gaze to the framed photo. "You want to take it with you?" he asked. "I mean, that or anything else on the walls, it's all yours. Take it."

Lester slowly shook his head. He wasn't even tempted. "Uh-uh. They belong right here. Permanent keepsakes of this office. I've got plenty at home."

"Sure. Sure." Schneider nodded and shuffled his feet, looking down at the top of his desk, which was already stacked with mounds of printout, operations manuals, and logbooks. Good luck, chump, Lester thought. You're going to need it if you're going to run this operation. Another thought occurred to him; something that had been in the back of his mind since the end of the strike, yet which up to now he had not been able to articulate. He looked straight at Schneider. "Let me ask you something, Jeremy . . . " he began.

Schneider's eyes darted back to him. Lester held his gaze for a couple of moments, long enough to begin to make Schneider sweat; then he cocked his head to his side. "How did you do it?" he asked quietly. "Really."

"Well . . . " Schneider reached up and scratched at an imaginary itch under his chin as his eyes traveled to the wall again, running across the pictures to the ceiling and then to the window. "It's kind of a long story, y'know, and . . . "

"And I've got to catch the *Collins*. Right." Lester sighed, grabbed the strap of his duffel bag, hoisted it over his shoulder, then bent to pick up the handle of his attaché case. "Listen, let me give you a single word of advice. . . ."

"And that is . . . ?"

"Honesty," Lester finished. Schneider visibly flinched at the word. Almost everything Riddell suspected about Jeremy Schneider was confirmed right then.

"That's my single word of advice," he continued. "I don't know how you managed this score, and I don't know if I even give a shit. But from here on out, you're going to have to play by a different set of rules if you want to keep this place. You may have been able to screw Wall Street and Skycorp, but if you ever try to screw the people who work here . . . " He tugged at the strap of the duffel bag. "You're going out of here *in* a bag, not carrying one. Y'got me on that?"

"Sure, sure . . . "

"Right." Lester turned toward the door. "Good luck, You're going to . . . "

"Need it," Butch Peterson said from behind him. "Les, don't you ever come up with any new lines?"

She was standing in the corridor outside the office; she had probably been there for several minutes without his being aware of it. Mighty Joe Young and Monk Walker were standing behind her, but for the moment he hardly noticed them. Riddell closed the door on Schneider and turned directly toward her. "Excuse me, guys," he said as he took Butch's arm and gently pulled her into the science lab. "Give us a minute alone, okay?"

"Okay." Mighty Joe settled against the corridor wall, his arms folded. "But if we hear her screaming . . . "

Lester slammed the lab door against the rest of it. He dropped the duffel bag from his shoulder and put down the attaché case. "Last chance," he said softly, looking straight into her eyes. "We've been through this before, but this is my last try, so just listen to me."

"Go on." Her face and voice were as bland as a sample of ilmenite. "Let's hear it."

He took a deep breath. "I can stall the lander for a few more minutes. The *Collins* won't launch without me . . . without us on it. There's one more couch available in the mid-deck. Grab your stuff, put it in a bag, and let's get out of here together. We can settle the paperwork when we get home. I'm not making any long, messy goodbyes and neither should you."

Peterson rested her hands on her hips and stared back at him in silence "Okay?" Lester pleaded. "Yes? No? Say what's on your mind."

Butch smiled, closed her eyes, and shook her head. "Les, don't drive me into a corner like this. I gave you my final answer last night and . . ."

"That was last night, Susie. This is—"

"Now. Right." She slowly let out her breath and looked around the lab. "Try to understand this, all right? I spent the better part of my life getting here. Right *here*, to *this* room. That meant years of posing in fishnet bikinis to pay my way through school, dumping a second career which could have made me rich, and breaking an engagement with a world-famous tennis jock. I'm talking about *sacrifices*, Les. . . ."

She shook her head disbelievingly. "And now you're asking me to ditch all that, just to come live with you in a trailer behind some backwoods New Hampshire campground? Get *real*, man."

Lester looked down at the floor. Damn, but she was right. He had been on the Moon for too long; it was beginning to fry his brain, even without a steady diet of pills. "I take it," he said, slowly, "that it's still a definite no."

Peterson stepped forward, slid her arms around his neck, and planted one of her memorable kisses on his mouth. "I mean that it's a definite maybe," she replied as she stepped back, taking his hands in hers. "I could get tired of this place in a year or two. Maybe I'll chicken out on the expedition to 2024 Garbo, or maybe the company will decide that it doesn't want to support a basic research program anyway. Maybe I'll just decide that I miss you after all. In that case . . . "

She shrugged. "You might expect to find me showing up at your campground after all."

Lester nodded, squeezing her hands. "You just want to leave it at that? Definite maybe?"

"Definite maybe," Butch repeated. She released his hands and perched herself up on a stool. "You better get out of here now. They might not hold the boat if you keep hanging around like this."

He bent down, picked up his bags, and stepped back toward the door. "You're . . . uh, not going to see me off?"

Butch shook her head. "No. Might not be a good idea." She

ducked a little so that her corn rows and beads fell down over her face; when she looked up at him again there was a sly smile on her face. "See ya around, boss."

"Be seeing you, tough guy." He forced a smile, turned and walked out the door, closing it behind him. She hadn't said whether or not she loved him. But, come to think of it, neither had he.

"Now look," Lester said to Mighty Joe as he slid his hands into his hardsuit gloves and let the suit tech buckle the wrist-rings, "you're gong to have to promise me that still doesn't get used except on Saturday nights, you understand? You let these people get drunk on that evil shit every night, and before you know it you're going to have a bunch of deadbeats on your hands. So . . ."

"Okay, okay, you made your point. It's a promise, I swear it." Mighty Joe took the helmet off the rack and waited while the tech clamped shut the back of the suit and checked the air mixture. "Hey, y'know, I might start experimenting with making sour-mash whiskey with that thing. Might turn out to be a good batch, if I can . . ."

"One more thing," Riddell continued. "I know they're making you general administrator. . . ."

"*Senior* administrator."

"Senior administrator, or whatever they want to call it, but you're going to have to pay stricter attention to the maintenance of the tugs. Even if you're buying your spare parts from Skycorp now, they might not be sending you quite so many in the future."

"They never did in the first place."

"So you're probably going to be holding those things together with rubber bands and epoxy." Lester held up two bulky fingers. "Just in the time that I've been here, you've had two crashes because of mechanical breakdowns, and you dinged your ribs on one of 'em. That should teach you a lesson. Don't trust your mechanics. Get the job done right the first time and you won't have any regrets. And look over the things yourself before you fly 'em, or get someone else to. . . ."

"All right! Okay! Jesus, get out of here already. You're beginning to sound like you're the—"

Mighty Joe stopped short of completing his sentence. A smile slowly grew on Lester's face. "Like I'm the general manager?"

"Senior administrator," Joe replied. He handed the helmet to Lester. "They retired the old title after the last GM decided to quit and go home."

"Uh-huh." Lester juggled the helmet in his hands. "Must have been a real shit, that guy," he said, peering down into the headpiece.

"He sure was," Joe replied. "But he got the job done right. Know what I mean?"

Lester nodded, feeling a lump in his throat. Mighty Joe stuck out his hand and Lester caught it in his fist. They shook hands silently, then Riddell raised the helmet and pulled it down over his head. When he looked through the faceplate, he saw that the new general manager—that is, the new senior administrator—of Descartes Station had turned his back on him and was walking away.

For a second, he thought about pulling off the helmet, calling Young back and telling him—what? Anything that really mattered? Maybe there was nothing left to be said between them. Even in the stifling warmth of the hardsuit, though, the ready-room now seemed like a much colder place. Maybe I could have used a big send-off after all, Lester mused, glancing down at his suit to switch on the electrical system while the suit tech turned the oxygen-nitrogen feed valves on his back. But what the hell were you expecting? A brass band? A cake? Tearful moondogs throwing themselves at your feet, begging you not to . . . ?

Muffled by the helmet, he suddenly heard loud laughter and applause. Lester looked up again and laughed out loud. Across the room, Mighty Joe Young had stopped, dropped his trousers and boxer shorts, and was bending over to exhibit one of the biggest, hairiest asses Riddell had ever seen.

A new tradition had been born.

"Crude but effective," Lester murmured. Who needed a damn cake anyway?

Out on Pad Two, the rats were reeling away the fuel lines and shutting the last few service hatches on the underside of the *Collins*. Alli James had been chiding Lester about his tardiness ever since he had emerged from the airlock; hauling his duffel bag and attaché case, Riddell bunny-hopped out to the waiting lander, relishing for one last time the freedom of one-sixth gravity, sand skipping up and away from his booted feet. Good old Moon, he thought. Nice place to visit, but what a bitch to live here. Gimme a morning in the White Mountains any old day. . . .

He reached the shadow of the lander and found the ladder leading up the hull to the crew compartment. Standing in the long, black shadow, a single moondog was waiting for him. "Better get out of here," Lester said as he reached for the lowermost rung. "Thanks, but I don't need a . . . "

The solitary moondog walked back a couple of steps, out of the shadow and into the sunlight, and in the instant just before he evaporated, Lester Riddell glimpsed the face of Sam Sloane for one last time.

He couldn't be sure, but he was almost positive that Sam had been smiling.

Who're you talking to down there? James demanded. *C'mon, Les, enough with the farewells. I got a ship to launch here.*

Lester stared at the place where Sam had been standing. "Just an old friend of mine," he said at last. "He's gone now. Let's go." He clipped the briefcase to his utility belt, tugged the duffel bag's strap securely over his left shoulder, and began to make the climb up to the open airlock of the *Michael Collins*.

"Fourteen . . . thirteen . . . "

"Engines armed and ready . . . hydraulics on, pumps one two three up and functional . . . "

"Twelve . . . eleven . . . "

"Final telemetry check, go . . . guidance IU set and functional . . . "

"Ten . . . nine . . . "

"Auto-abort on . . . autopilot sequence loaded and go . . . "

"Eight . . . seven . . . "

Head against the backrest of his couch, listening to the patter of the final countdown sequence between Alli James and Ray Carroll, Lester looked around at the other passengers in the rear seats of the flight deck. Tina McGraw sat stiffly in her seat, dreading yet another sickening flight into lunar orbit, although Riddell doubted that she would get as ill as she had when they were coming to the Moon . . . what was it, eight, nine weeks ago? Seemed like so much longer now. Next to her, Honest Yuri looked as if he was asleep; his eyes were shut, his head lolling languidly on his neck. Awaiting him back home were endless chemotherapy and radiation treatments for his cancer; compared to what faced the artist on Earth, a launch into space from the Moon was the least of his concerns.

"Six . . . five . . . " Alli said, then snapped, "You got a headset back there, Les?"

"Uhhh . . . no. I gave mine up when I left . . . "

"Four . . . three . . . guess we'll all have to listen to this on the way up, then."

She snapped a switch on the communications board, and Harry Drinkwater's voice boomed out of the audio speakers: *. . . request from a li'l lady from Kansas City going out to the gent from New Hampshire who's goin' on home . . .*

"Two . . . one . . . "

"Ignition and liftoff . . . "

. . . with love. And no razzberries this time, Les.

As the *Michael Collins* lofted into orbit, the first riffs of an old Chuck Berry tune ripped through the cabin.

Lester closed his eyes, feeling the vessel gently rock back and forth on its engine-thrust as it climbed the gravity well. He smiled, and didn't bother to look out the windows to see the Moon receding below him. He could see the Moon any time he wanted to look at it now.

The job was done. No regrets.